A TEXAS-SIZED SECRET

BY
MAUREEN CHILD

MILLS & BOON®

First Published in Great Britain 2017
By Mills & Boon, an imprint of HarperCollins*Publishers*
1 London Bridge Street, London, SE1 9GF

© 2017 Harlequin Books S.A.

Special thanks and acknowledgement are given to Maureen Child for her contribution to the Texas Cattleman's Club: Blackmail series.

ISBN: 978-0-263-92823-5

51-0617

Maureen Child writes for the Mills & Boon Desire line and can't imagine a better job. A seven-time finalist for a prestigious Romance Writers of America RITA® Award, Maureen is an author of more than one hundred romance novels. Her books regularly appear on bestseller lists and have won several awards, including a Prism Award, a National Readers' Choice Award, a Colorado Romance Writers Award of Excellence and a Golden Quill Award. She is a native Californian but has recently moved to the mountains of Utah.

To the readers,
because you are the reason we have stories to tell.

One

"What did I ever do to this Maverick?" Naomi Price kicked at the dirt, then gave a heavy sigh. "Why's he after me?"

Toby McKittrick glanced from the horse he was saddling to the woman standing on the other side of the corral fence. Even furious and a little scared, Naomi made quite the picture.

She was nine inches shorter than his own six feet two inches, but she had a lot of interest packed into her five-foot-five frame. Her long, copper-brown hair draped over her shoulders like fire, and her chocolate-colored eyes snapped with intelligence and, at the moment, worry. She wore white summer slacks and a loose, pale green shirt with some white lacy thing over it. The boots she wore were ankle-high, pale cream and fit only for walking down clean city sidewalks. Here on the ranch, they'd be ruined in a day or two. But Naomi was a city girl, so no worries.

"This Maverick," he said, "he—or *she*, for all we know," Toby pointed out, "is after everybody, it seems. Guess it was just your turn."

"Maverick" had been creating turmoil in Royal, Texas, for the last few months. Exposing private bombshells, taunting people with their innermost worries and fears, whoever it was not only knew the people of Royal, but didn't give a good damn about them.

Somehow this person—whoever—uncovered people's darkest secrets and then published them. Toby had no idea what the mysterious Maverick was getting out of all this— okay, some people had paid Maverick to keep his mouth shut—but Toby had the feeling the whole point was simply to try to destroy people's reputations. If that was it, he was batting a thousand.

"Great," Naomi muttered. "Just great."

"What exactly did he say to get you running out here first thing in the morning?" Toby gave her a long look. Usually, Naomi wasn't up and moving until the crack of noon. She didn't go anywhere unless she was completely turned out from the top of her head to the toes of her stylish shoes.

She sighed, then reached into her shoulder bag for her cell phone. "Look at it for yourself," she said, handing it over.

Toby gave the horse a pat, took the phone and keyed it up.

"It's ready to go," she said, "just push Play."

Frowning, Toby tipped the brim of his hat back and tapped the phone screen. Instantly, he saw what had Naomi as jumpy as a spider on a hot plate.

For the last year or so, Naomi had been the star, writer and producer of a small-town cable fashion show. She was making a name for herself, doing what she did best—advising women on how to look good. Naomi was proud of what she'd accomplished, and she had a right to be. She'd built herself an audience and she worked hard every day to put out the best show possible.

He scowled at the screen as the video played. Maverick had turned what she did into a parody. He'd found an actress who resembled Naomi to star in it, and the woman was cooing and sighing over a rack of dresses like she was having an orgasm on camera. Then she stepped out from behind that rack and Toby knew instantly what had *really* set Naomi off.

The actress looked about two years pregnant. She waddled across the stage, both hands supporting a belly so huge there might have been a baby elephant tucked inside.

"Oh, man…"

"Wait for it," Naomi ground out. "There's more."

A deep frown etched on his face, Toby watched and listened as the actress began talking with a slow, overblown Texas accent.

"And for summer," she said, simpering at the camera, "maternity wear just got more exciting! Our big ol' bellies won't keep us from looking stylish, ladies." She flipped long reddish-brown hair behind her shoulder, then rubbed both hands over that comically distended belly before slipping behind that rack of dresses again, still talking. "Remember, accessorizing is key. Drape a pretty belt around that baby belly. Draw attention to it. Be proud. Show the world what a fashionable pregnant woman should look like."

Toby's own temper was starting to spike for Naomi's sake.

She stepped out from behind the dress rack again to model an oversize tent dress with a gigantic black belt enveloping that belly. "Tell the world, Naomi," the woman said, smiling into the camera. "Do it fast, or Maverick will do it for you."

Gritting his teeth, Toby turned the phone off and handed it back to her. "Okay, I see what's got you all churned up."

She tucked her phone back into her purse and then reached out to grab the top rail of the corral fence. Her hands tightened on the weather-beaten wood until her knuckles went white.

"It's not just that he's threatening to tell everyone I'm pregnant, Toby," she said, her voice tight but low enough that he had to lean in to hear her. "It's that he's making fun of me. He's turning my show into a joke. He's *laughing* at me."

Toby laid his hand over one of hers and squeezed. "Doesn't matter what he thinks of you, Naomi. You know that."

"Of course I know," she said, giving him a grim smile that was brave, if not honest. "But I watched that video and wondered if I really sound like that. All know-it-all and prissy. Am I prissy?"

One corner of Toby's mouth quirked up. "I wouldn't say so, but you've had your moments…"

She looked at him for a long minute, then let her head fall back and a groan escape her throat. "You're talking about the mean girls thing, aren't you?"

He shrugged and went back to tightening the cinch on his horse's saddle. Naomi had been his best friend for years. But that didn't make him blind to her faults, either. Of course, *nobody* was perfect. Toby knew Naomi better than anyone else, and he knew that she had spent a lifetime hiding a tender heart beneath a self-protective layer of cool disdain.

"You, Simone and Cecelia have a reputation you more than earned. You've gotta admit that."

"Wish I didn't have to," she muttered and dropped her chin on top of her hands.

Shaking his head, Toby let her be, knowing her thoughts were racing. So were his own. Naomi and he had been best friends for years now. They'd grown up knowing each other in a vague, from-the-same-small-town kind of way. But in college, they'd connected when he was a senior and she a freshman. He knew her in a way not many people did, so Toby also knew that Naomi was shaken right down to her expensive, useless boots.

"Things are different now," Naomi insisted a moment later. She straightened up, and Toby was glad to see a fierce gleam in her eyes. "People change, you know."

"All the time," he said, nodding.

"Cecelia and Deacon are together now—she's pregnant, too," Naomi pointed out unnecessarily. "And Simone and Hutch have worked things out and she's pregnant with triplets, for heaven's sake." She threw up both hands and let them fall to her sides. "It's a population explosion with the three of us. We're not the mean girls anymore. We're…" She sighed. "I don't know what we are anymore."

"I do," Toby said, watching her with a smile. "You're Naomi Price—the woman who wears useless boots that cost more than my saddle…"

She laughed, as he'd meant her to.

Staring directly into her eyes, he continued. "You're also the woman who started her own television show and worked her behind off to make it a success."

"Thank you, Toby." She smiled at him, and he felt a sharp tug inside in response.

"Okay," she said, nodding to herself as she pushed away from the fence, giving that top rail one last slap. "You're right. I'm strong. I'm ready. I can do this."

"Yes, you can." Finished saddling his horse, Toby stroked the flat of his hand along the animal's sleek neck.

"I don't know how to tell them," she said, all the air leaving her body in a rush. "The whole strong, independent feminist thing just goes right out the window when I know I have to face down my parents and tell them I'm pregnant."

Toby turned, braced his forearms on the top rail of the fence and tugged the brim of his dark brown hat down low over his eyes. "You should have already told them."

"This is so not the time for cool logic," she snapped. Pacing back and forth along the fence line, she crossed her arms over her middle like she was hugging herself. "What happened to Mr. Supportive?"

"I'm being supportive," he argued. "I'm just not patting your head, because you don't need it."

She muttered something he didn't quite catch and kept pacing. If she'd stop walking so damn fast, he'd give her a hug himself. But the minute he considered it, Toby pushed the thought aside. Hell, he'd been burying his attraction for Naomi for years. He was a damn expert. She'd come to his ranch looking for a friend, so that was what he'd be for her. Which meant telling her what she didn't want to hear.

"Naomi," he said, "you knew you couldn't keep this a secret forever."

She stopped directly opposite him, with the fence separating them. A soft summer wind lifted the ends of her hair, and she squinted a bit into the sunlight, those beautiful brown eyes of hers narrowing. "I know, but…"

"But nothing," he said, yanking his hat off to stab his fingers through his hair. "Somebody else took the reins from you. You don't have a choice now in when to tell your folks. Time's up."

"How did Maverick even find out?" She took a breath and exhaled on a heavy sigh. "You're the only one—or so I thought—besides me who knows about the baby."

That sounded like an accusation. His gaze snapped to hers. "I didn't tell anyone."

"I know that." She waved that away with such casualness he relaxed again. Toby was a man of his word. Always. The one thing he always remembered his father saying was, "Without his honor, a man's got nothing." That had always stuck with him, to the point that Toby never made a promise unless he was sure he could keep it.

"You know, you're the only man in my life who's never let me down, Toby," she said softly. "The one person I can always count on."

He nodded but didn't say anything, because knowing Naomi, she had more to say.

"I tried to contact Gio again."

And there it was. Irritation spiked inside him, and Toby didn't bother to hide it. Gio Fabiani, a one-night stand who had left Naomi pregnant and wasn't worth the dust on her fancy boots. But Naomi being Naomi, for the last couple of months she'd been trying to track the man down to tell him about the baby. Even if she did finally find him, though, Toby was sure that Gio wouldn't give a flying damn.

"You've got to let that go," he ground out. "Just because the man fathered your child doesn't mean he's good enough to *be* its father."

"I know, but—"

"No buts," he said, interrupting her. "Damn it, Naomi, you told me yourself that sleeping with that sleaze was a mistake. You really want to make another one by bringing him back into your life?"

"Shouldn't he *know* that he has a child?"

"If he hadn't blown in and out of your life so fast, he *would* know," Toby said, though in truth he was damned grateful that Gio hadn't been more than a blip on Naomi's radar. She deserved better. "I did some checking of my own when you first told me about this."

"You checked? Into Gio?"

"Who else?" He calmed himself by stroking his palm up and down the length of his horse's neck. "The man's a worthless user. He goes through women like we go through feed for the horses."

She flushed, and he knew she didn't like hearing it, but true was true.

His voice low and soft, Toby added, "He's never going to stand with you, Naomi."

She took a breath and huffed it out again. "I know that, too. And I don't want him to, anyway." Shaking her head, she started pacing again. "One night of bad judgment doesn't make for a relationship. But I should tell him about the baby before this Maverick person sends that video out into the world and it goes viral." She stopped opposite him again and laid one hand against her belly. "Viral. People *everywhere* will see that awful video.

People will be laughing at me. Feeling *sorry* for me. Or, worse, cheering, because like you said, I haven't always been the nicest human being on the planet. Oh, God, my stomach's churning and it has nothing to do with the baby."

"You'll survive this," he said.

"Why should I have to *survive*? Who *is* this Maverick? Why has nobody found him yet?"

"I don't know—to all those questions."

Shooting another speculative look at his friend, Toby wondered exactly what she was thinking. With Naomi it was never easy to guess. She'd long since learned to school her features into a blank mask that could convince her disinterested parents that all was well. But usually with him, she was more forthcoming. Still, things were different now. She was more shaken than he'd ever seen her. It wasn't just the pregnancy—it was how her life seemed to be spinning out of her control.

And Naomi liked control.

"The video he sent me was just…" Her sentence trailed off as she shook her head. "If he puts that out on the internet like he threatened, everyone in town's going to know my secret in a few hours."

Toby sighed, braced both forearms on the top rung of the corral fence and waited until her gaze met his to say, "Honey, they were all going to know within another month or two anyway. It's not like you could hide it much longer."

He was repeating himself and he knew it, but sometimes it took a hammer to pound the truth into Naomi's mind when she didn't want to admit to something. That hard head of hers was one of the things he liked most about her. Which made him a damn fool, probably. But there was something about the look she got in her eye when she was set on something that twisted his guts into knots. Knots he couldn't do a damn thing about, since she was his best friend. But he did wonder from time to time if Naomi's insides ever twisted over him.

Naomi stopped pacing, spun around to look at him and blurted, "You're right."

That surprised Toby enough that his eyebrows lifted high on his forehead. She saw it and laughed, and blast if the sound didn't light fires inside him. Fires he deliberately ignored. Hell, of course his body responded as it did. She was a beautiful woman with a laugh that sounded like warm nights and silk sheets. A man would have to be dead six months to not be affected by Naomi.

"I'm not so stubborn—or delusional—I can't see the truth when it takes a bite out of me," she said. Leaning her arms on the fence rail alongside his, she said, "That's really why I came out to see you this morning. I know what I have to do, and I wanted to ask you to come with me to tell my parents."

He frowned a little, because he didn't much care for Naomi's folks. They were always so prissy, so sure of their own righteousness they put him off. Their house was like a damn museum, quiet, still, where a dust speck wouldn't have the nerve to show up. Always made him feel like a clumsy cowboy.

But he knew how they made Naomi feel, too. She'd never quite measured up to parents who probably shouldn't have had a child to begin with. From everything Naomi had told him and from what he'd seen firsthand, they'd been showing her for years in word and deed just how disappointing she was to them. The announcement she had to make today wasn't going to help the situation any.

She was watching him, waiting for an answer, and Toby saw a flicker of unease in her eyes. He didn't like it. "Sure," he said, "I'll come along."

"Thanks, Toby," she said, reaching over to lay one hand on his forearm. "I knew you'd do this for me. You really are my best friend."

A best friend probably shouldn't experience a jolt of lust with just a touch of her hand on his arm. So he'd just keep that to himself.

Naomi was nervous. But then, she'd *been* nervous since opening the email with the subject line Your Secret Is Out. She'd known the moment she saw the blasted thing in her inbox that Maverick had finally turned his talons toward her. For the last few months, she'd watched as people she knew and cared about had had their lives turned upside down by this malicious phantom. And somehow she'd managed to keep hoping he wouldn't turn on her. Now that he had, though, she was forced to tell her parents the truth and live through what she always thought of as the "disappointment stare." Again.

Her entire life, Naomi had known that she was continually letting her parents down. Oh, no one had actually *said* anything—that would have been distasteful. But parents had other ways of letting their children know they didn't measure up, and the Prices were masters at silent disapproval.

No matter what Naomi had done in her life, her mother and father stood back and looked at her as if they didn't have a clue where she'd come from. Today was going to be no different.

Thank God Toby was coming with her to face them. She glanced at his stoic profile as he drove his Ford 150 down the road toward her family's mini mansion. He was the only one who knew her secret. The only one she'd trusted enough to go to when she realized two months ago that she was pregnant. And didn't that say something? She hadn't even told Cecelia Morgan and Simone Parker, and the three of them had been close for years.

But when she was in trouble, she always had turned to Toby. Even though telling him she was pregnant because of her own stupid decision to spend one night with the fast-talking, too-handsome-for-his-own-good Gio made her feel like an even bigger idiot.

Naomi still couldn't believe that one night of bad judgment and too much champagne had brought her to this. Toby was right, though. Even without Maverick shoving his nose into her business, she wouldn't have been able to hide her pregnancy for much longer. Loose tops and a strategically held handbag weren't going to disguise reality forever.

She shuddered a little in her seat. Naomi *hated* being pushed around by some nameless bully.

"You okay?" Toby asked, shooting her a quick look before turning his gaze back on the road in front of him.

"Not really," she admitted. "What the hell am I going to say to them?"

"The truth, Naomi," he said, reaching out to cover her hand with his. "Just tell them you're pregnant."

She held on to his hand and felt the warm, solid strength of him. "And when they ask who the father is?"

His mouth worked as if he wanted to say plenty but wasn't letting the words out. She appreciated the effort.

He couldn't say anything about Gio that she hadn't been feeling anyway.

When she told Toby about the baby, he'd instantly proven to be a much better man than the one she'd slept with. Toby offered to help any way he could, which was just one of the things she loved most about him. He didn't judge. He was just *there*. Like the mountains. Or the ancient oaks surrounding his ranch house. He was sturdy. And dependable. And everything she'd never known in her life until him. Now she needed him more than ever.

The Prices lived in Pine Valley, an exclusive, gated golf course community where the mansions sat on huge lots behind tidy lawns where weeds didn't dare appear and "doing lunch" was considered a career. At least, that was how Naomi had always seen it. Growing up there hadn't been easy, again because her parents never seemed to know what to do with her. Maybe if she'd had a sibling to help her through, it might have been different. But alone, Naomi had always felt…unworthy, somehow.

Her thoughts came to an abrupt halt when Toby stopped at the gate. When he lowered the window to speak to the guard, a wave of early-summer heat invaded the truck cab.

"Who're you here to see?" the older man holding a clipboard asked.

Naomi knew that voice, so she leaned forward and smiled. "Hello, Stan. We're just coming in to see my parents."

"Naomi, it's good to see you." The man smiled, hit a button on the inside of his guard hut, and the high, wide gate instantly began to roll clear. "Your folks are at home. Bet they'll be happy to see you."

He waved them through, and she sat back. "Happy to see me? I don't think so."

Toby, still holding her hand, gave it a hard squeeze. She held on tightly, even when he would have released her. Because right now she needed his support—his friendship—more than ever.

The streets were beautiful, with big homes, most of them tucked behind shrubbery-lined fences. Even in a gated community, some of the very wealthy seemed to want their own personal security as well. Of course, not everyone's home was hidden away behind a wall of trees, hedges or stone. The palatial homes were all different, all custom designed and built. And the closer Toby's truck drew to the Price mansion, the more Naomi felt the swarms of butterflies soaring and diving in the pit of her stomach.

God, she couldn't remember a time when she'd felt at ease with her parents. It had always seemed as though she was putting on a production, playing the part of the perfect daughter. Only she never quite measured up. She wished things were different, but if wishes came true, she wouldn't be here in the first place, would she?

The driveway to her parents' house was long and curved, the better to display the banks of flowers tended with loving care by a squad of gardeners. The sweep of lawn was green and neatly trimmed, and trees were kept trained into balls on branches that looked as though they were trying to remember how to be real trees. The house itself was showy but tasteful, as her parents would accept nothing less—it was a blend of Cape Cod and Victorian. Pale gray with white trim and black shutters, it stood as graceful as a dancer in the center of the massive lot. The front door was white without a speck of dust to mar its surface. The windows gleamed in the sunlight and displayed curtains within, all drawn to exactly the same point.

It was like looking at a picture in an architectural magazine. Something staged, where no one really lived. And of course, she told herself silently, *no one did.* Instead of living, her parents existed on a stage where everyone knew their lines and no one ever strayed from the script. Well, except for Naomi.

Naomi herself had been the one time anything unexpected had happened in her parents' lives. She was, she knew, an "accident." A late-in-life baby who had caused them nothing but embarrassment at first, followed by years of disappointment. Her mother had been horrified to find herself pregnant at the age of forty-five and had endured the unwelcome pregnancy because to do otherwise would have been unthinkable for her. They raised her with care if not actual love and expected her not to make any further ripples in their life.

But Naomi had always caused ripples. Sometimes *waves*.

And today was going to be a tsunami.

"You're getting quiet," Toby said with a flicker of a smile. "Never a good sign."

She had to smile back. "Too much to think about."

She stared at the closed front door and dreaded having to knock on it. Of course she would knock. And be announced by Matilda, the housekeeper who'd worked for her parents for twenty years. People didn't simply walk into her parents' house.

And her mind was going off on tangents because she didn't want to think about her real reason for being here.

"You've already made the hard decision," Toby pointed out. "You decided to keep the baby."

She had. Not that she cared at all about the baby's father, Naomi thought. But the baby was real to her. A person. *Her* child. How could she end the pregnancy? "I couldn't do anything else."

He reached out and took her hand for a quick squeeze. "I know. And I'll help however I can."

"I know you will," she said, holding on to his hand as she would a lifeline.

"You know," he said slowly, his deep voice rumbling through the truck cab, "there's no reason for you to be so worked up. You might want to consider that you're nearly thirty—"

"Hey!" She frowned at him. "I'm twenty-nine."

"My mistake," he said, mouth quirking, eyes shining. "But the point is, you've been on your own since college, Naomi. You don't have to explain your life to your parents."

"Easy for you to say," she countered. "Your mom and sister are your own personal cheering squad."

"True," he said, nodding. "But, Naomi, sooner or later, you've got to take a stand and, instead of apologizing to your folks, just tell them what's what."

It sounded perfectly reasonable. And she knew he was right. But it didn't make the thought of actually doing it any easier to take. She dropped one hand to the slight mound of her belly and gave the child within a comforting pat. If there was ever a time to stand up to her parents, it was now. She was going to be a mother herself, for God's sake.

"You're right." She gave his hand another squeeze, then let go to release her seat belt. "I'm going to tell them about the baby and that the father isn't in the picture and I'll be a single mother and—" She stopped. "Oh, God."

He chuckled. "For a second there, you were raring to go."

"I still am," she insisted, in spite of, or maybe because of, the flurries of butterflies in her stomach. "Let's just go get it over with, okay?"

"And after, we'll hit the diner for lunch."

"Sounds like a plan," she said.

Two

Naomi took a deep breath in what she knew was a futile attempt to relax a little. There would be no relaxation until this meeting with her parents was over.

Toby came around the front of the truck, opened her door and waited for her to step down before asking, "You ready?"

"No. Yes. I don't know." Naomi shook her head, tugged at the hem of her cool green shirt as if she could somehow further disguise the still-tiny bump of her baby, then smoothed nervous hands along her hips. "Do I look all right?"

He tipped his head to one side, studied her, then smiled. "You look like you always do. Beautiful."

She laughed a little. Toby was really good for her self-esteem. Or, she thought, he would be, if she had any. God, what a pitiful thought. Of course she had self-esteem. It was just a bit like a roller-coaster ride. Sometimes up, sometimes down. Naomi'd be very happy if she could somehow reach a middle ground and stay there. But it was a constant battle between the two distinctly different voices in her head.

One telling her she was smart and talented and capable while the other whispered doubts. Amazing how much easier that dark voice was to believe.

And she was stalling.

"You're stalling," Toby said as if reading her mind. Her gaze snapped to his.

"Think you know me that well, do you?"

"Yeah," he said, a slow smile curving his mouth. "I do."

Okay, yes, he really did. Probably the only person she knew who could make that claim and mean it. Even her closest girlfriends, Cecelia and Simone, only knew about her what she wanted them to know. Naomi was really skilled at hiding her thoughts, at being who people expected or wanted her to be. But she never had to do that around Toby.

Taking her hand in his, he started for the front door. "Come on, Naomi. We'll talk to your folks, get this out in the open, then go have lunch so I can get a burger and you can nibble on a lettuce leaf."

She rolled her eyes behind his back, because damn it, he really *did* know her. All women watched their diets, didn't they? Especially *pregnant* women? At that thought, memories of that vile video Maverick had sent her rushed into her mind again. She saw the actress waddling, staggering across a mock-up of Naomi's own television set, and she shivered. She *refused* to waddle.

Naomi swallowed a groan and took the steps to the

wide front porch beside Toby. He was still holding her hand, and she was grateful. A part of her brain shrieked at her that it was ridiculous for a grown woman to be so nervous about facing her parents. But that single voice was being systematically drowned out by a *choir* of other voices, reminding her that nothing good had ever come from having a chat with Franklin and Vanessa Price.

"You ready?"

She looked up into his eyes, shaded by his ever-present Stetson, and gathered the tattered threads of her courage. She had to be ready, because there was no other choice. "Yes."

"That'd be more believable if you weren't chewing on your bottom lip."

"Blast," she muttered and instinctively rubbed her lips together to smooth out her lipstick. "Fine. Now I'm ready."

"Damn right you are." He grinned, and her nerves settled. Really, Naomi wasn't sure what she'd ever done to deserve a best friend like Toby, but she was so thankful to have him.

Before she could talk herself out of it or worry on it any longer, she reached out and rapped her knuckles on the wide front door. Several seconds ticked past before it swung open to reveal Matilda, the Price family housekeeper and cook.

Tall, thin and dressed completely in black, Matilda wore her gunmetal-gray hair short and close to her head. Her complexion was pale and carved with wrinkles earned over a lifetime. She looked severe, humorless, although nothing could have been further from the truth. Matilda smiled in welcome.

"Miss Naomi," she said, stepping back to open the

door wider. "You and Mr. Toby come in. I'll just tell your parents you're here. They're in the front parlor."

Of course they were, Naomi thought. She knew the Price family schedule and was aware that it never deviated. Late-morning tea began at eleven and ended precisely at eleven forty-five. After which her mother would drive into town to one of her charities and her father would go to the golf course or, on Tuesdays, the Texas Cattleman's Club to visit with his friends.

Waiting in the blessedly cool entry hall, Toby took his hat off, then bent to whisper, "Always makes me twitch when she calls me Mr. Toby."

"I know," Naomi said. "But propriety must be maintained at all times." Appearances, she knew, were very important to her parents. It had always mattered more how things looked than how things actually *were*.

She glanced around the home she'd grown up in. The interior hadn't changed much over the years. Vanessa Price didn't care for change, and once she had things the way she wanted them, they stayed.

Cool, gray-veined white marble tile stretched from the entry all through the house. Paintings, in soothing pastel colors, hung in white frames on ecru walls, their muted hues the only splash of brightness in the decorating scheme. A Waterford crystal vase on the entry table held a huge bouquet of exotic flowers, all in varying shades of white, and the silence in the house was museum quality.

Idly, Naomi remembered being a child in this house and how she'd struggled to find her place. She never really did, which was why, she supposed, she still felt uncomfortable just being here.

Toby squeezed her hand as Matilda stepped into the hall and motioned for them to come ahead. Apparently,

Naomi told herself, the king and queen were receiving today. The minute that thought entered her mind, she felt a quick stab of guilt. Her parents weren't evil people. They didn't deserve the mental barbs from their only child and wouldn't understand them if they knew how she really felt.

But at the same time, Naomi couldn't help wishing things were different. She wished, not for the first time, that she was able to just open the front door and sail in without being announced. She wished that her parents would be happy to see her. That she and her mom could curl up on the couch and talk about anything and everything. That her dad would sweep her up into a bear hug and call her "princess." That she wouldn't feel so tightly strung at the very thought of entering the formal parlor to face them.

But if wishes were real, she'd be sitting on a beach sipping a margarita right now.

Her parents were seated in matching Victorian chairs, with a tea table directly in front of them. The rest of the room was just as fussily decorated, looking like a curator's display of Louis XIV furniture. Nothing in the house invited people to settle in or, God forbid, put their feet on a table.

The windows allowed a wide swath of sunlight to spear into the room, illuminating the beige-and eggshell-colored furniture, the gold leaf edging the desk on the far wall, the white shades on crystal lamps and the complete lack of welcome in her parents' eyes. It was eleven thirty. They still had fifteen minutes of teatime left, and Naomi had just ruined it.

She was about to ruin a lot more.

"Hello, Mom, Dad." She smiled, steeled herself and

released Toby's hand to cross the room. She bent down to kiss the cheek her mother offered, and then when her father stood up to greet Toby, she kissed her dad's cheek, too.

"Hello, dear," Vanessa Price said. "This is a surprise. Toby, it's nice to see you. Would you like to join us for tea? I can have Matilda brew fresh."

"No, ma'am, thank you," Toby said after shaking Franklin's hand and stepping back to range himself at Naomi's side.

Franklin Price was a handsome man in his seventies. He wore a perfectly tailored suit and his silver hair was swept back from a high, wide forehead. His blue eyes were sharp but curious as they landed on his daughter. Vanessa was petite, and though in her seventies, she presented, as always, a perfect picture. Her startlingly white hair was trimmed into a modern but flattering cut, and her figure was trim, since she had spent most of her life dieting to ensure it. Her jewel-bright blue summer dress looked casually elegant and at the same time served to make Naomi feel like a hag.

"Is there something wrong, dear?" Vanessa set her Limoges china teacup down onto the table and then folded her hands neatly in her lap.

There was her opening, Naomi thought, and braced herself to jump right in.

"Actually, yes, there is," she admitted, and glanced at her father to see his concerned frown. "You've both heard about this Maverick who's been contacting people in Royal for the last several months?"

"Distasteful," Vanessa said primly with a mild shake of her head.

"I'll agree with your mother. Whoever it is needs to

be apprehended and charged," her father said. "Prying into people's private lives is despicable."

"He's caused a lot of trouble," Toby said and took Naomi's hand to give it a squeeze.

Her mother caught the gesture, and her eyes narrowed in suspicion.

"Maverick contacted *me* this morning," Naomi blurted out before she could lose her dwindling nerve entirely.

"You?" Vanessa lifted one hand to the base of her throat, her fingers sliding through a string of pearls. "Whatever could he do to you?"

Still frowning, Franklin Price looked from Naomi to Toby and back again. "What is it, girl?"

Oh, here it comes, she told herself. And once the words were said, everything would change forever. There was no choice. Toby was right—she couldn't keep hiding her baby bump with loose clothing. There would come a time when the truth just wouldn't remain hidden.

"I'm pregnant," she said flatly, "and Maverick is about to send a video out onto the internet telling everyone."

"Pregnant?" Vanessa slumped back against her chair, and now her hand tightened at the base of her throat as if she were trying to massage air into her lungs.

"Who's the father?" Franklin's demand was quiet but no less fierce.

"Oh, Naomi," her mother said on a defeated sigh. "How could you let this happen?"

"Who did this to you?" her father asked again.

As if she'd been held down against her will, Naomi thought on an internal groan. Oh, she couldn't tell them about Gio. About how stupid she'd been. How careless. How could she say that the baby's father was an Italian gigolo with whom she'd spent a single night? But what else *could* she say?

They were waiting expectantly, her mother just a little horrified, her father leaning more toward cold anger. She'd proven a disappointment. Again. And it was only going to get worse.

"I'm the father," Toby said when she opened her mouth to speak.

"What?" she whispered, horrified.

Toby gave her a quick smile, then fixed his gaze on her father. "That's why I came here with Naomi today. We wanted to tell you together that we're having a baby and we're going to be married."

Naomi could only stare at him in stunned silence. She hadn't expected him to do this. And she didn't know what to do about it now. A ribbon of relief shot whiplike through her, and even as it did, Naomi knew she couldn't let him do this. As much as she appreciated the chivalry, this was her mess and she'd find a way to—

"We wanted to tell you before anyone else," Toby went on smoothly. "Naomi's going to be living with me at my ranch."

"Toby—"

He didn't even glance at her. "No point in her staying at her condo in town, so she's moving to Paradise Ranch in a few days."

"But—" She tried to speak again. To correct him. To argue. To say *something*, but her mother spoke up, effectively keeping Naomi quiet.

"Living together isn't something I would usually approve," she said primly, "but as you're engaged, I think propriety has been taken care of."

Propriety. Naomi had often thought her mother would

have been happier living in the Regency period. Where manners were all and society followed strict rules.

"Engaged." Her mother said the word again, as if savoring it. "Oh, Naomi, you're marrying Toby McKittrick. It's just wonderful."

Vanessa rose quickly, moved to stand beside her husband and then actually beamed her pleasure.

Naomi had never been on the receiving end of that smile before, so it threw her a little. Then she realized exactly what her mother had said. She wasn't thrilled about the baby, but about her daughter marrying Toby. Handsome. Stable. *Wealthy* Toby McKittrick. That was the kind of announcement Vanessa Price could get behind.

And that realization only made Naomi furious. At Toby. She hadn't expected her parents to be supportive, but having Toby ride to the rescue felt, after that first burst of relief, more than a little annoying. She'd only wanted him here for moral support. Not to sweep in and lie to save her. The whole purpose of coming here to tell her parents the truth was to get it over with.

Now not only had the moment of truth been postponed, but Toby had added to the mess with a lie she'd eventually have to answer for.

"Toby—"

He looked down at her, gave her a smile, then surprised her into being quiet with a quick, hard kiss that left her lips buzzing. Shock rattled her. He'd never kissed her before, and though it hadn't been a lover's kiss, it wasn't exactly a brotherly kiss, either.

When he was sure she was shocked speechless, he turned to face her parents. "Naomi's a little upset. She wanted to be the one to tell you about us getting married, but I just couldn't help myself. And we're heading over to her place today to start packing for the move, so we wanted to see you first."

"Understandable," Franklin said with an approving nod at Toby, followed by a worried glance at Naomi. "I'll say, you worried me there for a moment with news of a pregnancy. But since you're marrying, I'm sure it's fine."

Great. All it had taken to win her parents' approval was the right marriage. God. Maybe they *were* in the Regency period.

"I don't see your ring," Vanessa pointed out with a deliberate look at Naomi's left hand.

Naomi sighed, then lifted her gaze to Toby as if to demand, *this was your idea—fix it.*

Then he did. His way.

"We're going right into town to see about that. And if I can't find what I want there," Toby announced, "we'll drive into Houston." He dropped one arm around Naomi's shoulders and pulled her up close to him. "But we wanted you to know our news before you heard about Maverick's video."

"No one pays attention to people of that sort," Vanessa said with assuredness.

Naomi wondered how she could say it, since the whole town of Royal had been talking about nothing else *but* Maverick for months. But Vanessa didn't care to see what she considered ugliness, and it was amazingly easy for her to close her eyes to anything that might disrupt her orderly world.

"Now, Naomi, don't you worry over this Maverick person," her mother said firmly. "You and Toby have done nothing wrong. Perhaps you haven't done things in the proper *order*—"

Meaning, Naomi thought, courtship, engagement,

marriage and *then* a baby. Still, her mother was willing to overlook all that for the happy news that her daughter would finally be *settled*, with a more than socially acceptable husband. Which meant that when she had to tell them that she absolutely was *not* going to marry Toby, the fallout would be epic.

"We should be going now. We need to get Naomi all moved in and settled at the ranch. Sorry for interrupting your tea," Toby was saying, and Naomi told herself to snap out of her thoughts.

He was going to hurry her out of the house before she could tell her parents the truth. And she was going to let him. Sure, she'd have to confess eventually, but right this minute? Naomi just wanted to be far, far away.

"Nonsense," Franklin said. "You're always welcome here, Toby. Especially now."

Naomi muffled a sigh. All it had taken was the promise of a "good" marriage to fling the Price family doors wide-open. She could only imagine how fast they would slam shut once they knew the truth.

"I appreciate that, Mr. Price."

"Franklin, boy. You call me Franklin."

"Yes, sir, I will," Toby promised, but didn't. "Now if you'll excuse us, I think we'll just go get Naomi's things and find that ring we talked about before Naomi changes her mind and leaves me heartbroken."

Vanessa's eyes widened. "Oh, she wouldn't!"

Toby winked at Naomi, completely ignoring how tense she'd gone beside him. To her parents, this suddenly imagined marriage was very real. She knew Toby thought he'd made things better, but in reality, he'd only made the whole situation more…complicated.

"You two enjoy yourselves, and, Naomi, we'll talk

about a lovely wedding real soon," her mother called after her. "We'll want to have the ceremony before you start...*showing.*"

"Oh, God," Naomi whispered.

Toby squeezed her hand and hurried her out of the house. Once outside, he bundled her into his truck before she could say anything, so it wasn't until he was in the truck himself, firing the engine, that Naomi was able to demand, "What were you thinking?"

He blew out a breath, squinted into the sun and steered the truck away from the front door and back down the flower-lined drive. "I was thinking that I didn't like the way your folks were looking at you."

His profile was stern, his mouth tight and a muscle in his jaw flexing, telling her he was grinding his teeth together. Naomi sighed a little. She hadn't thought he'd take her parents' reaction so personally on her behalf, though in retrospect, she should have. He'd always been the kind of man to stand up for someone being bullied. He took the side of the underdog because that was just who Toby was. But she didn't want to be one of his mercy rescues.

"I appreciate the misguided chivalry," she said, striving for patience. "But it just makes everything harder, Toby. Now I'm going to have to tell them that I'm not moving in with you, our engagement is off and make up some reason for it—which my mother will never accept—and then I'll still be a single mother and they'll be even more disappointed in me than ever."

"They don't have to be." He shot her one fast look. "We move you out to Paradise today. We get married. Just like I said."

Naomi just stared at him. Since he was driving, he didn't take his eyes off the road again, so she couldn't see if he was joking or not. But he *had* to be joking. "You're not serious."

"Dead serious."

"Toby," she argued, "that's nuts. I mean, it was a sweet thing to do—"

"Screw *sweet*," he snapped with a shake of his head. "I wasn't doing it to be sweet and, okay, fine, I didn't really think about it before saying it, but once the words were out, they made sense."

"In a crazy, upside-down world, maybe. Here? Not so much."

"Think about it, Naomi."

She lifted one hand to rub her forehead, hoping to ease the throbbing headache centered there. "Haven't been able to do much else since you blurted out all that."

"Then think about *this*. There's no point in you raising a baby on your own when I'm standing right here."

"It's not your baby," she pointed out.

"It could be," he countered just as quickly. "I'd be a good father. A good husband."

"That's not the point."

"Then what *is*?"

She lifted both hands and tugged hard on her own hair. Nope, she wasn't dreaming any of this, which meant she had to get through to him. What he'd just said had touched her. Deeply. To know that he was willing to throw himself on a metaphorical grenade for her meant more than she could say. But that didn't mean she would actually allow him to claim another man's child as his own. It wouldn't be fair to him.

"There are many, many points to be made, but the main one is, I'm not your responsibility," she said, keeping her voice calm and firm.

"Never said you were," he said. "You are my friend, though."

"Best friend," she corrected, still looking at his profile. "Absolutely."

"Then accept that as your friend I want to help you."

"Toby, I can't let you do that."

"You're not *letting* me, I'm just doing it." He stopped at a four-way intersection and, when it was clear, drove on toward Royal. "It makes sense, Naomi. For all of us, the baby included. You really want to be all alone in that snazzy condo in Royal? Or would you rather be with me out at the ranch? If we're living together, that baby has two parents to look out for it. And, big plus, you can stop tying yourself into knots over your folks."

"So you're trying to save me." Just as she'd suspected. "This is all some grand gesture for my sake."

"And my own," he said, then muttered something under his breath and pulled the truck over to the side of the road. He parked, turned off the engine, then shifted in his seat to face her.

His eyes, the clear, cool aqua of a tropical sea, fixed on her, and Naomi read steely determination in that stare. She'd seen him this way before. Whenever he had an idea for one of his inventions, he got that *I will not be stopped* look on his face, in his eyes. If someone told him no about something, he took it as a personal challenge. Once Toby decided on a course of action, it was nearly impossible to get him to change his mind. This time, she told herself, it had to be different.

"I'm not a saint, and I'm not trying to rescue you."

"Could have fooled me," she murmured.

He sighed heavily, turned his gaze out on the road stretched out in front of them for a long second or two, then looked back at her. "Hell, Naomi, we're best friends. We're both single, and we can raise the baby together. Helping each other. This could work, if you'll let it."

A part of her, she was ashamed to admit, wanted to say yes and accept the offer he shouldn't be making. But he was her friend, so she couldn't take advantage of him like that. "I don't need a husband, Toby. I can raise my child on my own."

Now he sent her a cool, hard stare. "You forget, my mother was a single mom after my dad died. I watched how hard it was for her to be mother and father to me and my sister. To work and take care of the house. To run around after me and Scarlett with no one to help out. You really think I want to sit by and watch you go through the same damn thing?"

She bit her lip. She had forgotten about Toby's family. His mother, Joyce, was a smart, capable, lovely woman who had worked hard to raise her kids on her own. Now Toby was not just a successful rancher, but a wealthy inventor, and his younger sister, Scarlett, was a veterinarian. "Your mother did a great job with both of you."

His features evened out, and he gave her a smile. "And we thank you. But my point is, you don't have to do it the hard way like my mom did. Mom didn't have anyone to help her. You have me."

"I know," she said, taking a breath to calm the anger bubbling inside. "I really do know. But you don't have to marry me, Toby."

"Who said anything about *have* to?" he asked. "I want to. We're good together, Naomi. There's plenty of room at the ranch. You can take over one of the bedrooms for an office. It's not far from the studio where you film your show…"

True. All true. There was a small studio at the edge

of Royal where her cable TV show, *Fashion Sense*, was recorded once a week. And to be honest, being at the ranch would get her away from most of the gossiping tongues in town, and once Maverick's video hit, she'd be grateful for that.

"It's a great idea, Naomi. Hell, even your parents liked it."

She choked out a laugh. "Of course they did. Toby McKittrick—inventor, rancher, wealthy. I'm surprised my mother didn't squeal."

He gave her a half smile and a slow shake of his head. "You're being too hard on her. On both of them."

"I know that, too," she said with a sigh. She smoothed her fingertips over her knees. "They're not evil people. They're not even really mean. They just live in a very narrow world and it's never had room for me."

He reached out and took her hand, stilling nervous fingers. "There's room for you with me."

"Toby…" Naomi didn't know what to think. Or feel. He was right in that they were good together. They were already friends, and maybe a marriage of convenience would be good for both of them. But was it fair to him? "If we're married, you can't find someone for real."

"Not interested," he said firmly with a shake of his head. "Been there already, and it didn't end well."

Naomi sighed again. She couldn't blame him for feeling burned in the love department. She could, however, blame the woman who'd hurt him enough that Toby had built a wall around his heart that was so tall and thick it had taken Naomi months to reach past it.

"Fine. You're not looking for love. Neither am I," she added in a mutter. "But that doesn't mean…"

"Think about it."

"But no one will believe it."

"Your parents did."

She waved that aside. "That's because they don't know me. My friends—"

"Are so wrapped up in their own happily-ever-afters they won't question it."

"Your family—"

He scowled thoughtfully, but a moment later, his expression cleared. Those amazing eyes fixed on her, he said, "Okay, I'll tell my family the truth. Don't want to lie to them anyway. Does that work for you?"

"They won't like it," she said, and silently added, *they'll blame me.*

"Mom and Scarlett both like you already, so what's the problem?"

"I don't know if I want to be married," she said simply. "You're my best friend, Toby. It'll be...*weird.*"

He laughed and shook his head. "Doesn't have to be. Think of it as a marriage of convenience. We're together because of the baby. No sex. Just friends who live together."

No sex. Well, it wasn't as if she was a wildly sexual person anyway. In fact, until that single night with Gio, she hadn't been with anyone in more than a year. And since Gio, she'd avoided *all* men except for Toby. So going without sex wouldn't be that terrible, would it? Oh, God.

"I'm not saying we become monks," Toby pointed out as though he could read her thoughts. "If one of us meets someone, we'll work that out then. In the meantime, we're together."

Toby watched her and wondered what the hell she was arguing about. Anyone could see this was a good idea. Though he could admit that he hadn't come up with it until that moment when Vanessa Price gave her daughter the cool look of disappointment at news of the baby. Damned if he could just stand there while Naomi tried to explain about the baby's father and how he was a worthless player. So, before he'd really considered it, he'd blurted out the lie. And it had felt…right.

Why not get married to his best friend? Whether she knew it or not, she was going to need help with the baby. And as long as they kept things between them platonic, everything would work out fine. Yeah, he was attracted to her. What man wouldn't be? But he wasn't going to act on that attraction, so a marriage of convenience was the best solution here.

"Well?" he asked, gaze fixed on hers. "What do you think?"

"I think you're crazy," she said on a half laugh.

"That's been said before," he reminded her. "People have been talking about crazy Toby and his weird inventions for years."

Nervously, she pushed her hair back from her face, and the early-afternoon sunlight caught a few threads of copper, making them gleam. "If we do this, we'll both be crazy."

"Worse things to be, Naomi."

She smiled. "Are you sure about this?"

He tipped his head to one side and gave her a look. "When have you ever known me to say something without meaning every damn word?"

"Never," she said, nodding. "It's one of the things I like best about you. I always know what you're thinking, because you don't play games."

"Games are for kids, Naomi. Neither one of us is a kid."

"No, we're not." She met his gaze squarely and took a deep breath. "I'm a city girl. What'll I do on a ranch?"

"Whatever needs doing," he said.

She laughed shortly. "We really must be crazy. Okay. I'll marry you and not have sex with you."

He grinned and winked. "Now, how many people can say that?" Turning in his seat, he fired up the truck, put it in gear and steered out onto the road again, headed for town. "We'll go get lunch, and then we'll go ring shopping."

"No."

"No?" He glanced at her, surprised.

"No ring," she said, shaking her head. "We don't need an engagement ring, Toby, and I don't want you buying one for me when it wouldn't really mean what it should. You know?"

He understood and couldn't say he disagreed. Their marriage would be a joining of friends, not some celebration of love, after all. "What's your mama going to say?"

Smiling sadly, Naomi said, "Even if we'd gotten one, she'd have found something wrong with it anyway."

They slipped into silence. Toby took her hand for the rest of the drive but left her to her thoughts.

Three

Toby opened the door to the Royal Diner, steered Naomi inside and stopped. Every person in the place turned to look at them, and he knew. Maverick had done as promised. That stupid video was on the internet, and it seemed clear that it was the hot topic in Royal.

The welcoming scents of coffee, French fries and burgers greeted them. Classic rock played on the old-fashioned jukebox in the corner, and noise from the kitchen drifted out of the pass-through, but other than that, the silence was telling.

"Let's go," Naomi said, and tugged at his hand.

"Not a chance," Toby countered. Then, bending his head down to hers, he whispered, "Do you really want them to think you're scared?"

He knew it was just the right note to take when she squared her shoulders, lifted her chin and stood there

like a queen before peasants. Toby hid a smile, because
in just a second or two the woman he knew so well had
reemerged, squashing the part of her that wanted to run
and hide.

A couple of seconds ticked past and then the diner
customers returned to their meals, though most of them
looked to be having hushed conversations. It didn't take
a genius to guess what they were talking about.

He gave Naomi's hand a squeeze, then took off his hat
and smiled at Amanda Battle as she hurried over. Married
to Sheriff Nathan Battle, who was doing everything he
could to find out who this Maverick person was, Amanda
owned the diner, along with her sister, Pam.

"Well, hi, you two," she said with a deliberately bright
smile. "Booth or table?"

"Booth if you've got it," Toby said quickly, knowing
Naomi wouldn't want to be seated in the middle of the
room. Hell, he still half expected her to make a break
for the door.

"Right. Down there along the window's good."
Amanda gave Naomi a pat on the shoulder and said,
"I'll get you some water and menus."

They walked past groups of friends and neighbors,
nodding as they went, and Toby felt Naomi stiffening
alongside him. She was maintaining, but it was costing
her. She wasn't happy, and he couldn't blame her. Hell,
he hated this whole mess for her.

The familiarity of the diner did nothing to ease the
tension in Naomi's shoulders. The Royal Diner hadn't
changed much over the years. Oh, it had all been updated,
but Amanda and Pam had kept the basics the same, just
freshening it all up. The floor was still black-and-white
squares, the booths and counter stools were still bright

red vinyl, and chrome was the accent of choice. The white walls held pictures of Royal through the years, and it was still the place to go if you wanted the best burger anywhere.

Once they were seated, Amanda came back quickly, set water glasses in front of them and handed out menus. Smiling down at them, she said, "I guess congratulations are in order."

"Oh, God," Naomi murmured, and her shoulders slumped, as if all the air had been let out of her body. "You've seen the video."

Amanda gave her a friendly pat and said, "I'm not talking about the video, honey. Don't worry about that. That nosy bastard has been poking into too many lives, so everyone here knows they could be next. Looks like this Maverick is moving around pretty quick, so he'll be onto someone new before you know it and you'll be old news."

Toby could have kissed her. "She's right."

Naomi looked at him, and he read resignation and worry in her eyes. "Doesn't help much, though. The whole town knows I'm pregnant now."

"Naomi, most of us guessed anyway," Amanda said. At Naomi's stunned expression, Amanda added, "You've never worn loose shirts and long cover-ups in your life."

Toby grinned. "She's got a point."

Naomi blew out a breath and gave him a rueful smile. "So much for my brilliant disguises."

"Oh—" Amanda waved one hand "—it probably fooled the men." She gave Toby an amused glance. "You guys don't really notice much. But women know a baby bump when they see one being hidden."

Naomi nodded. "Right."

"But I wasn't congratulating you on the baby anyway,"

Amanda continued. "Though sure, best wishes. I was talking about your engagement to Toby here."

Now it was his turn to be stunned. "How did you find out about that already?"

"Remember where we live, honey," Amanda said with a shake of her head that sent her dark blond ponytail swinging behind her. "Naomi's mother called one of her friends, who called somebody else, who called Pam's sister-in-law, who called Pam, who told me."

Naomi just blinked at her. Toby felt the same way. He had always known that gossip flew in Royal as fast as the tornadoes that occasionally swept across Texas. But this had to be a record.

"We just left my parents' house twenty minutes ago," Naomi complained.

"What's your point?" Amanda asked, grinning.

Helplessly shaking her head, Naomi said, "I guess I don't have one."

"There you go," Amanda said. "And so you know, most everybody's talking more about the engagement than that video. I mean, really." She laughed a little. "Maverick thought he was being funny, I guess, but him mocking you like that? Didn't make sense. People in Royal know Naomi Price has got style. So making that woman look so big and sloppy just didn't have the smack he probably thought it would."

Toby saw how those words hit Naomi, and once again, he could have kissed Amanda for saying just the right thing. She was right, of course. Naomi, even with her pregnancy showing, would be just as stylish as ever. That video was meant to hurt her, humiliate her, but he knew Naomi well enough to know that after the initial embarrassment passed, she'd rise above it and come out the winner.

"But you two engaged," Amanda said with a wink. "Now, that's news worth chewing on."

"I hate being gossiped about," Naomi muttered.

"In a small town," Amanda pointed out, "we all take our turn at the top of the rumor mill eventually."

"Doesn't make it any easier," she said.

"Suppose not, but at least people are pleased for you," Amanda said.

"Well, it's good the news is out." Toby spoke up, getting both women's attention. "And to celebrate our engagement, I'll have the cowboy burger with fries and some sweet tea."

"Got it. Naomi?"

"Small salad, please," she said. "Dressing on the side. And unsweetened tea."

"That's no way to feed a baby," Amanda muttered, but nodded. "And not even close to a celebration, but okay. Be out in a few minutes."

When she was gone, Toby took a drink of water, set the glass down and said, "She's right. That baby needs more than dry lettuce."

"Don't start," she warned, and turned her gaze on the street beyond the window. "I'm not going to end up waddling through the last of this pregnancy, Toby."

Irritation spiked, but he swallowed it back. Naomi had been on a damn diet the whole time he'd known her. In fact, he could count on the fingers of one hand how many times he'd seen her actually *enjoy* eating. She was so determined to stave off any reminders of the chubby little girl she'd once been, she counted every calorie as if it meant her life.

But it wasn't just her now. That baby was going to need protein. And once she was living with him on the ranch, he'd make sure she ate more than a damn rabbit did. But that battle was for later. Not today.

"Fine."

"I can't believe people already know about the engagement," Naomi said, looking back at him. Reaching out, she grabbed her paper napkin and began tearing at the edges with nervous fingers.

"At least they're talking about us, not the video," Toby pointed out and took another sip of water. His gaze was fixed on hers, and he didn't like that haunted look that still colored her eyes.

Scowling, she muttered, "I don't want them talking about me at all."

Toby laughed, and laughed even harder when she glared at him.

"What's so funny?" she demanded.

Scrubbing one hand across his face, he did his best to wipe away the amusement still tickling him. Keeping his voice low, he said, "You, honey. You *love* being talked about. Always have."

When she would have argued, he shook his head and leaned across the table toward her. "You were homecoming queen and a cheerleader—at college you were the president of your sorority. Now? You still love it. Why else would you have your own TV show? You like being the center of attention, Naomi, and why shouldn't you?"

"I didn't do all that just to be talked about," she argued.

"I know that," he said and slid one hand across the table to cover hers. "You did all of it because you liked it. Because you wanted to." *And because it was the at-*

tention you never got at home and that fed something in
you that's still hungry today.

"I did. And I like doing my show, knowing people
watch and talk about it." She leaned toward him, too, even
as she pulled her hand from beneath his. "But there's a
difference, Toby, between people talking about my work
and talking about my life."

"Not by much, there isn't," he said and leaned back,
laying one arm along the top of the booth bench. "Naomi,
we live in a tiny town in Texas. People talk. Always have.
Always will. What matters is how you deal with it."

"I'm dealing," she grumbled, and he wanted to smile
again but was half-worried she might kick him under
the table if he did.

"No, you're not." He tipped his head to one side and
gave her a look that said *be honest*. "You're nearly five
months along with that baby, and you just now told your
folks."

"That's different." Her fingers tore at the napkin again
until she had quite the pile of confetti going.

"And when we walked in here and people turned to
look, you would have walked right back out if I hadn't
gotten in your way."

She frowned at him, and the flash in her eyes told him
he was lucky she hadn't kicked him. "I don't like it when
you're a know-it-all."

"Sure you do." She lifted one eyebrow again, and he
had to admire it. Never had been able to do it himself.
"Look, either you can let this Maverick win, by curling
up and hiding out…or you can hold your head up like the
tough woman I know you are and not let some mystery
creep dictate how your life goes."

"Using logic isn't fair."

"Yeah, I know."

She sat back in the booth and continued to fiddle with the paper napkin in front of her. It was nearly gone now, and he told himself to remember to ask Amanda for more.

"Toby, I don't want to let Maverick win. To run my decisions. But isn't that what I'm doing by agreeing to marry you?"

"No." He straightened up now, leaned toward her and met her gaze dead-on. "If you were doing what he wanted, you'd be locked in a closet crying somewhere. Do you think that bastard wants you to be with me and happy? Do you think he wants you turning the whole town on its ear so they don't even think about his stupid video?"

"No, I suppose not," she murmured.

"Damn straight." He laid his hand over hers again and quieted those nervous fingers. "You're taking charge, Naomi."

"That's not how it feels."

"I can see that. But trust me on this—you're the one calling the shots here. You've left Maverick in your dust already, and he's only going to get dustier from here on out." He squeezed her fingers until he felt her squeeze back. "Us getting married? That's a good thing. For all of us, baby included."

She sighed. "I just don't know how this day got away from me. One minute I'm dreading talking to my parents, and the next I'm engaged to *you*."

"I don't know why you think marriage to me is such a damn hardship."

Her gaze narrowed on his. "I didn't say that—fine," she said when he smiled. "Make jokes. We'll see how funny you think it is when I'm living at the ranch with you."

He shrugged to show her he wasn't bothered. "You're a good cook and you're already pregnant, so all I need to do is keep you barefoot and in the kitchen."

She laughed then slapped one hand to her mouth to hold the rest of it inside. Toby grinned at her. God, he loved hearing that wild, deep laughter come out of such a wisp of a woman.

"You're making me laugh so I won't obsess about what a mess my life is."

"Is it working?"

Thinking about it for a second or two, she finally said, "Yes. So, thanks."

"You're welcome."

He watched her as, still smiling to herself, she looked out the window at the little town still buzzing over their news. Royal had seen a lot of upheaval over the last few months. Thanks to the mysterious Maverick, things had been changing right and left. It wasn't just him and Naomi making a major shift in their lives. Some of Toby's friends had made sudden changes that at the time had completely surprised Toby.

Hell, there was Wes Jackson for one. Toby never would have thought that man would settle down and get married, and now the man had a wife, a daughter and another baby on the way. Tom and Emily Knox had worked out their problems and seemed stronger than ever, and even Naomi's best friends, Cecelia and Simone, were happy and settled into real relationships.

Toby knew that Maverick had been at the heart of all those changes. Sure, the man had been trying to ruin people, but in a roundabout way he'd helped them instead.

Toby had stood on the sidelines, watching his friends take steps forward in their lives, and wondered when he would be Maverick's target. But the nameless bastard hadn't come for him at all, but Naomi. Seeing her worried, upset, had torn at him enough that he was willing to put aside his anti-marriage stance. And actually, the more he thought about it, the more marrying Naomi made sense. He'd get a family out of it without having to worry about getting in too deep emotionally.

All he had to do was make sure she didn't back out.

"Hey, Toby," Clay Everett called out, "you got a minute?"

"Sure." Toby glanced at Naomi. "I'll be right back."

She nodded when he slid out of the booth and walked to the table where Clay and Shane Delgado were having lunch. Toby's strides were long and easy, as if he had all the time in the world. He was tall and confident and seemed so damn sure that they were doing the right thing, and Naomi really wished she shared that certainty.

Clay, Shane and Toby were all ranchers, so no doubt they were talking about horses or grazing pastures or summer water levels. Her gaze swept them all quickly. Shane had long brown hair, a perpetual five o'clock shadow and a killer smile. He was both a rancher and a real estate developer. Clay was the strong, silent type with short brown hair, a lot of muscles and a limp he'd earned riding the rodeo circuit. After the accident that had ended his rodeo career, Clay had started a cloud computing company and had found even more success. Then there was Toby. Toby was both an inventor and a rancher and, from Naomi's point of view, the most gorgeous of them all.

She blinked at that thought and realized that for the first time she was looking at Toby without the filter of the best friend thing. And it was an eye-opener. When he looked up at her and gave her a slow smile, something inside her lit up—so Naomi instantly shut it down.

Surprise at her own reaction to him had her tearing her gaze from his and reminding herself that this marriage was a platonic one and now was *not* the time to start noting things she never had before. Toby was standing for her like no one else ever had. He was being the friend he always had been, and she should be grateful. Maybe, eventually, she would be.

But at the moment, her own pride was nicked, and Naomi hated knowing that she needed the help. He was right, of course. Raising a baby on her own was a daunting idea, but she would have done it. Now she didn't have to face the future alone. She had her best friend standing beside her. The only real question was, was it fair to *him*?

"Here's your tea," Amanda said, sliding two tall glasses of icy amber liquid onto the table.

"Oh, thanks." Naomi reached for her glass and took a sip.

"It's decaf tea for you, sweetie." Amanda tossed a glance at Toby, Clay and Shane, deep into a conversation, then looked back at Naomi. "I'd expect to see a smile on your face, just getting engaged and all."

Naomi sighed a little. Amanda Battle was a few years older than her, but growing up in the same small town meant they'd known each other forever. Amanda's blond hair was pulled back into a ponytail, and her eyes were sharp and thoughtful as she studied Naomi. "What's going on, Naomi? A woman engaged to a man like Toby McKittrick should be all smiles—and you're not."

"It just happened so fast," Naomi said, already leaning into the lie she and Toby had created out of thin air.

"Not too fast, since you're carrying his baby," Amanda reminded her.

"True." Toby had claimed the baby as his already, so that didn't even feel like a lie. Especially since the baby's actual father didn't even know about the pregnancy. "But he sort of sprung the proposal on me just this morning and I haven't gotten used to it yet, I guess." The best lies had a touch of truth in them, right?

"I know it must feel like a lot," Amanda said, laying one hand on Naomi's shoulder in sympathy. "But I was in your shoes once, remember?"

She did remember, and because she did, Naomi couldn't understand why Amanda was being so nice to her. Several years ago, Amanda had been pregnant and agreed to marry Nathan Battle for the sake of the baby. But then she miscarried and called the wedding off. Amanda had left town after that but had come back a few years later when her father died, and almost instantly, she and Nathan had reconnected and set the gossip train humming. Today, though, Nathan and Amanda had two kids and were so happily married there were practically hearts and flowers circling Amanda's head.

But back then, Naomi and her friends Cecelia and Simone were at the height of their mean girl reputations, and though it shamed her to admit it, Naomi had spread every ounce of gossip about Amanda that had come her way. Shaking her head at the crowd of memories that made her want to cringe, she managed to ask, "Why are you being so nice to me?"

Amanda threw another glance at Toby to make sure he wasn't on his way back, then she slid onto the bench seat opposite Naomi. Tipping her head to one side, Amanda studied her for a second, then said, "Because I've been the center of gossip and I know how ugly it can make you feel. And, Naomi, you're not who you were back then."

"How can you be sure?"

"Because the old Naomi wouldn't be feeling bad about any of it."

Yes, she would have, Naomi thought. Even back then, when she'd been the queen bee, guilt had haunted her whenever she allowed herself to think about what she'd said or done. Now Naomi released a pent-up breath she hadn't even realized she'd been holding. All the years she'd been coming to the Royal Diner, she'd never really had an actual conversation with Amanda. Years ago, it was because they were too far apart in age, and Naomi was too busy mocking people to make herself feel better. And then later, she'd been too ashamed of her past actions to talk to her. A small smile curved Naomi's mouth. "Thanks for that."

Amanda smiled again, shot a quick glance at the kitchen pass-through, then looked at Naomi. "Most of us did things when we were young and stupid that we come to regret." Her smile turned rueful, but her green eyes never left Naomi's. "So if you're lucky enough to grow out of the stupid, then you have a second chance to be who you want to be."

"You make it sound easy."

"It's not," the other woman said. "But you already know that. You started that fashion show—which, by the way, I never miss—and you're building a future with Toby."

"True." But if you were planning that future on a lie, did it count? Could it work? Not questions she could ask out loud. "Thanks. For the pep talk and, well, everything."

"No problem." Amanda scooted out of the booth, stood up and patted Naomi's shoulder again. "Toby's a good guy. You should celebrate."

Nodding, Naomi watched Toby laughing with his friends. Texas cowboys, all three of them. And handsome enough to have women lining up just to take a look at them. Her heart twisted as her gaze landed on Toby just as he lifted his head, caught her eye and winked. That flicker of something bright and hot sparkled inside her again, and though she fought to ignore it, the heat lingered.

In reflex, Naomi returned that smile and quietly hoped that this marriage didn't cost her her best friend.

Toby knew he'd catch his mom and sister off guard with his announcement. After lunch, where he'd finally convinced Naomi to take a small bite of his burger, Toby dropped her off at her condo to start packing. Then he'd driven straight to Oak Ridge Farms, his family ranch.

It was smaller than his own spread, but the ties binding him to the land ran strong and deep. His mother rented out most of the acreage to other ranchers and farmers, and his sister had her veterinary clinic in the remodeled barn. But no matter what changes took place, it would always be the McKittrick Ranch, and steering his truck up the drive would always make him feel the tug of memories.

He knew that he would beat the news of his engagement home, because it didn't matter how fast word was spreading throughout Royal. His mother, Joyce McKittrick, didn't approve of gossip, so she'd been cut out of the rumor loop years ago. As for his sister, Scarlett was too busy caring for the local animals to waste time or interest on gossip.

Toby had told Naomi that he wouldn't lie to his family. So after he explained the whole situation to his mom and sister, he waited for the reaction. He'd expected they'd be surprised. He hadn't expected them to be so happy about it. Especially since he'd made it clear that love didn't have a thing to do with his reasons for this marriage.

"You're marrying Naomi?" Scarlett McKittrick squealed a little, then leaped up from her chair at the kitchen table and ran around to hug her brother. "It's about time."

"What?" Toby looked at his younger sister when she pulled back to grin at him.

"Well, come on," Scarlett said. "You two have been tight for years, and even a blind person would have seen the sparks between you."

Sparks? There were sparks? Toby frowned a little as he realized that maybe all the lustful thoughts he'd been entertaining for so long had been obvious. Well, that was lowering, if his sister noticed something that he'd never seen himself—or allowed himself to see.

"Scarlett," he said, automatically returning his sister's hug, "there are no sparks. I told you it's a marriage of convenience."

"Yeah, I heard you," she countered and gave his cheek a pat as she straightened up. "Doesn't mean I believe you. I've seen the way you look at Naomi, Toby. And it's not like you're thinking *hey, good buddy.*"

"That's exactly what it is. She's my friend. That's all."

Shaking her head, Scarlett glanced at the wall clock and said, "If that's how you want to play it, fine. Look, I've got to run. There's a cow giving birth, and if she manages to pull it off before I get there, people will think they don't need to call me for this stuff." She grabbed her huge black leather bag and headed for the back door.

Once there, she stopped, ran her fingers through her short honey-brown hair and narrowed wide hazel eyes on him. "But I'll want more details later, you hear? 'Bye, Mom. Don't know when I'll be back."

And she was gone. Scarlett McKittrick was a force of nature, Toby thought, not for the first time. She'd always moved through life like a whirlwind, and now that she was a vet, it was even worse. Answering calls for help at all hours, she was dedicated to the animals she loved and as caring as their mother.

Scarlett did everything at a dead run, moving from patient to patient and keeping a grin on her face while she was doing it. Most people looked at her and thought she was too slight to do the kind of work she did. But Toby had seen his sister in action. When one of his mares got into trouble during labor, Scarlett had been there to save the foal and the mother. He knew she had the strength, determination and pure stubbornness to do a job most often thought to be a man's purview.

When the door slammed behind her, silence settled on the homey kitchen. He glanced around quickly while he grabbed a chocolate chip cookie from the plate in the middle of the table. The walls were sky blue and the cabinets were painted bright white. Toby himself had painted the kitchen for his mother the summer before, and he figured she'd be ready for another change by next year. The floor was wide oak planks, and the fridge and the stove had been replaced with top-of-the-line new ones. But there were old pictures attached with magnets to the new fridge, and when he looked at the images of him and Scarlett as kids, he had to smile. His mom's old mutt, Lola, was napping on a cushion under the bay window, and her snores rattled in the room.

Toby had grown up in this house and spent too many hours to count sitting at this very table. He'd done his homework here, had family dinners, come in late from a date to find his mother awake and waiting up for him. So it made sense to him that it was here that he and his mother had the conversation he could see building in her eyes.

Joyce McKittrick was short, with golden-blond hair that fell in waves to her shoulders. Her blue eyes were as sharp as ever, and she never missed a thing. She was, he thought, beautiful, strong and smart. Hadn't she stepped up when Toby's father died, to raise Scarlett and him on her own? Thanks to her husband's life insurance, they hadn't had to worry about money, but Joyce had never been one to sit back and do nothing. She'd boarded horses and given riding lessons to local kids. And she'd encouraged both Scarlett's love of animals and Toby's inventive nature. In fact, she was the one who'd made sure he got a patent on his very first invention—a robotic ketchup dispenser he'd come up with at the age of ten.

Joyce was his touchstone, the heart of their family, and she had given his sister and him the kind of home life that Naomi had missed out on.

"When you first said you were marrying Naomi, I was pleased. She's a good person, and I'm glad she's finally letting that side of her out to shine instead of hiding behind a mean streak that wasn't natural to her."

He smiled to himself. Trust Joyce to see past the surface to the truth beneath. Not many had, really. Naomi,

Cecelia and Simone had been like a trio of mean for a long time. They had always seemed to enjoy setting people back a step. To strike quick with a sharp word or a hard look.

But times, like everything else, changed, and now the three of them seemed to be coming into their own. Naomi, especially, he thought, had done well by letting go of her past enough to carve out the future she wanted for herself.

"Should have known you'd see through all that drama she used to be a part of," Toby said ruefully.

"Of course I did." Joyce waved that aside. "Her parents are…difficult and they made Naomi's life a misery for her, I know. It says something about her character that she's come so far all on her own." She reached out and smoothed his hair back from his face. "Though she had a good friend, these last few years, to be there for her."

"I have been," Toby said, wanting her to understand. "And I'm going to continue."

"I know that, too," his mother said, sitting back in her chair to give him a long look. "But, Toby, starting a marriage with a lie isn't the best way to go."

"We're not lying to each other," he countered. "Or to you and Scarlett." He'd known she'd feel this way, and he couldn't blame her. But he could convince her he knew what he was doing. "Naomi needs me, Mom. That baby does, too. I watched you struggle as a single mother, and I don't want to watch Naomi do the same. We get along great. We're good friends."

Apparently with sparks, he warned himself silently, and then dismissed the warning. "We're good together, and this is what I want."

"Then I want it for you," she said, though her eyes

said different. "All I ask is that you be careful. That you really think about what you're letting yourself in for."

He grinned and winked. "I'm always careful."

"Not nearly enough," she said, laughing a little.

"Honestly," Toby said, stealing another cookie and taking a bite. No one made cookies like Joyce McKittrick. "I figured you'd have the most trouble with me claiming the baby as mine."

"Not a bit," she said, shaking her head firmly. "That baby is an innocent, and you and Naomi are doing the right thing for it. I just want to be sure it's the right thing for *you*."

"It is, Mom," he said, his tone deep and serious. "I never figured to get married…"

She snorted a laugh. "Men always seem to say that, yet the world is filled with husbands."

His eyebrows arched. "*Anyway,*" he said pointedly, "Naomi and I are good together. I think we'll make this work for all of us."

"I always liked Naomi," Joyce said, nodding. "She's got a lot of spirit and a little sass, and that's a good thing. But she's also got a heart that's not been treated very gently over the years."

"I'm not going to hurt her."

"Not purposely, of course," she said. "And she wouldn't intentionally hurt you, either. Still, I'm your mother, so I'll worry a little, and there's nothing either of us can do to stop that. But if it's my blessing you were after, you have it."

"You're amazing," he said softly.

"I just know my son." She stood up, walked to a cupboard and came back with a plastic zip bag. She dumped every last cookie into the bag and sealed it before handing it over to Toby. "You take these home with you. And when you get home, you have a good long talk with yourself. Make sure this is what you want."

"I have. I will." He reached out and patted her hand. "I know what I'm doing."

Joyce shook her head and smiled wryly. "Scarlett was right, you know. There's always been sparks between you and Naomi."

"Mom…"

"I'm just saying, don't be surprised if those sparks kindle a fire neither of you is expecting."

Four

The next morning, Naomi was at the local cable studio outside Royal. No matter what else was going on in her life, she had a job to do—the fact that she loved her job was a bonus.

The station was small but had everything you could need. Local businesses used it to film commercials, the high school football games were broadcast from the studio, and Naomi's own show had been born there. The studio was so well set up they had community college students as interns, helping the professional staff.

She tried to focus on the upcoming taping of her show, but it wasn't easy to concentrate when she knew that Toby would be coming by her condo that afternoon to help move her things to the ranch. Naomi stopped on the walk across the parking lot, just to allow her brain to wheel through everything that was happening. She'd worked hard to buy her little condo in Royal and then to fix it up just as she wanted it. Sure, it was small, but it was *hers*. Her own place. And now she was giving it up to move to the country.

Granted, growing up in a small town in Texas, she was used to being in the country. But she'd never *lived* there. And not only was she giving up her home, but she was marrying her best friend, and that still was enough to make her bite her bottom lip and question herself.

In fact, Naomi had spent most of the night before pacing through her home, mind spinning. Was she doing the right thing? She didn't know. There were plenty of doubts, plenty of questions and not many answers. All she could be sure of was the decision had been made and there was no backing out now—since the whole town was talking about her engagement to Toby.

Of course, she told herself, since everyone was busy with Toby's lie, no one was talking much about the hideous video Maverick had put out. And today she was taping her first maternity-wear show—fighting fire with fire. Maverick had wanted to make her look foolish, but she would take his announcement and make it her own. Toby had been right about that. If Maverick wanted her crying in a corner somewhere, he was going to be really disappointed.

Truthfully, it was a relief to no longer have to hide the fact that she was pregnant. Disguising a growing baby bump wasn't easy. Loose shirts, pinned slacks and an oversize bag to hold in front of the rounding part of her body could only work for so long. Knowing her secret was out was…liberating in a way she hadn't expected.

Taking a deep breath, she headed for the building, stepped into the air-conditioned cool and came face-to-face with Eddie, the lead cameraman. He was an older man, with grizzled salt-and-pepper hair that stuck out around his head like he'd been electrocuted.

"We're ready for the run-through, Naomi." He gave her a smile and a thumbs-up. "You good to go?"

"I really am, as soon as I stop by makeup," she said. Twenty minutes later, she walked to the set, hair perfect, makeup just as she wanted it and her wardrobe displaying that bump she'd been hiding for too long.

Local cable channel or not, Naomi's show, *Fashion Sense*, was catching on. In the last year, she'd managed to get picked up by affiliates in Houston and Dallas, and just this week a station in Galveston had contacted her about carrying her show. And, thanks to social media, word about her show was spreading far beyond the Texas borders. Her Facebook page boasted followers from as far away as New York and California and even a few in Europe.

Naomi had plans. She wanted to take her show national. She wanted to be featured in magazines, to be taken seriously enough that even her parents would have to sit up and take notice. And she was going to make those dreams come true. Lifting her chin, Naomi walked in long, determined strides to the center of her set and turned to face the camera and her growing audience. The lights were bright, hot and felt absolutely right.

"In five, four," Tammy, the assistant sound engineer, said, counting down with her fingers as well until she reached one and pointed at Naomi.

"Hi, and welcome to *Fashion Sense*. I'm Naomi Price." She was comfortable in front of the camera. Always had been, a small part of her mind admitted quietly. Toby had been right about that, too. She enjoyed being the center of attention when it was *her* idea.

And she had a lot of ideas. Just last night, while she wandered her condo hoping for sleep, her mind had raced with all kinds of possibilities. To grow her audience, she had to grow the show itself. Make it appeal to as many people as possible. There were plenty of women out there, she knew, who didn't give a damn about fashion—though she found that hard to believe. But those women did care about their homes, decorating. Just look at all the DIY programs that were so popular.

Well, she couldn't build a staircase or install fresh lighting, but she knew how to find those who could. So today, she was going to announce a few of the changes she had in mind. Starting, she told herself, with the biggest announcement of all. With Maverick's video out and viral by now, she had to assume that her viewers had seen it, or would have by the time this show aired. So she was taking control of the situation.

"As you can see," she said, turning sideways to show off the baby bump proudly displayed beneath a tight lavender tank, "my own personal fashion style will be undergoing some drastic transformations over the next few months. My fiancé, Toby McKittrick, and I are both very happy about our coming baby and we're excited to greet all the new things in our future."

Smiling into the camera, she faced the audience head-on again and continued. "And to keep up with the changes in my life, I'm going to be doing a lot of shows focusing on contemporary, fashionable maternity wear, obviously."

Again, that brilliant smile shot into the camera and into homes across Texas. "But don't worry. It's not going to be all babies all the time. As our lives grow and evolve, we have to keep up. So here on *Fashion Sense*, we're going to be branching out—dipping into home furnishings and gardens and even designing your own outdoor living space." She tossed her hair back from her face and winked. "Since I'm expanding, I thought it was only right the show did a little growing, too."

Off camera, she heard a chuckle from one of the grips and knew she'd hit just the right note.

"So I hope you'll come with me on this journey of discovery. Over the next few months, we'll all be in new territory—should be fun!"

"And cut."

When Eddie gave her the go-ahead, Naomi looked at him and asked, "Well, how'd I do?"

"Great, Naomi, seriously great." Eddie winked at her. "I think you're on to something with this house stuff. My wife's always watching those home shows, coming up with things for me to do. So I already know she'll be hounding me to do whatever it is you show her."

"Good to know," Naomi said, laughing.

"We're gonna set up for the next shot. Be about fifteen minutes," Eddie said as the crew scurried around, making TV magic happen.

As long as most women felt as Eddie's wife did, this new direction Naomi was determined to take would work out. All she had to do was bring in experts to interview and to demonstrate their specialties. She could already see it. Gardeners, painters, tiling specialists. She would push *Fashion Sense* to the next level—and at the bottom of it, didn't she have Maverick to thank for the push?

Unsettling thought. Naomi wandered off to a chair in a quiet corner of the studio, sat down and turned her phone on. She checked her email, sighed a little at the number of them and wondered halfheartedly how many of them were because of Maverick's video. With that thought in mind, she closed her email program. She didn't need to deal with them right this minute, and she really didn't want to ruin the good mood she was in.

Because she felt great. She'd taken Maverick's slap at her and turned it around. She was taking ownership of her pregnancy, pushing her show to new heights—and marrying her best friend.

Okay, she could admit that she was still worried about that. Toby had been such an important part of her life for so long that if she lost him because of a fake marriage, it would break her heart. So maybe they needed to talk again. To really think this through, together. To somehow make a pact that their friendship would always come first.

The rumble and scrape of furniture being moved echoed in the building, letting her know the guys were still hard at work. So when her phone rang, Naomi checked the screen and felt her heart sink into a suddenly open pit in her stomach.

Wouldn't you know it? Just when things were starting to look up.

Answering her phone, she said, "Hello, Gio."

"Ciao, *bella*." The voice was smooth, dark and warm, just as she remembered it from that night nearly five months ago now.

Naomi closed her eyes as the memory swept over her, and she shook her head to lose it again just as fast. It wasn't easy admitting that you'd been stupid enough to have a one-night stand with a man you *knew* would be nothing more than that. And even though they'd used protection, apparently it wasn't foolproof.

Gio Fabiani, gorgeous, lying player who'd sneaked past her defenses long enough to get her into bed. Even now Naomi felt a quick stab of regret for her own poor choices. But moaning over the past wouldn't get her anywhere. She opened her eyes, looked across the room at the crew busily working and kept her voice low as she spoke to Gio. As much as she'd prefer to just hang up on the man, she had to do the right thing and tell him about the baby.

"I have your many messages on my phone, *bella*," Gio was saying. "What is so important? Is it that you miss me?"

She rolled her eyes and ground her teeth together, silently praying for patience. Behind his voice, she heard the telltale clatter and noise of a busy restaurant. With the time difference between Texas and Italy, it was late afternoon for Gio and he was probably at his favorite trattoria, sitting at a table on the sidewalk where he could see and be seen. She frowned at the mental image and then instantly shut down everything but the urge to get the truth said and done.

"I've been trying to get hold of you for months, Gio," she said softly.

"*Sì, sì*, I have been very busy."

Getting other foolish women into his bed, no doubt, and oh, how it burned to know she'd been just one of a crowd.

"Yes, me too. Gio," she said, taking a breath to say it all at once. "I'm pregnant."

Silence on the other end of the line and then, "This is happy news for you, *sì*?"

She skipped right over that. None of his business how she was feeling. "You're the father."

A longer silence from him this time, and she heard the street sounds of Italy in the background. She could see him, lounging in a chair, legs kicked out in front of him, a glass of wine in one hand and the phone in the other. What she couldn't see was his reaction. She didn't have long to wait for it, though.

"I am no one's father, *bella*," he said softly enough that she had to strain to hear him. "If you carry the baby, the baby is yours, not mine."

She hadn't expected anything else, but still, hearing it felt like a slap. How many women, she wondered, had made this call to Gio? How many times had he heard about a child he'd made just before he walked away from all responsibility? He was a dog, but it was her own fault that she'd fallen for his practiced charm. Toby had been right about him, of course. He'd called him a user, and that described Gio to a tee.

Naomi didn't actually *want* Gio in her life or her baby's. It seemed she would get what she wanted. But she had to be sure they both understood right where things were. "You're not interested?"

"*Bella*, you must see that I am not a man who wishes the encumbrance of a child."

The tone of his voice was that of a man trying to explain something to a very stupid person. And maybe she had been stupid. Once. But she wasn't anymore.

"That's fine, Gio. I'm not the one who made this phone call, Gio. I don't want anything from you," she said, flicking a glance toward the set, making sure no one was within earshot. "You had a right to know about the baby. That's it."

"Ah," he said on a long sigh of what she assumed was satisfaction. "Then we are finished together, yes?"

Big yes, she thought. In an instant, her mind drew up an image of Toby and what had happened yesterday. How he'd stood with her to face her parents. The difference between the two men was incalculable. Toby would always do the right thing. Always. Gio did the expedient thing. And Naomi herself? She would do what was best for her baby. And that was ridding them of the man who was, as he'd pointed out, *no one's* father.

"Yes, Gio," she said, her grip on the phone tightening until her fingers ached. "We're finished."

And she was relieved. She'd never have to see him or deal with him again. There was no worry about him coming back at some later date, wanting to be a part of her baby's life. The minute he hung up the phone, Gio would forget all about this conversation. He would forget *her*. And that was best for everybody.

"*Arrivederci, bella,*" Gio said and, without waiting for a response from her, disconnected.

She expelled a breath, looked at her phone for a long minute, then shook her head. Naomi had been trying to reach Gio for weeks, and when she finally did manage a conversation with him, it had lasted about three minutes. It felt as if a huge weight had been lifted off her shoulders. "It's over."

Of course it had *been* over for months. Heck, it had never even started with Gio, really. You couldn't count one night as anything other than a blip on the radar that appeared and disappeared in the blink of an eye. If she hadn't gotten pregnant, would she even have given Gio a single thought? "No, I wouldn't have," she said out loud.

Really, she'd have done everything possible to never think about one night of bad judgment. She looked down at the phone in her hand as a wave of relief swept over her. Gio was well and truly out of her life. Naomi knew Toby would be pleased to hear it.

Toby.

The familiar noises of the crew working registered in one part of her mind as her thoughts swirled as if caught in a tornado. What did it say, she asked herself, that the first person she wanted to tell about the call from Gio was Toby? That he was her best friend. That he was the one person in her life she always turned to first.

Maybe marrying him would be all right, she told herself now. Maybe it would be good for all of them. She trusted him, she loved him—as a friend—and she knew she'd always be able to count on him. So what was she so worried about? No sex? Not that big a deal, she assured herself silently. Heck, it wasn't as if pregnant women had red-hot sex lives anyway.

Was it fair to Toby? Wasn't that up to him? she reasoned. If he wanted to marry her, why shouldn't she? Yes, she could be a single mother. She was perfectly capable of raising a child on her own. But as Toby had pointed out, why deliberately take the hard route when there was another answer? And knowing that Toby would be with her, sharing it all, seemed to make the niggling fears of impending motherhood easier to conquer. But what to do with the fears she had of losing her best friend because of a convenient lie?

"We're ready, Naomi," Tammy shouted from across the room.

Pushing herself out of the chair, still wrestling with her thoughts, Naomi walked to the set. Distracted, she took her place in the center of the stage.

"Hey, hey," Eddie said. "Find your smile again, Naomi. We've got to finish this segment."

"Right." She shook off the dark thoughts, focused again on the moment and resolved to put all her energies into making this the best show she could.

Toby led the way into the stable, glancing over his shoulder at Clay Everett. As a former rodeo champ, Clay was the best judge of horseflesh in the county—not counting Toby himself, of course. Clay had left the rodeo behind after a bull-riding accident that had been bad enough to leave him with a slight limp. And a part of the man still missed it, Toby knew. The competition, the intensity of a seven-second ride that could win a trophy or break your heart. But he was settled now in Royal on his own ranch, and horses were still a big part of his life.

Of course there was more to Clay than being a successful rancher. His company, Everest, installed cloud infrastructure for corporations and was in demand by everyone with half a brain. Though Clay was a hell of a businessman, his heart was still at his ranch. The man was much like Toby in that way. Didn't matter how many inventions Toby came up with or how his business interests ate up his time, the ranch fed his soul.

There were twenty stalls in Toby's stables, but only eleven of them were occupied at the moment. Clay was here to see one of Toby's treasures—a beautiful chestnut mare called Rain.

"I brought her in from the south pasture this morning. Thought you'd want to take a close look at her before sealing the deal."

"You thought right," Clay said and stopped alongside Toby at the stall's half door. Inside the enclosure, the beautiful horse stood idly nosing at the fresh straw on the floor. When Toby clucked his tongue, the mare looked up, then moved to greet him.

"She's a beauty," Clay said, reaching out to stroke the flat of his hand along the horse's neck.

The mare actually seemed to preen under the attention. Clay laughed. "Yeah, you know you're something special, don't you?"

"She does." Toby watched Clay feed the mare an apple he'd brought along just for that reason. "She's two years old, good health—Scarlett did a full physical on her last week."

"Scarlett's word's good enough for me," Clay said, stroking the horse's nose. "Yeah, you still want to sell her, I want her."

"Deal," Toby said and gave the mare one longing look. Raising horses also meant you had to sell them, too. You couldn't keep them all. But every time he sold a horse, he felt the loss like a physical pang. Still, he knew Clay would be good to her, and Toby would get a chance to see her once in a while.

"We'll go up to the house, have a beer and take care of business."

"Sounds good," Clay said. Then he slanted Toby a look. "I hear you and Naomi are getting married."

Getting married. The words didn't send a clawing sense of dread and panic ripping through him. After Sasha walked out on him, Toby had pulled back from anything even remotely resembling a relationship. Now here he was, engaged, going to be a father, and it felt... good.

Toby blew out a breath, tipped the brim of his Stetson back a bit and nodded. Here it was. He was going to look into his friend's eyes and lie to him. But, hell. A lie to protect Naomi didn't bother him a bit. "When you've got a baby coming, it's time to get married."

Clay's eyebrows lifted. "Hadn't heard the baby part of the rumor. My source is slipping."

Toby grinned. "Times are sad when you can't count on the gossip chain to be thorough."

"Can't believe how the men in this town are getting caught in the marriage trap." Clay shook his head as if very sad for all his friends. The man's smile, though, told Toby he was enjoying all this. "Wes Jackson is a man I thought would never go down that road, and look at him now."

Toby had been thinking the same thing just a few months ago. Watching Wes reconnect with the woman he loved and discover he had a daughter had hit Toby hard at the time. Back then he'd felt the same way Clay did now, that somehow Wes had set himself up for pain. Funny how your ideas could change so dramatically in just a few months. Of course, he reminded himself, he wasn't in love with Naomi. This was a bargain between friends. Which was why it would work.

"He's happy." Toby braced both feet wide apart, folding his arms across his chest. Just because he wasn't looking for love didn't mean he couldn't recognize it when he saw it. "Hell, he practically *glows* when he's around Belle. And as for his daughter, Caro, he's become such a whiz at sign language he's talking about teaching it to a few of us so we can talk secretly to each other in the TCC board meetings."

Sunlight speared through the open stable doors, pouring spears of gold into the shadowy interior. The building smelled of horses and hay—one of Toby's favorite scents.

Nodding thoughtfully, Clay said, "Not a bad plan

there. But not the point of what I was saying. It's this whole wedding plague that's sweeping through Royal. It's picking the men off one by one."

"A *plague*?" Toby laughed.

"It sure as hell seems contagious," Clay said. Ticking them off on his fingers, he continued. "There's Deacon and Hutch and Tom Knox."

"Tom doesn't count," Toby interrupted. "He and Emily were already married."

"Yeah, but they were separated, now they're not," Clay pointed out. "Then there's Shane and now *you*."

Toby laughed shortly and shook his head. "I'm not sick—so not contagious, no worries there. I'm not caught in a trap, either, man. I'm marrying my best friend." And as he said it, Toby again felt the rightness of it. There was no risk in this marriage. No worry about falling for a woman and having her walk out, taking half his heart with her.

He'd already done that. Already lived through betrayal and having his heart smashed under the boot of a woman who decided some loser wannabe country singer was a better bet than a Texas inventor/cowboy. When Sasha walked out, she'd burned him badly enough that Toby hadn't wanted anything to do with women. But Naomi had been there with him, through all of it.

He didn't give a damn about Sasha anymore and figured he'd made a lucky escape in spite of the pain and fury he'd survived. And Naomi had helped him get clear of all that. So marrying her was not just a perfect solution to the current problem—it was also a way to stand by Naomi. To thank her for being there for him when he needed it most. This marriage meant he got his best friend living with him. He got a child to raise and love, and he didn't have to worry about whether or not he could trust his wife.

"Yeah, well," Clay said wryly, "she's your best friend *now*. That'll stop when she's your *wife*."

A flicker of doubt sputtered into life inside him, but Toby squashed it flat. "Not Naomi. I trust her."

"Your funeral," Clay said with a shrug.

"You talk a hard game," Toby retorted with a half laugh. "But then there's Sophie."

Sophie Prescott. Clay's secretary.

The other man shrugged, stuffed his hands into his pockets and said, "What about her?"

"Oh, man, don't try to look innocent. You can't pull it off." Toby laughed. "I've seen the way you look at her."

"Looking's one thing. Marrying's another," Clay allowed with a grin. "The rest of you may get picked off one by one, but you can bank on me being the last single man standing."

"Yeah," Toby said, heading for the house, waiting for Clay to follow, "that's what we all say. But you know what? You're going back to a cold, empty ranch, while I'll be here with Naomi."

He smiled to himself as he realized he was looking forward to having her here. To her being a part of his everyday life. Of watching that baby inside her grow. With Naomi, he could have the life he wanted with none of the dangers or risks. What man wouldn't want that?

Five

"So," Simone asked as she set an empty box down on Naomi's bed, "how excited is Toby to be a father?"

Simone had her nearly blue-black hair pulled back into a thick tail that hung down between her shoulder blades. The woman's amazing ice-blue eyes shone with a kind of happiness Naomi was glad to see there. Simone had the kind of face that made most people think she was gorgeous but empty-headed. It didn't take her long to prove just how brilliant she really was.

"He says he's really happy about it." Which was true, but not the whole truth. A flicker of unease rippled through her as Naomi realized that to keep her bargain with Toby, keep her baby safe, she'd have to lie to her closest friends.

It wasn't that she didn't trust Simone and Cecelia both. They'd been friends forever, and heaven knew the three of them had shared so many secrets, there really wasn't much they didn't know about each other. But she had to think about her baby, too. The baby who would grow up knowing Toby as its father. Was it fair to her child to let other people in on the fact that Gio Fabiani had been her sperm donor? And that was really all he had been, she assured herself. He wasn't a father in any sense of the word, so did he really deserve to even be mentioned? Now that she'd actually spoken to him and knew without a doubt that he'd never have anything to do with the baby, wasn't it better for everyone to just forget about his involvement completely?

"I can't believe you managed to keep your pregnancy a secret. From *us*," Simone added. "I mean, you're nearly five months, right?"

"It's because she never eats," Cecelia put in, playfully sticking her tongue out at Naomi. She was any man's dream woman, Naomi thought. Gray-green eyes, long wavy platinum hair, a curvy figure and long legs. She was also driven, ambitious and funny. "She's pregnant and still skinnier than I am."

Skinny. That had been Naomi's goal for most of her life. Now her body would be doing as much changing as her life, and she found she wasn't too concerned about it. Maybe it was having Toby standing with her. Maybe it was finally accepting and being proud of the fact that she was going to be a mother. Whatever the reason, though, Naomi thought it was about time she stopped worrying so much about the scale. She had more to think of than herself now, right? Hadn't Toby said just the other day that the baby needed more than a lettuce leaf to grow on?

"Naomi?" Cecelia asked. "You okay?"

"What? Yeah. Sorry. I'm fine. I'm just—" She paused, looked around at the chaos strewn around the bedroom of her condo and realized it was the perfect metaphor for her life. "Overwhelmed."

"Easy to understand," Simone said, folding another sweater and laying it in a box. "It's not every day you get slammed in a viral video, get engaged and announce a pregnancy."

"God," Naomi whispered. "It sounds even crazier when you say it out loud."

"Yes, but you're handling it," Cecelia said, pushing her hair back and kicking back onto the bed to get comfy. She crossed her feet at the ankle, grabbed a pillow and held it against her belly. "Simone and I have had our share of crazy lately, too, remember?"

"Absolutely," Simone muttered and pushed Cecelia's feet out of the way to reach for a stack of folded T-shirts. "Honestly, I didn't know what was going to happen with Deacon, but now look at us."

Cecelia tossed Simone more shirts while Naomi zipped her cosmetics case closed.

"Heck, look at *all* of us," Cecelia said with a wide smile. "The mean girls are done, and we're all in love."

Naomi sighed a little.

"Plus," Cecelia added, "we're all pregnant at the same time. Our kids can grow up friends."

"I'm more pregnant," Simone pointed out. "There's three in here." She patted her slightly rounded tummy. "Remember?"

Cecelia laughed. "You always were a show-off."

Naomi smiled, too, because it was so easy to be with these women. They'd been a trio for so long she couldn't even imagine her life without them in it. She had great friends. Cecelia, Simone—and Toby.

Bottom line, worries and all, it came down to the fact that she was marrying her best friend. How bad could it be?

"Is it time for a break?" Cecelia asked from the bed. "Come on, let's let the new fiancé finish this up when he gets here."

"Cec," Simone said, "if you'd pack as much as you talk, we'd be finished by now."

"Talking's more fun," Cecelia said, but she dutifully pushed herself off the bed, walked to the closet and dragged Naomi's garment bag down off the high shelf. "Fine. I'll get as much of her stuff into this thing as I can. But there's no way we'll get all your clothes in one trip, Naomi."

"I know." Her condo was small, but the closets were huge. It was really what had sold her on the place. "You know what?" she said, making up her mind on the spot. "Cec, do what you can with that bag. Simone, when we fill up this box, we're stopping. That's it. I've got enough to live on, and it's not like I'm moving to the moon. Toby and I can come back to get the rest another time."

"Deal. I feel ice cream coming on," Cecelia said from the depths of the closet.

Simone sighed. "Ice cream. I love ice cream. And I'm going to be *much* bigger than you guys will be, so I shouldn't have any. But I'm weak."

"You're safe, then," Naomi told her with a shrug. "I don't have ice cream in the house." In fact, she didn't have anything fattening in the condo. She'd never seen the point in testing her own willpower.

"Oh, that's just wrong." Cecelia came out of the closet,

laid the garment bag on the bed, then picked up her purse. "I'm going up to the store for ice cream and maybe cookies. I'll be back in fifteen minutes."

When she was gone, Simone said, "Thank goodness for Cec. I really do want ice cream now."

Naomi laughed. "I guess we do have to have some priorities, huh?"

"Ice cream is top of the list," Simone said. Then she hooked one arm around Naomi's shoulders. "I know what you're thinking. Everything's changing."

"Yeah," Naomi agreed, wrapping one arm around her friend's waist, "that's it exactly."

"I was feeling the same way just a few weeks ago, but then I remembered the most important thing."

"What's that?" Naomi asked.

"Change can be *good*, too."

"You're right," Naomi said and looked around the room again.

This condo had been perfect for her once. When she was single, with nothing more to think about than the career she was trying to forge. But the condo wasn't who she was anymore.

It was time to figure out who she was becoming.

"We can't sleep in the same bed."

Later that night, Naomi was at Paradise Ranch, staring up at Toby in stunned surprise. Sure, they had a no-sex agreement, but *look* at him.

He took a breath and blew it out again in obvious exasperation. "Naomi, you know I've got a housekeeper. If Rebecca sees we're not staying in the same room, how long do you figure it'll be before the rest of Royal knows it?"

"But—" She looked at the gigantic bed against the far wall of Toby's bedroom and shook her head. Sure, it was big enough for four or five people, but was it big enough for the two of them?

The room was cavernous, just right for the master of the house. There was a black granite fireplace tall enough for Naomi to stand up in, with two chairs and a table sitting in front of the now cold hearth. Along one wall were bookcases stuffed with hard-and soft-backed books, family pictures, and framed patents Toby had received for his many inventions. Across from the bed, a gigantic flat-screen TV hung on the wall, and French doors on the far wall led out to a wide wooden balcony that overlooked the fields behind the house and the really spectacular pool.

But her gaze kept sliding back to that bed. A massive four-poster, with heavy head-and footboards, the mattress was covered in a dark red quilt that looked as if it had been hand stitched. Toby's mother, Joyce, was a quilting fiend, so she was probably behind that. And there was a small mountain of pillows propped against that headboard, practically begging a person to climb up and sink in.

The whole room was inviting, and Naomi had to at least partially blame herself for that, since she'd helped him decorate the house. But she'd never imagined herself sleeping in the master bedroom.

"I thought I'd be staying in one of the guest rooms," she argued. "You've got seven bedrooms in this place."

"Yeah." He scrubbed one hand across the beard stubble on his jaw. "But married people sleep together. That's what folks expect."

He had a point, and why hadn't she considered it before? She hadn't counted on this at all. How was she supposed to share a bed with her best friend?

"Okay, look," he said, clearly reading what she was thinking. "We'll try this. You can sleep in the room next to mine, but all your stuff stays here, in my room. That should throw Rebecca off the scent. Especially if we keep that guest room looking like nobody's been in it."

"Okay. I can do that." This was crazy and getting worse by the minute. Enforced closeness was going to push their friendship places it had never been before, and it really worried her that the relationship might just snap from all the tension.

Reaching out for him, she laid one hand on his forearm and waited until his gaze shifted to hers. "You have to promise me, Toby. You have to swear that no matter what else happens between us, we stay friends."

"That's not even a question, Naomi." He pulled her in close for a hard hug, and Naomi surprised herself by leaning into him, relishing the feel of his strength wrapping itself around her. So much was changing so quickly that he was her stable point in the universe, and if she lost him, Naomi didn't think she could take it.

"We're gonna do fine, Naomi. Don't worry." His hands moved up and down her back, and tiny whips of heat sneaked beneath her defenses. Startled by that simmering burn, she stepped away from him, told herself that she was just tired. Distracted. Vulnerable. But that heat was still there, and Naomi knew she needed some distance.

And she didn't think the guest room was going to be far enough away.

Naomi hadn't been awake at 6:00 a.m. in...*ever*. And couldn't understand why she was now.

An avowed town girl, Naomi had always believed the only reason to be up with the sun was that your house was on fire. Yet now she was going to be a rancher's wife. She was in the country, where the quiet was so profound it was almost alive. There were no cars roaring down the street, no neighbors with a too-loud stereo. Here the night was really dark and there were more stars in the sky than she'd ever known existed.

She hadn't slept well, either. Lying there in the dark, listening to the quiet, knowing Toby was just on the other side of the wall, had kept her too on edge to do more than doze on and off. So this morning, it was too early, she was too sleepy and felt too off balance. Clutching the single measly cup of coffee she allowed herself each day she stepped out onto the back porch, where the soft, morning breeze slid past her.

The only reason she was up early enough to watch the sun claim the sky and begin to beat down on Texas with a vengeance was that Toby had woken her in the guest room so she could move into his bedroom while he went to work.

Once in Toby's bed, she'd tried to get back to sleep, but the pillows carried his scent and the sheets were still warm from his skin, and none of that was conducive to sleeping. She could have stayed upstairs and unpacked, but instead she'd grabbed one of Toby's T-shirts and pulled it on over her maternity jeans—that thankfully didn't *look* like maternity jeans unless you saw the elastic panel over the belly. She wore slip-on red sneakers and left her hair to hang in a tumble over her shoulders.

Now she looked around in the early morning heat and thought how beautiful Paradise Ranch was. There were live oaks studding the yard, providing patches of shade under the already blazing Texas sun. A kitchen garden behind the house was laid out in tidy rows and surrounded by a low white picket fence in the hopes of discouraging rabbits. The corral was enclosed by a high fence, also painted white, and the barn as well as the bunkhouse used by the cowboys who worked for Toby were freshly painted in a deep brick red. Toby's workshop was on the other side of the property from the barn and was the same farmyard red as the rest of the outbuildings.

The yard in front of the house boasted a neatly tended green lawn. Summer flowers in bright jewel tones hugged the base of the big house. But the house itself was the masterpiece. Two stories, it was the kind of house you expected to see in a mountain setting, with cedar walls, river rocks along the foundation and tall windows that opened the house up to wide views of the ranchland. To one side of the house was a pool, surrounded by rocks and waterfalls so cleverly designed that it looked like a naturally formed lagoon, and the whole thing was shaded by more oaks and a vine-covered pergola. A wraparound porch held tables and comfortable chairs that signaled a welcome and silently invited people to sit and relax.

This wasn't her first visit to Toby's ranch. She'd helped him design it. Helped to decorate it. Yet it all felt…different to her now. Not surprising, she told herself, since now she was *living* here. And awake way too early.

She took another sip of her coffee and let her gaze slide across the trees, the field beyond the barn and then back to the corral where Toby was grooming one of his prized horses.

Toby stood near the fence, brushing down a golden-brown horse whose coat seemed to shine in the sunlight.

But as beautiful as the horse was, Naomi couldn't take her eyes off Toby. He wasn't wearing a shirt. She took another gulp of coffee and struggled to swallow past the knot in her throat.

His chest was broad and chiseled, skin tanned, and every move he made had his muscles rippling in a way that made her think of those cool sheets and the wide bed.

"Oh, God…" Hormones, she told herself. Had to be hormones running amok inside her. Pregnancy was making her crazy. It was the only explanation for why looking at her best friend could suddenly turn her insides to mush.

She laid one hand on her rounded belly, and touching her baby seemed to ground her. Remind her of why she was here. What she'd agreed to. And for heaven's sake, Toby was her *friend*. She had no business getting all ruffled over a muscular chest and a tight butt encased in worn blue denim. She shouldn't even be noticing how the shadows thrown across his features by his cowboy hat made his face look sharply dangerous. And if she had any sense at all, she'd turn right around and go back in the house.

"Naomi?"

Oh, thank God. She turned to the open back door where Rebecca stood, holding out a sturdy wicker basket. "Yes?"

Rebecca had graying red hair, bottle-green eyes and freckles sprinkled liberally across her nose and cheeks. She was a widow in her midfifties with two grown kids who lived in Houston. She'd been working for Toby for five years and lived in a set of rooms off the kitchen. And she couldn't be more excited at the prospect of having a baby in the house to take care of.

"I've got to get breakfast going, and you could do me a huge favor if you'd go collect some eggs for me."

"Eggs?"

Rebecca wiggled the basket. "The chicken coop is on the other side of the barn. Just gather what's there. Should be enough with what's still in the fridge."

Naomi walked over, took the basket and handed her now-empty coffee cup to the other woman. "You know, I've never actually gathered eggs before," she admitted, wondering why it sounded like an apology.

"Nothing to it." Rebecca was already darting back into the coolness of the house. "Just reach under the chickens and grab them up." She let the screen door slam behind her, then closed the wood door as well.

"Reach under the chickens." Naomi looked at the empty basket, then lifted her gaze to the side of the barn where she could just make out another structure. A chicken coop. With chickens in it. Did chickens bite?

"I guess I'll find out," she muttered and started walking. If nothing else, this should take her mind off Toby. For now, anyway. She was headed across the yard, in no hurry to find out what *reaching under a chicken* was like, when Toby's voice stopped her.

"Hey, Naomi, come on over here a minute."

She changed course and walked to the corral, swinging the wicker basket with each step. Toby watched her approach, and even in the shadow of his hat, she saw those aqua eyes of his shining. Then Toby flashed a grin that made her heartbeat jolt a little, and Naomi told herself to get a grip.

Honestly, she'd always known he was a good-looking man. You'd have to be blind not to notice. But did he have to be *gorgeous*? Up close, his chest looked broader, his skin tanner, and every muscle seemed to have been carved out of bronze. She swallowed hard, forced a smile and said, "I'm supposed to be gathering eggs. Do the chickens mind?"

He laughed.

"Seriously," she said. "How do you gather eggs?"

Shaking his head, he said, "You're a smart woman. You'll figure it out." Toby opened the corral gate so she could step into the paddock with him. "I wanted you to meet Legend."

The horse he held by the bridle was tall and golden brown, with a dark streak down the center of his nose. His big dark eyes locked on Naomi, and she said, "He's beautiful."

"He is," Toby agreed. "I've had Legend with me since I was a kid. He's been living out at Mom's ranch, but I brought him here to Paradise a couple months ago. He's old, and I wanted him to live out the rest of his life here. With me."

"He doesn't look old." She reached out one hand to stroke the horse, but Toby grabbed her hand and pulled her back. "What's wrong?"

"Probably nothing. You just have to be careful around him. Like I said, he's an old man now and pretty damn crotchety." Toby held the horse's bridle tightly so she could slide her hand across the big animal's neck. "He gets so he doesn't like anybody—even me," he said, with a chuckle. "So I just want you to be cautious with him."

"Oh, you're not dangerous, are you?" Naomi was no stranger to horses. It would be impossible to grow up in Royal, Texas, and not be at least comfortable around them. She'd never had her own horse and hadn't really ridden much since high school, but she'd always liked them. And Legend, she could see, meant a lot to Toby.

"You just like getting your own way, don't you?" she cooed as she stroked and petted the horse. "Well, I do, too, so we'll get along fine, won't we?"

"You the horse whisperer now?" Toby asked.

She shot him a look from the corner of her eye. "He's male, isn't he? A woman always knows her way around a crabby man."

"Is that right?" One corner of his mouth tipped up.

God, he smelled good. He shouldn't smell good after standing out in the early-morning sun, sweat already pearling on his chest and back.

"I've talked you out of every bad mood you've ever had."

He laughed again and stroked Legend's nose. "Not much of a test, since I'm not a moody guy."

"Oh, really?" She tucked her arm through the handle of the basket and looked up at him. "When you couldn't get the hydraulic lift to work on the patio table you built to go below ground?" It had been a terrific invention and one of her favorites that he'd come up with.

A picnic table that seemed to dissolve into a patio, with the push of a button, it lifted, pieces sliding into place until it was a concrete-topped table big enough to seat six. When you wanted it, there it was. When you didn't need it, it disappeared, leaving only a patio behind.

"That was different," he said, a slight frown on his face.

"How?"

"That wasn't moody. That was frustration."

"Frustration *is* a mood," she pointed out, pushing her hair back from her face. "But did I talk you out of it or not?"

That frown slid into a smile of remembrance. "You did. Took me to the roadhouse for a beer and karaoke."

"You're a terrible singer."

"But I make up for it with enthusiasm."

Naomi laughed and felt everything in her settle. This was good. Hormones aside, this was what she needed, wanted. This easy affection. They were friends, and they always would be. She'd see to that.

"Okay," she said, giving Legend one last pat, "now that I've won an argument—"

"Not an argument. No one shouted."

"A debate, then," she amended. "I have chickens to assault and eggs to kidnap. If you don't hear from me in half an hour, come and find me."

"You're taking this whole rancher's wife thing to heart, aren't you?" he asked, and his mouth was still curved in a smile.

"If I'm living here, I'm doing my share of chores," she said. "As long as the chickens don't kill me." She looked past him to the horse. "Legend, it was nice meeting you. Toby, I'll see you at breakfast."

She headed for the corral gate and stopped when Toby laughed. Turning around, she saw that Legend had pulled free of Toby's grip to follow her. "I've never seen him do that before," he admitted.

"I'm new here, that's all," she said and kept walking. But now she heard the horse's hooves plopping onto the powder-soft dirt right behind her. Naomi stopped again and this time waited for the horse to come close. Staring up into those chocolate-brown eyes, she smiled and said, "You're on my side, aren't you?"

The horse lifted his huge head then laid it gently on her shoulder as if giving her a hug. Touched, Naomi whispered to the big animal and stroked his neck as she would have a puppy.

She looked over at Toby and saw amazement on his face as he watched her. And Naomi thought that maybe this was all going to work out, after all.

Six

The next couple of weeks were harder than Toby had thought they would be. Living with Naomi was both torture and pleasure.

She was his friend, but more and more, he was noticing her breasts, her butt, her smile, her low, full-throated laugh that tugged at something deep inside him. Lust, pure and simple, he told himself. Now that she'd relaxed about her pregnancy and he'd gotten her to loosen up and actually eat real food, she was curvier than ever, and that was giving him some bad moments.

He didn't want to feel for her. Didn't want to start feeling a need for more. But he didn't seem to have a choice in that. Cursing under his breath, Toby grabbed a screwdriver, stepped behind his latest project in the workshop and tightened the screws there. He smoothed his thumb over them to make sure they were deep set, then took a long walk around the piece, inspecting every inch before moving to test the design. Better to keep busy, he told himself. To keep his brain so full of work it didn't have time to pick apart thoughts of Naomi.

The workshop was his sanctuary. When Toby had the ranch built, he'd had this shop done to his specifications. The floor was hardwood, as it was easier to stand on for hours than concrete. The windows were wide enough to let in plenty of natural light, plus there were skylights in the roof. The walls were peppered with sketches he'd stuck there with pieces of tape. There were walls full of shelves holding every kind of supply he might need. And the wall behind his bench was covered in Peg-Board so he could hang his favorite tools within easy reach.

On the far side of the building, he had lumber, plastic, metal and vinyl and a table saw to let him cut anything down to whatever size he needed. This building was the one spot in the universe that was all his. No one came in here, so he was always guaranteed peace and quiet and the solitude he needed to spark ideas. He'd come up with some of his best stuff in this shop, and whenever he was here, his brain kicked into gear.

Until lately.

"Just keep focused." He studied the raw version of his design, looking for areas he could improve. If it worked as it was supposed to, of course, he'd redo the whole thing in finer materials and, with patent in hand, get it onto the market. It was what he did, what he'd been doing most of his life. Taking ideas and making them real. A few of those inventions had helped him amass a fortune that had allowed him to buy this ranch and live exactly the way he wanted to.

"And nothing's going to change just because Naomi's

here," he muttered. But hell, even he didn't believe that. Things had already changed.

Having Naomi around constantly was like having an itch he couldn't scratch. He hadn't counted on that. Her scent was everywhere. It was like she was stalking him. In his sleep, in the kitchen, hell, even here in his workshop he couldn't get her out of his mind. She'd invaded every part of his life, and what was worse, he'd *invited* her in. He'd done this to himself by coming up with that marriage-of-convenience idea. Now his skin felt too tight, his mind was constantly filled with images of her and she was looking at him as she always had. As good ol' Toby.

"And that's how you've got to stay," he said tightly. Once he got used to her constant presence, he'd get over the whole want-to-strip-her-naked thing and their relationship would smooth out again. That would be best. He didn't want any more from her than friendship, because anything beyond that was too damn risky. He could deal with the sexual frustration. But if she got any deeper under his skin, Toby could be in trouble. And he'd had enough female trouble to last him a lifetime already.

So he deliberately pushed everything but the moment at hand out of his head. All he needed was to keep his distance from her once in a while. Clear his head. Get some space. Like today. Some time spent in the workshop, focused on what he loved doing.

"Toby," Naomi called, walking into the workshop. "You in here?"

"So much for that idea," he muttered. "Yeah." He raised his voice. "In the back."

Sanctuary was gone now, so he braced himself for being near her. It was just as well she was sleeping in the stupid guest room, he thought. He didn't know if he could take it, having her in his bed every night and *not* touching her.

He heard her footsteps and could have sworn he smelled her perfume rushing toward him. Toby didn't dare take a deep breath to steady himself—he'd only draw more of her into him. And he was already on the slippery edge of control.

"Wow, you've been busy," she was saying as she got closer.

He turned to watch her as she approached and asked himself how any man could keep his mind on work when Naomi Price was around. Hell, she was his friend, and right now it felt like a damned shame to admit it.

Shaking his head at his own disturbing thought, he turned back to the shelf unit.

"I've got a few more projects hitting the market in the next couple months," he said.

"Like what?"

One thing he gave Naomi, she'd always been interested in his inventions. Wanting to know what they did, how they worked and how he'd come up with them.

"There's a self-leveling measuring cup—" He glanced at her as she came closer. "My mom loves to bake and complains that there are different kinds of cups. For dry or liquid. This cup does both and levels itself so you know you're always right."

She gave him a smile, and it lit up her eyes. Toby looked away fast, but not fast enough. The pit of his stomach jittered, and a little lower, his body went rock hard. Damn it.

"Your mom'll be happy. What else?"

She picked up a wood dowel and twirled it in her fin-

gers. Those long, slender fingers with the deep red polish on the nails. He looked away again.

"Something Scarlett wanted," he said and made a
minor tweak to the hydraulic system. Anything to keep
his brain focused. "She keeps her vet tools in the trunk
of her car and had one of those flimsy trunk organizers.
The one I designed is heavy acrylic, with a hinged lid
and compartments that slide out with a button push." He
checked the mechanism on the back of the piece again.
"I figure it'll be a hit with carpenters, plumbers, artists, even fishermen. They'll be able to keep their stuff
handy and safe."

"Wow." She dropped the dowel onto the workbench.
"Okay. Made your mom and Scarlett—not to mention
millions of others—happy. What've you got for me?"

He looked at her in time to see a wide smile flash
across her face. *What did he have for her?* Well, now,
that was a loaded question, wasn't it? Rather than face
it, he asked, "What do you need?"

She propped one hip against the workbench, threw her
amazing long copper-streaked brown hair back behind
her shoulders and said, "Surprise me."

Damn. Everything she said now tempted him, and he
knew she hadn't meant it that way. "I'll do that."

"So, what're you working on now?"

"This? It's a prototype for a new piece of furniture,"
he said, relieved to shift his thoughts back to safe territory. He stood back, folded his arms over his chest and
said, "Look at it. Tell me what you see."

Frowning a little, she moved to get a better look. Sadly,
she moved closer to him, and her scent wrapped itself
around him.

After a second or two, she shrugged. "It looks like

a bookcase. At least the top half does. The bottom half looks like it's a cabinet door, but you don't have any pulls on it yet."

He grinned. "Don't need them. See that switch on the side there? Give it a turn."

She did, and the machinery inside hummed into life. Naomi moved out of the way and watched, a smile on her face, as the cabinet door swung out and up until it was horizontal, jutting out from the bookcase itself. "Cool. It converts to a table."

"There's more," Toby said and, stepping forward, reached under the table and pushed another switch to one side. Instantly, hidden benches lowered from beneath the table and took their places, one on each side.

She laughed. "I love it. Table and chairs in a bookcase."

He liked that approving smile and took a seat on one of the benches as he waved her toward the other one. "In a small place? Buy this bookcase, and you have a table when you want one and it's gone when you don't."

She propped her elbows on the table and rested her chin on her joined hands. "For a man with a gigantic house, you're really into space-saving mode, aren't you?"

He ran his hand over the table surface. "I like coming up with things that can be multifunctional."

"It's brilliant. I love it." She looked at the top half. "And the bookcase stays in place so you don't have to unload it before using the table. Very cool."

"Thanks." He looked at the piece again. "There are some products like this on the market, but none that include benches along with the table and none that use hydraulics like I'm using them."

"Another patent for the boy inventor."

"Haven't been a boy inventor for a long time," he said, shifting his gaze back to hers.

For one long, humming second, the air between them nearly bristled. Toby stared into her eyes and wondered if she could read the hunger no doubt shining in his. She licked her lips, huffed out a breath and opened her mouth to speak. But whatever she might have said was lost, and the mood between them shattered, when another voice called from the doorway.

"Hey, you two! I'm on the clock here. No canoodling."

"Canoodling?" His eyebrows lifted. "Scarlett's here?"

Ruefully, Naomi smiled. "That's what I came to tell you. She's here to give Legend a checkup. I took him from the corral into his stall to make it easier on her. You know, out of the sun. It's really hot out there."

Toby shook his head again. "You mean you walked to the stall and he followed you."

"Pretty much. What can I say? He finds me irresistible."

A lot of that going around, Toby thought grimly. His horse loved her, and Toby couldn't stop thinking about her. Naomi Price was making life on the ranch a hell of a lot more interesting than he would have believed.

"Hello? You coming out or do I have to come in?" Scarlett's shout was tinged with laughter.

"We're coming!" Naomi called back and got up. She headed for the front door, then stopped and looked back at Toby.

Through the skylight, sunlight poured down over her like a river of gold. It highlighted the copper streaks in her brown hair and made her brown eyes glow like aged whiskey. Her body was curvier than he'd ever seen it, and the rounded mound of the baby made her seem softer, more alluring than he wanted to admit. She stood there, watching him, the hint of a smile on her face, and everything in Toby tightened into a hot fist.

"You coming?" she asked.

"Nearly," he muttered, and stood up slowly, trying to mask the signs of his body's reaction to her. "Yeah. Be right there."

As soon as he could walk again.

A few days later, Naomi had her files—folders with clippings and printouts of websites she was interested in—scattered across the dining room table. The room, just like every other one in the house, was perfect. At least to Naomi. The table was a live edge oak, long enough to seat twelve and following the natural contours of the tree it had been made from. The grain was golden and gleaming from countless layers of varnish and polish. A fireplace along the wall was unlit, and in the cold hearth were ivory candles on intricate wrought-iron stands. The windows across from Naomi gave her a view of the paddock and the fields stretching out beyond.

Naomi had the whole house to herself, since Toby was at Clay Everett's and Rebecca was in Royal doing some grocery shopping. Funny, Naomi used to be alone so much of the time she had convinced herself she loved it. Now that she lived with Toby and had the ranch hands popping in and out and Rebecca to sit and talk to, the house today seemed way too...*quiet* with everyone gone. On the other hand, she told herself, she could get some of her own work done with no interruptions.

With her new plans for the show, Naomi wanted to line up guests who could come in and demonstrate different ideas. And she knew just where she wanted to start. There was a place in Houston that specialized in faux stone finishes. It was owned and operated by a woman who'd started her business out of her garage. The show would be good for Naomi and good for the woman's company.

She shuffled through a pile of papers looking for the number, and when her cell phone rang she answered without even looking at caller ID. "Hello?"

"Ms. Price?"

"Yes." Frowning slightly at the unfamiliar voice, she said, "If this is about a survey or something, I'm really not interested—"

"I'm calling from Chasen Productions in Hollywood."

Naomi swallowed hard and leaned back in her chair. Panic, curiosity and downright fear nibbled at her. Hollywood? She took a breath, steadied her voice and said calmly, "I see. What can I help you with?"

"My name is Tamara Stiles, and I think we can help each other."

"How so?" *Wow.* She silently congratulated herself on sounding so calm, so controlled, when her insides were jumping and her mind was shrieking. Hollywood. Calling *her.*

"I've seen your show, and I'd like to talk to you about perhaps taking it national."

Naomi lurched up from her chair and started walking, pacing crazily around the long table. This couldn't be happening. Could it? Really? Her show. On national TV?

"National?" Did her voice just squeak? She didn't want to squeak. Oh, God, she couldn't seem to catch her breath and she really wanted to sound professional.

"That's the idea," Tamara answered. "Do you think you could come to Hollywood next week? I'd like to meet in person to see what the two of us can come up with."

Clapping one hand to the base of her throat, Naomi said, "Um, sure. I mean, yes. Of course. That would be great. I'd love to meet with you." *Understatement of the century.*

"Fine, then. Give me your email and I'll send you my contact information. I can arrange for your flight and hotel—"

"Not necessary," Naomi said, instantly wanting to stand on her own two feet. Sure, it would be nice if a Hollywood producer paid for her travel, but if Naomi did it herself, *she* remained in charge. They exchanged information, and then Naomi said, "I'll email you when I have particulars."

"Excellent. If you could be in town Monday, that would work well for us here."

"Monday is doable." Even if it wasn't, she'd find a way to make it work. Hollywood? Taking her show national?

People had enjoyed her local cable show, and it was getting more popular, but Naomi knew that her parents considered it more a hobby than anything else. This would convince them that she was so much more than they thought.

There were too many emotions crowding around inside her. Too many wheeling thoughts and dreams of possibilities. She was starting to shake, so she got off the phone as quickly as possible. There was no one there to tell. She needed to tell Toby, but she couldn't do it over the phone.

So Naomi just sat there in the silence. Alone. Smiling.

Later that night, Toby listened and watched as Naomi paced back and forth in the great room. She hadn't stopped talking since he got home, and honestly, he couldn't blame her. Pretty big deal getting a call out of the blue from Hollywood. Good thing the great room was as big as it was, though. Gave her plenty of space to walk off her nerves.

"Can you imagine?" she asked. "Hollywood? Calling me?"

"Well, why wouldn't they?" Toby said from his position on the couch. He was slouched low, feet crossed at the ankles, hands folded on top of his belly. "Even California's got to hear about it when a show takes off like yours has."

She stopped, threw him a grin that was damn near blinding. "You have to say that. You're my best friend."

There it was. Best friend. No lust. No need. Just pals. As it should be. If only his brain would get the memo. "You're great at what you do, Naomi. Half of Texas is talking about you, and the other half will be soon. Why not Hollywood?"

"You're right. Why not?" She started pacing again, her steps getting quicker and quicker as her words tumbled over each other. "Tamara," Naomi said, "isn't that an elegant name? Very showbizzy."

"Showbizzy?"

She shot him another wide smile. "I'm rambling and I know it. Heck, I can hear myself babbling and I can't seem to stop. Until you got home, I was talking Rebecca's ears off. She was too nice to tell me to be quiet and go away."

"Maybe she's pleased for you," he pointed out.

"She is. I know. But you're the one I wanted to tell, Toby." Naomi stopped dead, looked at him from across the room and said, "It about killed me waiting for you to get back from Clay's, because I just couldn't tell you this over the phone."

"Next time you need me," he said, sitting up, leaning his forearms across his knees, "call. I'll come home."

"Okay. Thanks. I will." She took a deep breath, laid one hand on her rounded belly and sighed. "Toby, this is just so crazy. Am I crazy?"

"Not that I've ever noticed."

"I've got to get tickets. And a hotel reservation."

"For both of us," he said, and she looked at him in surprise. Didn't she know that he would stand with her? Didn't she realize that Toby knew what this meant to her? That everything she'd been working toward for the last few years was finally coming true?

"Really? You'd come with me?"

"I'm not going to let you go alone." He shifted on the couch and dropped one arm along the back. "Naomi, I get it. This show, it's who you are. And someone noticing, wanting to talk to you about making it even bigger? I know what it means to you, so no, you're not going alone."

"You really are the best, Toby," she said, her voice soft, almost lost.

He shook his head, smiling wryly. "Who'll you talk to while you pace a hole through your hotel room floor?"

At that, she stopped pacing, darted across the room and dropped onto the chocolate-brown leather couch beside him, curling her feet up beneath her. She was so close he could see the excitement glittering in her eyes. Feel the warmth radiating from her and the scent of her, drawing him in again.

Laying one hand on his forearm, she admitted, "It was so surreal. Hollywood wants *my* show, Toby. It's a dream. And okay, maybe nothing will come of it, after all, and I'm completely prepared for that, but it's a *chance*. It tells me people are noticing."

"I know." He covered her hand with his.

"You know," she went on, "when Maverick first started all his trouble, I thought for sure the world was ending, and now look at me. I'm marrying my best friend and going to Hollywood to talk about my show."

Best friend. He took a breath and let it slide from his lungs. No matter what else happened, he would remain her friend, and that would be easier, he told himself, if he let go of her hand and slid just a bit farther away from her.

"Oh!" Her eyes went wide, and her mouth dropped open.

Instant panic clutched at his throat. "What? What is it? Is it the baby? Are you okay?"

She didn't answer him, just kept looking at him through wide eyes shining with something far more magical than the promise of Hollywood. Then she took their joined hands and laid them on her belly. "It moved. The baby moved, Toby."

His insides settled now that he knew she was okay. But then the baby moved again, the slightest ripple of movement beneath his hand, and he felt the magic still glittering in her eyes. "That was…"

"I know," she said breathlessly. "Wait for it."

She pressed his hand to her belly, and Toby held his breath, hoping to feel that rustle again, and when it came, they smiled at each other. Secrets shared and a moment of real wonder connected them more deeply than ever before.

"Isn't it amazing?" Naomi launched herself at him, planting a hard, fast kiss on his mouth that changed instantly from celebration to something else entirely.

Heat erupted between them, surprising them both. Toby's heart jolted into a fast gallop, and Naomi did a slow melt against him, parting her lips under his. His tongue swept in, tangling with hers, tightening the knots inside him until he was pretty sure they'd never come undone. His hands fisted at her back. Her hands stroked his shoulders and slid up into his hair, her fingers holding him tightly to her. Seconds passed, and the building heat between them became an inferno.

Toby had never felt anything like it, and he wondered how he'd been so close to her for so many years and never tried this. She moved against him, sliding onto his lap, and he knew she felt the hard proof of what he was feeling for her, because she squirmed on his lap, making it both better and worse all at the same time.

When that thought hit, Toby knew he had to end this. Before they completely crossed the line they'd agreed on to protect them both. He broke the kiss, lifted her off his lap and set her down on the couch. Then he got up, needing some space between them.

"Toby—"

He looked over his shoulder at her and nearly groaned. Her mouth was full and tempting, her eyes wide with surprise and her breath coming in short, hard gasps. He knew the feel of her, the soft curves, the warmth and eager response to his touch. And damned if he knew how he'd ignore that knowledge now.

"Just give me a minute here, Naomi," he ground out and pushed both hands through his hair. He dragged in a deep breath and shook his head.

"Why did you stop?" she asked.

Toby spun around and glared at her. "You're kidding, right?"

"No." She pushed herself off the couch and walked toward him.

Toby held up one hand to keep her at bay. Her hair was loose on her shoulders. The T-shirt she wore clung to her rounded belly, and her white shorts displayed way too much tanned leg. Her bare feet didn't make a sound on the floor, but it was as if every step thundered in his head, his chest, as a warning. Well, he was going to listen.

He'd been burned once by a woman he cared too much for, and he wasn't going to set himself up for that again. They were going to be friends. Nothing more.

"Toby, that was—"

"A mistake," he finished for her and walked to the bar in the far corner of the room. Yanking the mini fridge open, he pulled out a beer, opened it, then slammed the fridge closed again. He took a long pull of the cold, frothy brew and hoped to hell it served to put out the fire burning inside him. Somehow he doubted a beer was up to that task, though.

"Why does it have to be a mistake?" she asked. "We're engaged, aren't we?"

"Yeah," he said, taking another drink. "And it's a marriage of convenience, remember? We agreed to no sex. It'll just complicate everything, and you know it."

She scowled at him. "Nobody said anything about sex tonight, Toby. I'm talking about a kiss."

"A kiss like that?" He waved one hand at the couch where they'd been just moments ago. "Leads one place, Naomi."

"Wow. You're really sure either of yourself or of me." She tipped her head to one side to watch him like he was a bug on a glass slide. "You think kissing my brains out means I'm just going to leap into your bed shrieking, 'Take me, baby'?"

"I didn't say that."

"You didn't have to." She pushed that silky mass of copper-brown hair back from her face. The better to scowl at him, he guessed. "For God's sake, Toby, I'm not that easy."

He snorted, shook his head and took another gulp of his beer. "You are many things, Naomi, but I never thought *easy* was one of 'em."

"Right." She folded her arms across her middle, unconsciously lifting her breasts so that the tops peeked out of her T-shirt's neckline. "But you figured one hot kiss from you and I was going to toss my panties over my head?"

"You're twisting this up somehow," he said and tried to figure out exactly where he'd taken the wrong tack.

"Oh, I don't think so." She walked toward him, and as short as she was, she looked pretty damn intimidating when she had a mad on.

She stopped about five feet from him and said, "I liked kissing you—which, okay, surprised me a little—"

He snorted again and nodded. It had surprised the hell out of him, too. Hell, his mouth was still burning.

"—that doesn't mean I'm ready for more, though. But we are engaged, Toby." She wagged a finger at him. "You're the one who's waking me up at six in the morning so Rebecca won't find out we're not sleeping together."

"Yeah, so?" He frowned a little, not following her train of thought.

"Well, don't you think she'd expect to see an engaged couple kissing now and then?" she asked, sarcasm dripping from her tone. "Hugging? Looking like we're intimate even if we're not?"

He hadn't considered that, but she had a point. If he kept treating her like a pal or a little sister or something, Rebecca would notice and start wondering. "Damn it."

"Ah," she said, satisfied. "Good. Now maybe you won't freak out over a simple kiss. And you'd better get used to the idea, because we should do more of it."

Insulted, he countered, "A, I didn't freak out. B, there was nothing simple about that kiss."

"You don't think so?" she asked, turning around and heading toward the door. "For me, it was nice, but nothing special."

He stared after her, stunned. She was playing him. Had to be. Because that kiss had nearly lifted the top of his head off, and he'd damn well *felt* her heart beating a wild rhythm. No way was she as unmoved and blasé about it as she was pretending.

When she was at the door, she paused and looked back at him. "Seriously, Toby, if we're going to make Rebecca and everyone else believe this marriage is real, then we'd better practice kissing until we're good at it."

She gave him a half smile and left. Toby stared at the empty doorway for a long count of ten, then tipped his beer back for another drink.

"Practice? If we get any better at it, I'm a dead man."

Seven

Dinner at the TCC on Saturday night was a treat. Naomi had always liked the club, and once women were allowed in as members, she'd taken full advantage of her new rights. She, Cecelia and Simone had headed the redecorating committee, and they'd done what they could to spruce up the old place.

Not that they'd been given free rein. But painting the entryway and the restaurant and the ladies' room had helped to brighten things up. They were too steeped in tradition here to willingly let go of the Texas artifacts, documents and pictures decorating the walls, and a part of Naomi understood it. She was a Texan, too, after all. But at least those walls were painted a soft gray now, with fresh white trim, and it looked brighter in here even with the dim lighting.

Sitting across the table from Toby, she took a second to admire it. The dining room in the Texas Cattleman's

Club really hadn't changed much in decades, and even with a fresh coat of paint, it remained very much what it always had been—an upscale restaurant with roots in the past. Tables were draped in white cloth, and on every table was a bud vase with a single yellow rose in it. Soft jazz spilled out of overhead speakers, and the brass sconces on the wall threw out shafts of pale light. The atmosphere was old-world, but the clientele was a mixture of the older generation and younger. Conversations rose and fell like the tides, with a sprinkling of laughter now and then to keep things bright.

Naomi looked at Toby and just managed to squelch a sigh. He wore a white dress shirt, black jacket and black slacks. His black boots were shined to perfection, and he'd capped everything off with a black Stetson that made him look like a well-dressed outlaw. Her insides shivered, and her stomach did a long, slow roll. That sensation still caught her by surprise, despite how often she'd been experiencing it lately.

Desire pumped through her and she fought it down, because really, he hadn't said a word about that kiss since it happened two nights ago, so maybe he hadn't felt what she had. Wanted what she had—did.

And maybe she'd been trying to tempt him, to remind him of that kiss when she chose what to wear tonight. Her short, bright red dress hugged her breasts and her growing curves proudly. The neckline was square and deep and supported by inch-wide straps across her shoulders. Her red heels gave her an extra three inches of height, which she was always in favor of—plus, they made her legs look great.

He'd noticed, because she'd seen the flare of approval in his eyes when he first saw her tonight. But he'd been cool, controlled, even a little distant since they sat down at the restaurant.

Two days since she'd kissed him on impulse and found so much more than she'd expected. When his mouth fused to hers and his arms came around her, every cell in Naomi's body had come alive. Sitting on his lap, she'd felt his body tighten, and just remembering it now had her shifting slightly in her seat.

But long, luscious kisses couldn't make up for the sheer panic in his eyes when he pulled away from her. When he'd announced that for her own good, he was stepping back.

Infuriating to think about it even now. Naomi made up her own mind, and she didn't appreciate him making decisions for her. After all, she wasn't the type to just leap into bed without thinking about it. Although, she thought as she glanced down at her baby bump, she'd done it at least once. And maybe that was what Toby had been thinking. That she'd slept with Gio so easily, why wouldn't she jump *him*, too?

God, that was humiliating.

Especially when it was true. If he'd made the slightest move, Naomi would have willingly gone to bed with him, and forget the bargain they'd made. She'd never felt anything like that kiss before, and oh, how she wanted to know what else he could make her feel.

"What in the hell are you thinking about?" he asked, his voice a low rumble.

"What?" She jolted a little, immensely grateful he couldn't read minds.

"Just a tip, Naomi, but poker's not your game." He shook his head. "I'm sitting here watching your expression shift and change with every thought running through your brain. Want to tell me what's going on?"

"Nothing," she said. Though she wanted to talk about that kiss *and* the way he'd pulled back and shut her down, this wasn't the place for that conversation. Not when they were surrounded by half the town. "I'm just mentally packing, preparing for the trip tomorrow."

"Right." Clearly, he didn't believe her. But he was going to accept it. "Okay. Wes said he'd have his jet ready to leave whenever we get to the airport."

Toby had arranged to borrow Wes Jackson's private jet for the trip to LA, and Naomi was looking forward to it. She was so nervous about this upcoming meeting that being able to pace restlessly on the flight was going to be nice.

Actually, Toby had taken not only their flight but their hotel reservations out of her hands and didn't mention it until it was done. She should have been irritated, since she was completely capable of making reservations, but instead, she thought it was sweet. Which only went to prove that their kiss had seriously short-circuited her brain.

"You didn't have to ask Wes for the use of his plane."

Toby shrugged. "He wasn't using it. Said it was no big deal, and it's better than flying commercial."

"It would have to be," she said and tried a smile. His eyes gleamed in the candlelight as he watched her. "I'm glad you're still going with me."

"Why wouldn't I?"

"After the other night…" There, she'd brought it up anyway, despite vowing that she wouldn't. But then again, it was hard *not* to talk about something that was constantly on her mind.

"You were right," he said, tapping his fingers against the tabletop.

"That's unexpected," she said, keeping her voice even, soft, not sure where he was going with this. "But I'm always happy to hear it. What was I right about?"

He leaned closer. "About showing affection for each other. If we want to make this marriage look real to everyone, then you were right." As if to prove it, he reached across the table and took her hand in his.

Heat skittered up her arm to settle in her chest. His thumb stroked the back of her hand, and his gaze locked on hers. "I'm with you, Naomi. For the long haul. We made a deal, and I keep my word. You know that."

"I never doubted it," she said honestly. No matter what else, Toby McKittrick kept his promises. Which meant, she thought sadly, that he would not be the one to cross that no-sex line. If the line was to break, it was up to her to do it. Now all she had to do was figure out if it was what she really wanted or not.

"Good. So we'll show affection. Make this marriage as real as we can…" He paused, then added, "While keeping to the bargain we already made." As if everything were settled, he gave her hand a pat and let her go to sit back and pick up his after-dinner coffee.

Naomi stewed quietly. How was it possible to both win and lose at the same time?

"Naomi!" Cecelia, a wide smile lighting up her face, hurried up to their table with Deacon just a few steps behind her. "Oh, I'm so glad we ran into you tonight." She glanced across the table. "Hi, Toby. Don't mean to interrupt, but I just have to tell someone."

"What's going on?" Naomi asked, standing to hug her friend.

Cecelia gave her a squeeze, then reached back for Deacon's hand before looking at Naomi again. "We just found out today. We're having a girl." Her eyes filled with tears that she blinked furiously to keep at bay. "God, I've been tearing up all afternoon. Can't seem to stop myself. Don't really want to. I'm going to have a daughter, Naomi."

Happy for her friend, Naomi pulled her in for another hug and then kissed Deacon's cheek. "Congratulations, you two."

"Yeah," Toby said, "add mine to that." He shook Deacon's hand. "That's great news. Really."

"Yeah, it is," Deacon said, pulling Cecelia to his side and holding on to her as if worried she might try to make a break for it. "And if she's half as gorgeous as her mother, she's going to be a beauty."

"Deacon…" Cecelia sighed a little and went up on her toes to give him a kiss. "When will you find out, Naomi? Can't wait to see what you're going to have."

"I was thinking about being surprised," Naomi admitted, only because she couldn't say that up until a couple of weeks ago, she hadn't really allowed herself to think about the baby.

"Oh, how will you get things ready?" Cecelia asked. "No, you've got to know. The suspense would kill me."

Laughing, Naomi said, "I'll think about it."

"Okay, good. Now, we're going to have dinner and plan our baby girl's future, right up through college," Cecelia said, laughing. "Oh, Naomi, you can help me with the design and furnishings for the nursery…"

"I'd love to." It would be great practice for setting up a nursery at the ranch. She hadn't even begun to think of that, but that was not surprising, since there'd been so much more to concentrate on lately.

"Okay, we'll talk soon."

When Cecelia and Deacon walked off to their own

table, Naomi sat down again and watched Toby as he reached for the check folder.

Cecelia was in love and lucky enough to have Deacon love her back. Naomi shot a sidelong glance at Toby as he tucked several bills into the folder for their waiter. He loved her, she knew. But he wasn't *in* love with her, and that was the difference between her relationship and her friend's. Still, Naomi was lucky, too. Toby was here. With her. He'd changed his life around to be there for her.

And they'd had that kiss that had stirred up feelings she'd never suspected she had for him. Was there something more than friendship between them? Was it worth the risk of losing him to find out?

Los Angeles was big and noisy and crowded, and Naomi loved it. From the packed freeways to the mobs of tourists wandering down Hollywood Boulevard, everything was so different from what she knew that Naomi felt energized. Of course, being with Toby had that effect on her, too.

From flying on Wes Jackson's private jet to their penthouse suite at the Chateau Marmont in West Hollywood, it was as if she and Toby were wrapped up in some fantasy together. The two-bedroom suite was decorated in pale grays, with hardwood floors, beamed ceilings and glass tables. There was a tiled terrace off the living room and a waist-high concrete balcony railing. The gas fireplace in the main room flickered with dancing flames, because though it was June, it was also Southern California. The damp air coming in off the ocean meant the fire was welcome as well as beautiful.

Naomi spent that first night alone in her bedroom,

unable to sleep—not just because she was nervous about her meeting with the producer the following morning. But because Toby was right there with her and still so far away.

He'd been as good as his word, making small, affectionate gestures in front of Rebecca and the hands who worked for him. But when they were alone, he was careful to be...*careful*. He didn't seem to be having any difficulties keeping his distance from her. So maybe she was wrong about all this, she told herself. Maybe she was the only one who couldn't stop thinking about that kiss. Who couldn't help wondering what more might be like.

"How'd the meeting go?" Toby sat across from her, a sea breeze ruffling his hair as he watched her, waiting. He'd loosened the dark red tie at his neck and left off his steel-gray suit jacket. The long sleeves of his white dress shirt were rolled back to the elbows, and his long legs were stretched out, crossed at the ankle. Toby was probably the only man she knew who could pull off black cowboy boots in Los Angeles.

They were on the terrace of the penthouse suite, and evening was settling in. On the glass-topped table between them was a pitcher of iced tea and two tall glasses provided by room service. It had been a long day. Naomi'd had her meeting with the producer, and Toby had taken care of some business with his patent attorneys. This was really the first chance they'd had to talk since breakfast in the restaurant that morning.

Naomi took a breath and sighed it out. How did she explain what it had been like to hear Tamara Stiles praising *Fashion Sense*? All her life, she'd been striving to matter. Maybe it had started out as an effort to finally earn her parents' pride, but at some point her motivation had shifted. It wasn't only about them any-more, but about Naomi herself. She'd wanted to prove to everyone—including herself—that she was more than a rich man's daughter. That she had more to offer.

Okay, a cable television show about fashion wasn't curing cancer or ending nuclear war, but she *was* helping people, she told herself silently. Giving them ideas on how to improve not only their looks, but their lives. Looking your best meant that you *felt* your best. Sure, she enjoyed what she did, but knowing that other people did, too, was what made it all so good.

Now, here in Hollywood, she'd reached the very thing she'd been aiming for. There were people here who wanted to produce her, make the show bigger, get a larger audience, really help Naomi be *heard*. And she wasn't thrilled. She should be. This was the pot of gold at the end of her own personal rainbow. This was the X marks the spot on her private treasure map.

Looking at Toby, she tried to tell him what she was feeling, but she couldn't explain it, since she wasn't sure herself yet. Maybe she just needed time to think. Distance to put it all in perspective.

"Naomi?" His features reflected concern. "It didn't go well?"

"No," she answered quickly with a shake of her head. "It went fine. She loves the show—said it has great potential."

He frowned a little at that. "Potential? What's that supposed to mean? It's already a hit in Texas. Hell, it's why she wanted you to come talk to her."

"Thanks. That's what I thought, too." Naomi tried to settle and couldn't, so she stood up and walked the length of the private terrace. He was right when he'd once said she needed room to pace when she was thinking. But this time, she felt as though she could walk all the way back to Texas and things still wouldn't be clear.

When she came back up to the table, she didn't look at Toby, but instead turned to face the valley view, her hands flat atop the wide concrete rail. "Tamara says for the show to go national we'd naturally have to make changes. To the sets, the kind of shows we do, pretty much everything."

"If she loves it, why does she want to change it?"

She looked over her shoulder at him. "Funny, I asked myself that same question."

"You should." He stood up, too, and joined her at the railing.

A sea breeze drifted through Hollywood and brushed past them like a damp caress. Naomi pushed her hair back and lifted her face into that soft wind before looking up at Toby.

He was so steady. So strong. And she was so grateful he'd come with her. She was out of her element here. In Royal, even in Houston, she was fairly well-known. But here she was just one of a crowd of supplicants trying to take that next step up on a Hollywood ladder.

Resting one hip against the balcony rail, she said, "Tamara says the show had something on its own—and that the Maverick video and all the hype that happened after on social media really gave it the kind of push they need to bring up a local show."

"Okay…"

"But," she said, shifting her gaze again, out to the valley and the smudge of ocean she could see in the distance, "to go national, the show has to be polished, have less of a small-town feel, so that it will appeal to everyone."

"Small town?" he asked. "Houston, Dallas—they've signed on already. They're not exactly small town, and it works for them just as it is."

"It does," she said, and again, Toby was saying pretty much what she'd said to herself after leaving the meeting. "She says that with a bigger studio and professional crew—not to mention scriptwriters—we *might* make it big."

"Might."

"Well, she can't guarantee it, of course," Naomi admitted. "And I wouldn't have believed her if she'd tried. But I never saw a problem with our studio in Royal."

"Seems to work fine," he agreed.

"And the crew are very professional. Even the interns from the college know what they're doing." She'd already made these arguments to Tamara. Gone over them time and time again by herself after the meeting, too. But it didn't change anything.

"They do."

"She said," Naomi added after a long minute, "that at first, they'd want to do the taping here. In Hollywood."

He went still. "So you'd have to live here."

"That was part of it, yes." She looked at him again and tried to read what he was thinking. But except for the flash in his eyes, his features were cool, blank. "They would, in theory, tape a short season all at once, so I'd have to be here in California for at least a few weeks."

"Weeks." He nodded thoughtfully but didn't say anything else.

Seconds ticked past into minutes, and still the quiet between them grew. Naomi's own mind was racing, going over the meeting again, what living in California for weeks at a time might mean to her. To Toby.

The baby. There were too many questions and too few answers.

"This is Hollywood, Toby," she said a little wistfully. "They're the experts. And this chance, it's what I've been aiming for."

"Sounds like you got it." No inflection to his voice, giving no clue to what he was thinking.

"I don't know," she said softly. What was more, she didn't know if she wanted it anymore.

Yes, LA was exciting. Hollywood had such cachet, deserved or not. Even their hotel, the Chateau Marmont, was a legend in a town filled with them. Movie stars as far back as the '20s had stayed in this hotel, and it was as if their spirits remained, because the hotel felt…out of time somehow. The stars still flocked here—movie stars, TV actors, singers all flocked to this place, this city.

Dreams were born, lived…or died, all in this one city.

And Naomi didn't know anymore if she wanted what was offered here. "This all comes back to Maverick's video," she mused, shaking her head at the irony of having something she hated be at the base of what could be the realization of her dreams.

"Well," she amended, "I guess it was more about how we handled the video than the video itself. That's what caught her attention, really. Tamara said she liked how we turned it around, used that video to spark more changes on the show…"

"Not we, Naomi," Toby said softly. "*You*. You did it. You faced Maverick down, took that ugly video of his and made it work for you."

She smiled to herself and pulled a lock of windblown hair from across her eyes. "You know, I really did. But, Toby, without you I don't think I could have. You're the one who helped me see that hiding wasn't the answer. You were right there. Standing with me. Helping me. You gave my baby a father."

His eyes darkened, swirled with emotions that flashed past too quickly for her to read. And suddenly, she didn't care what he was thinking, feeling. Right now all she knew was what *she* felt.

"Ever since we kissed," she said softly, sliding her hand along the railing until she found his and covered it with her own. "I've been thinking about more."

"Me too." He looked down at their joined hands, then into her eyes.

"That no-sex line you talked about?" she said, despite the tightness in her throat, the galloping of her heart. "The one you said we shouldn't cross?"

"Yeah?" His eyes darkened again. A muscle in his jaw twitched.

"I want to cross it."

"Me too." Toby reached for her, and she went to him eagerly. He pulled her in close, locked his arms around her and kissed her with a raging hunger that shattered every last thread of control she might have clung to.

Naomi lifted her arms to hook around his neck and held him to her as his mouth took hers. Their tongues tangled together in a silent dance of passion that sent tingles of expectation skittering through her veins. Better even than the kiss that had filled her dreams for days, this one promised more than just a few minutes of heat. This kiss promised an inferno to come, and Naomi readily jumped into the flames.

She lost herself in the wonder of the moment, of having him touch her, hold her, kiss her. For days she'd been hoping to feel this again. For days she'd watched him try to keep a safe distance between them. And now at last, the wall separating them was coming down in a rush.

His hands swept up and down her back, and Naomi wanted to peel out of her sleeveless sunshine-yellow dress. She wanted his hands on her skin—those strong, rough hands that showed such gentleness. She wanted all of him against her, inside her.

He tore his mouth from hers, and for one horrible second, Naomi thought he was going to pull away from her again. To back off from what was happening. Breath catching in her lungs, heart pounding in her chest, she looked up at him and knew she needn't have worried.

"That's it," he muttered thickly and bent to scoop her up into his arms.

"Toby!"

"Quiet," he ground out through clenched teeth. "We're too far gone to stop now, Naomi. I swear I will stop, though, if you say no," he added. "So don't say no."

She shook her head, cupped his cheek in the palm of her hand. "I'm not. I'm saying hurry up."

"That's my girl."

Eight

He marched through the living area and straight into the big bedroom. There were two in the penthouse suite, and last night they'd been in those separate rooms. Not tonight, though, Naomi thought. Tonight, things would change. He walked to the wide bed, reached down and tugged the silky gray duvet off and let it slide to the floor. Then he set Naomi on her feet but kept a firm grip on her as if half-afraid she'd disappear if he stopped touching her. But she wasn't going anywhere.

Naomi turned in his grasp, pulled her hair to one side and said softly, "Help me with the zipper?"

He did, his fingertips trailing along her spine as the material fell open. She shivered when he bent to kiss the base of her neck, and an instant later, her dress was sliding off her body to lie on the floor like a puddle of sunlight. Wearing just her cream-colored bra and panties and a pair of three-inch taupe heels, she stood in front of him, letting him look his fill.

She was a little nervous, because her body was so different now. Naomi had been so careful for so long, counting every calorie, watching every bite, but since Toby's proposal, he'd been coaxing her to eat more. Now Naomi was rounder, fuller, and the mound of the baby was distinct enough that she actually thought to cover it with her hands.

He stopped her, though, holding her hands in his and tugging them aside. "No, don't hide from me." Shaking his head, he let his gaze sweep over her, top to toe and back again. A slow smile curved his mouth. "You make a hell of a picture, Naomi."

What she saw in his eyes made her feel beautiful. Desirable. She released a breath she hadn't known she was holding and reached for the buttons of his shirt. Then she pulled the tie from around his neck and tossed it onto a nearby chair. "You're wearing too many clothes," she whispered.

"Yeah, we can take care of that." He did. In what felt like a blink, he was undressed, laying her back on the bed and covering her with his body.

She sighed at the first contact of skin to skin. God, it felt good. Right. The cool sheets at her back, Toby's hot skin against the front of her. Sensations swarmed inside her, and she fought to breathe past the rush of them.

She smoothed her palms across the broad expanse of his chest, and he hissed in a breath in reaction. Naomi smiled, loving how much he was affected by her. Knowing that he was as swept away as she was. She rubbed her thumbs across his flat nipples until he groaned deeply, then dipped his head to take one of her hard nipples into his mouth.

Her smile slipped away, lost in the rising tide of heat enveloping her. His tongue swirled across her sensitive skin, and he ran the edge of his teeth across her nipple as well. Naomi moaned softly and arched her back, moving into him. When he suckled at her, she whispered his name, threaded her fingers through his hair and held him to her.

She didn't ever want him to stop. Naomi's eyes closed on a wave of heat swamping her senses. She'd never known anything like this before. The feel of his mouth on her was incredible, and when he ran one hand down the length of her body, she shivered. His hands, so scarred and callused from years of hard work, touched her skin with a rough tenderness that left her breathless.

He lifted his head, and she nearly whimpered at the loss of his mouth against her breast. But she stared up into his eyes and felt herself falling into that churning aqua sea of sensations. How had she gone so long, never knowing what they could create together? Never knowing what it felt like to have his hands on her skin?

"I've wanted this for a while now, Naomi," he whispered, stroking one hand across her breasts, down her rib cage. "But you've gotta be sure."

She actually laughed a little, to think that he was giving *her* a way out this time. But no, they were through turning from each other. For tonight, for now, all that was important was the two of them. She didn't even want to think about tomorrow, but there was one thing she had to reassure herself on.

"I'm absolutely sure. But, Toby—" She paused and took his face between her palms. "Remember what we promised each other. No matter what else happens, we stay friends."

"Honey, right now I'm feeling *real* friendly." He grinned, took her mouth in a long kiss that had her insides melting into a puddle, then said, "Yeah. Friends. Always."

She nodded, because she was too full of emotions to speak. Naomi couldn't even identify everything she was feeling. All she knew was that in this moment in time, she was right where she wanted to be. But neither of them needed words right now. All they needed was to *feel*. To explore. Experience.

As if he heard her thoughts, he slid one hand down her body to stop over the curve of the baby she carried. Naomi went perfectly still, wondering what he would do, what he was thinking. Pregnant women couldn't be very alluring, right?

"Stop thinking," he ordered in a hush.

"What?"

"You're worrying. About how you look, of all things." Toby shook his head as his gaze met hers. "Can't you tell that I think you're the most beautiful thing I've ever seen?"

"Toby—"

He smoothed his hand across her baby bump, then bent to kiss both her and the child within. There was so much tenderness in the action, in his eyes, that in that instant, Naomi was lost. Her heart filled to bursting, she felt the sting of tears in her eyes and impatiently brushed them away. She wanted nothing to blur this image of him. Instead, she etched it into her heart and mind so she'd never forget.

He looked up at her, his eyes shining, and all she could

think was that she loved him. Beyond friendship, beyond sense, beyond anything. Naomi was in love with Toby. With her best friend.

When had it happened? Had it always been inside her, just waiting to be recognized? And what was she supposed to do about this realization now? If Toby knew what she was feeling, he'd pull away again, and Naomi knew she wouldn't be able to stand that. So she'd hide what she felt. Keep it locked up inside her so she wouldn't have the pain of seeing him turn from her.

Reaching for him, she stroked her fingers over Toby's cheek, then across his lips, defining them with the lightest of touches. There was so much she wanted to say to him and couldn't.

Finally, though, when she was sure her voice wouldn't break, she said only, "You're going to make me cry."

"Oh, no," he assured her, giving her a slow smile and a wicked wink. "I'm going to make you scream."

"Promises, promises," she said, keeping it light, not wanting him to guess at what she'd just discovered.

"I always keep my word," he reminded her, then shifted his hand down to cup her center.

Naomi gasped and instinctively lifted her hips, rocking into his touch, wanting more, *needing* more. And he gave it to her. His thumb caressed that one sensitive spot while he speared two fingers into her heat. Within and without, Naomi felt on fire. She wouldn't have been surprised to see actual flames licking at the mattress beneath her.

She grabbed at his shoulders, her fingers flexing to hold on as gentle exploration gave way to desperation.

He kissed her, touched her, lavished attention on Naomi's breasts, her neck, her inner thighs, driving her wild with a kind of need she'd never known before. She'd never thought of herself as particularly sexual, but right now her body was pleading for release and the only man who could give it to her was bent on drawing out the torture of expectation.

"You smell so damn good," Toby whispered against her throat. "Your scent stays with me everywhere I go." He kissed her neck, licking, tasting. "You're there in my sleep, Naomi. I can't shake you."

"Then stop trying to," she told him, and he lifted his head to look at her.

"Yeah," he said, "I'm done with that. You're here to stay."

One breathless second passed, then two before he kissed her, taking her mouth in a celebration of need and passion. God, she wanted to drink him in, drown in him and what he was making her feel. She couldn't touch him enough. Hair, face, shoulders, back. She loved the feel of his muscles shifting beneath her palms.

Then he moved to kneel in front of her, and Naomi held her breath as he entered her. One long, slow thrust and he claimed everything she was, and she sighed as a shiver slid through her body. Lifting her legs, she wrapped them around him and pulled him deeper, higher.

His body moved in hers, in a rhythm that moved faster and faster. She groaned, sighed, at the luscious feel of his hard length taking her so completely. Silently, he offered her more, demanded the same. He looked down into her eyes, and she couldn't have looked away from that heated stare if it meant her life.

Anticipation coiled in the pit of her stomach as tension settled even deeper within. Naomi moved with him, racing to match his rhythm, rushing toward whatever was waiting for her. Always before, sex had been a quick bout of stress release. A subtle pop of pleasure that had left her mildly satisfied and silently wondering what all the big fuss was about.

Then she found out. His fingertips stroked her core while his body moved in hers, and she shattered, clawing at his back, whimpering his name through a throat so tight air could barely pass. Mind spinning, she held on to him and rode the pulsing flashes of brightness that seemed to blind her.

"Toby!" Her hips were still rocking with the force of that climax, and before she had time to adjust, to understand, he was pushing her past that pleasure to a place she'd never been before.

Her body felt raw, too sensitive, too *everything*, but Toby was relentless. "I can't," she whispered, shaking her head, looking up at him. "I mean, I already—"

"Again," he said tightly and drove himself deep inside her. He lifted her hips, tossed her legs over his shoulder and went even deeper than he had been.

Naomi wouldn't have thought it possible, but while her body was still quivering from the most amazing climax she'd ever experienced, she felt it preparing for another. She could barely breathe and didn't care. Her head tipped back into the mattress as her hands reached for his thighs. She was lifted so high she had no way to match his movements. She was at his mercy, and he was showing none.

Naomi had never been so at the mercy of her own body. She'd never known the kind of overwhelming sensations that were taking her over. Had never been so out of control with a man. Never let any man take her over as Toby was doing. And she hadn't even guessed that her body could feel so much.

He was unstoppable. Indefatigable. His hips were like

pistons, pumping into her, pushing her past all boundaries, all restrictions. Naomi stared up at him, licked her lips and knew that nothing would ever be the same again. Not after this. Not after Toby.

"Come on, Naomi," he whispered, voice low. "Let me watch you fly. Let go, Naomi. Just let go."

"I am, Toby," she said breathlessly, as her heels dug into his back. He was battering away the last of her defenses. Tension clawed at her. That first orgasm was as good as forgotten in her body's rush to claim another.

"Now, Naomi," he whispered, his big hands holding her bottom, squeezing soft flesh, giving her one more sensation to add to the mix. "Come now."

She laughed a little, but the sound came out as a sob for air. Her hands slapped at the sheets, clutching the fabric as if looking for a way to hold herself in place. "You're not giving me a choice. I feel—"

"Look at me," he said, and she heard the fight for control in his voice.

She opened her eyes, met his, and while their gazes were locked, he pushed her over the edge of desire into a completion that was so foreign to her that she was lost in the sweeping tide of it. Naomi stared into those aqua eyes as her world rocked and her body splintered. She screamed, unable to stop the wild rush of release as it grabbed her and shook her down to the bone.

Naomi watched him, lost in those eyes, as her body, still trembling, held on to his and cradled him as he let himself go.

When he collapsed on top of her, Naomi held him tightly. Their hearts raced in tandem, their bodies quaking as if they were shipwrecked survivors clinging to each other for safety. But it was so much more than that.

He rolled to one side, taking her with him, and Naomi laid her head on his chest, listening to the steadying beat of his heart. Loving him was going to be hard, she knew, but there was nothing she could do about it. He was in her heart forever. And she would never, for as long as she lived, forget what they'd shared here tonight. On the night she knew she loved him.

Toby lay there like a dead man. If the hotel had been on fire, he'd burn to a crisp because there was no way he could move. He doubted his legs still worked.

Hell, he'd been with plenty of women in his time, but not once had he experienced anything like what had just happened between him and Naomi. He scraped one hand across his face and stared at the ceiling. He'd crossed a line. Hell, he'd *erased* the line. And he didn't give a good damn. All he could think about was that he wanted her. Again. Now.

She curled on her side and slid one leg across his, and the silky glide of her skin against his stirred him into need in a flat second. Who knew that there would be such heat between them? He rubbed one hand down her back, and she cuddled into him, sliding her palm across his chest. She was…amazing. More than that, but he didn't have the words. What he had was need that only she could meet.

That was dangerous territory, though, and he had to lay out some signposts before they headed farther down this road. Now that the line was gone, new ones had to be drawn. To protect both of them.

"Toby…"

She whispered his name on a breathy sigh, and instantly his body tightened. Didn't seem to matter that he barely had his breath back from the most incredible sex of his life—his body was apparently raring to go again.

But right now he had to give his brain the upper hand. If he could manage it while she was looking at him through soft eyes, her tongue running across her bottom lip. *Oh, man.*

"Okay, we need to talk," he said and winced because he'd just sounded like a damn cliché.

"No, we don't," she said and smoothed her fingertips across his nipple.

"That's not helping." Muffling a groan, Toby caught her hand in his and held her still. If she kept touching him like that, talking would be the last thing on his mind. "Naomi, this changes things."

She chuckled, tipped her head back and looked up at him. "It sure does."

"Not funny," he warned, going up on one elbow and rolling her over onto her back. Still, seeing the softness and the humor in her eyes, he nearly smiled back. Then he remembered the line. Smoothing her hair back from her face, he ran his fingers through the long, silky threads and had to fight to concentrate. "We have to talk about what this is going to mean between us."

She sighed, stiffened a little, then said, "That it'll be even easier for us to show affection toward each other?"

Oh, he wanted to show her some affection right now. But before anything else got started, he had to make sure she knew there was a limit on how much he was willing to give. How much he was willing to risk.

He looked into her eyes—eyes that shone like warm whiskey—and shook his head. Taking a deep breath to center himself, he said, "Sure. Yeah. That's a good point.

But what I want to say is…" Hell. What *was* he trying to say?

Naomi pushed herself up slightly, bracing one hand against his chest. "Want me to say it for you? That I shouldn't let my little heart fall in love with you because you're not interested in love?"

"Naomi…"

"Or is it that you don't want me to make the mistake of thinking that our marriage is going to be real all of a sudden?"

"That's not what I was going to say," he argued, though he had to admit it was pretty damn close.

"Right." She tipped her head to one side. "You can stop panicking, Toby. We were friends and now we're friends plus. That's all. I get it. That about sum everything up?"

Sounded like it did. Although why it bothered him that she was being so reasonable about it all, he didn't know. He hadn't expected calm, and he should be grateful for it. Toby wasn't even sure why he felt oddly…disappointed. "Yeah, I guess it does. Look, the point is, we had the no-sex agreement, and that's shot to hell—"

"Not going to say I'm sorry about that," she put in.

"No, me either," he admitted. They could at least be honest with each other. "But I have to make sure you know that sex doesn't mean—"

She pushed herself off his chest into a sitting position, shoved her tangled hair back and looked him dead in the eye. "For heaven's sake, Toby. I'm not going to throw my heart at your feet. I know you, remember? I know that Sasha messed your head up so bad you don't even want to hear the word *love*."

His frown deepened. Was it a blessing or a curse that

Naomi knew him so well? "This isn't about Sasha," he ground out.

"Oh, please. It's always about Sasha. That miserable excuse for a woman was never right for you, and," she said, lifting one eyebrow meaningfully, "if you'll remember, I told you that at the time."

"Yeah. I remember." His expression soured. "Thanks for the *I told you so*."

"No problem." She scooted off the bed, stalked to the window and stared out at the deepening twilight.

The growing darkness seeped into the room as well, shadows filling every corner. Toby's gaze followed the line of Naomi's back and down to the curve of her behind. The woman had a great behind. Then, when she turned to look back at him, she was profiled and her breasts were high and full, the rounded outline of the baby on full display. She was beautiful. Even the fire in her eye couldn't dim his reaction to the woman.

Then she started talking. "Sasha leaving was the best thing to happen to you."

He gritted his teeth. "This isn't about Sasha."

"It's all about her," Naomi continued. "Has been since the day she walked out with her pretty-boy country singer. She's gone, Toby, but you're still caught up in that drama."

He sat up and leaned against the headboard, the sheet pooling at his hips. "What the hell are you talking about?"

"You." Naomi walked back to the side of the bed and glared down at him. "She's moved on, Toby, but you're still running your life by what happened to you with her."

"No, I'm not."

"Really? You haven't been involved in a single relationship since she left." She crossed her arms beneath her breasts. "Why?"

"Not interested."

"Liar." Now she frowned at him. "At least be honest and admit that you won't let yourself trust anyone anymore."

"I trust you," he pointed out. And why did he suddenly feel as though he had to defend himself?

She sighed as if disappointed, but damned if he knew what the problem was.

"Toby, you're cheating yourself out of maybe finding something amazing, all because Sasha convinced you that feelings weren't to be trusted." She bent down and tapped her index finger against his chest. "Well, you're wrong to give her so much power."

"How did this get to be about Sasha?" he asked, shoving himself off the bed to stare down at her. "She doesn't run my life. Never has. Never will. I stopped thinking about her the day she left Royal. I live my life the way I want to, Naomi."

"You're probably the most stubborn man I've ever met."

"Thanks."

"Not really a compliment." She sighed a little and chewed at her bottom lip.

He dropped both hands to her hips and pulled her in closer. She had to tip her head back to meet his eyes, but she did. "I trust *you*. That's good enough for me."

"Okay," she said, nodding, watching his eyes. "I just don't want you to be sorry one day for marrying me and cheating yourself out of love somewhere down the line."

"We're getting married, Naomi." He smiled softly. "And hell, if we get sex, too, all the better."

Her returning smile wasn't wide, but it was there. "Yeah, that works for me, too."

"I do love you, Naomi. Always will. I just don't want you to think of what we have as more than what we have."

"Got it. You're not in love with me."

"Right." He didn't know what the hell he was feeling at the moment, but it wasn't the kind of love that people built dreams around. He knew that much.

"Fine. Don't worry about it." She shook her hair back and said, "Oh, stop looking like you're kicking a puppy. I'm a big girl, Toby. I walked into this with eyes wide open, and I didn't ask for undying declarations of romantic love."

No, she hadn't, he realized. In fact, she was acting like what had happened between them was no big deal. And he didn't know how he felt about that. Damn it, Naomi had a way of turning everything around on him so that Toby didn't know whether he was coming or going, and she'd just managed it again. Was he worried about nothing?

"So, are we finished talking?" she asked, running one hand down his chest, across his abdomen and lower still, to curl her fingers around the thick, hard length of him.

He hissed in a breath through his teeth. "Yeah, I think that about covers everything."

"Good to hear," she said and kissed him while her fingers moved on him, sliding, caressing. "So don't just stand there, cowboy. Show me what you've got."

"Challenge accepted," he muttered. He felt like he was going to explode. How could he want her so desperately? Lifting her, he half turned and braced her back against the closest wall. "Not slow this time, Naomi. This time it's gonna be hot and fast."

She leaned into him, wrapped her legs around his waist and nibbled at his neck. "Show me."

Hard and aching, he slid inside her and instantly felt her body tighten around his. Silky heat surrounded him, and he groaned as Naomi scraped her nails across his skin and hooked her ankles behind his back. She met him eagerly, hungrily, and his brain short-circuited as he stared into the eyes of a woman he'd thought he knew.

Her body, his, moving together, in a mad, wild tangle of desire and need that gripped them both. One corner of his mind yelled at him to lay her down, take his time with her. But that calm, reasonable voice was shouted down by the other half of him demanding that he have her. Now.

"Toby, Toby…" She twisted her hips on him, increasing the friction, increasing the need until he thought he'd go blind with it.

"Come on, baby." He kissed her, hard and long and deep, and took her breath as his own, devouring her as she was devouring his body. "Come with me. Come with me now."

He felt her body tighten, felt the first flickering pulse of her climax and watched her eyes glaze. And while she rocked with the orgasm shaking through her, he forgot about control and emptied himself inside her.

Caught in the web spinning between them, Toby knew that in spite of what he'd said before, nothing would ever be the same.

Nine

After a few days in LA, Naomi was ready to be home in Texas. Now that she was back home, she might miss Hollywood a little, but it was good to be back. As summer heated up and June inched toward July, the days got longer and the people moved slower. It was an easier pace than the big city, and that was part of its appeal. She'd heard people say that anyone could live up north, but it took real character to make it through a southern summer.

Naomi wasn't so sure about that. But one thing she did know—she was grateful the Royal Diner had AC. The minute she and Toby's sister, Scarlett, stepped inside, Naomi almost whimpered.

"Oh, it's going to be one ugly summer," Scarlett said as she signaled to Amanda and then tugged Naomi to a booth.

Naomi flopped onto the red vinyl bench seat and

stacked her shopping bags beside her. "I let you talk me into buying too much."

"It's never too much," Scarlett said. "Besides, you're getting married. You need…stuff."

Stuff didn't begin to describe all the things Naomi had picked up that morning. She and Scarlett had spent the last several hours at the Courtyard Shops, a great collection of eclectic shops where you could find anything from antiques and crafts to fresh local produce. But there was also a new bridal shop owned by Natalie Valentine.

And *that* shop was where Scarlett had pushed Naomi into going a little nuts. She was only carrying a few of the things she'd bought. The rest were being delivered to the ranch. Naomi wanted a small wedding, in the evening, maybe, out at the ranch. She hadn't talked to Toby about it yet, and she knew her mother wouldn't be happy with the venue, but Naomi was. A small, simple wedding, with just their families and friends there, made the most sense to Naomi. After all, it wasn't as if this was ever going to be a *real* marriage.

Her heart ached at that thought, but she had to acknowledge the truth, no matter how painful. Toby was never going to know she loved him. Never going to love her back. And she had to find a way to be all right with that. If she couldn't…then maybe marriage wasn't the answer. For either of them.

"I love the dress you picked out," Scarlett said. "That pale yellow just looks gorgeous on you, and knee length will keep you from passing out in this heat."

"Thanks," Naomi said. "I like it, too. My mother will no doubt want me in yards of lace and tulle, but that doesn't make sense for a backyard ceremony. And besides," she added wryly, "it's tacky to wear white on your wedding day when your baby bump is showing."

Scarlett laughed a little, then shook her head. "You're going to be a beautiful bride. But are you really sure you want it held outside? Even in the evening it'll be hot."

"I'm sure," Naomi said. "We can have the reception by the pool, and if it gets too hot, people can go into the house for a break. Of course, I haven't talked to Toby about any of this yet, so he may have different ideas..."

Scarlett waved one hand at her. "He'll be good with whatever you want. He loves you, right?"

Sighing a little, Naomi leaned toward the other woman and whispered, "Scarlett, you know the truth. I know Toby told you."

"Sure, I know," she said. "And I know my brother. He's a great guy, Naomi, but he's not going to marry someone just to do her a favor. He cares for you. I can see it."

Care was a long way from love. Too long. Since they got back from California, they'd shared a bed and shared each other, every night, every morning and one memorable afternoon in the workshop. But they hadn't talked about Hollywood. Hadn't talked about their wedding. Hadn't talked about anything important. It was as if they were both holding back, and Naomi didn't know what to do about it.

"Hey, Naomi, you okay?"

"What?" Sighing, she shook her head. "Sorry. I drifted."

"To somewhere nice? Maybe cooler?" Scarlett asked.

"No, stayed right here in Royal. Scarlett, can I ask you something?"

"Sure."

"Are you good with this?" Naomi asked. "I mean, me and Toby getting married. You're okay about it?"

"Absolutely." Scarlett paused when Amanda Battle walked up to their table. She slid two tall glasses of ice water onto the table, and Scarlett sighed. "Bless you, my child."

"Thanks, I'll take it," Amanda said, laughing. "You two been running around buying out Royal's shops?"

"Just put a dent in a few of them," Naomi assured her. Her stomach rumbled, reminding her of why they'd come to the diner. And a salad just didn't sound the least bit appetizing. "Can I get a turkey sandwich? Potato salad?"

"Oh, me too, please," Scarlett said.

Amanda nodded and hurried off to tend to other customers. So when they were alone again, Scarlett took a long drink of her water, then said, "Anyway, why wouldn't I want you married to Toby? You're way better for him than Sasha was."

"Low bar there, but thanks," Naomi said drily.

"What's going on?" Scarlett watched her for a long minute. "You don't seem as excited as I thought you'd be over everything. I mean, you're engaged, pregnant and have Hollywood knocking on your door."

"It's complicated," Naomi said and thought that might be the understatement of the century. She still didn't know what she was going to do about the offer from Tamara Stiles, and she had to let them know soon.

But if she took it, she would be giving up the kind of control that had made the show *hers* in the first place. And did she really want to live in Hollywood for weeks at a time? If she did, what about Toby? Would he move there with her? Stay on the ranch? And what about when she had the baby? What then? Would she be dragging the baby from state to state?

"Wow. Judging by your expression, wish I could buy you a beer."

Naomi sighed. "Me too. Or the most gigantic glass of wine in the state of Texas." She took a long drink of her ice water, letting it soothe her dry throat. "There's just so much going on right now, and I'm still getting emails from people about that stupid video—"

"No one who knows you cares about that thing, Naomi," Scarlett said.

"I know, but millions of people who don't know me have seen it." Just thinking of that made her want to cringe. Didn't matter if she'd managed to turn the tables on Maverick. That she'd taken his vicious attack and made it work *for* her.

Whoever Maverick was had tried to ruin her life, and knowing that person was still out there made her nervous. He'd wanted to make her life a misery. Wouldn't it infuriate him to realize that he'd inadvertently helped Naomi rather than hurt her? Wasn't it likely that he'd try something else in order to make trouble for her?

"Okay, yeah," Scarlett allowed, "millions of people saw the video, but now they're tuning in to your show, so hey. Win for you." She picked up her water glass, waited for Naomi to do the same and then clinked them together in a toast. "Seriously, don't let that weirdo bother you. I'm sure Sheriff Battle's going to find out who Maverick is and stop him. Soon."

"I hope so," Naomi confessed. "I can't help wondering if he's going to be frustrated at how the video worked for me and try something else."

"I understand why you'd be worried about that, but

honestly, I don't see it happening." Thoughtful, Scarlett looked at her. "Why would he? There're still plenty of people in Royal to screw with."

"Talking about Maverick?"

Both women looked up at Gabe Walsh. He was tall and gorgeous and his hazel eyes always held a gleam of humor. His dark blond hair was militarily short, and he had a lot of intricate tattoos. Formerly FBI, he now owned a private security firm based in Royal.

"Sorry," he said, mouth curving into an unrepentant smile. "Didn't mean to eavesdrop, but I heard you talking as I was walking to my table. Maverick the subject of interest?"

"Who else?" Scarlett asked.

"Everyone's talking about him," Naomi said. "Especially those of us he's already attacked."

Gabe winced. "Yeah, I get that. And I know the guy's caused a lot of misery around here. But I just left my uncle Dusty, and I swear all the intrigue and mystery surrounding this Maverick guy is really sparking my uncle's will to live. It's even making his cancer treatments easier for him to deal with."

Dale "Dusty" Walsh was in his sixties and used to be a big bear of a man. But Naomi had seen him not so long ago, and the chemo he was undergoing had whittled him down until he hardly looked like himself anymore.

"I'm glad to hear he's doing better," Naomi said, knowing nothing she said could make things easier on Dusty's family.

"I don't know about better," Gabe admitted sadly, stuffing his hands into the pockets of his slacks. "But Maverick has sure perked Dusty up. The mystery of it has him intrigued and more interested than anything else has been able to do. I think he's trying to figure out who the guy really is."

"I hope he does," Naomi said with feeling. "I won't feel really safe until he's caught."

"He will be," Gabe assured her before he left to meet his friends for lunch. "No one can stay hidden forever."

Naomi wondered, though. For months, Maverick had proven elusive enough to avoid being caught. Who was to say anything would change? And if he came after her again...

Scarlett's cell phone rang, and when she glanced at the screen, she said, "It's Toby."

Naomi listened to the one-sided conversation, and when Scarlett hung up she asked, "What is it?"

"It's Toby's horse, Legend." All business now, she looked worried. "Toby says he's gone down and won't get up again. Sorry about lunch, but we have to get to the ranch." She waved a hand at Amanda and called, "We have to cancel. Sorry."

Naomi was already gathering her things, and when she pushed herself out of the booth, Scarlett was right behind her.

Toby hated feeling helpless.

Legend's labored breathing filled the air and brought Toby to his knees beside the failing horse. Fresh straw littered the floor and rustled with every movement. Toby rubbed his hands up and down the big animal's neck. He felt each shuddering breath and the thready beat of Legend's big heart. Hell. He was old. The horse had had a long, great life. Toby had brought him to live with him at the ranch because he knew that Legend's life was coming to an end. And God, Toby wished he could do *something* to change what was happening.

He heard his sister's approach before he saw her and recognized the quick, lighter steps of Naomi coming in with her. He'd hated to interrupt their day out together, but he didn't want Legend to suffer. He owed his old friend that much. And damn it, he'd wanted Naomi with him.

Scarlett came into the stall with her doctor's bag and instantly went to work. Toby stood up, making room, and walked to where Naomi stood at the open door. She didn't say a word, just wrapped her arms around his waist and nestled her head against his chest. Toby held on to her like a lifeline in a churning sea and felt everything inside him settle.

Holding Naomi, he watched his sister examine the horse, and as he looked at Legend, he saw his own life flash in pictures through his mind. The day Legend arrived at Toby's home. The first time they rode off together, down back roads and out through the fields. He could still feel the excitement of being astride Legend and pretending to be everything from a great explorer to a Western outlaw. Life had been easy and full of possibilities, and Legend had been with him through all of it.

That horse had been the most important thing to him for a lot of years, and now it was time to let him go. Toby didn't need the sympathy shining in his sister's eyes to know Legend had run out of time. His heart ached with the truth.

"I can put him down gently, Toby," Scarlett said. "He'll just go to sleep."

"Oh, God…" Naomi's voice was a whisper, but he heard the pain in it and was grateful she was with him.

"Give us a minute with him first, okay?"

"Sure." Scarlett stood up, kissed her brother's cheek and said, "Call me when you're ready. I'll be right outside."

"Thank you." Naomi squeezed Scarlett's hand as the woman slipped out of the stall.

Toby walked to Legend's side and held out one hand to Naomi for her to join him. The horse's breathing was more labored, and his eyes wheeled as if he were trying to understand what was happening.

"Poor Legend," Naomi whispered, then bent to kiss the horse's forehead. "You're such a good boy. Such a good horse."

"He loves you," Toby said simply, watching as Legend tried and failed to rest his head in Naomi's lap.

She lifted tear-drenched eyes to Toby's. "I'm so sorry. So sorry you have to lose him."

"I know. I am, too." He stroked the horse's side, then back up to his neck and face. Bending down to look into the big brown eyes of his oldest friend, he said, "We had a great life together, Legend. And I'll never forget any of it."

The horse jerked his head as if agreeing, then tried to stand, failed and fell back into the straw again. It broke Toby's heart to watch the valiant old horse try so desperately to stand and be what he once was.

"Easy, boy," he said quietly. "It's all right. You can go on now."

Naomi never stopped stroking him, whispering to him as the horse labored on until Toby couldn't stand it any longer. Glancing at Naomi, he saw her tears and felt his own. But it did none of them any good to drag this out. Best to say goodbye and let Legend go on to the next adventure.

"Scarlett?"

"I'm here." She stepped into the stall, sympathy etched into her features.

"Do it," Toby said. "But I'm staying with him."

"*We're* staying with him," Naomi said, gaze locked with his.

"Yeah. We." Toby nodded, his throat too full to speak.

"Not a problem," Scarlett said. "It won't take long and he won't suffer. I promise."

Toby tuned his sister out. He didn't want to think about it. Didn't want to watch her end the old guy's life, even though it was a blessing for Legend. Toby looked again into his horse's eyes, and he could have sworn he read a silent thank-you there.

Legend's breaths came slower, slower, then stopped, and the silence was almost unbearable. He was gone. A huge piece of Toby's life had just ended, and he felt like he'd been kicked in the gut. Naomi took his hand and held on. Scarlett kissed him again and silently left them alone.

"I'm so sorry," Naomi whispered, turning into him, wrapping her arms around him.

"I know," he said and held on to her, burying his face in the curve of her neck.

He'd wanted her there, with him, when he realized that Legend was dying. Toby had needed Naomi, and she'd come. Just as she always had. Her hand in his, he felt her warmth pouring into him and clung to it.

After the trip to California, things had definitely changed between Naomi and him. Sure, the sex was great. Amazing, even, but out of bed, he felt the strain between them. They hadn't talked again about the offer she'd had, and he had no clue what she was thinking. Planning. So he had to wonder what she was considering. Did she want that offer badly enough to leave Texas? Move to Hollywood? And if she did, what then? His life was here. In Royal. Living in California wasn't part of his game plan, but was it in Naomi's? That producer had offered a dream. Was she going to take it?

And if she wanted to, then maybe they shouldn't get married, after all. Was it fair to her?

That's bull, he told himself. All of it. He wasn't thinking about what was best for Naomi. It was about *him*. What he was feeling. Every time they had sex, he felt himself sliding farther down a steep cliff. Pretty damn soon, he'd find himself loving a woman and risking everything he'd promised himself he never would again.

Straightening up, he looked into those whiskey-gold eyes and knew he was in trouble. He just didn't know how to avoid getting in deeper. "Thanks, Naomi. For being here."

"I'll always be here, Toby."

He hoped so, but there was some serious doubt. Toby caught her cheek in the palm of his hand and realized that Naomi was really the only woman outside his immediate family whom he trusted completely. Why, then, was he so cautious about letting his feelings for her grow? Was it himself he didn't trust? Or was he just too damned cowardly to risk loving again?

Either way, he didn't come off too well.

Standing up, he drew her to her feet and said, "Come on. I have to get out of here."

"Okay." She held his hand and followed him out of the stall, where they both stopped and looked down at Legend one more time.

Then, together, they left the stable, and the pain, behind.

Ten

Two days later, Naomi was furious.

The text she'd received an hour before ran through her mind again.

Naomi, we must speak. Come to Oaks Hotel in Houston as soon as you can. Gio

The fact that he'd practically ordered her to come irritated her only half as much as the fact that she was going to see him at all. Why had Gio come to Texas? Why had he texted her out of the blue after making it perfectly clear he wasn't interested in her or her baby?

Temper spiked inside her. Naomi hadn't told Toby about Gio's text, because she knew he'd tell her not to go meet the man. But she had to, didn't she? Had to find out what he was up to. Why he was here. Had to tell him to go away and never come back. Once she had it all settled, she'd tell Toby about it, of course. She wasn't going to lie to him about this.

Over the past few weeks, Naomi had put Gio out of her mind completely. He had nothing to do with her or her baby. Toby was the man who would be her child's father. Toby was the man she loved. The man she was about to marry. Gio had no place in their lives. And the only reason she was going to see him was so she could tell him that to his face.

It was time to banish her past so she could go forward with her future.

She parked her car on the street, fed the meter and then hurried toward Gio's hotel. It was plush, of course, with a liveried doorman and a red carpet stretching from the sidewalk to the polished brass front door.

Naomi smoothed her palms over her cream-colored slacks, then tugged at the hem of her pale green blouse. The fabric was light but clung to the outline of her baby bump proudly. The doorman hurried to open the door for her, and she smiled at him as she stepped into the blessedly cool interior.

The spacious lobby was all wood, dark fabric and glass, giving the impression of old-world money and cool elegance. Naturally this was the kind of place Gio would stay. Looking around, she spotted the bar and headed for it. She was right on time for this meeting, and she didn't want to be here any longer than she absolutely had to.

The elegant bar held a luxurious hush. A long mahogany bar stretched along one side of the room, and a dozen or more small round tables dotted the gleaming woodplank floor. Her gaze swept the room, and since there were only a handful of people in the room, she spotted

Gio instantly. He had a table in the back, in a shadowed corner, and Naomi sighed. If he thought this was some kind of assignation, he was in for a disappointment. The only reason she'd agreed to meet him was that she wanted to look him in the eye and tell him to get lost.

Gio had been a blip in her life. A moment out of time in her past. He had no part in her future, and that was what she'd come to tell him. As she approached, her heels tapping on the floorboards, he noticed her, and Naomi stiffened in response. She still couldn't believe she'd been foolish enough to spend the night with the man, but in her defense, just look at him.

Not as tall as Toby, Gio had long jet-black hair, blue-green eyes and always just the right amount of beard scruff on his cheeks. He wore black slacks, a cream-colored silk shirt and looked, as always, very self-satisfied. The man was gorgeous, but he was as deep as a puddle.

"*Bella,*" he crooned as he stood to meet her, "you are so beautiful."

"Thanks, Gio." She avoided the kiss he aimed at her cheek and pretended not to notice his clearly false look of hurt and disappointment.

"Can I get you something to drink?" he asked, already signaling to the waitress.

"No, thanks."

He waved the waitress away again as Naomi took the seat opposite him at the small round table. She glanced around the room, making sure she didn't know anyone there, then focused on Gio again. Waiting.

"I'm so happy you came to meet me," he said and managed to look both pleased and disappointed.

"Gio," she said, "I don't know what this is about, but I'm only here to tell you I don't want anything from you—except," she added as she had a brain flash, "to have you sign away your parental rights to the baby."

"*Sì, sì,*" he said, waving his hand as if erasing the very thing she'd just asked for. "We will speak of all this. *After* we speak of something else…"

Okay, so it wasn't the baby he was interested in. No big surprise there, after the way he'd reacted when told he was going to be a father. So what had brought him all the way from Italy?

The room was quiet, and so was Gio's voice. He leaned toward her across the table, and Naomi had a moment to really look at him and wonder how she could ever have been attracted to the man in the first place. He was handsome, but in a stylized way that told her he spent a lot of time perfecting his look. The just long enough hair, the right amount of scruff on his face, the elegant, yet seductive pose he assumed, half lounging in the chair. He couldn't have been more different from Toby.

Toby was a man comfortable enough with himself that he didn't need to set a scene so that a woman would admire him. All he had to do was walk into a room and his confidence, his easy strength, would draw every woman's eye.

No, there was no comparison between Gio and Toby. And now all she wanted to do was wrap this up and get back to the man she loved.

"The baby is growing, yes?"

Hard to miss that, she thought, since her top clung to the rounded curve of her belly. And as if the baby was listening, it gave her a solid kick, as if to say *Let's get out of here, Mom. Go home to Dad.* She smiled at the notion, and Gio smiled back, assuming her expression was meant for him.

Shaking her head a little, she said, "Yes. Everything's fine. And no, I don't need anything from you, Gio. I'm getting married, and *he* will be my baby's father."

Gio tapped one manicured finger against his bottom lip, then gave her a reluctant smile. "Yes, I have heard of your marriage plans." When she looked surprised at that, he shrugged. "Gossip flies across oceans, too, *bella*. You have the marriage with a very rich man. I wish you well."

Frowning now as a ribbon of suspicion twisted through her, Naomi said, "What are you getting at, Gio?"

"Ah, so you are in a hurry. *Che peccato*—what a shame," he translated for her. "All right, then. I will sign your paper for you—"

"Good. Thanks."

"—*if*," he said, "you are willing to do something for me."

A cold chill swept along her spine, twining itself with the suspicion and quickly tangling into greasy knots that made Naomi shiver in response. Gio's eyes were fixed on hers, and she saw the speculative gleam shining in their depths.

"What do you want, Gio?"

"Ah. We will be businesslike, yes?" He smiled, and she saw briefly the man she'd slept with before he disappeared into a sly stranger. "*Bene*. We will be frank with each other. Is best."

"Then say it." She folded her hands together on the table in front of her and kept her gaze fixed on him.

"I will be quiet, *bella*, about being your bambino's daddy," he said with a wink, "*if* you agree to finance my next film."

She blinked at him. The one thing she hadn't expected

to hear from him was a threat of blackmail. Gio was a filmmaker, but she knew his last two films hadn't done well. So apparently, he was having trouble getting backing. Enough trouble that he was willing to fly to America for the sole purpose of blackmailing *her*.

Naomi was so furious with him, with herself, she could hardly draw breath. But Gio was oblivious of her thoughts and feelings, and went on outlining his business plan.

"Since you told me about the bambino," he said, "I felt it my duty to check on you. And I have found that your fiancé is the man who invents so many wonderful things…" He gave her another of his *I'm so disappointed* looks and said, "He is very rich and yet you did not mention this to me. Why is that?"

"Because it's none of your business?" she ground out.

"But yes, it is." He leaned toward her again, reached out and covered her hand with his, and smiled into her eyes. "You will marry this man soon, yes?"

"Yes." One word, squeezed past the knot of fury and humiliation lodged in her throat.

"Then you are able to afford to help me, *si*? I have a film in production, and I want you to finance it for me. We will be business partners, *bella*!" He released her hand, sat back and smiled benevolently at her. "You, me, our bambino."

Blackmail. Plain and simple. It was an ugly word, but it was the only one that fit. Naomi felt like an idiot for ever involving herself with this sad, shallow man. She could only hope that her genes would wipe out whatever of Gio was lingering in her baby. But even as she thought it, she realized that Toby would be her child's father. He would be the role model her child needed—the guiding hand, the understanding heart—and that would more than make up for Gio's faulty genes.

"Do we have an agreement, *bella*?" He pursed his lips, shook back his hair and positioned himself in the single slice of light piercing through a window. "I will keep your secret about the baby. I will not demand my fatherly rights. All you must do is help me with this. Is not such a bad bargain, *sì*?"

Naomi took a deep breath, shook her head and said, "No, Gio. It's not a bad bargain."

He smiled, clearly delighted with her.

"It's a terrible one."

His smile disappeared. "*Bella*, do not be foolish."

"You know when I was foolish, Gio?" she asked. "When I looked at you and saw more than was actually there. I'm thinking clearly now." Leaning across the table toward him, she said, "I won't give you a penny. You'll get nothing from me, Gio. Ever.

"So, you do your worst. Tell the world you're the baby's father. In fact," she said, as brilliance flashed in her mind, "I approve. Go ahead. Take out an ad in every paper...splash it across cyberspace, claim my baby as yours. It'll be easier to sue you for child support."

He gaped at her, his mouth opening and closing like a fish on a line. Oh, he hadn't expected this. He'd thought that Naomi would roll over and do just what he wanted to protect her own name. But she'd learned something with Toby's help. You stood up to bullies. You didn't let them dictate your actions. So she was taking a stand here, to protect herself *and* her baby.

He looked absolutely stunned, and the knowledge that she'd caught him off guard gave Naomi a huge rush of pleasure. Pushing up and away from the table, she looked down at him. "My husband will be my baby's father, and no child could ask for a better one. So do what you have to do, Gio. But you'll never get a dime from me."

Smiling, she turned around and stalked out of the plush bar. She felt…liberated, and she couldn't wait to get home to the ranch and tell Toby all about this meeting and how she'd handled it.

Naomi never noticed the man in the corner who'd been surreptitiously taking pictures during her encounter with Gio.

When his phone signaled an incoming text, Toby checked it, expecting to hear from Naomi that she was headed home from Houston. He opened it, stared and felt his stomach drop to his feet.

A picture of Naomi and a dark-haired man seated at a table together, looking cozy, as the man held her hand and looked meaningfully into her eyes. The message accompanying the photo was short and to the point.

You're a fool. She's meeting Gio Fabiani behind your back.

Gio. Her baby's father. Toby actually *saw* red. His vision blurred and darkened at the edges as he stared at the damning photo. Naomi was meeting the man who'd gotten her pregnant and turned his back on her. The man she'd claimed she didn't want anything to do with. Yet they looked pretty damn friendly, with him staring into her eyes while he held her hand.

She'd told Toby she was going to do some wedding shopping in the city. Instead, she'd gone to meet another man. She'd lied to him. So what else had she lied to him about? His heart felt as if it were being squeezed by a cold, tight fist. He couldn't breathe, because the cold rage rising inside was choking him.

This was exactly what he'd worried about. Getting closer to Naomi only set him up for the pain he'd felt the last time he allowed a woman into his life. Naomi knew what Sasha had put him through, and now she herself, the woman he'd thought of as his best friend, was doing the same thing?

Why was she meeting Gio? Was she playing both of them against each other? Was she planning on walking out on him in favor of the guy who'd gotten her pregnant?

"What the hell, Naomi? What the hell is going on?" He couldn't stop staring at the picture.

Maverick was behind this texted photo, he knew. Who the hell else would be watching Naomi and making sure Toby knew what was happening? Bastard had a lot coming to him when he was finally caught.

Shutting his phone down, he stuffed it into his pocket as if he could wipe the image of Naomi with another man from his mind if he just didn't have to look at it. Pain stabbed at him. This was so much worse than when Sasha had walked out. It cut deeper because Naomi was a part of him. She'd been his friend. His lover. His fiancée.

And now she was…what? He didn't know. All he was sure of was that he had some thinking to do. He wouldn't hold her to their engagement if this Gio was what she really wanted. But he'd be damned if he'd wish her well with the guy. Betrayal stung hard and settled in the center of his chest.

"Damn it, Naomi," he muttered. "What the hell were you doing with him?"

After all they'd shared, all they'd planned, she went to Gio in secret? Why? Naomi was *his*. They were building a damn life here. Didn't that mean anything? He had half a thought to drive to Houston, hunt down this Gio and beat his face to a pulp. But as satisfying as that would be, it wouldn't change the fact that Naomi had sneaked off to meet him.

Toby needed time to think. Space to do it in. Slamming out of the workshop, he stalked to the stables and saddled a horse. It'd be best for all involved if he wasn't at the ranch when she came back. Because he wasn't sure how he would handle it if she looked him dead in the eye and lied to him. Again.

Good thing he wasn't in love with her—or this would be killing him.

Astride the big black stallion, Toby headed out, and the horse's hooves beat out a rhythm that seemed to chant, *it's over, it's over, it's over...*

By the time Naomi made it home to the ranch, her anger at Gio had dissipated and she felt as if she was thinking clearly for the first time in days.

It was time to stand up to all the men in her life. She'd sent Gio packing, and heck, maybe she'd scare Toby into taking off, too. But she was tired of pretending, living a half life.

She was in love with Toby McKittrick, and today she was going to tell him just how lucky he was to have her. She didn't care if he wasn't in love with her right now. Naomi could wait. Because he loved her for who she was, and that was enough for her—for now. She had no doubt that he would come to feel the same way she did. He was only protecting himself after what Sasha had done to him.

Hardly surprising that he would keep his heart safe after having it crushed by betrayal.

But she was going to show him that love didn't have to be about pain. And she would *make* him listen.

She steered her car into the long, curved drive toward the ranch house and realized that in the past few weeks, Paradise Ranch really had become home. Her heart was here. In the wide-open spaces. In the stupid chicken coop and with Legend, lying buried under a live oak at the rear of the property.

Her heart was with the man who had always been her friend and was now her lover. The man who had offered to be a father to her child. How could she *not* love him and everything they'd found together?

She didn't need Hollywood. She didn't need dreams of fame and fortune. She didn't even need her parents' approval anymore. All she needed was Toby.

When she parked the car, Naomi raced into the house, calling for him as she went from room to room. She'd been longer than she'd planned and so she expected him to be in his office, as he was most afternoons, working on plans for another amazing invention. But he wasn't there, so she headed to the kitchen and tried not to hear how the heels of her shoes sounded like a frantic heartbeat against the wood floors. "Toby?"

"He's not here," Rebecca said, poking her head into the room from the walk-in pantry. "Took off on that big black of his a few hours ago. Haven't seen him since."

Disappointed, Naomi asked, "Do you know where he went?"

"Nope." Rebecca shook her head, then went back to whatever she'd been doing before. "He took off like a bat outta hell, though. Must be something bothering him."

Worry replaced disappointment, and Naomi chewed at her bottom lip. What could have happened while she was gone? "Okay, thanks. Um, I'll try his cell."

"Phones on horses," Rebecca muttered. "It's a weird damn world…"

Naomi called him as soon as she was in the great room, and she listened to the ring go on and on until finally his voice mail activated. She didn't leave a message, just hung up. And as she looked out the window at the sprawl of the ranch she considered home, she wondered where he'd gone. And why.

An hour later, Toby opened the front door and stalked into the house.

She'd tried to reach him a dozen times, but his phone went to voice mail and her texts to him went unanswered. By the time she heard him enter the house, Naomi's nerves were strung so tightly she could have played a tune on them.

She followed the sound of his footsteps and found him in his office, pouring scotch into a heavy crystal tumbler. He glanced at her when she walked into the room, but there was no welcome on his face.

"Toby? Is everything okay?"

"Interesting question," he said without answering at all.

The only light in the room came from the dying sun drifting through the wide windows at his back. He was a shadow against the light, and even at that, she saw the tightness on his features, the hard gleam in his eyes. And she wondered.

"I was worried," she said, walking a little closer.

"Yeah?" He laughed shortly, took a long drink of

scotch and said, "Me too. So, did you find some great wedding stuff in Houston?"

"Actually, that's what I wanted to talk to you about."

"Is that right?" His hand tightened around the glass, and even at a distance, she could see his knuckles whiten.

"I didn't really go to the city to shop."

He snapped his gaze to hers. "Yeah, I know. See, you weren't the only one texting me today."

"What do you mean?" Worry curled in the pit of her stomach and sent long, snaking tendrils spiraling through her bloodstream.

He pulled his phone from his pocket and held it out to her. "Here. Tell me what you think."

Naomi suddenly didn't want to know what was on his phone. What had made his eyes so cold and his mouth so relentlessly grim. But she forced herself to walk to him, take the phone and turn it on. The photo was already keyed up.

She and Gio at their shadowy table, leaning toward each other, his hand covering hers. They looked…cozy. Intimate. If she didn't know what had happened between them, she might believe that they were lovers, intensely focused on only each other.

Oh, God. What he must have thought when he saw this. She took a breath, looked up at him. "Toby—"

"You lied to me." His features were colder, harder than she'd ever seen them. Even when Sasha left him, he hadn't looked this closed off. Untouchable.

"I didn't lie."

"Semantics. By not telling me you were meeting Gio, you lied to me," he ground out through gritted teeth. "Damn it, Naomi."

He whirled around and threw the glass tumbler into

the empty fireplace, where it shattered, sounding like the end of the world. Despite the heat of that action, Toby was coldly furious. When he whipped around to look at her, his sea-blue eyes were stormy and glinting with banked fury. "You're meeting Gio behind my back?"

"It wasn't like that."

"Really?" He pushed both hands through his hair. "Because that's just what it looks like in that picture. Maverick said I'm a fool, and I'm starting to think he's right."

Stunned, she stared at him. "Until now, Maverick was a lowlife. Now you're ready to take his ugliness over what I'm trying to tell you?" She took a step toward him. She hated that he stepped back, keeping her at bay. "Gio texted me. Said it was important that I meet him. So I went there to tell him to leave me alone."

"Yeah?" He cocked his head and gave her a sour smile. "You needed a quiet little romantic corner to do that?"

"It wasn't romantic, Toby." She couldn't believe she was having to explain this. And wanted to kick herself for keeping it from him in the first place. "I don't want Gio. I want you."

"What's the matter? Gio not interested? Or, hey, maybe you're going to keep us both dangling. Is that the plan?" He shook his head and said, "Don't bother answering that. I don't need another lie."

"I'm not lying to you," she countered. God, she'd handled this all wrong. She should have gone to him, asked him to go to Houston with her. To face down Gio together. Instead, she'd wanted to clean up her own mess, and now it looked as though she'd simply traded one bad situation for a worse one. How could she make him see? Make him understand that he was wrong about all this?

Then she realized what she had to do. What she should

have done weeks ago when she'd first admitted the truth to herself. "Toby, I love you."

He laughed, but the sound was harsh, strained, as if it had scraped along his throat like knives. "God, Naomi, don't. You really think telling me that is going to convince me?"

Stung, she swallowed the ache and demanded, "Well, what will?"

"Nothing," he said, staring at her as if she were a stranger.

Naomi's heart hurt, and her breath was strangled in her lungs. She was losing everything and didn't know how to stop it. Toby's gaze was locked with hers, and through her pain, Naomi realized that she wasn't just hurt, she was *insulted*. She was closer to him than to anyone she'd ever known. He *knew* her and he was still going to take Maverick's word over hers?

She had to reach him. Had to fight for what they had, because if she gave up now, he'd never believe in her. Never accept that she loved him.

"You know me, Toby," she said and saw his eyes flash.

"Thought I did," he acknowledged.

"Well, thanks for the benefit of the doubt." She crossed her arms over her chest and hugged herself for comfort.

"What doubt? That picture says it all," he said.

"That picture says just what Maverick wanted it to say," she countered. His eyes were shuttered, his mouth tight and grim, and every inch of his tall, muscular body looked rigid with tension. She wasn't reaching him and she knew why. This wasn't Maverick and his nasty tricks. This went back much farther than that.

"This all comes back to Sasha," she said tightly.

"It has nothing to do with her." Toby stalked across

the room, as if he needed some distance from her. As if shutting her out wasn't enough. Then he turned around to face Naomi. "She's gone. Been gone for years."

"And she took your heart with her," Naomi said, though it cost her to admit it.

"Please." He snorted.

"I'm not saying you're still in love with her," she said, voice cold as steel. "I'm saying that the part of you that was willing to trust, to take a risk, left with her. You loved her, and she walked out."

"I don't need the recap," he said. "I was there."

"Yes, me too," she reminded him. "I was there for you. I saw what you did to yourself to get past her. You closed off a part of your heart. Your soul. You didn't want to trust anyone because you were afraid to be hurt again."

"Afraid? I'm not afraid."

"Come on, Toby," she said. "At least be honest."

"Oh, like you?" he asked with a snort of derisive laughter.

She winced, because even she knew she'd had that shot coming.

"Today was the first time I've ever lied to you, Toby, and I didn't like it. You know me. So whatever it is you're feeling right now isn't about me meeting with Gio."

"Is that so? Then what is it about, Naomi?"

"It's about you using Maverick's photo as an excuse to back away from me before I get too close."

If anything, his features tightened even further. "That's bull."

"Is it?" She stomped across the room, stopped right in front of him, tipped her head back and looked into his dark, angry eyes. "I didn't do anything wrong. Well, okay," she admitted, "I should have told you that I was meeting Gio today."

"Yeah, I'd say so."

"But," she continued as if he hadn't spoken at all, "other than that, I've done nothing to earn your mistrust, Toby. You're my friend. My lover. The man I trust to be a father to my baby."

A muscle in his jaw twitched furiously, but he didn't speak. That was fine by Naomi, because she wasn't finished.

"Sasha hurt you so badly you don't trust anybody."

"I trusted you," he said quietly. "Look where that got me."

"You didn't. Not really." Funny, she was only just seeing it now. "You've been holding back all along. Waiting for something to go wrong. For me to screw up. To prove to you that I was no better than Sasha."

"Not true."

"Of course it's true," she snapped. "My mistake was playing into it. I was afraid to tell you how I really felt because I thought you'd shut me out even more if you knew."

His eyes narrowed. "Knew what?"

"I should have told you in California, when I realized it for the first time," she admitted. "I *love* you, Toby. I'm *in* love with you."

"I don't want to hear this."

"Too bad," she said. "You need to." Naomi shook her head and stared up into his eyes, willing him to see the truth. "I'm not going to pretend anymore. I love you. If you don't believe me, I can't do anything about that.

"But I knew you'd react this way, and that's why I didn't tell you. I thought I could wait, that you would eventually come to love me back." She cupped his face in her palms and held on when he would have shaken her off. "I'm not so sure of that now, and you know what? I'm not going to wait for crumbs, Toby. I deserve more. We both do. I can't be with someone who doesn't trust me. Doesn't believe in me. Doesn't love me."

Turning around, she walked to the door, hoping with every step that he would stop her. Ask her to stay. But it didn't happen, and disappointment welled up inside her until it dripped from her eyes.

She paused briefly at the threshold to look back at him. So tall, so strong, so determined to cut himself off from love. Sadly, Naomi told herself she had nothing to gain by staying except more pain—and she'd had enough of that for one day.

"Congratulations, Toby," she said sadly. "You found a way out of this marriage, and you convinced yourself it was my fault. A win-win for you, right? You're using my stupid meeting with Gio as your excuse to not have to feel. It's easier that way. If you hold yourself back, you don't risk anything."

"Why did you meet Gio, then?"

She smiled sadly. "You should have just asked me that first, Toby. You should have trusted me. Believed in me. But you didn't. This marriage was a bargain. An act. But that's not enough for me anymore. I want it all. Or I don't want any of it. I deserve more. So does my baby." She took a breath and let it out. "Toby, so do you."

She didn't wait for an answer. Instead, she walked out, grabbed her purse off the hall tree in the entryway, then left the ranch, closing the door quietly behind her.

Eleven

"She's right, you know."

Toby looked over at his sister as she gave one of his pregnant mares a checkup. "Figures you'd say that. You're female."

Scarlett bit back a smile. "True, females are far more logical than males, but even a man should be able to see the truth here. You're just not letting yourself."

Why the hell had he talked to Scarlett about this? Answer? He hadn't slept, and he'd been on edge since the day before, when Naomi walked out, left him standing in his office, more alone than he'd ever been in his life. Temper still spiking, he'd roamed through his house like a ghost, haunting every room, seeing Naomi wherever he looked. Maybe *she* was the ghost, he corrected silently.

Either way, he felt like his head was going to explode with all the thoughts running through it. Then Scarlett had shown up, and he'd blurted it all out before he could stop himself. He and his sister had always been close. He'd expected some support. Instead, he was getting his ass kicked. Figuratively speaking.

Stubbornly, though, he reminded his sister, "She went into Houston to meet that sleaze Gio and didn't bother to tell me."

"Did you give her a chance to when you came home?" Scarlett asked. "Or did you just jump down her throat with accusations?"

He frowned and asked himself when Scarlett's loyalties had shifted to Naomi. Female solidarity? Made a man feel like he was standing outside, pounding on a door for someone to notice him.

When he didn't answer, Scarlett said, "Yeah, that's what I thought."

"I saw the picture, Scarlett," he argued, remembering that hard punch to the gut that had hit him when he first saw the photo Maverick had sent him.

"You saw exactly what that bastard Maverick wanted you to see," she corrected.

He looked at her and waited, because he knew she wasn't finished.

"Damn it, Toby, that guy's been creating chaos all over Royal for months and you know it." She smoothed her hands up and down the mare's foreleg to make sure the strain she'd suffered a few days before was healing well. When Scarlett stood up again, she said, "You reacted just the way he wanted you to. My God, could you be any more predictable?"

That was irritating, so he didn't address it. "Maverick's been hitting people with *truth*, hasn't he?"

"Uh-huh. The truth was, she met with Gio. She didn't

fling herself at him and run off to the closest hotel room. You're the one who filled in that blank."

He scowled at her, but she didn't stop.

"And you know, Maverick hit Naomi with truth and you stood by her." Tipping her head to one side, she stepped around the mare, running her hand across the animal's back as she moved. "You think maybe Maverick might have been ticked that she didn't fall apart? That her life wasn't ruined by his vicious little attack? You think it bothered the hell out of him that you went riding to the rescue?"

He scrubbed one hand across his jaw. His brain started working even through the sleep-deprived fog, and he had to admit that she might have a point. "Maybe."

"Uh-huh. And maybe he was mad enough to go after *you* this time? To get you to turn from Naomi so she could be as crushed as he'd planned in the first place?" She leaned her forearms on the stall's half door and looked up at him. "And then *you*, being male and not exactly logical when it comes to the women in your life, react just like he wanted you to."

Well, if any of that was true, it was damned annoying. Toby hated the thought that he'd done just what Maverick had wanted him to do. Hated being that predictable. He remembered the look in Naomi's eyes and wondered if Scarlett was onto something. Had his sister instantly understood something that he'd been too blind to see? Then Scarlett started talking again, and he was feeling less magnanimous toward her.

"Naomi was right about you and Sasha."

He shot her a single, hard look. "Leave it alone."

"Yeah, that's gonna happen," she said with a laugh as

she swung her hair back from her face. "You know Mom and I were worried about you when Sasha took off."

He did know that, and it didn't make him feel any better to recognize it. Sure, he'd taken it hard, but anyone would have. He remembered his family trying to make him see that Sasha leaving was the best thing that could've happened to him. But he hadn't been willing to admit that then.

"Yeah, so?"

"Naomi was the one you turned to back then."

"I know that, too." He remembered how Naomi had drawn him out of the dark fury that had held him in a grip for weeks after the woman he thought he'd loved left with another man. She'd stuck by him no matter what he'd done to make her leave. She'd stayed to be insulted when he was rude to her.

Naomi had just flat refused to leave him alone to brood. Instead, she'd dragged him out to the movies, to dinner, to picnics. He'd remembered how to laugh because of her. And eventually, he'd admitted that it hadn't been Sasha he had missed, but the idea of her. Of a wife. Family.

"But you're still holding on to what Sasha made you feel, Toby."

"The hell I am." He brushed that aside, stepped back and opened the stall door so his sister could exit. When she was out, he closed and locked the door behind her.

Sunlight speared through the open stable door to form a slash of pale gold along the center aisle. The scent of hay and horses was thick in the air, but it didn't give Toby the sense of peace it usually did. Hell, there was never peace when Scarlett was on a tear.

"You don't even realize it," his sister said, "but ever

since that woman, you've looked at everyone else like you're just waiting for them to turn on you. To prove themselves dishonest. Untrustworthy."

He shifted uneasily. He was long since over Sasha, but the lesson she'd taught him had remained fresh. "So being cautious is wrong?"

"That's not cautious, Toby," she said, laying one hand on his chest. "That's cowardly."

"Oh, thanks very much." He turned and headed for the next stall, opening it for her and holding it even when she didn't step inside.

"What would you call it if someone refused to care again because they might get hurt? Refused to trust again because they might be let down?"

He wanted to say careful, but he was afraid she had a point.

"Naomi loves you."

"How the hell do you know that?" he demanded. "She only told *me* last night."

"And you let her leave anyway?" Scarlett's eyes went wide in astonishment. "God, you really are an idiot. Of course she loves you. She always has. If you weren't such a stubborn *male*, you would have noticed it on your own."

She walked into the stall and slammed the door closed behind her.

"Love wasn't part of our deal," he argued, even knowing it was weak.

"Love isn't a bargain, Toby. It's a gift. One you just returned." She shook her head again and turned away to do another physical on the next mare. "Idiot."

Toby watched her but stopped listening to her frustrated muttering. He had a feeling it wasn't real flattering to him anyway. And maybe he didn't deserve flattery. Maybe he was the idiot his sister had called him.

And maybe, he thought in disgust, he'd tossed aside something he should have been fighting for.

When her cell phone rang, Naomi grabbed it, hoping to see Toby's name on her screen, and felt a swift stab of disappointment when it wasn't him. She answered on a sigh. "Hi, Cecelia."

Her friend started talking in a rush. "Naomi, you remember that guy Gio you told me and Simone about when you came home from that big fashion show?"

Naomi rolled her eyes and dropped into a chair. Curling her feet up underneath her, she said wryly, "Yes, I remember him." *Just saw him yesterday*, she wanted to add but didn't. "What about him?"

"I was watching that gossip channel on cable just now, and he's all over it." Cecelia paused for dramatic effect. "Can I just say wow? You didn't tell us how pretty he is."

"He's not that good-looking in person," Naomi assured her. Especially, she added silently, when you added in his personality. His character. Compared to Toby, Gio Fabiani was simply an attractive waste of space.

"Well, he looks good on camera," Cecelia said. "Except he's not looking real happy right now."

Naomi sighed again. She was tired, since she'd been up half the night reliving that argument with Toby. And the other half of the night, her dream self had done the same thing.

This morning, she'd been on the phone handling dozens of things, all the while letting the back of her mind work on what she would say to Toby when she talked to him again. Because they *were* going to talk. She wasn't going to let him end what they'd just so recently found because of a stupid lie. Should she have told him about meeting Gio? Sure. In hindsight, it was perfectly clear. But at the time, she'd been trying to handle things on her own. Clear up her past and set up her future. Why was that so hard to understand?

Resting her head against the back of the chair, she stared up at the ceiling and asked listlessly, "Why's he on the news?"

"Get this," Cecelia said, clearly settling in for a good gossip session. "There are *three* different women suing him for child support."

Surprised, but somehow comforted by the fact that she wasn't the only foolish woman to have landed in Gio's bed, Naomi chuckled a little to herself. "Really?"

"Oh, yeah, apparently it's huge news in Italy. He even left the country to get out of the spotlight for a while."

"If he's on the news, doesn't sound like that plan worked."

"I know, right? And you know what's weird?" Cecelia asked, and didn't wait for an answer. "Some photographer caught him at the airport in Houston. He was running to catch a plane headed to England. He was right here in Texas. Can you believe it?"

And now he was gone, Naomi thought with a pleased smile. Obviously, he'd taken what she said to heart and wasn't waiting around to see if she'd change her mind. "Well, I hope those women catch up to him."

"I think they will," Cecelia said. "He's got to go home sometime, right? Anyway, I just thought it was weird, seeing him on TV and knowing you'd met him—"

"It is weird." Beyond weird. But it explained why Gio

had been desperate enough for money to give extortion a try. The upside here was, with three other women and children to worry about, the man would certainly be willing to sign over his parental rights, so that was good for Naomi and her baby.

Cecelia was talking, but Naomi was only half listening. Instead, she was thinking about Toby. Maybe she should have stayed at the ranch last night and just had it out with him. But he'd hurt her, damn it. Hurt her by dismissing her when she told him she loved him. It had been a big moment for her, opening herself up like that, and he hadn't believed her.

Hadn't trusted her, and that, she thought, hurt most of all. He'd been waiting, or so it seemed to her, for Naomi to let him down. To prove that what they had couldn't be counted on. Scowling, she thought about the night before, and then something dawned on her.

A part of his mind and heart had been convinced that she would leave him. Walk away. To protect himself, he'd held back, committing to a marriage he didn't believe would work so that when it failed, he wasn't blindsided by it.

With a jolt, Naomi sat up straight. And what had she done? Walked away in the middle of an argument. She'd walked away. Just as he'd expected her to do. "Oh, God."

"Naomi, are you even listening to me?"

She winced. "Sorry, Cec, I'm just really distracted."

"Everything okay with you and Toby?"

She hesitated and almost lied but didn't want to get into the habit, so she said only, "It will be. We're just working out a few things."

Like our lives.

"Oh, I totally get it. Between weddings and babies

and the rush of hormones…we're all half-crazed these days. I'll let you go, sweetie. I just wanted to tell you about that Gio guy."

"And I appreciate the update," Naomi said. "We'll talk soon."

When the call ended, she stood up and walked through the condo, realizing that this wasn't her place anymore. Her place was with Toby. Whether he knew it or not.

Grimly, she turned her phone on and made a call. When a woman answered, she said, "Scarlett, this is Naomi. Where's your brother?"

"An hour ago, he was at the ranch, and he was pretty damn crabby, too."

Naomi smiled. "He's about to get a lot crabbier."

"Yay!"

Naomi drove straight to the ranch, telling herself if he wasn't there, she'd wait. She wasn't going to leave again without making him see the truth of what they had. What they *could* have. And if she'd just stayed right there last night, they'd be through this already. *Mental note: no more walking out.*

Her hair twisted wildly in the wind blasting through her open window. The Texas summer sky was a brassy blue with only a few stray clouds drifting aimlessly, looking lost and alone in that vast expanse. There was no traffic on the road, so she pushed the car as fast as she dared. The baby was moving around excitedly, almost as if he or she knew they were headed home. Naomi smiled fiercely and caught her own eye in the rearview mirror.

She was going to make Toby listen. Make him believe. Make him love her as much as she loved him. Naomi had waited for love her whole life, and she wasn't going to settle for less.

Gravel flew up from behind her tires as she took the long drive to the ranch. Her gaze swept the familiar, looking for Toby, and then she spotted him, getting into his truck.

"Oh, no," she murmured, "you're not leaving yet." She pulled to a stop directly in front of the truck, blocking him from leaving. Then she threw the gear into Park, jumped out and walked toward him with long, determined strides.

Toby's breath caught in his throat. When he saw her car flying down the drive, he thought he'd never seen anything that beautiful. She was coming home on her own. But now, watching the woman who held his heart, he had to admit that she looked both gorgeous…and dangerous. There was fire in her eye, and what did it say about him that he found that damned sexy?

It was so good to see her. To catch her scent on the wind. He wanted to tangle his hands in that thick hair of hers, slant his mouth over hers and feel that rush of *rightness* that always went through him when they were together.

Since she walked out the door yesterday, he'd felt only half-alive. Through his anger and pain, there was a constant ache for her. In spite of distrusting her, he wanted her. In spite of everything, he'd missed her.

And after talking to Scarlett today, he'd realized that he'd handled that talk with Naomi all wrong. He hadn't even listened to her, because he'd been so wrapped up in the surety that he'd been right to keep his heart locked away.

But he was wrong. About all of it. And it was long past time she heard everything he'd been keeping inside.

"You're not leaving, Toby," she said when she was close enough.

"No need to now," he said affably, one corner of his mouth lifting as her eyes spit fire at him.

"Not until we get a few things straight," she said, then asked, "What did you say?"

"I was coming to you, Naomi, so, no," he said, "I'm not going anywhere now."

Some of that temper that had been driving her melted away. He could see it in the way her shoulders relaxed some. "You were really coming to me?"

"Couldn't take the silence here, Naomi. The emptiness. I needed you to come home. And you have."

He grabbed hold of her, yanked her in close and kissed her, letting his body tell her everything that was so hard to say in words. She leaned into him, and he felt whole for the first time in hours. This was where he belonged. Right here, with her. The world righted itself, and every last, lingering doubt hiding in the shadows of his mind dissolved in the realization of what he had—what he had almost lost.

When he finally lifted his head, he looked down into her eyes and said, "I'm sorry."

"Excuse me? You're sorry?"

He grinned a little. "Is it so surprising?"

"Well," she admitted, "yes. I didn't expect you to say that. I thought we'd finish our argument and that I'd have to hold you down to make you listen to me. An apology wasn't in the game plan."

"I was wrong, Naomi. Expected or not, I am sorry. I never should have let Maverick get to me." He released her, jammed his hands in the back pockets of his jeans and admitted, "I reacted just the way he wanted me to. I shut you down. Wouldn't listen. Hell, I didn't even listen to myself, because of course I trust you, Naomi."

She blew out a breath, then pressed her lips together in an attempt to steady herself. Toby knew her even better than he knew himself, and that was just one more reason why he'd been the idiot his sister had called him.

Naomi didn't cheat. Naomi would never hurt him.

"Thanks for that," she said and gave him a tremulous smile.

"I saw that picture and I lost it," he admitted, jerking his hands free and tossing them in the air helplessly. "I didn't think. Didn't remember that the bastard's whole point is to create chaos and tear people apart."

"It wouldn't have done anything to us if I had just told you about Gio wanting to meet with me in the first place, Toby." Her eyes were shining as she looked up at him. "I should have asked you to go with me."

Watching her, he asked what he should have the day before. "Why didn't you?"

"Because I wanted to handle it myself." She laid both hands on the curve of the baby and rubbed, as if soothing the child within. "I wanted to kick him out of my life, *our* lives. Once I was there, I was wishing for you, though, if that helps."

"A little," he admitted. "I get you wanting to do it yourself, Naomi. But you could have told me."

"And should have, I know." She pushed her hand through her wind-tangled hair and sighed. "He wanted money. Threatened to tell the world that he's my baby's father if I didn't pay him off."

Toby felt a hard punch of anger and gritted his teeth against the helpless flood of it. He really wished he had five minutes alone with the man. "What did you say to that?"

"I told him to go ahead. It would make it easier to sue him for child support."

A laugh shot from Toby's throat. "You did?"

"Yes, and he wasn't happy," she said, smiling now. "But according to Cecelia, he's got bigger problems at the moment."

"What?"

"Not important," she said, shaking her head. "I'll tell you later. Toby. Why were you coming to see me?"

"Because sometime between last night and this morning, I finally figured something out." He reached for her again, laid both hands on her shoulders and held on. "I was coming to tell you that I love you, Naomi."

She gasped and clapped one hand to her mouth. Her eyes filled instantly with a sheen of tears. "Really?"

"Yes." His gaze moved over her face, taking in every detail. In the sunlight, the bright streaks in her hair shone like polished copper. Behind her hand, her mouth was curved in a small smile, as if she wanted to believe him but couldn't quite manage it. And her eyes, her beautiful eyes glittered with love and hope.

"I love you, Naomi," he said again, willing her to trust him. To believe him. "I was a jackass yesterday. I was so worried about losing you I forgot to fight to keep you."

"Toby…"

He had no clue what she was going to say, but Toby was determined to speak first. To tell her everything he should have told her when he first suggested they get married.

"I shouldn't have shut down like that yesterday. I do trust you, Naomi. It was my own stubbornness that didn't let me tell you that I think I've always loved you." He ran his hands up and down her arms, kept his gaze locked with hers. "I'm lucky enough to be in love with my best friend."

She pressed her lips together and reached up to impatiently swipe tears from her eyes. "When I left yesterday, Toby, I wasn't really *leaving*, you know. I always planned to come back."

"You walking away is something I never want to see again, Naomi. Don't think I could take it." Just the thought of losing her was enough to bring him to his knees.

When Sasha left, anger had driven him. If he lost Naomi, he'd lose his soul.

"You don't have to worry about that," she assured him, stepping in to wrap her arms around his waist. "I'm not going anywhere. I'm exactly where I want to be."

He held on to her for several long minutes, relishing the beat of her heart against his chest, the scent of her shampoo flavoring every breath and the thump of their child, kicking to get attention.

Finally, though, he pulled back, caged her face between his palms and said, "I want to adopt your baby, Naomi. As soon as it's born, I want to be its father. So that baby will never doubt that he or she belongs. That we're family."

"Oh, Toby…" Tears trickled down her cheeks, but she smiled through them, and his heart turned over to see the love beaming in her eyes.

"And about the California thing," Toby added quickly, wanting to say it all now while he was holding her close. "If you have to be there for weeks on end to tape your show, we'll manage. We can buy a house in the hills there and we'll have a California base for whenever we need it."

"You'd do that for me?" she asked.

"For *us*," he corrected, wiping her tears away with his thumbs.

"It means so much to me that you would," Naomi said and went up on her toes to kiss him, hard and fast. "But you don't have to. I called Tamara today to tell her thanks but no, thanks."

Now it was his turn to be surprised. "What? Why would you do that?"

"Because I don't need it in the desperate way I used to," she said. "Before, I wanted my show to succeed so badly so I could prove myself. To my parents. To myself. Because the show was all I had, I poured everything into it.

"But these past few weeks, I've discovered I'm more than my show, Toby. I don't need to make a point. I need you. *Us*."

"But, Naomi, this was your dream."

She shrugged and smiled. "If Tamara Stiles can get *Fashion Sense* on stations around the country, so can I. And doing it myself means it gets done my way. I don't have to leave Texas, leave what makes my show what it is to make it succeed. I'll get there. It'll just take a little longer."

"You're amazing," he said quietly. He'd always seen her strength, and he was glad she could see it now, too. "I believe in you, Naomi. You wait and see. In a few years, your show is going to put Royal on the map."

She grinned. "As long as you're with me, then everything will be perfect."

"Oh, I'm with you, honey. And you'll never shake me loose now."

"Good to hear," she said and moved to kiss him again.

He stopped her cold with a shake of his head. "Not yet. We've got something else to settle first."

"What's left?" she asked, but she was smiling and he was grateful. He never wanted to see her cry again.

"Just this." Toby went down on one knee in front of her and pulled a simply set sapphire ring from his pocket. Holding it up, he saw more tears and told himself this one last time was okay. "You didn't want an engagement ring before because it wouldn't have been real. I hope you'll take this one, though. This ring belonged to my grandmother, Naomi. It symbolizes the fifty years of love she and my grandpa shared."

"Toby…"

His gaze locked on hers, Toby said softly, "I'm offering you this ring, Naomi. I want to give you my name, my love and the future we'll build together. Marry me for real, Naomi. Trust me with your heart, with your baby. Give me more babies. Fill this big empty house with the kind of love that lasts generations."

"Oh, Toby, my heart hurts it's so full," she whispered brokenly.

"That's a yes, then?"

"Yes, of course it's yes."

He slid the ring onto her finger, where that cool sapphire caught the sunlight and winked up at both of them. Then he lifted the hem of her shirt and pressed a gentle kiss to the mound of her belly and heard her sigh as she stroked her fingers through his hair.

Then he stood up and looked into her eyes as he pulled

her into his arms. "I love you, Naomi," he whispered. "Always have. Always will."

She sighed again, smiled and lifted one hand to smooth his hair back from his forehead. "I love you, Toby. Always have. Always will."

"Good to hear," he said, lowering his head for a kiss.

Naomi grinned. "Talk, talk, talk. Show me what you've got, cowboy."

He grinned back, and then he showed her.

* * * * *

September 2017: TAKING HOME THE TYCOON
by USA TODAY *bestselling author Catherine Mann.*

October 2017: BILLIONAIRE'S BABY BIND
by USA TODAY *bestselling author Katherine Garbera.*

November 2017: THE TEXAN TAKES A WIFE
by USA TODAY *bestselling author Charlene Sands.*

December 2017: BEST MAN UNDER THE MISTLETOE
by USA TODAY *bestselling author Kathie DeNosky.*

* * *

If you're on Twitter, tell us what you think of
Mills & Boon Desire! #Mills&BoonDesire

"So you need a boyfriend," Rick Serenghetti said without preamble.

She itched to rub the smug smile off his face. "I don't need anything. This would be a completely optional but mutually advantageous arrangement."

And right after this conversation, she was going to have another serious talk with her manager. What had Odele signed her up for?

"You need me."

She burned. He'd made it sound like *You want me*.

"I've been asked to play many roles, but never a stud."

"Don't get too excited."

He grinned. "Don't worry, I won't. I have a thing for the doe-eyed, dark-haired look, but since Camilla Belle isn't available, you'll do."

The flames of temper licked her, not least because he was clued in as to her Hollywood doppelgänger. "So you'll settle?"

"I don't know. Let's kiss and find out."

"If the cameras were rolling, it would be time for a slap right now," she muttered.

He caught her wrist and tugged her closer.

"This isn't a movie, and you're no actor!" she objected.

"Great, because I intend to kiss you for real."

* * *

Hollywood Baby Affair
is part of the Serenghetti Brothers series:
In business and the bedroom,
these alpha brothers drive a hard bargain!

HOLLYWOOD BABY AFFAIR

BY
ANNA DePALO

First Published in Great Britain 2017
By Mills & Boon, an imprint of HarperCollins*Publishers*
1 London Bridge Street, London, SE1 9GF

© 2017 Anna DePalo

ISBN: 978-0-263-92823-5

51-0617

Our policy is to use papers that are natural, renewable and recyclable products and made from wood grown in sustainable forests. The logging and manufacturing processes conform to the legal environmental regulations of the country of origin.

Printed and bound in Spain
by CPI, Barcelona

USA TODAY bestselling author **Anna DePalo** is a Harvard graduate and former intellectual property attorney who lives with her husband, son and daughter in her native New York. She writes sexy, humorous books that have been published in more than twenty countries. Her novels have won the *RT Book Reviews* Reviewers' Choice Award, the Golden Leaf and the Book Buyer's Best. You can sign up for her newsletter at www.annadepalo.com.

For DeLilah & Bob,
thanks for the support & encouragement

One

Actress and Stuntman Lovefest! More Than Movie Pyrotechnics on Display.

The gossip website headline ran through Chiara Feran's head when it shouldn't have.

She clung to Stunt Stud's well-muscled shoulders, four stories up, wind blowing and helicopter blades whipping in the background—trying to act as if her life depended on it when the truth was that only her career did. After all, a gossip site had just written that she and Mr. Stunt Double were an item, and right now she needed the press distracted from her estranged father, a Vegas-loving card-sharp threatening to cause a controversy of his own.

She tossed her head to keep the hair out of her face. She'd learned Stunt Stud's first name was Rick when they'd rehearsed, but she thought *insufferable* was a better word for him. He had remarkable green eyes…and he looked at her as if she were a spoiled diva who needed the kid-glove treatment.

I don't want you to ruin your manicure.

Thanks for your concern, but there's a manicurist on set.

They'd had a few brief exchanges over the course of filming that had made her blood boil. If the world only knew... True, his magnetism was enough to rival that of the biggest movie stars, so she wondered why he was content with stunt work, but then again, his ego didn't need any further boosting. And the rumors were that he wasn't who he seemed to be and that he had a shadowy, secretive past.

There was even a hint that he was fabulously wealthy. Given his ego, she wouldn't be surprised if he'd put out the rumors himself. He was a macho stuntman ready to save a damsel in distress, but Chiara could save herself, thank you. She'd learned long ago not to depend on any man.

She opened her mouth, but instead of an existential scream, her next line came out. "Zain, we're going to die!"

"I'm not dropping you," he growled in reply.

Chiara knew his voice would be substituted later with her costar's by the studio's editing department. She took perverse satisfaction in calling him by her costar's character name. And since Rick was pretending to be her costar, and her costar himself was just acting, she was two steps removed from reality.

And one long fall away from sudden death.

Even though both she and Rick had invisible harnesses, accidents could and did happen on movie sets. As if on cue, more explosions sounded around them.

As soon as this scene was over, she was heading to her trailer for coffee and maybe even a talk with Odele—

"Cut!" the director yelled through a bullhorn.

Chiara sagged with relief.

Rick barely loosened his grip as they were lowered to the ground.

She was bone-tired in the middle of a twelve-hour day on set. She didn't dwell on the other type of tired right now—an existential weariness that made it hard to care about anything in her life. Fortunately filming on this movie was due to wrap soon.

Action flicks bored her, but they paid the mortgage and more. And Odele, her manager, never stopped reminding her that they also kept her in the public eye. Her Q score would stay high, and it would keep those lucrative endorsement deals flowing. This film was no exception on both counts. *Pegasus Pride* was about a mission to stop the bad guys from blowing up the United Nations and other key government buildings.

As soon as her feet hit the ground, she ignored a frisson of awareness and stepped away from Rick.

His dark hair was mussed, and his jeans clung low on his hips, a dirty vest concealing his tee. Still, he managed to project the authority of a master of the universe, calm and implacable but ready for action.

She didn't like her reaction to him. He made her self-conscious about being a woman. Yes, he was all hard-packed muscle and latent strength. Yes, he was undoubtedly in top physical shape with washboard abs. But he was arrogant and annoying and, like most men, not to be trusted.

She refused to be intimidated. It was laughable really—after all, *her* bank account must dwarf his.

"Okay?" Rick asked.

His voice was as deep and rich as the hot chocolate she wished she had right now—damn him. It was a surprisingly damp and cold early April day on Novatus Studio's lot in Los Angeles. "Of course. Why wouldn't I be?" Dozens of people milled around them on the movie set. "All in a day's work, right?"

His jaw firmed. "This one is asking for more than usual."

"Excuse me?"

He looked at her quizzically. "Have you spoken to your manager recently? Odele?"

"No, why?"

His gaze moved to her trailer. "You may want to give it a go."

Uh-oh.

He fished his cell phone out of his pocket and showed her the screen.

It took a moment to focus on the newspaper website's headline, but once she did, her eyes widened. Chiara Feran and Her Stuntman Get Cozy. Is It More Than High Altitudes That Have Their Hearts Racing?

Oh…crap. Another online tabloid had apparently picked up the original gossip site's story, and worse, now Rick was aware of it, too. Heat rushed to her cheeks. He wasn't *her* stuntman. He wasn't her anything. Suddenly she wondered whether she should have sent that first story into internet oblivion when she'd had the chance by denying it. But she'd been too relieved they were focusing on a made-up relationship rather than the real pesky issue—her father.

At Rick's amused look, she said abruptly, "I'll talk to Odele."

He lifted her chin and stroked her jaw with his thumb—as if he had all the right in the world. "If you want me, there's no need for extreme measures like planting stories in the press. Why not try the direct approach?"

She swatted his hand away and held on to her temper. "I'm sure there's been a mistake. Is that direct enough for you?"

He laughed at her with his eyes, and said with lazy self-assurance, "Get back to me."

As if. In addition to her deadbeat father making news, she had to contend with burgeoning rumors of a relationship with the last stuntman on earth she'd ever walk the red carpet with.

She turned her back on Rick and marched off. The man sent a red mist into the edges of her vision, and it had nothing to do with lust. She clenched her hands, heart pounding. Her jeans and torn tee were skintight—requisite attire for an action movie damsel in distress—and she was aware she was giving Rick a good view as she stomped away.

At her trailer, she banged through the door. She immediately spotted Odele sitting at a small table. The older woman lifted her head and gave Chiara a mild look from behind red glasses, her gray bob catching the light. If Chiara had learned anything during her years with her manager, it was that Odele was unflappable.

Stopping, Chiara touched her forehead. "I took pain medication for my headache an hour ago, and he's still here."

"Man problems have defied pharmacology for decades, honey," Odele replied in her throaty, raspy voice.

Chiara blurted out the gossip about her and Rick, and the stuntman's reaction. "He thinks he's God's gift to actresses!"

"You need a boyfriend," Odele responded cryptically. For a moment, Chiara had trouble processing the words. Her mind, going sixty miles an hour, hit the brakes. "What?"

She was one of those actresses who got paid to be photographed sporting a certain brand of handbag or shoes. She glanced around her trailer at the gleaming wood and marble countertops. She had more than she could possibly want. She didn't desire anything, especially a boyfriend.

True, she hadn't had a date in a long time. It didn't mean she couldn't get one. She just didn't want the hassle. Boyfriends were work…and men were trouble.

"We need to retain a boyfriend for you," Odele rephrased.

Chiara gave a dismissive laugh. "I can think of many things I need, but a boyfriend isn't one of them. I need a new stylist now that Emery has gone off to start her own accessories line. I need a new tube of toothpaste for my bathroom. And I really need a vacation once this film wraps." She shook her head. "But a boyfriend? No."

"You're America's sweetheart. Everyone wants to see you happy," her manager pointed out.

"You mean they want to see me making steady progress toward marriage and children."

Odele nodded.

"Life is rarely that neat." She should know.

Odele gave a big sigh. "Well, we don't deal in reality, do we, honey? Our currency in Hollywood is the stardust of dreams."

Chiara resisted rolling her eyes. She *really* needed a vacation.

"That's why a little relationship is just what you need to get your name back out there in a positive way."

"And how am I supposed to get said relationship?"

Odele snapped her fingers. "Easy. I have just the man."

"Who?"

"A stuntman, and you've already met him."

A horrifying thought entered Chiara's head, and she narrowed her eyes. "You put out the rumor that Rick and I are getting cozy."

OMG. She'd gone to Odele with the rumor because she expected her manager to stamp out a budding media firestorm. Instead, she'd discovered Odele was an arsonist...with poor taste in men.

Odele nodded. "Damn straight I did. We need a distraction from stories about your father."

Chiara stepped forward. "Odele, how could you? And with—" she stabbed her finger in the direction of the door "—him of all people."

Odele remained placid.

Chiara narrowed her eyes again. "Has he said anything about your little scheme?"

"He hasn't objected."

No wonder Rick had seemed almost...intimate a few minutes ago. He'd been approached by Odele to be her supposed love interest. Chiara took a deep breath to steady herself and temper her reaction. "He's not my type."

"He's any woman's type, honey. Arm candy."

"There's nothing sweet about him, believe me." He was obnoxious, irritating and objectionable in every way.

"He might not be sugar, but he'll look edible to many of your female fans."

Chiara threw up her hands. It was one thing not to contradict a specious story online, it was another to start pretending it was *true*. And now she'd discovered that said story had been concocted by none other than her own manager. "Oh, c'mon, Odele. You really expect me to stage a relationship for the press?"

Odele arched a brow. "Why not? Your competition is making sex tapes for the media."

"I'm aiming for the Academy Awards, not the Razzies."

"It's no different from being set up on a date or two by a friend."

"Except you're my manager and we both know there's an ulterior motive."

"There's always an ulterior motive. Money. Sex. You name it."

"Is this necessary? My competition has survived extramarital affairs, DUIs and nasty custody disputes with their halos intact."

"Only because of quick thinking and fancy footwork on the part of their manager or publicist. And believe me, honey, my doctor keeps advising me to keep my stress level to a minimum. It's not good for the blood pressure."

"You need to get out of Hollywood."

"And you need a man. A stuntman."

"Never." And especially not *him*. Somehow he'd gotten his own trailer even though he wasn't one of the leads on this film. He also visited the exercise trailer, complete with built-in gym and weightlifting equipment. Not that she'd used it herself, but his access to it hadn't escaped her notice.

Odele pulled out her cell phone and read from the screen: "Chiara Feran's Father in Illegal Betting Scandal: 'My Daughter Has Cut Me Off.'"

Oh…double damn. Chiara was familiar with yesterday's headline. It was like a bad dream that she kept waking up to. It was also why she'd been temporarily—in a moment of insanity—grateful for the ridiculous story about her budding romance. "The only reason I've kept him out of my life for the past two decades is because he's a lying, cheating snake! Now I'm responsible not only for my own image, but for what a sperm donor does?"

As far as she was concerned, the donation of sperm was Michael Feran's principal contribution to the person she was today. Even the surname that they shared wasn't authentic. It had been changed at Ellis Island three generations back from the Italian *Ferano* to the Anglicized *Feran*.

"We need to promote a wholesome image," Odele intoned solemnly.

"I could throttle him!"

Rick Serenghetti made it his business to be all business. But he couldn't take his gaze off Chiara Feran. Her limpid brown eyes, smooth skin contrasting with dark brows and raven hair made her a dead ringer for Snow White.

A guy could easily be turned into a blithering fool in the presence of such physical perfection. Her face was faultlessly symmetrical. Her topaz eyes called to a man to lose himself in their depths, and her pink bow mouth begged to be kissed. And then came the part of her appearance where the threshold was crossed from fairy tale to his fantasy: she had a fabulous body that marked her as red-hot.

They were in the middle of filming on the Novatus Studio set. Today was sunny and mild, more typical weather for LA than they'd had yesterday, when he'd last spoken to Chiara. With any luck, current conditions were a bellwether for how filming on the movie would end—quickly and painlessly. Then he could relax, because on a film set he was always pumped up for his next action scene. In a lucky break for everyone involved, scenes were again being shot on Novatus Studio's lot in down-town LA, instead of in nearby Griffith Park.

Still, filming wasn't over until the last scene was done.

He stood off to the side, watching Chiara and the action on camera. The film crew surrounded him, along with everyone else who made a movie happen: assistants, extras, costume designers, special effects people and, of course, the stunts department—*him*.

He knew more about Chiara Feran than she'd ever guess—or that she'd like him to know. No Oscar yet, but the press loved to talk about her. Surprisingly scan-dal-free for Hollywood...except for the cardsharp father.

Too bad Rick and Chiara rubbed each other like two sheets of sandpaper—because she had guts. He had to respect that about her. She wasn't like her male costar who—if the tabloids were to be believed—was fond of getting four-hundred-dollar haircuts.

At the same time, Chiara was all woman. He remem-bered the feel of her curves during the helicopter stunt they'd done yesterday. She'd been soft and stimulating. And now the media had tagged him and Chiara as a couple.

"I want to talk to you."

Rick turned to see Chiara's manager. In the first days of filming, he'd spotted the older woman on set. She was hard to overlook. Her raspy, no-nonsense voice and distinctive ruby-framed glasses made her ripe for cari-cature. One of the crew had confirmed for him that she was Odele Wittnauer, Chiara's manager.

Odele looked to be in her early sixties and not fight-ing it—which made her stand out in Hollywood. Her helmet hair was salt-and-pepper with an ironclad curve under the chin.

Rick adopted a pleasant smile. He and Odele had exchanged a word or two, but this was the first time she'd had a request. "What can I do for you?"

"I've got a proposal."

He checked his surprise, and joked, "Odele, I didn't think you had it in you."

He had been propositioned by plenty of women, but he'd never had the word *proposal* issue from the mouth of a Madeleine Albright look-alike before.

"Not that type of proposition. I want you to be in a relationship with Chiara Feran."

Rick rubbed his jaw. He hadn't seen that one coming. And then he put two and two together, and a light went off. "You were the one who planted that story about me and Chiara."

"Yup," Odele responded without a trace of guilt or remorse. "The press beast had to be fed. And more important, we needed a distraction from another story about Chiara's father."

"The gambler."

"The deadbeat."

"You're ruthless." He said it with reluctant admiration.

"There's chemistry between you," Odele responded, switching gears.

"Fireworks are more like it."

Chiara's manager brightened. "The press will eat it up. The stuntman and the beauty pageant winner."

So Chiara had won a contest or two—he shouldn't have been surprised. She had the looks to make men weak, including *him*, somewhat to his chagrin. Still, Odele made them sound like a couple on a C-rated reality show: *Blind Date Engagements.* "I've seen the media chew up and spit out people right and left. No, thanks."

"It'll raise your profile in this town."

"I like my privacy."

"I'll pay you well."

"I don't need the money."

"Well," Odele drawled, lowering her eyes, "maybe I can appeal to your sense of stuntman chivalry then."

"What do you mean?"

Odele looked up. "You see, Chiara has this teeny-weeny problem of an overly enthusiastic fan."

"A stalker?"

"Too early to tell, but the guy did try to scale the fence at her house once."

"He knows where she lives?" Rick asked in disbelief.

"We live in the internet age, dear. Privacy is dead."

He had some shred left but he wasn't going to go into details. Even Superman's alter ego, Clark Kent, was entitled to a few secrets.

"Don't mention the too-eager fan to her, though. She doesn't like to talk about it."

Rick narrowed his eyes. "Does Chiara Feran know you approached me?"

"She thinks I already have."

All right then.

He surmised that Odele and Chiara had had their talk. And apparently Chiara had changed tactics and decided to turn the situation to her advantage. She was willing to tolerate him…for the sake of her career at least. He shouldn't have been surprised. He'd already had one bad experience with a publicity-hungry actress, and then he'd been one of the casualties.

Still, they were in the middle of the second act, and he'd missed the opening. But suddenly things had gotten a lot more interesting.

Odele's eyes gleamed as if she sensed victory—or at least a chink in his armor. Turning away, she said, "Let me know when you're ready to talk."

As Rick watched Chiara's manager leave, he knew there was a brooding expression on his face. Odele had presented him with a quandary. As a rule, he didn't get involved with actresses—ever since his one bad episode—but he had his gallant side. On top of it, Chiara was the talent on his latest film—one in which he had a big stake.

As if on cue, his cell phone vibrated. Fishing it out of his pocket, Rick recognized the number on-screen as that of his business partner—one of the guys who fronted the company, per Rick's preference to be behind the scenes.

"Hey, Pete, what's going on?"

Rick listened to Pete's summary of the meeting that morning with an indie director looking for funding. He liked what he heard, but he needed to know more. "Email me their proposal. I'm inclined to fund up to five million, but I want more details."

Five million dollars was pocket change in his world.

"You're the boss," Pete responded cheerfully.

Yup, he was…though no one on set knew he was the producer of *Pegasus Pride*. He liked his privacy and kept his communications mostly to a need-to-know basis.

Right. Rick spotted Chiara in the distance. No doubt she was heading to film her next scene. *There* was someone who treated him more like the hired help than the boss.

Complications and delays on a film were common, and Rick had a feeling Chiara was about to become his biggest complication to date…

Two

"Hey."

It was exactly the sort of greeting she expected from a sweaty and earthy he-man—or rather, stuntman.

Chiara's pulse picked up. *Ugh.* She hadn't expected to have this reaction around him. She was a professional— a classically trained actress before she'd been diverted by Hollywood.

Sure, she'd been Miss Rhode Island, and a runner-up in the Miss America pageant. But then the Yale School of Drama had beckoned. And she'd never been a Hollywood blonde. The media most often compared her to Camilla Belle because they shared a raven-haired, chestnut-eyed look.

Anyway, with her ebony hair, she'd need to have her roots touched up every other day if she tried to become a blonde. As far as she was concerned, she spent enough time in the primping chair.

She figured He-Stuntman had gotten his education in the School of Hard Knocks. Maybe a broken bone or two. Certainly plenty of bumps and bruises.

Rick stopped in front of her. No one was around. They were near the actors' trailers, far away from the main action. Luckily she hadn't run into him after her talk with Odele two days ago. Instead, she'd managed to avoid him until now.

Dusk was gathering, but she still had a clear view of him.

He was in a ripped tee, jeans and body paint meant to seem like grease and dirt, while she was wearing a damsel-in-distress/sidekick look—basically a feminine version of Rick's attire but her clothes were extratight and torn to show cleavage. And from the quick perusal he gave her, she could tell the bare skin hadn't escaped his notice.

"So you need a boyfriend," he said without preamble.

She itched to rub the smug smile off his face. "I don't need anything. This would be a completely optional but mutually advantageous arrangement."

And right after this conversation, she was going to have another serious talk with her manager. What had Odele signed her up for?

"You need me."

She burned. He'd made it sound like *you want me*.

"I've been asked to play many roles, but never a stud."

"Don't get too excited."

He grinned. "Don't worry, I won't. I have a thing for the doe-eyed, dark-haired look, but since Camilla Belle isn't available, you'll do."

The flames of temper licked her, not least because he was clued in as to her Hollywood doppelgänger. "So you'll settle?"

"I don't know. Let's kiss and find out."

"If the cameras were rolling, it would be time for a slap right now," she muttered.

He caught her wrist and tugged her closer.

"This isn't a movie, and you're no actor!" she objected.

"Great, because I intend to kiss you for real. Let's see if we can be convincing for when the paparazzi and public are watching." He raised his free hand to thread his fingers through her hair and move it away from her face. "Your long dark hair is driving me crazy."

"It's the Brazilian-Italian heritage," she snapped back, "and I bet you say the same thing to all your leading ladies."

"No," he answered bemusedly, "some of them are blondes."

And then his mouth was on hers. If he'd been forceful, she'd have had a chance, but his lips settled on hers with soft, tantalizing pressure. He smelled of smoke from the special effects, and when his tongue slipped inside her mouth, she discovered the taste of mint, too.

She'd been kissed many times—on-screen and off— but she found herself tumbling into this one with shocking speed. The kiss was smooth, leisurely...masterful but understated. Rick could double for any A-list actor in a love scene. He touched his tongue to hers, and the shock and unexpectedness of it had her opening to him. As an unwritten rule, actors on-screen did not French kiss, so she was already in uncharted territory. The hard plane of his chest brushed against her, and her nipples tightened.

Think, Chiara. Remember why you don't like him.

She allowed herself one more second, and then she tore her mouth away and stepped back. For a fleeting moment she felt a puff of steam over his audacity. "All right, the screen test is over."

Rick curved his lips. "How did I do?"

"I don't even know your last name," she responded, sidestepping the question.

"I'll answer to anything. 'Honey,' 'baby,' 'sugar.'" He shrugged. "I'm easy."

"Clearly." This guy could charm his way into any woman's bed. "Still, I'd prefer your real one for when the police ask me to describe the suspect."

He grinned. "It's Rick Serenghetti. But 'darling' would add the appropriate air of mystery for the paparazzi."

Serenghetti. She knew an Italian surname when she heard one. "My last name was originally Ferano. You know, Italian."

His smile widened. "I'd never have guessed, Snow White."

"They used to call me Snow White, but I drifted," she quipped. "Not suitable for the role."

"No problem. I'm not Prince Charming. I'm just his body double."

She wanted to scream. "This is never going to work."

"That's why you're an actress." He looked curious. "And, Odele mentioned, a beauty contestant. Win any titles?"

She made a sour face. "Yes. Miss Congeniality."

He burst out laughing. "I won't ask what your talent was."

"Ventriloquism. I made my dummy sing."

"'Some Day My Prince Will Come'?"

"Nothing from *Snow White*! I was also Miss Rhode Island, but obviously that was on the state level." She'd gone on to be a finalist in Miss America, which was where she'd earned her title of Miss Congeniality.

"Rhode Island is the smallest state. Still, the competition must have been fierce."

"Are you mocking me?" She searched his face, but he looked solemn.

"Who, me? I never mock women I'm trying to score with."

"Wow, you're direct. You don't even like me."

"What's *like* got to do with it?"

"You have no shame." When it came to sex, she was used to men wanting to bed anyone in sight. This was Hollywood, after all.

"Is it working?"

"Nothing will work, except Odele convincing me this is a good idea."

Rick frowned. "You mean she hasn't already?"

It took Chiara a moment to realize he wasn't joking. "Please. She may have persuaded you to go along with her crazy scheme, but not me."

"I only went along with it because I thought you'd said yes."

Chiara watched Rick's dawning expression, which mimicked her own. "I believed you'd agreed."

"Stuntmen are made of sterner stuff." He threw her attitude right back at her.

Chiara realized they'd both been tricked by Odele into believing the other had agreed to her plan. Rick had dared to kiss her because he thought she'd already signed up for her manager's plot. "What are we going to do?"

Rick shrugged. "About the gathering media frenzy? We're already bickering like an old married couple. We're perfect."

Chiara's eyes widened. "You can't tell me you're seriously considering this? Anyway, we're supposed to act like new lovebirds, not a cantankerous old married couple."

"If we're already arguing, it'll make our relationship seem deeper than it is."

"Skip the honeymoon phase?" she asked rhetorically. "What's in this for you?"

He shrugged. "Have some fun." He looked at her lingeringly. "Satisfy my fetish for Snow White."

Chiara tingled, her breasts feeling heavy. "Oh, yeah, right…"

"So what's your take?"

"This is the worst storyline to come out of Hollywood."

For the second time in recent days, Chiara banged open the door of her trailer and marched in. "I can't pretend to be in a relationship with Rick Serenghetti. End of story."

Odele looked up from her magazine. She sat on a cushioned built-in bench along one wall. "What's wrong with him?"

He was too big, too macho, too everything—most of all, *annoying*. She still sizzled from their kiss minutes ago, and she didn't do vulnerability where men were concerned. But she sidestepped the issue. "It's the pretending part that I have trouble with."

"You're an actress."

"Context is everything. I like to confine my acting to the screen." Otherwise, she'd be in danger of losing herself. If she was always pretending, who was she? "You know I value integrity."

"It's overrated. Besides, this is Tinseltown."

Chiara placed her hands on her hips. "You misled me and Rick into thinking the other one had already agreed to this crazy scheme."

Odele shrugged. "You were already open to the idea.

That's the only reason it even mattered to you whether he was already on board with the plan."

Chiara felt heat rise to her face, and schooled her expression. "I'm not signing up for anything!"

Her conversation with Rick had had no satisfactory ending. It had sent her scuttling, somewhat humiliatingly, back to her manager. Chiara eyed the shower stall visible through the open bathroom door at the end of the trailer. If only she could rinse off the tabloid headlines just as easily.

"Fine," Odele responded with sudden and suspicious docility, putting aside her magazine. "We'll have to come up with another strategy to distract the press from your father and amp up your career."

"Sounds like a plan to me."

"Great, it's settled. Now…can you gain twenty pounds?" Odele asked.

Chiara sighed. Out of the frying pan and into the fire. "I'd rather not. Why?"

She'd gained fifteen for a film role two years ago in *Alibis & Lies*—in which she'd played a convicted white-collar criminal who witnesses a murder once she's released from jail and thinks her husband is framing her. To gain the weight, she'd indulged her love for pasta, creamy sauces and pastries—but she'd had to work for months with a trainer to shed the pounds afterward. In the meantime, she'd worn sunglasses and baggy clothes and had lain low in order to avoid an unflattering shot by the paparazzi. And she'd been disappointed not to get a Golden Globe nomination.

She wondered what movie project Odele had in mind these days… Usually her talent agent at Creative Artists sent projects her way, but Odele kept her ear to the ground, too.

"Last time I was heavier on-screen, I got a lot of backlash." Some fans thought she'd gained too much weight, some too little. She could never please everyone.

"It's not a film," Odele said. "It's a weight-loss commercial."

Chiara's jaw dropped. "But I'm not overweight!"

Odele's eyes gleamed. "You could be."

Chiara threw her hands up. "Odele, you're ruthless."

"It's what makes me good at what I do. Slender You is looking for a new celebrity weight-loss spokesperson. The goodwill with fans alone is worth the pounds, but Slender You is willing to pay millions to the right person. If you land this contract, your DBI score will go up, and you'll be more likely to land other endorsement deals."

"No." Her manager was all about Q scores and DBIs and any other rating that claimed to measure a celebrity's appeal to the public. "Next you'll be suggesting a reality show."

Odele shook her head. "No, I only recommend it to clients who haven't had a big acting job in at least five years. That's not you, sweetie."

For which Chiara would be forever grateful. She was having a hard enough time being the star of her own life without adding the artifice of a reality show to it.

"How about writing a book?" Odele asked, tilting her head.

"On what?"

"Anything! We'll let your ghostwriter decide."

"No, thanks. If I have a ghost, I won't really be writing, will I?" Chiara responded tartly.

"You're too honest for your own good, you know." Odele sighed, and then suddenly brightened. "What about a fragrance?"

"I thought Dior just picked a new face for the brand."

"They did. I'm talking about developing your own scent. Very lucrative these days."

"You mean like Elizabeth Taylor's White Diamonds?"

"Right, right." Odele warmed up. "We could call it Chiara. Or, wait, wait, Chiara Lucida! The name suggests a bright star."

"How much is an Oscar worth?" Chiara joked, because her idea of becoming a big star involved winning a golden statuette.

"Of course, an Academy Award has value, but we want to monetize all income streams, sweetie. We want to grow and protect your brand."

Chiara sighed, leaning against the walnut-paneled built-in cabinet behind her. There'd been a time when movie stars were just, well, movie stars. Now everyone was *a brand*. "There's nothing wrong with my brand."

"Yes, of course." Odele paused for a beat. "Well, except for the teeny-weeny problem of your father popping up in the headlines from time to time."

"Right." How could she forget? How could anyone fail to remember when the tabloids followed the story breathlessly?

"How about a lifestyle brand like Gwyneth Paltrow or Jessica Alba has?" Odele offered.

"Maybe when I win an Academy Award or I have kids." Both Alba and Paltrow had had children when they'd started their companies.

At the thought of kids, Chiara had an uncomfortable feeling in the pit of her stomach. She was thirty-two. She had an expiration date in Hollywood *and* a ticking clock for getting pregnant without spending thousands of dollars for chancy medical intervention. Unfortunately the two trains were on a collision course. If she was going to avert disaster, she needed to have a well-established career—er, Oscar—before she caved in to the public clamor for her to get a happily-ever-after with marriage and children.

Of course, she wanted kids. It was the husband or boy-friend part that she had a problem with. Michael Feran hadn't set a sterling example for his only child. At least she thought she was his only child.

Ugh. Her family—or what remained of it—was so complicated. It wouldn't even qualify as a Lifetime movie because there was no happy ending.

Still, the thought of a child of her own brought a pang. She'd have someone to love unconditionally, and who would love and need her in return. She'd avoid the mistakes that her parents had made. And she'd have something real—pure love—to hold on to in the maelstrom of celebrity.

"So," Odele said pleasantly, "your other options aren't too appealing. Let me know when you're ready to consider dating Rick Serenghetti."

Chiara stared at her manager. She had the sneaking suspicion that Odele had known all along where their conversation was heading. In all probability, her manager had been set on showing her the error of her ways and her earlier agreeableness had just been a feint. "You're a shark, Odele."

Odele chuckled. "I know. It's why I'm good at what I do."

Chiara resisted throwing up her hands. Some actresses confided in their personal assistants or stylists. She had Odele.

"So what's got you down?"

Rick figured he needed to work on his acting skills

if even Jordan was asking that question. "I don't know what you're talking about."

They were sitting in his kitchen, and he'd just handed his brother a cold beer from the fridge. He grabbed opportunities with his family whenever he could since he spent much of his time on the opposite coast from everyone else. Fortunately, since his current movie was being filmed on a Novatus Studio lot and nearby locations around LA, he was able to get to his place at least on weekends—even if home these days was a one-bedroom rental in West Hollywood.

"Mom asked me to check on you." Jordan shifted his weight on the kitchen barstool.

"She always asks you to check on me whenever we're in the same city. But don't assume the reconnaissance runs one way. She wants me to keep an eye on you, too."

"My life hasn't been that interesting lately."

Jordan was in town because his team, the New England Razors, was playing the Los Angeles Kings at the Staples Center. He was the star center player for the team. The youngest Serenghetti brother also had movie star looks, and hardly ever let an opportunity pass without remarking that their parents had attained perfection the third time around.

Rick followed hockey—family loyalty and all—but he wasn't passionate about it like Jordan and their older brother, Cole, who'd also had a career with the Razors until it had ended in injury. Rick had been a wrestler in high school, not a hockey team captain like his brothers.

The result was that he had a reputation as the family maverick. And hey, who was he to argue? Still, he wasn't intentionally contrary—though Chiara might want to argue the point.

An image of Chiara Feran sprung to mind. He'd been

willing to tease her about playing a couple, especially when he'd thought Chiara was going along with the idea. After all, it was nice, safe, *pretend*—not like really getting involved with an actress. And it was fun to ruffle Chiara's feathers.

If he was being a little more serious, he'd also acknowledge that as a producer, he had a vested interest in the star of his latest film maintaining a positive public image despite her problematic family members—not to mention staying *safe* if she really had a would-be stalker.

Still, being a *pretend boyfriend* and *secret bodyguard*, if Odele had her way, was asking a lot. Did he have enough to overcome his scruples about getting involved with a celebrity? Hell, even he wasn't sure. He'd been burned once by an aspiring starlet, and he'd learned his lesson—never stand between an actress and a camera.

For a long time, he'd counted actors, directors and other movie people among his friends. Hal Moldado, a lighting technician, had been one of those buddies. Then one day, Rick had run into Isabel Lanier, Hal's latest girlfriend. She'd followed him out of a cafe and surprised him with a kiss—captured in a selfie that she'd managed to take with her cell phone and promptly posted to her social media accounts. Unsurprisingly it had spelled the end of his friendship with Hal. Later he'd conclude that Isabel had just been trying to make Hal jealous and stay in the news herself as an actress.

The saving grace had been that the media had never found out—or cared—about the name of Isabel's mystery man in those photos. It had been enough that Isabel looked as if she were cheating on Hal, so Rick had been able to dodge the media frenzy.

Ever since, though, as far as he was concerned, starlets were only interested in tending their public image.

And up to now Chiara had fit the bill well—even if she hadn't yet agreed to her manager's latest scheme. After all, there was a reason that Chiara had partnered with someone like Odele. She knew her celebrity was important, and she needed someone to curate it.

But Odele had increased the stakes by referring to a possible stalker... It complicated his calculations about whether to get involved. He should just convince Chiara to get additional security—like any sane person would. Not that *sanity* ranked high on the list of characteristics he associated with fame-hungry actresses.

Jordan tilted his head. "Woman in your thoughts?"

Rick brought his attention back to the present. "Anyone ever tell you that you have a sixth sense where the other sex is concerned?"

His younger brother smiled enigmatically. "Sera would agree with you. Marisa's cousin is driving me crazy."

Their brother Cole had recently married the love of his life, Marisa Danieli. The two had had a falling-out in high school but had reconnected. Marisa's relatives were now an extension by marriage of the Serenghetti clan—including Marisa's younger cousin Sera.

Apparently that didn't sit well with Jordan.

"I'm surprised," Rick remarked. "You can usually charm any woman if you set your mind to it."

"She won't even serve me at the Puck & Shoot."

"Is she still moonlighting as a waitress there?" Rick had had his share of drinks at Welsdale's local sports bar.

"Off and on."

He clasped his brother's shoulder. "So your legendary prowess with women has fallen short. Cheer up, it was bound to happen sometime."

"Your support is overwhelming," Jordan replied drily.

Rick laughed. "I just wish Cole were here to appreciate this."

"For the record, I haven't been trying to score with Sera. She's practically family. But she actively dislikes me, and I can't figure out why."

"Why does it matter? It won't be the first time a family member has had it in for you." Jordan had come in for his share of ribbing and roughing up by his two older siblings. "What's to get worked up about?"

"I'm not worked up," Jordan grumbled. "Anyway, let's get back to you and the woman problems."

Rick cracked a careless smile. "Unlike you, I don't have any."

"Women or problems?"

"Both together."

Jordan eyed him. "The press is suggesting you have the former, and you look as if you've got the latter."

"Oh, yeah?"

"Who's the starlet on your latest film?"

"Chiara Feran."

His brother nodded. "She's hot."

"She's off-limits."

Jordan raised his eyebrows. "To me?"

"To anyone."

"Proprietary already?"

"Where did you get this ridiculous story?"

"Hey, I read."

"Much to Mom's belated joy."

Jordan flashed the famous pearly whites. His good looks had gotten him many modeling gigs, including more than one underwear ad. "*Gossipmonger* reported you two have been getting cozy, and the story has been picked up by other websites."

"You know better than to believe everything you

read." If the gossip had reached Jordan, then it was spreading wider and faster than Rick had thought. Still, he figured he shouldn't have been surprised, considering Chiara's celebrity.

"Yup. But is it true?"

Frankly, Rick was starting not to know what was true anymore, and it was troubling. "Nothing's happened."

Except one kiss. She'd tasted of peaches—fruity and heady and delicious. He'd gotten an immediate image of the two of them heating up the sheets, his trailer or hers. She challenged him, and something told him she'd be far from boring in bed, too. Chiara was full of fire, and he warmed up immediately around her. The trouble was he might also get burned.

Jordan studied him. "So nothing's happened yet..."

Rick adopted a bland expression. "Unlike you, I don't see women as an opportunity."

"Only your female stars."

"I'm done with that." Isabel had been the star of Rick's movie when they'd been snapped together. The fact that they'd both been working on the film—he as a stuntman and secretly as a producer, and she as an actress—had lent an air of truth to the rumors.

Jordan looked thoughtful. "Right."

Rick checked his watch because he was through trying to convince his brother—or himself. In a quarter of an hour, they needed to head to dinner at Ink, one of the neighborhood's trendy restaurants. "Just finish your damn beer."

"Whatever you say, movie star," Jordan responded, seemingly content to back off.

They both took a swill of their beers.

"So, the new digs treating you well?" his brother asked after a moment.

The apartment had come furnished, so there wasn't a hint of his personality here, but it served its purpose. "The house is nearly done. I'll be moving in a few weeks."

Jordan saluted him with his beer bottle. "Here's to moving up in the world in a big way." His brother grinned. "Invite me to visit when the new manse is done."

"Don't worry. I'll tell the majordomo not to throw you out," Rick replied drily.

Jordan laughed. "I'm a babe magnet. You'll want me around."

Privately, Rick acknowledged his brother might have a point. These days, the only woman he was linked to was Chiara Feran, and it wasn't even real.

Three

For two days, Rick didn't encounter Chiara. She and Adrian Collins, the male lead, were busy filming, so today Rick was hitting the gym trailer and working off restless energy.

So far, there'd been no denial or affirmation in the press that he and Chiara were a couple. As a news story, they were stuck in limbo—a holding pattern that kept him antsy and out of sorts. He wondered what Chiara's camp was up to, and then shrugged. He wasn't going to call attention to himself by issuing a denial—not that the press cared about his opinion because for all they knew, he was just a stuntman. They were after Chiara.

After exiting the gym trailer, Rick made his way across the film set. He automatically tensed as he neared Chiara's trailer. Snow White was a tart-tongued irritant these days—

He rounded a corner and spotted a man struggling with the knob on Chiara's door.

The balding guy with a paunch was muttering to himself and jiggling the door hard.

Frowning, Rick moved toward him. This section of the set was otherwise deserted.

"Hey," he called, "what are you doing?"

The guy looked up nervously.

All Rick's instincts told him this wasn't a good situation. "What are you doing?"

"I'm a friend of Chiara's."

"Does she know you're here?"

"I've been trying to see her." This time there was a note of whininess.

"This is a closed set. Do you have ID?" Rick didn't recall seeing this guy before. He was within a few feet of the other man now. The guy stood on the top step leading to the door of the trailer. Rick could see perspiration had formed on the man's brow. Was this the creepy fan Odele had referred to?

Rick went with his gut. "I'm her new boyfriend."

The other guy frowned. "That's impossible."

Now that he was closer, Rick could see the other man was definitely not the glamorous or debonair celebrity type that he would expect an actress like Chiara to date.

In the next second, the guy barreled down the trailer's steps and shoved past him.

Rick staggered but grasped the trailer's flimsy metal bannister to keep himself upright.

As Chiara's alleged friend made a run for it, Rick instinctively took off after him.

The man plowed past a crew member, who careened back against a piece of lighting equipment. Then two extras jumped aside, creating a path for the chase.

The guy headed toward the front gate of the studio lot, where Rick knew security would stop him. Rick could only guess how the intruder had gotten onto the lot. Had he hidden in the back of a catering truck, as paparazzi had been known to do?

Gaining on Chiara's admirer, Rick put on a final burst of speed and tackled the guy. As they both went down, Rick saw in his peripheral vision that they'd attracted the security guards' attention at the front gate.

The man struggled in his grasp, jabbing Rick with his elbow. "Get off me! I'll sue you for assault."

Rick twisted the man's arm behind his back, holding him down. "Not before you get written up for trespassing. Where's your pass?"

"I'm Chiara's fiancé," the guy howled.

Rick glanced up to see that two security guards had caught up to them. "I found this guy trying to break into Chiara Feran's trailer."

"Call Chiara," her alleged fiancé puffed. "She'll know."

"Chiara Feran doesn't have a fiancé," Rick bit back.

Someone nearby had started filming with his cell phone. *Great.*

"We're together. We're meant to be together!"

Nut job. Rick was in great physical shape due to his stunt work, so he wasn't out of breath, but Mr. Fiancé was no teddy bear, either; he continued to put up a struggle.

Suddenly the trespasser wheezed. "I can't br-breathe! Get off me. I have asthma."

Great. Rick eased back and let one of the security guards take over while the other spoke into his radio.

Things happened slowly but methodically after that. Police were summoned by the studio's security, and Chiara's special fan—who'd given his name as Todd Jeffers—was led away. Eventually Rick was questioned by a police officer. Chiara materialized soon after and was similarly prodded for details by the officer's partner.

Before the police left, Rick gleaned that Chiara's overly enthusiastic fan would be charged with criminal trespass, disorderly conduct and harassment. *Well, that's something.* But by the time Rick had finished talking about the incident to Dan, the director, Chiara had holed up in her trailer.

Rick eyed Chiara's door, twisted his mouth in a grim line and made his way to the trailer for some answers.

He didn't bother knocking—chances were better for a snowstorm in LA right now than for her rolling out the red carpet for him—and simply marched inside.

He came up short when he found Chiara sitting at a cozy little table, a script in front of her.

She was memorizing her lines? He expected her to be rattled, upset…

He looked around. The trailer was a double-decker, and with walnut paneling, it was swankier than his own digs, which were done in a gray monochrome and had no upper level.

When his gaze came back to rest on Chiara, she tilted her head, and said, "People weren't sure when you tackled him whether it was a stunt, or if you were rehearsing a scene from the movie."

"You're welcome." Leaning against a counter, he folded his arms, like a cop getting ready for an interrogation. He wanted answers only she could provide, and after getting into a fight with her admirer, he was going to get them. "Luckily you weren't in your trailer when he got here."

"I was rehearsing. We're shooting a difficult scene."

Rick figured that helped explain why she was sitting with a script in front of her, though he imagined her concentration was shot.

"I can only imagine the press coverage that today will

get." A horrified look crossed her face, and she closed her eyes on a shudder.

So she wasn't as unaffected as she seemed. In fact, Rick had already dealt with suppressing the video of him tackling Jeffers. The person who'd been taping had turned out to be a visiting relative of one of the film crew. But even if those images didn't become public or weren't sold to the tabloids, the media would get wind of what happened from the police report and show up for Jeffers's court hearing. Then, of course, Jeffers himself might choose to make a public statement…

"Hey, at least it'll take attention away from your father's latest losses at the gambling tables." He wondered if Chiara appreciated just how close she'd come to danger. It had been dumb luck that her overly enthusiastic fan hadn't found her earlier.

She opened her eyes and raised her head. "Yes, how can I forget about my father? How can anyone?"

"So you have a stalker." He kept his tone mild, belying the emotions coursing through him. *Damn it*. Chiara was slender and a lightweight despite her mouth and bravado. His blood boiled just thinking of some jerk threatening her.

"Many celebrities have overly enthusiastic fans." She waved her hand, and Rick could practically see her walls going up. "But my property has a security gate and cameras."

Rick narrowed his eyes. "Have you dealt with this Todd Jeffers guy before? What kind of unstoppable fan is he? The sort who writes you pretty letters or the type who pens twisted ones?"

She shrugged. "He tried to scale my property fence once, but he was spotted by a landscaper and shooed away even before he got within view of the security cameras. I haven't heard from him in the months since."

So today's guy was the same person who'd shown up at Chiara's house once, and yeah, she wasn't understanding the risk… Still, Rick strove for patience. "How do you know it was Jeffers at your house that day?"

She hesitated. "He wrote to me afterward to say he'd tried to see me."

"He wrote to you about an attempted criminal trespass?" Rick let his tone drip disbelief. "Have you gotten a temporary restraining order?"

Chiara sighed. "No. He's never been a physical threat, just a pest."

"Just because he *only* tried to jump the fence doesn't mean that's what he'll settle for doing in the future. There's often an escalation with these nut jobs once they figure out that plan A isn't working."

Chiara raised her chin. "He's probably a lonely, starstruck guy. Plenty of fans are."

"Probably? I don't deal in probabilities. Your run-of-the-mill serial killer often starts out torturing animals before moving to the big time. As I said, escalation."

"Like A-list stars starting out in B movies?" she asked snippily.

"Right," he said, his voice tight even as he ignored her flippant attitude. "Listen, Snow White, there are villains out there aside from the Evil Queen."

Rick raked his fingers through his hair. He could understand why this guy was besotted with Chiara. Unfortunately Chiara herself wasn't appreciating the gravity of the problem. They were like two trains on parallel tracks. "You've got a stalker. It's time you acquired a boyfriend. Me."

He'd been mulling things over, his mind in overdrive

ever since he'd tackled Jeffers. If he pretended to be Chiara's boyfriend, he could stick close and keep an eye on her. Maybe once this guy realized Chiara had a supposedly real boyfriend, he'd back off. Odele may have been onto a good idea.

Chiara opened and closed her mouth. "You're not in the protection business."

"I'm appointing myself right now. Besides, I've got the right background. I used to do security." He'd worked as a guard at an office building during his college days and beyond in order to earn extra cash. He'd been a good bouncer, too. His parents had instilled the value of hard work in their children even though they'd been well-off.

Chiara slid off her seat and stood. In the confined space, she was within touching distance. "You can't unilaterally decide to be my protector." She spluttered as if searching for words. "I won't agree to it."

"You could solve two problems at once. The bad press from your father, and the issue of your stalker and needing security. Don't quibble."

"I'll get a restraining order."

He took a step forward. "Damn straight, you will."

"So I don't need you."

"You need physical protection, too, unless you have seven dwarves hanging around, because a court order is just a piece of paper." He didn't want to think about how many news stories there'd been concerning an order of protection being violated—and someone getting hurt or killed.

She looked mutinous. "I'll hire professional security."

"It still won't solve the problem of your father and distracting the press."

Chiara threw up her hands.

"Don't worry. I'll always be a step behind you, like a good prince consort—I mean, bodyguard."

"Hilarious."

"I'll make sure to hold an umbrella open for you in the rain," he added solemnly.

"What's in this for you?"

"Let's just say I have a vested interest in the star of my next blockbuster staying safe until the end of filming. Everyone working on this movie wants to see it finished so they can get paid."

"I thought so. Well, my answer is still no."

He'd given her the wrong answer, and she'd responded in kind. "Do you just act contrary, or is this your best side?"

"How can you say that about the damsel in distress you helped save from a helicopter?" she asked sweetly.

"Exactly."

They were practically nose-to-nose, except because she stood several inches shorter than his six-foot frame, it was more like nose-to-chin. But then she raised her face to a stubborn angle, and he abandoned his good intentions about keeping himself in check during this conversation.

Hell, here goes nothing.

He tugged her forward and captured her mouth. It was just as good as before, damn it. There was a little zap of electricity because they were differently charged, and then he was kissing her in earnest, opening that luscious mouth and deepening the kiss.

She smelled faintly of honeysuckle, just like Snow White ought to. He caressed her cheek with the back of his hand. She was petal-soft, and he was getting hard.

After what felt like an eternity, she pushed him away.

Her chest rose and fell, and he was breathing deeply with arousal.

She touched her fingers to her lips and then shot fire at him with her eyes. "That's twice."

"Are we getting better? We've got to be convincing if we're going to pull this off."

"We're not practicing scenes, but if we were, try this response on for size." She stretched out her arm and pointed to the door of the trailer, giving him his marching orders.

It was a proverbial slap in the face, but Chiara was wrong if she thought he was backing down. "Let me know when our next scene is scheduled for filming. It might be time to throw a plate or break something. For real, not pretend."

After this parting shot, he turned and headed to the door, almost laughing as he heard her bang something behind him.

"She doesn't want to get extra security." Rick ran his hand through his hair. "She's stubborn."

"Hmm." Odele nodded. "And I'm her manager, so I don't know this?"

"And reckless, too." They were sitting in Novatus Studio's commissary having coffee before lunchtime. Rick had asked to meet and had told Odele not to mention it to Chiara. "How long has this guy Todd been hanging around thinking he's her special friend?" *Or fiancé.*

Odele shrugged. "Several months. I had staff look at Chiara's fan mail after he showed up at her house. He'd sent an email or two, and my assistant says he's cropped up on social media, too. Then he started a fan club and wanted autographed photos."

"And now he's moved on to believing he's her fiancé."

Odele sighed. "Some people buy into the Hollywood celebrity stuff a little too much."

Right. Rick leaned back in his chair. "Besides trying

to scale the fence at Chiara's house, has he made any other moves?"

"Not until yesterday. At least not that I know of." Odele took a sip from her cup. "I've already instructed Chiara's attorney to go for a restraining order."

"You and I both know it's only a piece of paper, but she doesn't want to consider additional physical security. Not even if I appoint myself." Rick didn't hide the frustration in his voice. Damn it. Who was he kidding? Chiara would resist, especially if it was him.

"So you're considering my idea of being a pretend boyfriend? You need to move in."

Rick shook his head in exasperation because Odele was a bulldozer. "If she doesn't want a fake relationship and won't tolerate a bodyguard, she definitely won't have someone living in her house."

If he and Chiara lived under one roof, they'd drive each other crazy. He'd alternate between wanting to shake some sense into her and take her to bed. And she'd... Well, she'd just rage at him and deny any sparks of a simmering attraction.

It was a recipe for disaster...or a Hollywood movie.

Odele gave him a mild look. "It's all a matter of how it's presented to her. If you're going to distract the press as her new boyfriend, the story will play even bigger in the media if you move in. There'll be more opportunities for the two of you to be photographed together."

"*Pretend* boyfriend." Everyone needed to be clear on the fake part, including and particularly *him*, if he was going to get involved with another actress.

Odele inclined her head. "Leave convincing her to me. I won't say anything more about having you function as a bodyguard. But believe me, the press attention surrounding her father is really upsetting her."

In Rick's opinion, Chiara should be spending more time worrying about her stalker than about her estranged father. Still… "Tell me about Michael Feran."

Odele set aside her coffee cup. "There's not much to say. Chiara's parents divorced when she was young. Chiara and her mother were in Rhode Island until Hollywood beckoned. Her mother died a few years ago. She developed sepsis after an illness. It was a shock for everyone."

"But her father continues to make waves."

"Last year, he accepted money from a third-rate weekly to dish about Chiara."

Rick cursed.

Odele shot him a perceptive look from behind her red glasses. "Yes, Chiara felt betrayed."

So Chiara's was far from a fairy-tale upbringing. No wonder she was prickly around him, and no doubt distrustful of men.

"Take it from me. Be the good boyfriend that she needs and keep an eye on her. Just don't bring up the bodyguard part to her."

"A pretend boyfriend." *Pretend* being the operative word there. He wasn't sure if he was reminding himself or Odele, though.

"Right."

Right.

Chiara took Ruby out of her box and perched her on her knee. The dummy wore a sequined gown, and her hair and face were worthy of a Vegas showgirl.

Chiara sat at the writing desk occupying one corner of her master bedroom. There'd been a break in filming for the weekend, and she was happy to retreat to her sanctuary. She needed time away. First her father, then Rick and finally a stalker had frayed her nerves.

Still, even though it was a beautiful and sunny Saturday afternoon, and she should have been in a great mood, she…*wasn't*. She was irritable and restless and anxious. She'd been having trouble memorizing her lines ever since the attempted break-in at her trailer. *Pegasus Pride* was an action flick, so the script wasn't heavy, but there was still dialogue that she had to be able to say without prompting.

Frustrated, she'd finally resorted to using Ruby to help her relax. She hadn't taken the dummy out in months, but ventriloquism kept her in touch with her former life—and at moments like these, let her deal with her present concerns.

Chiara searched the dummy's face. "What am I going to do?"

Ruby tilted her head.

"I must be out of my mind to be talking to a dummy by myself."

"You're not alone if you're having a chat with someone," Ruby responded in her singsong voice. "I just help you figure things out, sugar."

"I thought that's what Odele is for."

Ruby waved her hand. "You already know where Odele stands. She's on the hunk's side, and frankly, I don't know why you aren't, too." Ruby tossed her hair—because rolling her eyes was out of the question. "He's delicious."

"Annoying. You're reading too much gossip."

"I have to, it's about you," the dummy chirped. "Anyway, it's time you let someone under your skin, and back into your bed. And Rick…that body, that face, that kiss. Need I say more?"

"You are saucy and naughty, Ruby."

"And you wish you could be. Let your hair down, sugar."

Chiara's gaze fell to the laptop at her elbow. "I have too many responsibilities…and plenty of problems."

The headline on the computer screen spoke for itself: Chiara Feran's Father Thrown Out of Casino.

Maybe now that he couldn't gamble because he'd been caught counting cards, Michael Feran would stay out of trouble. But Chiara knew that was wishful thinking.

The public thought she had an enviable life—helped by Odele's relentless image craftsmanship. But the truth…

She'd never thought of herself as a beauty queen, for one. Oh, sure, she'd been blessed with good genes—a nice face and a fast metabolism that meant it wasn't impossible to adhere to Hollywood standards of beauty. But she also considered herself an outsider. She'd been raised by an immigrant mother, grown up enduring cold New England winters and would have still been doing theater but for a quirk of fate and Odele risking taking her on as a client.

She liked her privacy, her best friend was a smart-mouthed talent manager ripe for caricature and her sidekick was a doll made of wood. Obviously Todd Jeffers was crazier than she gave him credit for if he couldn't pick a better-credentialed starlet to stalk. And now she had a rumored *boyfriend*—a muscle-bound stuntman who looked as if he could enter a triathlon.

She'd already ignored a text from Odele about the latest headline, but Chiara knew her manager was right— they needed a distraction *fast…*

Her lawyers were due in court in the coming days to get a temporary restraining order—so there'd be more unwanted press attention because of her unpleasant fan.

Still, Rick Serenghetti? *Argh.*

Her cell phone buzzed again, a telltale ringtone, and this time Chiara knew she couldn't ignore it. With an apologetic look, she propped Ruby on a chair and took the call. "Hello, Odele."

"Enjoying your time off?"

"Define *enjoy*. I'm memorizing my lines." Among other things. She cast Ruby a hush-hush look.

"Rick needs to move in if we're going to make this fake relationship work. It'll help believability."

"No." The refusal fell from her lips without thought. Rick in her house? They'd throttle each other…if they weren't jumping into bed. And the contradiction of trying to make a *fake* relationship *work* was apparently lost on her manager.

Odele sighed. "We need to move quickly. I'm going to tell my assistant to break the story on social media accounts so we can control the initial message. I took an amateur shot with my cell phone of you and Rick seemingly engaged in an intimate conversation on the Novatus Studio lot."

"Of course you did."

"It looks great. Really like the two of you having a tête-à-tête," Odele added, warming to her subject and ignoring the sarcasm.

"Did it also look as if I was going to kick him in the shins?"

"And I've already set up a print interview for the two of you with a trusted reporter," Odele went on as if she hadn't heard.

"I'm not looking for a protector. And have you even done a background check on Rick Serenghetti? Maybe he's the one I need safeguarding from!"

Rick was dangerous to her tranquility, but she didn't care to delve into the reasons why. He had a way of looking at her with a lazy, sultry gleam that she found…annoying—yes, definitely annoying.

She'd done a quick search online for him—*only* for the purpose of satisfying herself that he didn't have a criminal record, she told herself—and had come up with nothing. She supposed no news was good news.

"Who said anything about a bodyguard?" Odele said innocently. "This is to help everyone believe you two are an item."

So Rick had backed off the part about offering personal protection? Somehow she had her doubts. "He doesn't need to move in to do that. What ever happened to dating? We're going from zero to sixty."

"It's Hollywood. Pregnancies last five months, and babies arrive right after the wedding. Everything is fast here."

Chiara couldn't argue. Celebrities were well-known for trying to hide their pregnancies from the press until the second trimester or beyond.

"Do I need to resend you the latest headline about Michael Feran?" Odele asked.

"I've already read it. I should have taken a different surname when I started my career."

"Too late now, sweetie. Besides, the media would have found him anyway, and he'd still be giving you trouble."

"Yes, but it would have made the connection between us seem less close."

"Well, time to distance yourself by cozying up to a hot stuntman."

"I know I'm going to regret this," Chiara muttered.

"I'll arrange for him to move in at the end of the week," Odele responded brightly.

"The guest bedroom, Odele!"

Four

Rick roared up on his motorcycle.

Since he was in temporary digs, and most of his stuff was in storage, he didn't have much to bring to Chiara's house in the affluent Brentwood neighborhood. Instead, he'd had a taxi deposit his suitcases and duffel bags at the foot of Chiara's front steps shortly before his arrival midafternoon.

Looking up, he eyed the house. It was a modest size by Tinseltown standards. Three bedrooms and three baths, according to the write-up on a celebrity gossip site. Reminiscent of an English cottage, it had white stucco walls, an arched doorway and a pitched roof with cross-gables and a prominent chimney. Lush gardening added to the atmosphere of a place that might be featured in *Architectural Digest*.

He'd taken Odele's advice and planned to say nothing about being a bodyguard. As far as Chiara was concerned, he was here only as a pretend live-in boyfriend. He had no idea, however, how Odele had convinced Chiara to let him move in.

By the time he'd taken off his helmet, Chiara was standing on the front steps.

"Of course you'd ride a motorcycle," she commented.

He gave an insouciant smile.

"I thought it was an earthquake."

"I rock your world, huh?"

"Please."

He looked at her house. "Nice digs. I should have guessed a typical English-style cottage for you, Snow. But where's the thatched roof?"

"Wrong century," she responded. "Where do you call home?"

He gave a lopsided grin. "Technically a small apartment in West Hollywood, but my heart is always where there's a beautiful woman."

"I thought so."

He couldn't tell what she meant by her response. Still, he couldn't resist provoking her further. "Shouldn't we kiss for the benefit of the paparazzi and their long-range lenses?"

"There are no photographers," she scoffed.

"How do you know? One could be hiding in the bushes."

She eyed his suitcases. "I'll put you in the guest bedroom."

"Relegated to the couch already," he joked. "Are you going to do a media interview about our first lovers' spat?"

The temperature between them rose ten degrees, and even the planted geraniums perked up—they apparently liked a good show as much as anybody.

"Hilarious," Chiara shot back, "but it's a perfectly fine bed, not a couch."

"And you won't be in it."

She cast him a sweeping look. "Use your imagination. A make-believe relationship means pretend sex. But something tells me you have no problem with letting your dreams run wild."

"Will you still awaken me with a kiss, Snow White?"

She huffed. "You're hopeless. I don't do fairy tales, modern or otherwise."

"That's obvious."

"Don't act as if you're disappointed. Your forte is action flicks, not romantic comedies."

"Then why do I feel as if I'm trapped in a romance?" he murmured.

"Go blow something up and make yourself feel better."

"It's not that type of itch that I need to scratch."

She huffed and then turned toward her front door. "I'll have you checked for fleas then."

Rick stifled a grin. This was going to be one interesting stay.

After he got settled in the guest bedroom, he found Chiara in the large country-style kitchen. Warm beige cabinets and butcher-block countertops added to the warm atmosphere. Sniffing the air, he said, "Something smells delicious."

She glanced up from a saucepan on the range, edible enough herself to be a food advertiser's dream. "Surprised?"

"That you cook? Gratified."

"Dinner is beef Stroganoff."

"Now I'm surprised. You're an actress who eats."

"Portion control is everything."

"Can cook. I'll check that little detail off my list."

She cast him a sidelong look, her cloud of dark hair falling in tantalizing waves over one shoulder. "What list?"

"The one that Odele gave me. A little quiz for the both of us...so we can get acquainted. Be believable as a couple."

Chiara frowned, and then muttered, "Odele leaves nothing to chance. Next thing, she'll have us convincing the immigration service that we're not in a sham marriage for a residency card."

"Because you need one...being from the Land of Fairy Tales?" He almost got a smile out of her with that.

"What do you—I mean, Odele—want to know?"

Rick consulted his cell phone. "What first attracted you to me?"

Chiara spluttered and then set down her stirring spoon with a *clack*. "This is never going to work."

"Come on, there must be something that you can tell the reporters."

She looked flustered. "Does she ask you the same question about me?"

He lowered his eyelids. "What do you think?"

As the question hung there, Rick's mind skipped back to their stunts...the rehearsals...every single moment, in fact, that he'd become aware of her close by. The air had vibrated with sexual energy.

Chiara wet her lips. "I'll take that as a 'Yes, she did ask.'"

Rick gave her a seductive smile. "When you showed up for the rehearsal of our first stunt, I knew I was in trouble. You were beautiful and smart and had guts." He shrugged. "My fantasy woman. The perfect match."

Chiara blinked.

After a pause, he asked, "Sound good enough for an interview answer?"

She seemed to give herself a mental shake, and then pursed her lips. "Perfect."

He focused on her mouth. *Kissable, definitely.* "Great."

She slapped the lid on the saucepan and made for the kitchen door. "Things are simmering. Dinner will be ready in thirty minutes."

"It'll give you time to think of your own answer to Odele's question," he called after her, and could swear she muttered something under her breath.

But when she was gone, Rick acknowledged that much as he enjoyed teasing Chiara, the joke was on him. Because she was his dream woman. If only she wasn't also a publicity-hungry actress…

Through dinner, he and Chiara trod lightly around each other. The beef Stroganoff was delicious, and he helped clean up—a little surprised she didn't keep a full-time housekeeper even if she traveled a lot. Afterward, she excused herself and retreated to her room, announcing that she had to memorize her lines.

Left to his own devices, he took a quick tour of the house and grounds, familiarizing himself with its security…and possible vulnerability to intruders. Then, with nothing more to do, he headed to bed.

Passing Chiara's door, he could see a light beneath, and shook off thoughts of what she wore to bed and how her hair would look around her bare shoulders above a counterpane… Still, in the guest bedroom, he found himself punching his pillow multiple times before he drifted off to sleep.

"Rick?"

He opened his eyes and saw Chiara's shadowy silhouette in his bedroom doorway. His lips curved. Apparently she'd had a hard time sleeping, too.

She walked toward him, and he made no attempt to disguise his arousal—he'd been thinking about her. Her short slip with spaghetti straps hid little, her nipples jutting against the fabric. She had a fantastic figure. High breasts and an indented waist...softly curved hips. His fingers itched to touch her.

Instead, he propped himself on the pillows behind him.

She sat down on the side of the bed, and her hand brushed his erection.

He saw no prickliness—just need...for him.

"What can I do for you?" His voice came out as a rasp.

Chiara's eyes glowed in the dim light afforded by the moon. "I think you know."

She leaned closer. Her lips brushed his and her pretty breasts tantalized his bare chest.

He cupped the back of her head and brought her closer so he could deepen the kiss. His tongue swept inside her mouth, tangling and dueling with hers.

She moaned and sank against him, breaking the kiss just long enough to say, "Love me."

He needed no further invitation. He pulled her down onto the mattress next to him and covered her body with his.

She responded with the lack of inhibition that he'd hoped for, arching toward him and opening in invitation, her arms encircling his neck as she met the ardor of his kiss.

His only thought was to get even closer...to sink into her welcoming warmth and find oblivion.

It would be sweet release from the restless need that had been consuming him...

Rick awoke with a start. He couldn't tell what had jerked him from his fantasy, but the room was empty, and he was alone in his bed.

He was also frustrated and aroused.

He groaned. *Yup.* It was going to be torture acting as if he were Chiara's boyfriend and hiding the fact that he was her protector.

The next morning, Chiara was up early for the drive to Novatus Studio. She donned jeans and a knit top. No use prettying up since she'd be sitting in a makeup chair at work soon enough. In fact, it was so early, she figured she might be able to get in a few minutes to study today's lines of dialogue before the drive to the lot.

Concentrate, that's what she had to do. But she hadn't slept well. In bed last night, she'd stared up at the ceiling, very aware of Rick's presence in her house.

What attracted her to him?

He was the epitome of rough manliness—cool, tough and exuding sex appeal. His green eyes were fascinatingly multihued, and even the hard, sculpted plains of his face invited detailed study by touch and, yes, taste.

A woman could feel safe and sheltered in his arms.

And there was the problem. She'd learned a long time ago not to rely on any man. Starting with her father, who'd disappeared from her life at a young age, and had become a gambling addict and reprobate.

She didn't hear a sound from Rick's room, so she tiptoed downstairs with script in hand.

When she reached the kitchen, she was taken aback to spot him sitting outside on the veranda, gazing at the sunrise, dressed in black denim jeans and a maroon tee. He looked peaceful and relaxed, so far from the constant motion and barely leashed energy that she was used to from him.

As if sensing her presence, he turned and met her gaze.

Rising, he gave a jaunty salute with the mug in his hand and said, "Good morning."

"I didn't hear you," she blurted as he entered through the French doors.

"We stuntmen can be stealthy."

She lowered her lashes and swept him with a surreptitious look. His jeans hugged lean hips and outlined muscular legs. The tee covered a flat chest and biceps that were defined but not brawny. He had the physique and face for a movie screen, except there was nothing manicured about him. Rick had a rough male aura instead of polish.

She looked at the cup in his hands. "I didn't even smell the brew."

"It's not coffee. It's a vitamin power drink."

Ugh. "For your superhero strength."

"Of course." He gave her a wicked smile. "Helps with the stamina. Sleep well?"

"For sure. And you?" She refused to give an inch, treating him with cool civility, even if that smile made her body tighten.

"Naturally."

The truth was she'd lain awake and tossed around for close to two hours. She wondered how she was going to maintain this charade…especially since Rick was adept at provoking her. And she refused…*refused*…to dwell on his kiss.

"Nice story about your father in the news. I had time to catch up on the headlines while I waited for you to come down, Sleeping Beauty."

Damn it. She should have gotten up even earlier. "My father?"

"Yeah, you know, the guy who shares a last name with you."

"That's all we have in common," she muttered.

"Nice story about the card counting recently."

"Maybe he'll stay out of trouble now that he's been barred from his favorite haunts." Casinos were Michael Feran's drug of choice.

"Is that what you're hoping?"

"Why are we discussing this?"

He shrugged. "I figured we should talk about the reason we're together." A smile teased his lips. "It seems logical."

So he wanted an extension of yesterday's get-to-know-you? *No, thanks.* Not that last night's question had haunted her sleep or anything. "We're not together."

"It's what the tabloids think that matters."

Argh.

"So Michael Feran is a sensitive topic."

Chiara walked to the kitchen cabinets. "Only in as much as he's a liar, gambler and cheat."

"Hmm…must be hard to share the same surname."

She got a glass and poured herself some water from the fridge's water filter.

"Eight glasses a day?"

She glanced at him. "What do you think? It's good for the complexion."

"You're very disciplined."

She took a sip. "I have to be."

"Because your father isn't?"

"I don't define myself relative to him."

Rick's lips twitched. "Okay, so you're not your father."

"Of course."

"How old were you when he walked out?"

She put down the glass. "Nearly five. But even when he was there, he wasn't really. He disappeared for stretches. Some of it was spent touring as a sax player with a band. Then he moved out for good a few days before my fifth birthday."

"Must have been rough."

"Not really. The party went on without him." She remembered the pink heart piñata. Her first major role was putting on a smile for the photos when it was just her and her mother.

"Did he ever try coming back?"

"There were a few flyovers until I became a teenager."

"Brief?"

"Very." Either her parents would argue, or Michael Feran would quickly move on to his next big thing.

"Right." Rick looked as if he'd drawn his own conclusions.

"Why are we talking about this?" she asked again, her voice sharp.

"I need to get the story straight so I'm not contradicting you when I speak."

"Well, there's nothing to tell."

"That's not what the press thinks."

Yup, he had her there. Which was the crux of her problem. Straightening her shoulders, she grabbed her car keys from the kitchen counter. On second thought, she could have breakfast at the studio—there was always food around. "Well, I'm off. See you on set."

"I'm coming with you," Rick responded casually. "Or rather, you're coming with me."

She stopped and faced him. "Excuse me?"

"My car or yours?"

"Do you have an endless supply of pickup lines?"

"Do you want to find out?"

"No!"

"That's what I thought you'd say." He took a sip from

his mug. "How can we be two lovebirds if we don't arrive together?"

"We're trying to be discreet at work."

"But not for the press."

"Anyway, you own a motorcycle."

"Look outside. I had my car deposited here early this morning by a concierge service."

Rats. He'd been up even earlier than she'd thought. She tossed him a suspicious look and then walked over to peer out the French doors. She spotted a Range Rover in the drive. "Lovely."

"I think so."

She glanced back at Rick with suspicion, but he just returned a bland look. Another of his sexual innuendoes? Because it was impossible to tell what he'd been referring to—her or the car.

Then she sighed. She had to pick her battles, and it was clear the drive to the office was not one worth fighting over.

Rick walked toward her, pausing to glance at a script that she'd left on the counter yesterday. "It's early. Want me to quiz you on your lines?"

"No!" Not least because there was a scene were the leads got flirty.

Rick raised an eyebrow and then shrugged. "Suit yourself but the offer stands. Anytime."

Yup, he was an anytime, anywhere kind of guy.

"What else are we supposed to do while we're shacked up together?" he asked, his eyes laughing at her.

She raised an eyebrow. "Go to work?"

Within the hour, she and Rick pulled up to the gate to Novatus Studio in his car.

Rick rolled down his window in order to give his identification to security, and with a sixth sense, Chiara turned her head and spotted a hovering figure nearby. The flash of a paparazzi camera was familiar.

"Odele," she muttered, facing forward again.

There was a good chance that her manager had tipped off a photographer so someone could snap her and Rick arriving *together* at the studio. Odele was determined to give this story her personal spin.

Rick gave an amused look. "She thinks of everything."

Rick tried to be on his best behavior, but having some fun was oh-so-tempting…

The Living Room on the first floor of The Peninsula Beverly Hills was nothing if not a den for power brokers, so he supposed it was perfect for a print interview over afternoon tea with *WE Magazine*—which wanted the dishy scoop on Chiara's new relationship.

Rick eyed the sumptuous repast set out on the coffee table before them: finger sandwiches, scones and an assortment of petite pastries. Arranged by Odele, of course, the afternoon tea in The Living Room was worthy of a queen. Of course, all of it went untouched.

This wasn't about food, but business. *Showtime in Hollywood.*

When he and Chiara had arrived at Novatus Studio that morning, Odele had surprised them with the news that she'd arranged a friendly press interview for them later the same day. Chiara was already scheduled to have the cover of the next issue of *WE Magazine* in order to promote the upcoming release of *Pegasus Pride*, but Odele had deftly arranged for it to become a joint interview about her new relationship. He and Chiara had left work early, because Odele had already spoken to Dan, the director, about their appointment. Dan had been happy to oblige if it meant more positive ink ahead of the release of the film—everyone was banking on it opening big at the box office.

Rick had to hand it to Chiara's manager—she wasted no time. But he knew what Odele was thinking—better to get ahead of the gossip by getting your own version of the story out there before anyone else's. So he'd gone along with the whole deal.

Too bad Chiara herself didn't want him here. But Odele had insisted, arguing his presence would make the relationship more believable. As Odele had put it, *Readers inhale romance. Touch each other a lot.* To which Chiara had responded, *Odele, I'm not making out in public for the benefit of gawkers.*

Now, at his sudden grin at the recollection, Chiara shot him a repressive look. She'd already told him she saw his role here as a yes-man supporting player. He figured he could bridge the gap between stuntman and Prince Charming easily enough, but if Chiara thought he'd toady to a gossip columnist, she had another think coming. He stretched and then settled one arm on the back of the sofa—because he knew it would drive Chiara crazy.

The couch was in a cozy and semiprivate corner. The interviewer, Melody Banyon—who looked to be in her late forties and was a dead ringer for Mindy Kaling—leaned forward in her armchair. "So was it love at first sight?"

From the corner of his eye, Rick noticed Chiara's elbow inching toward him, ready to jab in case he made a flippant comment. But then Chiara just smiled at him before purring, "Well, I don't usually notice the stuntmen on my movie sets…"

Rick glanced at the interviewer and a corner of his mouth lifted. "You could say Chiara's manager played matchmaker. She thought we'd be perfect for each other."

Chiara's eyes widened, but then she tossed him a grateful look. "Yes, Odele is always looking out for my best interests…"

Melody gave a satisfied smile. "Great, just great." Repositioning the voice recorder on the table before them, she looked back and forth between her interview subjects. "And I understand you two just moved in together?"

"Yup," Rick spoke up, unable to resist. "Like yesterday." It was also roughly when their whole "relationship" had started.

Chiara shot him a quelling look, and he tossed back an innocent one. He moved his arm off the sofa, gave her shoulder a squeeze, and then leaned in and nuzzled her temple for a quick kiss.

"Mmm," Melody said, as if tasting a delicious story, "you two move fast."

Rick relaxed against the sofa again, and responded sardonically, "You don't know the half of it."

He knew he risked Chiara's wrath, and he was surprised to find himself relishing the challenge of sparring with her again. No doubt about it—they set sparks off in each other. And it would probably carry over to the bedroom.

He glanced at Chiara's profile. She was a beautiful woman. Winged brows, pink bow lips, thick, rich chocolate hair and a figure that was hourglass without being voluptuous. She was also talented and tough enough to play a kick-ass action movie heroine and do her own stunts. He had to respect that—all the while being attracted as hell—even though he knew celebrity actresses like her couldn't be trusted.

They were duplicitous—they had to be for the press. *Like right now.*

Chiara seemed chummy with Melody—as if they

were friends, or at least acquaintances from way back. Melody asked a few questions about *Pegasus Pride*, and Chiara answered, while Rick threw in a few sentences at the end.

He wasn't the star attraction here, and there was no use pretending otherwise. Sure, he had a lot riding on this film—money and otherwise—but he wouldn't be why this movie succeeded, or not, at the box office. Chiara was the public face of *Pegasus Pride*.

After a few minutes, Melody changed the subject, mentioning the upcoming Ring of Hope Gala to Benefit Children's Charities, for which half of Hollywood turned out. "So give me the scoop, Chiara." Her voice dipped conspiratorially. "What will you be wearing?"

"I haven't decided yet. There are two dresses…"

"Give me the details on both!" Melody said, her face avid with anticipation.

Rick suppressed a grunt. As far as he was concerned, a dress was a dress. He didn't care what it was made out of—whether a pride of lions had to be sacrificed for the embellishment, or the designer used recycled garbage bags. His youngest sibling might be an up-and-comer in the fashion business, but it was all the same to Rick— or as his sister liked to say, *Bless your style-deaf soul.*

"There's a one-shoulder pale blue column dress from Elie Saab. The other gown is a red chiffon—"

"Oh, I love both! Don't you, Rick?"

If it wasn't for Chiara's significant look, Rick would have answered that *naked* was his first preference. Chiara had a body that invited fantasies even, or especially, if she was aiming verbal barbs at him.

He settled back. "I don't know…isn't pale blue the color for Cinderella?"

Chiara turned to him and smiled, even as her eyes shot a warning. "Wrong fairy tale."

When Melody just appeared confused, Chiara cleared her throat. "Well, keep your eyes open on the night of the gala to find out which dress I go with."

The reporter pressed Stop on her recorder. "So when am I going to see you again, Chiara? Girls' night sometime at Marmont? Paparazzi snapped Leo there just last week."

Rick raised his eyebrows. From the lack of a ring, Rick deduced Melody was divorced, widowed or had never married. "You ladies do go for the chills and thrills."

Chateau Marmont was a trendy celebrity haunt. Some booked one of the hotel rooms for privacy, and others just went to party and be seen. But he preferred his thrills a little more real than a Leonardo DiCaprio sighting.

"I'd love to, Melody," Chiara said, "but can I take a rain check? This movie is wearing me out—" she looked down demurely "—when Rick isn't."

Yup, strong acting chops.

Melody laughed. "Of course. I understand."

When Melody excused herself a moment later in order to freshen up, Rick regarded the woman who'd been driving him crazy. "So…I wear you out?"

Chiara flushed. "Don't look at me that way."

"Mmm. The image of us and a bed is sort of stuck in my mind."

Chiara shifted, and her skirt rode up her leg.

He focused on her calves. She had spectacular legs. He'd seen them encased in skintight denim on set, and in a barely there miniskirt in a photo that had circulated online. He imagined those legs wrapped around him as he lost himself inside her…

On a whim, he reached out and took her hand, and caressed the back of it with his thumb.

"What are you doing?"

Was it his imagination or did her voice sound a little uneven?

"Move closer," he murmured. "There's a photographer watching us from across the room."

Her eyes held his. "What? Where?"

"Don't look." Then he leaned in, his gaze lowering.

Chiara parted her lips on an indrawn breath.

Rick touched his mouth to hers.

When Chiara made a sound at the back of her throat, he deepened the kiss. He stroked and teased, wanting more from her, craving more and not caring where they were. When she opened for him, he fanned the flames of their passion, cupping her face with his hand as she leaned closer.

When her breast brushed his arm, he tensed and stopped himself from bringing his hand up to cup the soft mound in public. He wanted to crash through her barriers, making his head spin with the speed of it.

As if sensing someone approaching, Chiara pulled back and muttered, "We have to stop."

Rick spotted Melody walking back from across the room, a big grin on her face. Obviously the reporter had seen the kiss. Odele would be pleased. "Not if we're going to pretend to be a couple."

When the reporter drew near, she teased, "Did I say you two are fast? Now, that moment would have provided some photo op for the magazine!"

Rick settled back and forced a grin for the reporter's benefit. "We'd be happy to give a repeat performance."

"No, we wouldn't," Chiara interjected, but then she smiled for Melody's benefit. "I'll make sure you get plenty of good pictures for the cover story at the photo shoot tomorrow."

"Of course," Melody said politely, maintaining her perkiness as she sat down to gather her things.

Rick hadn't gotten an invitation to the photo shoot—which was just as well. They were boring and went on for hours. Apparently, though, even Odele had drawn the line at a cozy tableau of him and Chiara with their arms around each other.

"Do you have a cover line yet for this article, Melody?" Chiara asked, her face suddenly turning droll. "Or has Odele already suggested one?"

Rick knew from his experience with movie promotions that the cover line was the front cover text that accompanied a magazine article: *From Tears to Triumph, I'm Lucky to Be Alive*, or even the vague but trustworthy standby, *My Turn to Talk*.

"No," Melody said, "Odele hasn't offered anything."

"How about 'Chiara Feran—True Love at Last'?" he offered drily.

Melody brightened. "I love it. What about you, Chiara?"

Chiara looked as if she was ready to kick him out of this interview, and Rick suppressed a laugh.

Oh, yeah, this was going to be a roller coaster of a relationship. *Make-believe* relationship.

Five

Soon after she and Rick arrived at her house—a place that she used to consider her haven and sanctuary until Rick moved in—she decided to escape to the exercise room to let off steam. Every once in a while, the urge to do the right thing and work out for the sake of her career kicked in, so she changed into a sports bra and stretchy pedal pusher exercise pants.

It had been a long day, and she'd risen early only to find Rick in her kitchen. At the studio, she'd gotten prepped in her makeup chair and then shot a few scenes. Afterward, she'd still had to be *on*, public persona in place, for the interview with Melody. It hadn't helped that the whole time she'd been aware of Rick lounging beside her—his big, hard body making the sofa seem tiny and crowded.

He'd enjoyed toying with her, too, during the interview. She'd been on pins and needles the whole time, wondering whether he'd say the wrong thing and Melody would see through their charade.

Except the kiss at the end had been all too real. She'd tasted his need and his slow-burn desire underneath the playfulness, and she'd responded to it.

I have to be more careful.

And on that thought, she entered the exercise room and came to a dead halt.

Apparently Rick had had the same idea about burning off steam. And in a sleeveless cutoff tee, it was clear he was in phenomenal shape.

She'd seen her share of beautiful people in Hollywood. But Rick was…impressive. He had washboard abs, a sprinkling of hair on his chest and muscles so defined they looked as if they could have been sculpted by a Renaissance master.

She shouldn't be once-overing him. She was still annoyed with his behavior in front of Melody that afternoon.

Rick looked up and gave her a careless lopsided smile. "Enjoying the view?"

A wave of embarrassment heated her face. "Nothing I haven't seen before."

"Yeah, but I'm not airbrushed."

And there was the problem in a nutshell.

"Need an exercise buddy?"

Oh, no. They were so not going to do this together. "I don't need you to act as my workout instructor. I've been doing fine on my own."

"Yeah," he drawled, "I can tell."

She gave him a quelling look and walked toward the weight bench.

He followed her and then scanned the weights. He

lifted one of the lighter ones as if it were a feather and placed it on the bar.

She put her hands on her hips. "What do you think you're doing?"

"Helping you out, but not as much as I'd like."

"You're already doing more than I want, so let's call it a draw and say we're splitting the difference."

He quirked his lips. "Just trying to get you to release that pent-up energy and frustration."

She narrowed her eyes and then lay back on the bench as he fixed the weight on the other side. Unfortunately she hadn't anticipated how much he seemed to be looming over her from this angle.

She flexed and then grasped the barbell. Before she could do more, however, Rick adjusted her grip.

"I started with sixty pounds," he said, stepping back. "That's about right for a woman your size."

Chiara wondered how much he lifted. He'd hoisted her with amazing agility and ease during their stunts…

Then she turned her attention back to the weights, took a breath and began lifting. Once, twice… Rick faded into the background as she brought the same attention to the task as she did to acting.

"Slow and smooth," he said after a few minutes. "Slow and smooth… That's right."

Damn it. Chiara's rhythm hitched as she brought the weight back up again and then down. She refused to look at Rick. He was either a master at sexual innuendo or set on unintentionally making her lose her mind.

She gritted her teeth and lifted the weight a few more times. After what seemed like an eternity, during which she refused to show any weakness, Rick caught the barbell and placed it on the nearby rack.

Chiara concentrated on slowing her breathing, but her chest still rose and fell from the exertion.

Rick leaned over her, bracing himself with one hand on the metal leg of the weight bench. "Nice work."

They weren't touching but he was a hair's breadth away—so close that she could get lost in the gold-shot green of his eyes. Her mind wandered back to their last kiss…

He quirked his lips as if he knew what she was thinking. "Want to indulge again?"

She pretended not to understand his meaning. "No, thanks. I'm dieting. You know Hollywood actresses. We're always trying to shed a few pounds."

Rick's eyes crinkled. "Seems more like fasting to me."

Damn him. As a celebrity, it wasn't as if she could just get online, or even on an app, and hook up with someone. There was her public image to consider, as Odele never stopped reminding her, and she didn't want to be exploited for someone else's gain. As a result, she'd had far fewer romantic partners than the press liked to imagine. These days, a lot of men were intimidated by her status. But not Rick. He was just a lone stuntman, but he had enough ego for an entire football team.

Still, need hummed within her, and her skin shivered with awareness. What was it with this man? He had a talent for getting under her defenses, and together they were combustible.

"Have I been doing it right?" His eyes laughed at her.

"What?"

"The kissing."

If the response he stirred in her was any indication, then…yeah. She tingled right now—wanting him closer against her better judgment. "All wrong."

"Then we need to practice." His lips curved in a sultry smile. "For the photographers and their cameras."

She'd walked into that one. "There isn't one here right now."

"Then we'll need to make this real instead of make-believe," he muttered as he focused on her mouth. "You have the fullest, most kissable lips."

Chiara inhaled a quick little breath. It was heady being the focus of Rick's attention. He brought the same intensity to kissing as he did to his stunts.

But instead of immediately touching his mouth to hers this time, he surprised her by smoothing a hand down her side.

She shivered, and her nipples puckered, pushing against her sports bra. She itched to explore him the way he was doing to her. She raised her hand to push him away, but instead it settled on his chest, where she felt the strong, steady beat of his heart.

"That's right," he encouraged. "Touch me. Make me feel."

She parted her lips, and this time he did settle his mouth on hers. She felt a little zing, and was surrounded by his unique male scent.

His chest pressed down on the pillow of her breasts, but he didn't give her all his weight, which was still braced on his arms.

Wrapped in his intoxicating closeness, she felt him everywhere, even on the parts of her body that weren't touching his.

His hand cupped her between her thighs, where her tight spandex shorts were the only barrier between her heat and his. He stroked her with his thumb, again and again, until she tore her mouth from his and gasped with need.

She grasped his wrist, but it was too late. Her body splintered, spasming with completion and yet unfulfilled desire.

When she looked up, she was caught by his glittering gaze. She was vulnerable and exposed, more so even than when they'd been hanging from a helicopter and his embrace had been a haven.

She could tell he wanted her, but he was holding himself in check, his breathing heavy.

Sanity slowly returned. This was so wrong.

"Let me up," she said huskily.

He straightened, and then tugged on her hand to help her up.

"I don't want this," she said, standing and knowing the last thing she needed was to feel this way—especially when wrong felt…right.

"Sometimes what we think we should want is beside the point."

She wanted to argue, but for once, she didn't know what to say.

"I'm going to take a cold shower," he said with a rueful smile, and then turned.

She half expected a teasing addition—*Want to join me?*

But he said nothing further, and somehow she found his seriousness more troubling than his playfulness.

Bed & Breakfast in Brentwood. Chiara Feran and Her Stuntman Seen Moving in Together.

Chiara stalked back to her trailer along a dirt path, her scene complete. Filming had moved for today from the Novatus Studio lot to nearby Griffith Park.

The blog *Celebrity Dish* had scooped *WE Magazine* and run a relationship story about her and Rick. Melody should still be happy about her exclusive interview, but it hadn't taken long for the gossip to start making the rounds...

Chiara attributed her bad mood to lack of coffee... and a certain stuntman.

Yesterday afternoon, they'd had a near tryst on her weight bench. There was no telling what he was capable of if he stayed in her house much longer.

She'd shown up at work at six in the morning intent on avoiding Rick, and had sat in the makeup chair. It was now ten, and there was still no sign of him. After their encounter in the exercise room, she'd heard him shower and leave her house. He still hadn't returned when she'd gone to bed hours later.

Perhaps he'd met and hooked up with a woman. Not that it was her business. Even if it meant he'd gone straight from her arms to those of another... *Damn it*.

At least *Pegasus Pride* would wrap soon. They were in the last days of filming. The scenes that she'd been in with Rick acting as a body double for her costar Adrian had been thankfully few.

Head down, she turned a corner...and collided with a solid male chest.

The air rushed out of her, and then she gasped.

But before she could wonder whether her favorite fan had made a surprise appearance again, strong arms steadied her, and she looked up into Rick's green eyes.

"You."

"For two people who are roommates, we hardly ever run into each other," he said in an ironic tone.

Chiara blinked. His hands were still cupping her upper arms, the wall of his chest a mere hair's breadth away. The heat emanated from him like a palpable thing.

"It's a big house and an even larger movie location."

She sounded breathless and chalked it up to having the air nearly knocked out of her.

He was irritating but also impossible to ignore—and she'd been throwing her best acting skills at the problem.

"Miss me?" he teased drily. "I thought we were supposed to be joined at the hip these days."

How could she answer that one? After he'd left last night, she'd succumbed to a restless night's sleep. He'd left her satisfied and bereft at the same time. Sure, she'd gotten release, but they'd missed out on the ultimate joining, and hours later, her body had craved it. At least he wasn't openly chastising her for her artful dodge that morning.

He stepped closer and eased her chin up, his gaze focused on her lips. "I missed you."

"The mouth that can't stop telling you off?"

He gave her a crooked smile. "We'd be good in bed. There's too much combustible energy between us. Admit it."

"Can't you tell good acting when you see it?"

"That was no act. If that wasn't an orgasm last night, I'll stand naked under the Hollywood sign over there." With a nod of his head, he indicated the iconic landmark in the distance.

"We are acting. This is fake. We're on a movie set!"

"Yup," he drawled and glanced around, "and I don't see any cameras rolling right now. Just because we're playing to the media doesn't mean we can't have fun along the way."

She didn't do *fun*. She left that to her dice-rolling father, who'd run away from responsibility—a wife, a child, a home...

"Oh, I like it!"

Chiara turned and spotted Odele.

"Did I interrupt something? Or let me rephrase that one—I hope I was interrupting something!"

"He needs to go," Chiara retorted.

Odele looked from her to Rick and back. "What went wrong? It's only been—" she checked her watch "—two days."

"A lover's spat," Rick joked. "We can't keep our hands off each other."

Odele's eyes gleamed behind her red glasses. "You can't quit now. The press is reporting Chiara's father was tossed out of a Vegas casino."

Rick quirked a brow at Chiara.

"On top of it," Odele went on, "there's a big fundraiser tomorrow night, and I managed to secure a ticket for Chiara's date."

"And let's not forget *WE* just got the exclusive interview that *we* are an item," Rick continued drolly.

Chiara faced her nemesis. "You are impossible."

"Just acting the part."

"You're giving an Oscar-worthy performance in a B movie."

"I believe in doing my best," Rick intoned solemnly. "My mother raised me right."

She wanted to claim his *best* wasn't good enough, but the truth was he'd been…impressive so far. "This isn't working."

"You don't want me?" He adopted a wounded expression, but his eyes laughed at her.

Grr. "I'm stuck with you!"

"Then why don't you make the most of it?" His voice was smooth as massage lotion. "Who knows? We might even have fun together."

The last thing she needed was his hands on her again.

"*Fun* is not the word that comes to mind. This is crazy. Are we nuts?"

"You know the answer to that question. I hang from helicopters for a living—"

"Clearly the altitude has addled your mind."

"—and you are an actress and celebrity."

"*Fame* is a dirty word in your book?"

Rick shrugged. "I'm camera-shy. Call it middle-child syndrome. I leave the high-profile celebrity stuff to my older and younger brothers."

She frowned. "You're an agoraphobic stuntman?"

He bit back a laugh. "Not quite, but putting on the glitz isn't my thing."

"Odele just mentioned we have a big fund-raiser to attend tomorrow night," she countered. "And since you signed up for the boyfriend gig, you'll need to put on a tux."

"Trust me, you'll like me better naked."

Chiara felt her cheeks heat, and on top of that, her manager was tracking everything like a talent agent on the scent of a movie deal.

She narrowed her eyes at Rick. "Oh? Is that the usual attire for reclusive stuntmen?"

He gave a lazy smile. "If we live together much longer, you'll find out."

She hated his casual self-assurance. And what was worse, he was probably right…

Chiara gave her manager a what-have-you-gotten-me-into look, but Odele returned it with a beatific one of her own.

"I came to tell you that you're needed. Dan wants to reshoot a scene," Odele said.

Chiara wasn't normally enthusiastic about retakes, but right now she thought of it as a lucky break…

* * *

Hours later, during some downtime in his schedule, Rick sat in a chair outside the gym trailer, his legs propped on a nearby bench. He consulted his cell phone to make sure he was caught up on work.

Often his emails were mundane matters sent by a business partner, but today, lucky him, he had something more salacious to chew over. All courtesy of *Celebrity Dish*—and a specific actress who'd occupied way more of his thoughts than he cared to admit.

After his encounter with Chiara in her exercise room yesterday afternoon, he'd done the only thing that he could do in the face of frustration and lack of consummation: he'd taken a cold shower and then sat alone at a nearby sports bar to have dinner.

Still, now that the story had progressed in the media to him and Chiara shacking up, Rick knew he'd better tackle his family. In the next moment, his cell phone buzzed, and Rick noted it was Jordan before answering the call.

"Wow, you move fast," his brother said without preamble. "One day you're denying there's anything going on, the next you're moving in together."

"Hilarious."

"Mom asked. Has she rung you yet?"

"Nope." Camilla Serenghetti was probably vacillating between worry and being ecstatic that her middle son might have gotten into a serious relationship—preferably one heading toward marriage and children.

"She's concerned some temptress has worked her wiles on you, and not just on the big screen, either. I told her that you're not innocent and naive enough to resist a beautiful woman."

"Finger-pointing never got you anywhere, Jordan."

"Except for some scratches and bruises from you and Cole in retribution. But don't worry, I bounced back."

"Clearly," Rick responded drily.

"Mom is talking about coming to the West Coast to tape an episode of her cooking show. You know, do something different and expand the audience, and if I'm not mistaken—" his brother's voice dripped dry humor "—she wants to check up on you."

No, no and no. The last thing he needed was for his mother to add a sideshow to the ongoing drama with Chiara—though Camilla Serenghetti would no doubt easily become best buds with Odele. Two peas in a pod. Or as the Italians liked to say, *due gocce d'acqua*—like two drops of water. *In a pot of boiling pasta water.* Still, the thought gave him an idea...

"Mom can't come here."

"She's worried about the show. The station is under new management and she wants to make a good impression."

"Fine. I'll go to her."

The idea was brilliant. If he delivered Chiara Feran to his mother's show, he'd drive up ratings for a program that was only in local syndication. And it would add steam in the press to his and Chiara's supposed relationship. All while getting Chiara out of her house in LA and away from her crazy fan.

It was fantastic...clever...an idea worthy of Odele.

Rick suppressed a smile. Chiara's manager would love it.

"You're serious?" his brother asked.

"Yup." If he was going to engage in this charade, he was going to be all in.

With that in mind, he ended his call with Jordan and went looking for his favorite actress.

Things had slowed down on set because Adrian Collins didn't like some of his lines and had holed up in his trailer with a red pen. Rick would have gotten involved and gone to read the riot act to the male lead, but he didn't like to blow his cover. Not even Dan knew how much he had invested in this movie.

Besides, Adrian's antics were mild in comparison to other off-camera drama he'd witnessed on movie sets—stars kicking each other, hurling curses and insults, and throwing tantrums worthy of a two-year-old while breaking props. Yet another reason he hadn't gotten involved with mercurial actresses…until now.

As luck would have it, he soon caught up with Chiara some distance from the parked movie trailers. She was walking back alone, picking her way along a dusty path, apparently having finished filming another scene.

Maybe it was unfulfilled sexual desire, maybe it was the picture she presented, but his senses got overloaded seeing her again. Since this morning, she'd changed into business attire because her scenes called for her to have escaped from a federal office building. She was wearing a pencil skirt paired with sky-high black pumps and a white shirt open to show a bit a cleavage. The effect was sexy in an understated way.

He liked the way the light caught in her dark halo of hair—which was just the right length for him to run his fingers through in the throes of passion. His body tightened.

He wasn't one to be overcome by lust—particularly where actresses were concerned—but Chiara was just the package to press his buttons. He hadn't been kidding when he'd said she was his type. His brothers would say he was attracted to women who were a study in contrasts: dark hair against a palate of smooth skin; humor and passion; light and hidden depths… On top of it all, Chiara was blessed with a great figure, which was emphasized at the moment by a come-hither outfit made for the big screen…and male fantasies.

He, on the other hand, was in his usual stunt clothes for this movie: a ripped tee, makeup meant to resemble dirt smeared on his abs, an ammo belt across his chest and another one slug low on his hips with an unloaded gun. He felt…uncivilized.

And the setting was appropriate. They were at the bottom of a canyon, surrounded by mountain roads and not far from actual caves. Only the presence of the Hollywood sign spoiled the effect of unspoiled nature.

Still, he tried for some semblance of polite conversation when they came abreast of each other. Thanks to Jordan, he had a brilliant idea—one that should deal with multiple problems at once. "I have a favor to ask."

She looked at him warily. "Which is?"

He cleared his throat. "I'd like you to appear on my mother's cooking show."

Her jaw went slack. "What?"

He shrugged. "If you appear on her show, it'll feed the rumors that we're involved. Isn't that what you want?"

"Your mother has a cooking show?"

He nodded. "It's on local TV in Boston and a few other markets, and it films not far from my hometown of Welsdale in western Massachusetts. *Flavors of Italy with Camilla Serenghetti.*"

Chiara's lips twitched. "So you're not the Serenghetti closest to fame? I'm shocked."

"Not by a long shot," he returned sardonically. "Not only is Mom ahead of me, but my brothers and sister are, too."

Chiara looked curious. "Really?"

He nodded. "You don't watch hockey."

"Should I?"

"My kid brother plays for the New England Razors, and my older brother used to."

She seemed as if she was trying to pull up a recollection.

"Jordan and Cole Serenghetti," he supplied.

"And your sister is…?"

"The youngest, but determined not to be left behind." He cracked a grin. "She's a big feminist."

"Naturally. With three older brothers, I imagine she had to be."

"She had a badass left kick in karate, but these days she's rechanneled the anger into a fashion design business."

Chiara's eyes widened. "Ooh, I like it already it."

So did he… Why hadn't he dreamed it up before? He had an opening with Chiara that he'd been too blind to see till now. "Mia would love it if you wore one of her creations."

"I thought I was helping your mother."

"Both." He toasted his brilliance. "You can wear Mia's designs on the cooking show."

Chiara threw up her hands. "You've thought of everything!"

Rick narrowed his eyes. "Not everything. I still need to figure out what to do about your overenthusiastic fan and your Vegas-loving father. Give me time."

Number three on his list was getting her into bed, but he wasn't going to mention that. He didn't examine his motives closely, except he was nursing one sad case of sexual frustration since their truncated tryst on her weight bench late yesterday. He tucked his fingers into his pockets to resist the urge to touch her…

He cleared his throat. "It would mean a lot to her if you made an appearance as a guest. The show is doing well. The name recently changed from *Flavors of Italy* to *Flavors of Italy with Camilla Serenghetti*. But the station is under new management, and Mom wants to make a good impression."

"Of course," Chiara deadpanned. "It's a slow climb up the ladder of fame. I can relate."

"Mom's is more of a short stepladder."

"What happens when your mother and I land on the cover of *WE Magazine* together?" Chiara quipped. "Will you be able to deal with being caught between two famous women?"

"I'll cross that bridge when I come to it," Rick replied drolly. "And knowing Mom, she'll want to be on the magazine with the both of us, like a hovering fairy godmother."

"She sounds like a character."

"You don't know the half of it."

"This is serious," she remarked drily. "You're bringing me home to meet Mama."

"In a sense," he said noncommittally—because what he wanted to do was bring her home to bed. "She'd be even more impressed if you'd starred in an Italian telenovela."

"A soap opera?" Chiara responded. "Actually I was a guest on a couple of episodes of *Sotto Il Sole*."

Rick's eyebrows rose.

"It was before I became known in the States," she added. "My character wound up in a coma and was taken off life support."

"They didn't like your acting?"

"No, they just needed more melodrama. My character was an American so it didn't matter if I spoke Italian well."

"Still, my mother will eat it up." He flashed a grin. "No pun intended."

In fact, Rick suspected his mother would love everything about Chiara Feran. Their relationship "breakup," which inevitably loomed on the horizon, would disappoint his mother more than a recipe that didn't work out. He'd have to fake bodily injury and blame the rupture with Chiara on the distance created by their two careers...

"What about filming?" Chiara asked with a frown.

"We're in the last few days. Then Dan will move to editing. I can arrange with Odele for us to fly to Boston once you're done with your scenes. Mom's taping can wait till then." He didn't add he still had to broach the subject with his mother, but she'd no doubt be thrilled to move heaven and earth with her producers in order to fit a star of Chiara's caliber into the schedule.

"Where will we stay?" Chiara pressed.

Rick could tell she was debating her options, but the wavering was a good sign. He shrugged, deciding to seem nonchalant in order to soothe any doubts she had.

"I've got an apartment in Welsdale."

"Oh?"

"It has a guest bedroom." Still, he hoped to entice her into making their relationship in the bedroom more real—purely for the sake of their romantic believability in front of the press, of course.

"Naturally."

"Don't worry, though," he said, making his tone gently mocking. "There'll be enough luxuries for an A-list celeb."

Chiara narrowed her eyes. "You think I can't rough it?"

He let his silence speak for him.

"As a matter of fact, I was born and raised in Rhode Island. I'm used to New England winters."

"Of course, Miss Rhode Island should visit her old stomping grounds."

"I was an undergraduate at Brown."

"Rubbing shoulders with other celebrity kids?"

"Financial aid. Where did you get your stunt degree?"

He quirked his lips. "Boston College. It's a family tradition."

"Now you've surprised me. I expected the school of hard knocks… So, what have you told your family about us?"

He shrugged. "They read *WE Magazine*." He flashed a smile. "They know I have the goods."

Chiara rolled her eyes. "In other words, they think we really are an item?"

"My ego wouldn't have it any other way."

"I'm not surprised."

Rick heard a noise, and then felt a telltale little jolt, followed by a gentle rocking.

Chiara's eyes widened.

"Did you feel that?"

She nodded.

Earthquakes were common in Southern California, but only a few were strong enough to be felt. "We may have sensed it because we're at the bottom of a canyon." Rick looked around, and then back at her with a wry smile. "I'm surprised you didn't fling yourself into my arms."

"We actresses are made of sterner stuff," she said, tossing his words from days ago back at him.

He stifled a laugh. "We made the ground move."

"It was a truck rumbling by!"

"My motorcycle sounds like an earthquake, but an earthquake is just…a truck rumbling by?" he teased.

"Well, it's not us making the ground move, much as you have faith in your superpowers!"

Rick laughed and then glanced around again. "This earthquake didn't seem like a strong one, but you might want to rethink your position on my rocking your world."

"Your ego wouldn't have it any other way?" she asked archly.

"Exactly. Good follow-up, you're learning." He glanced down at her impractical footwear. "Need a hand…or a lift?"

She raised her chin. "No, thanks."

He doubted she'd thank him if he said she looked adorable. "You know, if you left one of those shoes behind…"

"A frog would find it?"

"Some of us are princes in disguise—isn't that how the story goes?"

"Well, this princess is saving herself," she said as she walked past him, head held high, "and not kissing any more frogs!"

Six

The Armani suit was fine, but Rick drew the line at a manicure. He did his own nails, thanks.

In his opinion, premieres and award ceremonies were an evil to be endured, which was another reason he liked his low-profile, low-key existence. Tonight at least was for a good cause—the Ring of Hope Gala to Benefit Children's Charities.

The fund-raiser also explained why Chiara's spacious den was a hub of activity on a Saturday afternoon. The room was usually a quiet oasis, with long windows, beige upholstery and dark wood furniture. Not now, however.

Chiara sat in the makeup chair. Someone was doing her hair, and another person was applying polish to her nails, and all the while Chiara was chatting with Odele. A fashion designer's intern had dropped off two gowns earlier, and at some point, Chiara would slip into one of them, assisted by plenty of double-sided tape and other tricks of the Hollywood magic trade.

Rick figured this amounted to multitasking. Something women were renowned for, and men like him apparently were terrible at—when the reality was probably that men just preferred to do their own nails.

Suddenly Odele frowned at Chiara. "Have you gone through your normal skincare regimen?"

"Yes."

Rick almost laughed. For him, a regimen meant a grueling workout at the gym to get ready for stunts on his next film. It didn't apply to fluffy skincare pampering.

Odele rolled her eyes. "I imagine you raided the kitchen cabinets for sugar and coconut oil, and threw in some yogurt for one of your crazy DIY beauty treatments."

From her chair, Chiara arched her eyebrows, which had been newly plucked. "Of course."

Rick studied those finely arched brows. He hadn't known there was such a thing as threading, and especially not applied to eyebrows. He was a Martian on planet Venus here. Still, he could understand that for an actress like Chiara, whose face was part of her trade, the right look was everything. Subtle changes or enhancements could impact her ability to express emotional nuances.

His gaze moved to Chiara's mouth. Their interlude in the exercise room still weighed on him. She'd been so damn responsive. If she hadn't put a stop to things, he would have taken her right there on the weight bench. In fact, it had been all he could do to keep a cool head the past few days. If it hadn't been for work on the movie set and coming back exhausted after a fourteen-hour day...

Odele sighed. "You're the bane of my existence,

Chiara. You could be the face of a cosmetics and skin-care line. You're throwing away millions."

"My homemade concoctions work fine," Chiara responded.

"You make your own products?" Rick asked bemusedly.

Chiara shrugged. "I started when I was a teenager and didn't have a dime to my name, and I saw no reason to give it up. I use natural items like avocado."

"Me, too," Rick joked. "But I eat them as part of my strength-training routine."

Chiara peered at him. "I could test the green stuff on your face. You might benefit."

Rick made a mock gesture warding her off. "No, thanks. I'm best friends with my soap."

"Not everyone is blessed with your creamy complexion, Chiara," Odele put in. "Have a little sympathy for the rest of us who could use expensive professional help."

The hairstylist and manicurist stepped away, and Chiara stood, still wrapped in her white terry robe. "Well, time to get dressed."

Rick smiled. "Don't let me stop you."

Odele steamed toward him like a little tugboat pulling Chiara's ship to safe harbor. "We'll call you when we need you."

He shrugged. "More or less explains my role."

Without waiting for further encouragement, he stepped out of the room. For the next half hour, he made somewhat good use of his time by checking his cell phone and catching up on business. Finally, Odele opened the door and motioned him into the den again.

Rick stepped back into the room...and froze, swallowing hard.

Chiara was wearing a one-shoulder gown with a short

train. The slit went all the way up one thigh, and the deep red fabric complemented her complexion. She had the ethereal quality of, well, a fairy-tale princess naturally.

"I can't decide which gown," she said.

"The one you're wearing looks good to me."

He knew what the big minefields were, of course. *Do I look fat in this dress?* The automatic answer was *no*. Maybe even *hell, no*. Still, he was ill-equipped for the bombshell that was Chiara Feran—sex poured into a gown.

"You look spectacular," he managed.

She beamed. "I'm wearing a Brazilian designer. I have a platform, and I want to use it."

He knew what *he* wanted.

He'd like nothing better than to swing Chiara into his arms and head for the bedroom. He wasn't particular about *where* frankly, but he didn't want to scandalize her entourage. And if Odele was tipped off, she would be on the phone with Melody Banyon of *WE Magazine* in no time to report his and Chiara's relationship had become serious—never mind that it was make-believe.

Still, the evening was young, and Chiara's manager wouldn't be here at its close…

Flashbulbs went off around them in dizzying bursts of light. The paparazzi were out in full force for this red-carpet event. Chiara gave her practiced smile, crossed one leg in front of the other and tilted her head, giving the photographers her best side.

Her one-shoulder silk organza gown had a deep slit revealing her leg to the upper thigh. It was a beautiful but safe choice for an awards show. Invisible tape ensured everything stayed in place and she didn't have a wardrobe malfunction. Her hair was loose, and her jewelry was limited to chandelier earrings and a diamond bracelet.

The Ring of Hope Gala to Benefit Children's Charities was being held at The Beverly Hilton Hotel. The hotel's sixteen-thousand-foot International Ballroom could seat hundreds—and did for the Golden Globe Awards and other big Hollywood events. Soon she and Rick would be inside, along with dozens of other actors and celebrities.

Rick's hand was at the small of her back—a warm, possessive imprint. It was for the benefit of the cameras, of course, but the reason didn't matter. He made her aware of her femininity. She'd never been so attuned to a man before.

Despite the presence of plenty of well-known actors tonight, Chiara saw women casting Rick lingering looks full of curiosity and interest. He had a blatant sex appeal that was all unpolished male...

Chiara put a break on her wayward thoughts—aware there were dozens of eyes upon them. Not only were bulbs constantly flashing, but the press kept calling out to them.

"Chiara, look this way!"

"Who's the new guy, Chiara?"

"Can you tell us about your gown?"

"Who's the mystery man?"

Chiara curved her lips and called back, "We met on the set of *Pegasus Pride*."

"Is it true he's a stuntman?"

She cast Rick a sidelong look, and he returned it with a lingering one of his own. She could almost believe he was enraptured for real...

"I don't know," she murmured, searching Rick's face. "Do you know some stunts, honey?"

"Not for the red carpet," he said, smiling back. "Maybe I should practice."

Ha. In her opinion, he was doing just fine with his *publicity stunt* for the red carpet. He was *too* believable in the role of boyfriend.

She knew what the headlines would say, of course. *Chiara Feran Makes Debut with New Man.* She and Rick had given their interview to *WE Magazine*, but every media outlet wanted their own story.

Chiara smiled for another few moments. Then she linked hands with Rick and moved out of the spotlight so the next prey—uh, *celebrity*—could take her place. She knew how these things worked.

She and Rick walked into the Hilton, where sanity prevailed in contrast to the paparazzi and fans outside. They followed the crowd toward the International Ballroom. Fortunately she didn't cross paths with anyone she knew well. She wasn't sure if she was up for further discussion of her ultimate accessory—namely, Rick.

When they reached their table, she sighed with relief. *So far, so good.*

"Rick, sugar!"

Chiara turned and spotted an actress she wasn't well-acquainted with but whose name she'd come across more than a few times. *Isabel Lanier.*

She'd never heard Rick's name said in the same breath as *sugar* before. In her opinion, *spice* was more appropriate.

"Wow, I haven't seen you in ages!" Isabel said—and though she addressed Rick, she directed her crystalline blue gaze to Chiara. "And you're one half of an item, too, I hear."

"Isabel, this is—"

"Chiara Feran," Chiara finished for him.

She assessed the other woman. Isabel Lanier had a reputation in Hollywood, and there wasn't enough Botox in LA to make it pretty. She'd slept with directors to land supporting roles. She'd broken up a costar's marriage by having an affair with him during filming. And she'd been named in a lawsuit involving back rent on a house in the Hollywood Hills.

Isabel looked her over in turn, and then, directing her gaze to Rick, murmured, "I'm so glad you've moved on, sugar, and to another actress, too. No bad feelings, hmm?"

Rick seemed to tense, but then Chiara wondered whether she was imagining it.

Isabel fluttered her mascara-heavy eyelashes. "I'd love to talk to you about—"

"Isabel, it was a surprise running into you. Glad you're well."

The dismissal on Rick's part was polite but unmistakable.

Chiara wondered about his past tie to Isabel. It gave her a bad feeling—though, of course, not jealousy. What had Rick been thinking? Isabel? *Really?* The woman's reputation followed her like a trail of discarded clothing in a tacky Vegas hotel room.

Isabel gave them a searching look, and then nodded as if reaching a conclusion. "It's time I got back to my date."

"Hal?" Rick inquired sardonically.

Isabel tossed her head, her smile too bright. "Oh, sugar, you know better." She flashed her hand and a ring caught the light. "But this time, I did find one who is for keeps."

"Congratulations."

The smile stayed on Isabel's lips but her eyes were sharp. "Thank you."

When the other woman moved off, Chiara turned to Rick. "Should I ask?"

"Will you be able to stop yourself?"

"Do you date all your leading ladies?"

"In Isabel's case, it was more her trying to hook up with me. Misguidedly, as it turned out."

Chiara raised her eyebrows.

"Isabel is the reason that I don't get involved with starlets. They're trouble."

"Men are trouble."

"Finally, a topic that we agree on," he quipped. "The opposite sex is trouble."

Chiara shrugged. "Isabel Lanier seems an odd choice for you."

Chiara definitely wasn't jealous. The irony wasn't lost on her, though. Usually her dates were the ones having to contend with overeager male admirers. Now the shoe was on the other foot—sort of.

"Possessive?" Rick asked, lips quirking, as if he'd read her mind.

"Don't be silly," Chiara retorted.

"It's not like you to get territorial, but I like it."

"So what is the connection between you and Isabel Lanier?" she tried again.

Rick regarded her for a moment. "Isabel made a play for me in front of some photographers. Unfortunately her boyfriend at the time was also a good friend of mine. End of friendship."

"Why would she do that?"

Rick gave her a penetrating look. "Fame, public image, to make Hal jealous. You know, all the likely ulterior motives."

She didn't want to dwell on their own ulterior motives right now.

"Shall we sit down?" Rick asked.

She felt compelled to go on. "If you were more high profile, the organizers here would have made sure your path didn't cross Isabel's, and that you were seated on opposite sides of the ballroom."

"Fortunately I'm not. High profile, that is."

"But I am." Chiara made a mental note to put the word out that she and Isabel should be kept apart—at least until her "relationship" with Rick came to an end.

Rick pulled out a chair for her, and she sat down. As Rick turned to acknowledge a waiter, Isabel fished the cell phone out of her clutch and typed a quick text to Odele. No time like the present to make sure a viper stayed in her tank, she thought, her mind traveling back to Isabel.

After that, the evening passed quickly and painlessly. The master of ceremonies was a well-known comedian, and he drew regular laughs from the crowd, who dined on butterfly salmon pâté with caviar and peppered chateaubriand with port wine glacé.

Before long, Chiara found herself heading home with Rick. She'd never had a live-in significant other, and in the past, it had been easy enough to say goodbye at the end of a date. Not this time, however. *Awkward.*

When they entered the hushed silence of her foyer, she faced Rick. She reminded herself that she held the cards here. She was the celebrity. This was *her* house. And he, for all intents and purposes, was *her* employee, thanks to Odele.

Still, it was of little help when faced with Rick's overwhelming masculinity.

He was tall and broad, and all evening she'd been ignoring how he filled out his tux. Should she be surprised he even owned one?

Rick quirked his lips. "I guess this is the part where I kiss you good-night—" he glanced past her to the stairs "—except I'm staying here." His gaze came back to hers, and he looked at her with a slow deliberateness.

All of a sudden, she was searching for air. They hadn't been this close since their encounter in the exercise room, and she'd vowed it was an experience that would never, ever be repeated.

But the memory of how easily he'd aroused her—her body tightening and then finding blessed release—played havoc with her senses and scruples right now.

He bent his head, and said in a low voice, "It would aid in believability."

There was no need for him to elaborate. If he kissed her…if he excited her…if they became lovers…

Yes…no. She mentally shook her head.

He looked down at her gown, and she felt his gaze everywhere—on her breasts, her hips and lower…

"Do you need help with that dress?" he muttered, his eyes half-lidded. "There's no Odele here, no designer's assistant or fashion stylist."

Didn't she know it. They were alone, and the quiet of the night and the empty house surrounded them. The only illumination was the dim light that she'd left on in the foyer.

Chiara cleared her throat. "You did well tonight for an agoraphobic stuntman."

"Isn't this the time in the movie for a love scene?" he teased.

She tried gamely for her typical maneuver. She did *outrage* really well. "This isn't a movie and we're not—"

"Actors," he finished for her. "I know."

He took her hand and drew her near. Another smile

teased his lips. "That's what's going to make this so great. No pretending."

She swallowed. "I don't know how not to pretend."

The brutal honesty escaped her before she could help herself.

"Just feel. Go with your instincts."

"Like method acting?"

"Like real life." He settled his hands and massaged her shoulders. "Relax. We stuntmen are not so bad."

"Are you the baddest of the bunch?" she asked, her voice husky.

His smile widened. "Want to find out if I'm the Big Bad Wolf?"

"Sorry, wrong fairy tale again."

She could feel the heat and energy coming off him even though only his hands touched her. She was attuned to *everything* about him. As an actress, she was trained to observe the slightest facial sign, the subtlest inflection of voice, the intention behind a touch. But with Rick, she quivered with sensation approaching a sixth sense.

Slowly he raised her chin, and her gaze met his.

They'd been working up to this moment ever since the exercise room, and she saw in his eyes that he knew it, too.

He searched her face and then, focusing on her mouth, he brushed her lips with his.

She parted for him on an indrawn sigh, touched her tongue to his and twined her arms around his neck. She needed this, too, she admitted, and for tonight at least she couldn't think of a reason to deny herself.

He settled his hands on her waist, and she felt the press of his arousal. He deepened the kiss, and she met him, not holding back. Her evening clutch slipped from her limp hand and hit the ground with a small *thump*.

He broke the kiss, only to trail his mouth, whisper-soft, across her jaw and to her temple.

"Rick…"

"Chiara."

"I…"

"This isn't the time to start one of your arguments."

"About what?"

"About anything."

He nuzzled the side of her neck, and she angled her head to afford him better access. She fastened her hands on his biceps in order to anchor herself, and the hard muscle under her fingers reminded her that he was built… and right now primed to mate with her.

Chiara felt that last realization to her core, even as Rick's lips sent delicious shivers down her spine.

One of his hands shifted lower and settled on her exposed thigh. She felt the caress of his slightly callused fingers.

He kissed the shell of her ear, and then whispered, "Your dress has been giving me a thrill all evening."

"Oh?" she managed.

"The slit is so high…playing peekaboo all the way up…making me wonder whether this time I'll get a glimpse…"

She gave a throaty laugh. "I'm not commando. I don't take those kinds of risks."

His hand moved lower, slid under the slit and covered her. "Oh, yeah? But I want you to go on all kinds of adventures with me. Let me show you, baby…"

Chiara's eyes closed and her head fell back as Rick's finger slipped inside her and the pad of his thumb brushed her in a wicked dance. Her lips parted. *Oh, my.* They hadn't even made it past the inside of her front door and all she wanted to do was strip for him and let him take her against the hard wall of the foyer, pounding into her until she wept with the pure ecstasy of it, her legs wrapped around him and holding him close.

"Ah, Chiara." His voice sounded rough with arousal as he nipped and nibbled along her jaw. "So hot. There's nothing cold about you."

His words wrapped around her like a warm caress. She'd worked all her life to get her walls up and, most of all, be independent and succeed. But with Rick, her defenses came crashing down, and in their place rushed in powerful need.

Rick snaked his free hand beneath the one-shoulder bodice of her gown and cupped her breast. He kneaded her soft flesh and she peaked for him.

A moan escaped her.

"I should have stuck around earlier tonight so I'd know how you got into this gown, and how to get you out," he muttered.

A laugh caught in her throat, but then the buzz of a cell phone interrupted the mood like the beam of car headlights slicing through the night.

It took a few moments for Chiara to clear her head and get oriented. And then she flushed. She and Rick had gone from zero to sixty in minutes, and any longer…

As her phone continued to buzz from the inside of her clutch on the floor, she pulled away from Rick, and he dropped his hands and stepped back.

"You don't have to answer it," he said roughly.

"It's Odele. I can tell from the ringtone." She started to bend down, but Rick was faster and retrieved the clutch for her.

"You don't have to answer it," Rick commented, his voice edged with frustration.

Flustered and still aroused, Chiara gathered her scattered thoughts. "She's used to having her calls answered. I—I've got to take this. I've…got to go."

"Of course." His expression was sardonic, knowing, and he raked his hand through his hair. "I'm guessing it's time for another cold shower."

Turning away from Rick to regain her composure, she hit the answer button. "Odele, hello?"

"Hello, sweetie. How are you? Did you have a fine evening?"

"Yes, of course," she answered as she hurried up the stairs. "What can I do for you, Odele?"

"I'm responding to your request, hon."

For a moment, Chiara was confused, but then she remembered her text to Odele earlier in the evening.

"From what I could see on TV, you and Mr. Stuntman were doing an excellent job at your first public appearance together. But then I got your message about keeping you and Isabel Lanier separated at future social events. Did something happen that I'm not aware of?"

Chiara didn't know whether to be relieved or frustrated. If not for Odele's untimely—or rather, timely—call, she'd have been moments away from inviting Rick to follow her to the bedroom. A mistake that she would have regretted.

"Not that I don't have sympathy," Odele went on in her trademark raspy voice. "Isabel Lanier reeks of tacky perfume, and her manager is worse."

Chiara smiled weakly. Leave it to Odele to be competitive with even Isabel's snarky manager.

"So, honey, are you going to tell me what the story is, or make me guess? I have my sources, you know."

Chiara lowered her voice even as she reached the privacy of her bedroom and flipped on the light. "Rick and Isabel were involved at one point."

"Really?" The word was a long, drawn-out drawl.

"Well, not really." Chiara dropped her clutch on the vanity table. "She sort of threw herself at him in a publicity stunt and that was the end of his friendship with her then boyfriend."

"Damn it, I knew her manager was cunning."

"It takes one to know one, Odele."

"Okay, all right," her manager responded grumpily. "Now that I've got the details, I'll put the word out about Isabel and file away the information for any future events that I book you for."

"You're a doll, Odele."

"Oh, stop," her manager rasped. "I'm a barracuda in a town infested with sharks."

When she ended the call with Odele, Chiara sighed. The conversation had let sanity back in. She couldn't get involved with Rick. Sweet heaven, she didn't even like him. She *couldn't* like him.

Too bad she was having an increasingly hard time remembering why.

Seven

Welsdale was a quaint New England town with brick buildings dotting the main streets and colorful homes lining the back roads.

Chiara could hardly believe she was here except that Odele had, of course, loved Rick's idea for an appearance on his mother's cooking show. Before Chiara had caught her breath, she and Rick had been on an early flight from Los Angeles to Boston.

She supposed it was just as well. Ever since the Ring of Hope Gala last weekend, she'd done her best to keep Rick at arm's length. Only a long couple of days on set had saved her. She'd collapsed into bed, exhausted, late at night.

From the airport, where Rick had a car in long-term parking, they drove to Welsdale and then, after no more than twenty minutes on oak-lined roads, to a stunning home on the outskirts of town. Rick had mentioned that his parents were hosting a small party at their house.

The elder Serenghettis lived in a Mediterranean-style mansion with a red-tile roof and white walls. Set amidst beautiful landscaping, the house greeted visitors with a stone fountain at the center of a circular drive.

Chiara didn't know what she had expected, except perhaps a humbler abode. Clearly she'd been wrong in her assumptions. Rick came from an established family and a comfortable background, unlike her.

When they stepped inside, Rick stretched out his arms and joked, "Welcome to the Serenghetti family reunion."

Chiara blinked. "They're all here?"

"We like to support Mom."

Oh, sweet heaven. She wasn't prepared for this. The gathering was larger than she'd expected, and it seemed that assorted Serenghettis were sprinkled among the crowd.

There'd be no Feran family reunion, of course. Or if there were, it would be at a Las Vegas gaming table, where she'd be settling her father's debts.

People were standing around chatting in the family room and adjacent living room, and she noticed in particular how two of the men were as attractive as Rick. It appeared the Serenghetti men came in one variety only: drop-dead gorgeous.

"Come on," Rick said, cupping her elbow. "I'll introduce you."

As they approached, one of the two men glanced at them and then came forward. "Ah, the prodigal son returning to the fold…"

"Stuff it, Jordan." Rick's tone was good-natured—as if he was used to being ribbed.

Jordan appeared unabashed and gave Chiara an openly curious look. "Well, this time you've outdone yourself. Mom will be pleased. But how you managed to convince a beautiful actress that you've got the goods, I'll never know." He held out his hand. "Hi, I'm Jordan Serenghetti, Rick's better-looking brother."

"Which one of us was a body double for *People*'s Sexiest Man Alive?" Rick retorted mildly.

"Which one is featured in an underwear ad on a billboard in Times Square?" Jordan returned.

"Nice to meet you," Chiara jumped in with a light laugh. "I've been putting up with his humor—" she indicated Rick "—for days. Now I see it's a family trait."

"Yes, but I'm younger than Rick and our older brother, Cole, so I like to say our parents achieved perfection only the third time around."

When Rick raised his eyebrows, Chiara laughed again. It was good to see Rick getting back some of his own.

Rick's gaze went to the arched entrance to the family room, and Chiara spotted an attractive woman with honey-blond hair caught in a ponytail, a nice figure showcased in tights and a short-sleeved athletic shirt. Unlike many women in Hollywood, she seemed unaware of her beauty, sporting a fresh-faced natural look with little makeup.

"Your nemesis is here," Rick murmured.

Jordan followed his brother's gaze. "Heaven help us."

At Chiara's inquiring look, Rick elaborated. "Serafina is related to us by marriage. She's Cole's wife's cousin. She also happens to be the one woman under the sun Jordan can't charm."

Jordan wore an unguarded look that said he was attracted like a bee to nectar—and befuddled by the feeling. Chiara hid a smile. She suspected that like her, Jordan lived in a world with plenty of artifice—big-time sports likely resembled Hollywood that way—and Serafina was a breath of fresh air.

Serafina was something different, and Jordan appeared at a loss as to how to deal with her. Relative? Friend? Lover? Maybe he couldn't make up his mind—and it wasn't only his choice to make, either.

"Excuse me," Jordan announced. "Fun just walked in."

"Jordan," Rick said warningly.

"What?" his brother responded as he stepped away.

"Just make sure that while you're getting a rise out of our newest in-law, you don't come in for a pounding yourself."

Jordan flashed a quick grin. "I'm counting on it."

Chiara watched Serafina's eyes narrow as she noticed Jordan step toward her. It seemed as if Jordan wasn't the only one who was aware of someone else's every move…

Then Chiara quashed a sudden self-deprecatory grimace. She couldn't judge Serafina. She herself was attuned to Rick's every gesture.

At that moment, the other attractive man Chiara had spotted earlier approached.

"Hi, I'm Cole Serenghetti," he said, holding out his hand.

"Chiara Feran," she responded, shaking hands.

She could tell on a moment's acquaintance that Cole was the serious brother.

Unlike Jordan and Rick, Cole's eyes were more hazel than green. Still, the family resemblance was strong. But Chiara noticed that Cole sported a scar on his cheek.

A beautiful woman walked up to them, and Cole put his arm around her. She had the most translucent brown eyes that Chiara had ever seen, and masses of brown hair that fell in waves and curls past her shoulders.

"This is my wife, Marisa," Cole said, looking affectionately at the woman beside him. "Sweet pea, I'm sure you've heard of Chiara Feran."

"I loved your movie *Three Nights in Paris*," Marisa gushed, "and I follow you online."

Chiara smiled. "It's good to meet you. So you like romantic comedies?"

"I adore them." Marisa threw a teasing look at her husband. "Though it's hard to get Cole here to watch them with me."

"Ouch." Cole adopted a mock-wounded expression. "Hey, I'm just showing family loyalty to Rick for his adventure flicks."

"A great excuse," Marisa parried before turning back to Chiara. "You aren't filming a romantic comedy now, are you?"

Chiara sighed. "Unfortunately no." Unless she counted the banter that she had going on with Rick offscreen. "Blame Hollywood. Action movies bring in the big bucks at the box office."

Marisa made a sympathetic sound.

"You're a woman after my own heart," Chiara said.

"I've had my tenth grade students watch you in the film adaptation of *Another Song at Dawn*," Marisa added enthusiastically. "I've taught here in Welsdale."

Chiara warmed to the other woman. "I'm so glad. That's the nicest compliment—"

"Anyone's ever paid you?" Rick finished for her.

Cole cast Rick a droll look. "Quite the romantic boyfriend, aren't you?"

Chiara flushed. "I meant the best professional praise."

Cole and his wife just laughed.

"Cole's gotten better with sharing warm thoughts since we've gotten married," Marisa added, throwing a playful look at her husband, "but I'm still not finding little heart drawings in my lunchbox."

Chiara envied Cole and Marisa's obvious connection.

In contrast, she and Rick pushed each other's buttons. Then she reminded herself there was no *her and Rick*. They had a fake relationship for the benefit of the press.

When Cole and Marisa excused themselves, another woman approached, and Chiara again saw a resemblance to Rick.

"Chiara, this is my younger sister, Mia," Rick said.

Mia was slender and lovely, with arresting almond-shaped green eyes. She could have qualified as a model or actress herself.

"I wish I could say Rick has told me a lot about you," Mia quipped, "but I'd be lying."

"Family," Rick muttered. "Who needs enemies?"

Mia tossed her brother a droll look that made Chiara smile.

"Rick mentioned you're a designer," Chiara said.

"He did?"

"I'd love to see some of your creations."

"I'm based in New York."

"Do you have something that Chiara could toss on for an appearance on Mom's cooking show?" Rick prompted.

When Mia rolled her eyes, Chiara held back a grin.

"Leave it to my brother to give me the professional opportunity of a lifetime, and no fair warning."

"Hey," Rick said, holding up his hands, "I did tell you to bring a trunk of stuff to show a friend of mine."

"Yeah, but you didn't say who!"

"Don't you read any of the celebrity glossies or supermarket tabloids?" Rick countered. "I'm dating one of the hottest actresses around."

Chiara felt a wave of heat at the word *hottest*.

"How am I supposed to know what's true and what isn't?" Mia responded. "It's a good thing I know my way around a needle and thread for a little nip and tuck if necessary."

"I'm not that thin," Chiara chimed in.

"Yeah, she has the appetite of a lumberjack," Rick agreed jokingly. "I should know. I've carried her out of exploding buildings and onto a helicopter with one hand."

"Hilarious, Rick," Mia said. "Next you'll be telling us that you have real superpowers."

Rick arched an eyebrow. "Ask Chiara."

Chiara flushed again. The last thing she wanted to do was discuss Rick's prowess—sexual or otherwise—with his siblings.

When Chiara didn't immediately reply, Mia laughed. "I guess you got your answer, Rick."

An older woman came bustling over, clapping her hands. "*Cari, scusatemi.* I'm sorry, I was speaking on the phone with my producers."

Rick's face lightened. "Don't worry, Mom. We're all good here. Just introducing Chiara to everybody."

Rick's mother clasped her hands together. "I'm Camilla. *Benvenuti.*"

"Thank you for the welcome, Mrs. Serenghetti," Chiara said.

"Camilla, please. You are doing me a huge *favore.*"

"She mixes Italian and English like they're flour and water," Rick said in a low voice. "Interrupt at your own risk."

"Now, Chiara—what a lovely name! You are Italian and Brazilian, no?"

She nodded her head.

"You are a celebrity, yes? And beautiful, too, no?"

"Um…"

"*Basta, così.*" Camilla nodded her head approvingly.

"It is enough. You are doing me a huge *favore*. Anything else will be extra filling in the cannoli, no?"

"Mrs. Serenghetti—"

"Camilla, please. Do you want me to demonstrate a recipe to you on the show, or—" Camilla brightened hopefully "—you have one to share?"

"Actually I do." Chiara had been thinking about the show on the plane ride. She didn't want to disappoint. It had nothing to do with Rick, but rather her own high standards and integrity, she told herself. "I used to visit relatives in Brazil when I was growing up. Italian food is very popular there."

Camilla beamed.

"Brazilian barbecue—" Chiara began.

"Churrascaria, sì."

"—is well-known, but we also have *galeteria*. It's chicken and usually an all-you-can-eat pasta and salad. So I would like to make a pasta dish that sounds Italian, but was really popularized by the Italian immigrant community in Brazil. *Cappelletti alla romanesca.*"

"Perfetto." Camilla nodded approvingly.

Mia linked arms with her mother. "Excuse us while I get Mom's opinion on how to finish the tagliatelle salad."

When his female relatives had departed, Rick turned to Chiara with a bemused expression. "I'm impressed. Have you actually made this dish before?"

"Please." Chiara gave him a long-suffering look. "Do I look Brazilian and Italian to you?"

"Yes, but—"

"Trust me." The words were out of her mouth before she could stop them.

"Isn't that my line?" he mocked.

She felt the heat rise in her cheeks and turned away. "Rick!"

Chiara spotted an older version of Rick coming toward them.

"Brace yourself," Rick murmured. "You have yet to meet the most colorful member of the family. Serg Serenghetti."

Oh, dear.

"So the prodigal son has returned."

"Wrong script, Dad," Rick quipped. "This is *The Son Also Rises*."

Serg Serenghetti fastened his eyes on Chiara. "What do you see in this guy?"

Chiara gave a weak smile.

"How do you know about us?" Rick retorted, addressing his father.

"I read *WE Magazine*," Serg grumbled. "Same as everyone else. Your mother leaves copies lying around." Serg lowered his brows. "And with my recovery, I have plenty of time to surf the internet for news about my wayward children."

Rick looked at Chiara and jerked a finger in his father's direction. "Do you believe he knows about surfing? He's keeping up with those teenagers that make action flicks such blockbusters at the box office."

As Rick poked fun at his father, his tone was laced with affection.

Serg grumbled again. "I've known a lot about a lot for a lot longer than you've been around, but all I get is guff from the young pups."

Rick pulled out a chair, and Serg sank into it.

"He's still recovering from a stroke," Rick murmured for her benefit.

Oh. Chiara felt a tug at her heartstrings. Beneath the bluster, the affection between father and son sounded loud and clear. In contrast, her relationship with her father was a distant echo.

Chiara realized that with the Serenghettis, she was in for something new and different from her own experience. And as she settled into a conversation with Serg, she realized that might not be such a bad thing—except for the fact that meeting his family made Rick even more likable and attractive, and she was already in danger of succumbing to him…

Rick couldn't believe his eyes, but then he should have known Chiara would be a natural in front of the cameras—even on Camilla Serenghetti's cooking show.

He was also tense. He wanted this episode to boost ratings for his mother, but he had little idea about Chiara's cooking skills, let alone how they'd play out on television. And he also wanted Chiara and his mother to get along.

So far so good.

"The reason I'm not wearing an apron," Chiara said brightly into the camera, "is because this outfit is too scrumptious to cover up." She gestured at her V-neck berry-colored top with clever draping, the cream trousers underneath barely visible above the kitchen counter. "It's courtesy of Camilla's daughter, Mia Serenghetti, whose clothes are mouth-watering."

Camilla laughed, and because she sat next to him in the audience, Rick could tell his sister looked amused.

"I guess Camilla is not the only talented one in the family."

"*Grazie tanto*, Chiara *bellissima*," his mother said.

"*Prego.*" Chiara acknowledged the thanks and then dumped prosciutto in a blender before smiling at the studio audience. "I sometimes prefer an electronic device to hand-chopping. Goes faster, too."

As she scanned the buttons on the blender, Rick realized something was wrong and started to rise from his front-row seat.

Chiara pressed a button, and prosciutto pieces started flying everywhere.

Chiara yelped, and Camilla covered her mouth with her hands. The audience exploded in shocked laughter.

Rick stared, and then sank back into his seat.

Chiara quickly pressed another button to turn off the blender, and then she and Camilla stared at each other… before dissolving into peals of laughter.

"Oops." Chiara looked into the camera and shrugged, a teasing smile on her face. "Next time I'll remember to put the top on the blender first. But first let's get this cleaned up."

Moments later, after help from behind-the-scenes staff, Chiara raised a wineglass, and she and Camilla toasted each other.

Rick watched, fascinated by the interplay between the two women. Looking around him, he realized everyone else was entertained, as well.

After that, Chiara proceeded to prepare the cappelletti recipe without another hitch. She chopped more prosciutto, by hand this time, and added it to a shallow pan containing peas, mushrooms and a light cream sauce. With a saucy look, she added a touch of *vino* from the open wine bottle, and said with a wink, "Do try this at home, but not too much."

His mother laughed, and then both she and Chiara took more sips from their wineglasses.

Rick couldn't imagine what they were both thinking, but when Chiara motioned for his father, Serg, to join them from the audience, Rick knew things were only going to get more interesting. His father was a character, but this was the first time Serg had been so public since his stroke.

Rick made to help his father out of his seat, but Serg just batted his hand away.

"Bah!" Serg said, doing a comical rendition of a grumpy old man even though he had the grin of an eager fan.

"I hear Camilla's husband, Serg, knows his way around wine," Chiara announced. "Perhaps he can suggest a vintage to pair with my dish."

"I'd be happy to," Serg replied as he climbed the two steps to the stage. "It's not every day that my son brings home a beautiful actress."

Rick suppressed an embarrassed groan. His and Chiara's pretend relationship had just gotten a major advertising boost from his father. Odele would be overjoyed.

When Serg reached the stage, he sampled the cappelletti dish from a plate Camilla handed to him. After taking a moment to savor, he declared, "Bianco di Custoza, Verdicchio or Pinot Bianco."

Chiara beamed. "Thank you so much for the wine suggestions, Serg."

Serg winked at the audience. "You know I'm Italian, so I suggest Italian wines. I like them on the dry side, but you can pair this dish with a lighter Chardonnay if you like."

Getting the signal from a producer offscreen, Camilla addressed the camera in order to wrap up the show. "*All prossima volta.* Till next time, *buon appetito.*"

As the show's support staff approached to remove Camilla's and Chiara's mics, Serg returned to his seat.

"Good job, Dad," Rick remarked with a smile. "I didn't know you had it in you."

He was still trying to process Chiara's interaction with

his parents on camera. It was like she'd known them for-ever, it had been so natural.

"Bah!" Serg said, though his expression again belied his grumpiness. "Don't be jealous I was the one called on stage by a beautiful woman. You've got to work it, Rick."

"And a star is born," Rick replied with dry humor to his sister, who gave a knowing smile.

"Do you want my autograph?" Serg chortled, picking up his sweater from his seat as Mia moved to help him.

Rick stepped off to the side, and when Chiara ap-proached, minutes later, he remarked, "That was quite a scene-stealing performance."

"It's why I'm an in-demand actress."

She looked sexy in Mia's designs, and he liked her even more for lending her celebrity to help his family.

"So it was all planned?"

"Planned? Like reading lines?" She shook her head. "No. More like improv and stand-up comedy."

"It worked."

"I hope the show's ratings reflect it." She shrugged. "Viewers want drama and action. Or maybe I just think that because I've been doing too many adventure mov-ies."

"Hey—" he chucked her under the chin "—that's how you met a hunky stuntman who's given you a new lease on life in the press."

"Oh, yes, the media." She made a disgruntled sound that he didn't expect. "Of course, I have to attend to my public persona."

He tucked his hands in his denim pockets—because the urge to comfort and, even more, get closer to her, was overwhelming. "So who is the real Chiara Feran? Odele mentioned a few details about your childhood and parents."

She sighed, and there was a flash of pain. "My mother was in some ways a typical stage mother, but in other ways, she wasn't. She had thwarted dreams of being a star, so she was ambitious for me."

"Things didn't work out for her?"

"Well, she had some modest success in Brazil, so she went to Hollywood. But the Portuguese accent didn't help when it came to acting roles. Who knows what would have happened if she'd stayed in South America."

Curious, Rick asked, "Your mother didn't want more kids?"

Chiara sobered. "No. Her marriage broke up, and I was enough for her to handle as a single parent living far from her family in Brazil. Plus, I was her spitting image in many ways, so she already had a Mini-Me. She died a few years ago, and I still miss her a lot. I have mixed feelings about my childhood, but I loved her with my whole heart. She did the best she could in raising me."

Rick was starting to understand—a lot. Chiara's upbringing couldn't have been more different from his own. While he'd been tossing around a football in the backyard with his siblings, she was probably being prepped and groomed for a chance to appear in a national commercial or catalog.

"Your mother should think of doing a food blog," Chiara commented, changing the subject. "She needs to think of branching out and building the Camilla Serenghetti food empire."

"Empire?" he repeated in a sardonic tone. Because while it was one thing for his mother to have a local cooking show, it was another for her to be an empress in the making. Still… "She'll like the way you think, and appreciate the pointers on building a brand."

"Of course. That's what we're about in Hollywood.

Building a brand." Chiara looked around. "You, on the other hand, are about wholesomeness, surprisingly enough. Or at least your family is. You come from a nice little town in Massachusetts that's ages away from the Sunset Strip."

"You grew up in Rhode Island, not far from here. You're not so different."

Chiara shook her head. "I'm all about performing these days. The show must go on."

"Whatever the cost?" Rick probed.

Chiara nodded. "Even if the show is a sham."

"And yet, I think of you as real and vital," Rick replied, stepping closer. "And my physical reaction to you definitely is."

She gave a nervous laugh and shook her head. "You must be mistaken. I'm Snow White, remember? A make-believe character."

Rick's lips twitched. He wasn't sure when they had gotten so mixed up. Suddenly *she* was insisting she was a make-believe character, and *he* was arguing the opposite.

One thing was for sure: he was more determined than ever to finish exploring their very real attraction. He'd kept his distance since they'd left Los Angeles, but he wanted her with a need that was getting hard to ignore.

In the now nearly empty television studio, Chiara stood to one side, waiting for assorted Serenghettis to depart. Rick was speaking to his mother and one of her producers, no doubt making sure everything was in order with respect to today's guest appearance.

Chiara was glad for the respite. Minutes ago, her conversation with Rick had devolved into a far more intimate and personal exchange than she'd been prepared for. What had she been thinking?

She'd revealed more about her background and her mother than she'd intended. And then she hadn't been able to keep out the wistfulness when contrasting her circumstances with Rick's own family. *Wholesome. Warm. Loving.* She felt relaxed here, in the embrace of the Serenghettis and away from her problems—the limelight, her father, her would-be stalker...

Still, she'd dodged the very real emotional and sexual currents between her and Rick by making light of the matter. *The show must go on.* She doubted Rick would be satisfied with that response, however. Awareness skated over her skin as she remembered the gleam in his eyes followed by his words: *I think of you as real and vital. And my physical reaction to you definitely is.*

Her resolve to keep him at a distance was weakening, aided by her very real yearning for what he'd had— still had—in comparison: a tight-knit family who cared about each other.

As if on cue, Rick's sister appeared, her face wreathed in a wide smile. "Thank you for the on-air plug, Chiara. You are the perfect model to bring out the best in my designs."

Chiara smiled back and then touched the other woman's arm. "Don't mention it."

"I've never dressed someone so high profile before. You have a great sense of style."

"I owe a lot to my former stylist Emery. But she went off to start her own accessories line, so I'm open to new ideas." Chiara's eyes widened, as an idea struck. "I should connect the both of you. Emery would be a natural complement to your clothing line."

Mia gave a look of wry amusement. "I can see it now—'ME by Mia Emery... Not Your Mom's Everyday.'"

"Perfect." So this was what it might be like to have a sister. Chiara let the wistful feeling wash over her again.

Mia tilted her head. "Rick isn't the only maverick in the family, though he likes to think so. I've abandoned the family construction business and run off to New York to follow the bright lights of fashion."

"You make *maverick* sound like a bad thing. It's not so terrible."

"Not so wicked, you mean?" Mia gave a sly grin. "So Rick's worked his charm on you then?"

Chiara's face warmed. Was it *charm*—or something more? Just a short time ago, she'd have called Rick the least charming man she knew, but somehow her feelings had been changing. Now with his family, she was even more...charmed.

Mia leaned in conspiratorially. "You're beautiful, smart and famous. How did you and Rick wind up together?"

"We...um..." Somehow she couldn't bring herself to lie to Rick's sister, so she finished lamely, "Don't believe everything you read in the press."

What could she say? *We're not really a couple. It's a big fat lie.* Even if she was having increasing trouble remembering that, especially surrounded by the Serenghettis.

"I see," Mia responded, and then nodded as if satisfied. "Well, you two bounce off each other in a charming way. It's as if Rick has met his match."

Even if that were true, it meant one of them was going down for the count...

"You're someone who can't be impressed by his money," Mia added.

What? Chiara mentally shrugged, and said carefully, "I'm not sure how much money Rick has."

Mia laughed. "Neither am I, but after making a killing with his hedge fund, he's got enough to play with."

Hedge fund? Chiara felt her head swim. Rick was a gritty rolling stone of a stuntman as far as she knew. If he had millions, what was he doing…?

"He's a stuntman," she blurted. "He jumps off buildings, leaps from moving cars…" *And embraces actresses while hanging from a helicopter.*

"And takes big risks with money by betting things are going up or down in value." Mia shrugged. "Same thing."

Chiara froze. Mia made it seem as if Rick was a risk taker—which wasn't far from her gambling father. She'd never seen the similarity, and now she was in a very public relationship with Rick. She needed therapy…and not the kind provided by pretending to talk with a wooden dummy, either. *Sorry, Ruby.*

But even more shockingly, Rick wasn't merely a stuntman, he was—

"*Pegasus Pride* is his baby right now," his sister said.

Chiara blew out a breath and tried to keep her voice steady. "He's got money invested in the film?"

Mia nodded. "You didn't know?"

Nope. Otherwise she'd never have spent her time insulting the boss—the producer of her current film—who could have had her fired any day.

Mia gave a choked laugh. "That's just like Rick. He always wants to keep a low profile." Her eyes suddenly danced. "We're still talking about his favorite childhood Halloween costume. You know, he just tossed a brown paper bag over his head and made cutouts for eyes."

"And the school play?" Chiara nearly squeaked.

"Stage crew, or he'd play the tree, of course."

"Well, he's graduated to leaping from speeding motorcycles and hanging from airplanes," Chiara replied drily. *And tricking unwary actresses.*

She glanced over at Rick. Why hadn't he told her? She'd thought...they'd... Chiara nearly closed her eyes on a groan.

She *really* needed to talk to him. But not around his family. No, she'd have to wait for the right moment...

Eight

Chiara somehow managed to keep her silence until they were at Rick's place.

At least now she understood why he might be checking his phone all the time. He was a behind-the-scenes Hollywood power player who liked to keep his name out of the press. And perhaps he needed to keep track of his substantial financial investments, too.

When they arrived at his condo, she was impressed all over again. But at least now she was prepared for what she found, unlike when they'd first arrived in Welsdale. The airy space had the stamp of muted luxury: exposed brick, rich leathers, recessed lighting and electronics hidden behind sliding panels of artwork. Nearly floor-to-ceiling windows made the most of the apartment's perch on the top floor of a block of high-priced condos, and Welsdale's evening lights twinkled outside.

How was it possible she'd been in the dark? She'd researched Rick again online after her conversation with Mia, and nothing had come up. He was good at covering his tracks. Except she was on his trail, thanks to his sister.

She sauntered into the muted light of the living room ahead of Rick. He was dressed in slacks and an open-collar navy shirt. A five o'clock shadow made him look even sexier.

Chiara smoothed her hands down the front of her pants. Then, taking a deep breath, she pinned Rick with a steady gaze. "You didn't tell me you're the producer of *Pegasus Pride* as well as doing its stunt work."

When he didn't react, she didn't know whether to stamp her foot or applaud his acting skills.

"Surprise."

"Now is not the time for humor, Serenghetti."

"When is?" He continued to look relaxed.

She placed her hands on her hips. "You misled me."

"You didn't ask. Anyway, does it matter?"

"I never date the boss," she huffed. "I don't want the reputation of being the actress who slept her way to the top."

On the long list of what he'd done wrong, it was one of the lesser of his transgressions, but she was nearly speechless and didn't even know where to begin.

Rick, though, had the poor grace to smile. "Does it help to know I'm only the behind-the-scenes guy? I'm an investor in Blooming Star Productions."

"Why don't you get your mother a cameo in a movie then? She could play herself. A cook with a local television show trying to make it big."

"God help us."

Chiara narrowed her eyes. "And where did you get the money to be the financial backer for a film production company?"

She'd heard it from Mia—and hadn't quite believed it—so she wanted confirmation from the source himself.

He shrugged. "I worked on Wall Street after Boston College and created a hedge fund."

She felt light-headed when he told her this, just as she had at the television studio. How much money were they talking about? Millions? Billions?

As if reading her mind, he said, "I've made a few best-of lists, but I left New York before joining the billionaires' club."

She figured he had serious bank dwarfing that of a run-of-the-mill actress. "It's unheard of to be both a producer and a stuntman!"

"They're not as different as you think. Both involve calculated risks. One with money, the other physically."

His words echoed Mia's earlier. What was this, a Serenghetti press release? Or did Rick and his siblings just think alike?

She should have been able to read the signs and put them together. They were all there. The expensive car. The apartments on two coasts.

He shrugged again. "I'm a maverick."

"You said you lived in a rental in West Hollywood!"

"Until the house is finished. It's under construction."

"And where is this house?" she asked suspiciously.

"Beverly Hills."

But of course. "Brentwood must seem...quaint to you."

There were plenty of celebrities in her section of LA but it was a little more low-key than the brand-name neighborhoods where tourists flocked—Beverly Hills, Bel Air...

Rick's lips twitched. "Brentwood has its charms, particularly if there's a thatched English cottage...and fairytale princess involved."

"She's the kick-ass modern variety," she sniffed—because she should be verbally demolishing him right now for letting her believe he was just an *aw-shucks* stuntman living for the next thrill and its accompanying paycheck.

"Don't I know it." His eyes laughed at her.

"Why would you give up New York, the financial industry and your own hedge fund to go out West to Hollywood?"

He smiled a little, still unflappable. "New challenges. Hollywood is not that different from Wall Street. The studios take major gambles with movies. Different rules, but the same game. And it's still about trusting your instincts and making money—or not."

"Well, it all makes sense now—" sarcasm crept into her tone "—except for the part where you led me to believe you were a regular Joe."

"Is this our first argument?"

She nearly snorted. "Or our hundredth."

He sauntered closer. "Would it have made a difference if you'd known?"

"You could have hired a stable of bodyguards for me with your bank!"

"Ah," he drawled, "but then I wouldn't have had the pleasure of…your company."

"The joy of sparring with me, you mean? And living in a humble cottage instead of a castle in Beverly Hills?"

He burst out laughing. "I'm paying you enough to live in more than a humble cottage."

"But are you paying me enough to put up with you?"

He gave a sultry smile and reached for her. "I don't know. Let's find out."

She should be mad at him. She *was* angry with him. Still, it didn't matter. The truth was she'd been lured in by the seductive cozy family life of the Serenghettis. She yearned for it. They were miles removed from her existence in Southern California, and the distance wasn't just a matter of geography.

When Rick's lips met hers, Chiara was transported, winging through the clouds as if they were performing another one of their stunts. Exhilaration ran through her, the feeling humming alongside one of safety, family... and coming home.

He molded her to him with his hand on her back, making her feel his need—his desire. She rested her hands on his shoulders, and then, caving, slid her arms around his neck, bringing his head closer.

Rick lifted his head slightly, and muttered against her mouth, "We need props."

She gave a choked laugh. "This is not a film scene."

Rick raised his eyebrows. "You're an actress who's not into role-playing?"

"I like to keep it real. Well, except for this pretending about being a couple that Odele has me doing!"

"Believe me, this is as real and raw as it's going to get."

Awareness shivered through her. "Okay, what if I'm a chilly A-list actress and you're...the help who is intent on seducing me?"

"There's nothing cold about you, Snow," he said, tilting up her chin. "Well, except for maybe your nickname."

"But you're here to melt me?"

He flashed his teeth. "I'm trying."

It had been safer to pretend he was the help. Just the movie stuntman. Or the make-believe boyfriend. Not a man whose wealth dwarfed hers. One who had no use for her money or her fame and celebrity. One who'd put himself on the line to protect her—just because.

She didn't know what to do with a man like that. She'd

spent years living as if she didn't need any man. Because she could provide for herself, thanks. But with Rick, she was at a disadvantage. He'd come to her defense against a stalker, and now it turned out he was her boss. She didn't have the upper hand. He didn't need her for anything, either.

Well, except for sex. He clearly wanted her *badly*.

And what was wrong with making herself feel feminine and powerful for an interlude? After all, it wasn't as if she was giving up something. Except she risked falling for him.

The pent-up desire that she'd been feeling these weeks and refusing to acknowledge slipped from its shackles. Rick drove her crazy, and it was a thin line between being irritated and jumping his bones. Giving in meant easing some of the frustration, and suddenly nothing else mattered.

Seeming to read the assent in her eyes, Rick slowly took off her clothes, tossing the pieces aside one by one onto nearby furniture and peeling away her defenses to find what was in no way artifice. Then he shed some of his own clothes until they were both down to underwear.

She shivered as the cool air hit her.

"Let me warm you up," he muttered.

She wanted to say he already had, and that that was the problem. She was melting, her defenses flowing away like so much ice under a hot sun.

Chiara stepped out of the clothes pooled at her feet. Clad in just a lacy black bra and the barest slip of underwear, she had no mask. But if she felt nervous, the naked appreciation stamped on Rick's face put an end to it. She straightened her shoulders, and the resulting movement thrust her breasts forward, their peaks jutting against their thin covering.

Rick's face glowed with appreciation, and then he muttered what he wanted to do with her, his prominent arousal testimony to his words. Waves of heat washed over her, and she sucked in a breath.

He stepped forward, and when the backs of her legs hit the sofa, she let herself fall backward, bracing herself with one hand on a pillow. Rick followed, bent and took one of her nipples in his mouth through her bra, fabric and all, suckling her gently.

Chiara gasped, a strangled sound caught in her throat, and need shuddered through her. Her head fell back when he pushed aside her bra and transferred his attention to her other breast. She was awash in sensation, the universe popping with a kaleidoscope of color.

Rick knelt, pulled her to the end of the sofa arm so that her legs straddled it, and then pushed aside her underwear to use his mouth to love her some more. Cries of pleasure were ripped from her throat…and she felt herself splintering—until she bucked against him with her release.

Afterward, Rick straightened and shed his underwear like a man possessed. Watching him, Chiara stood up and did the same, her remaining garments melting away.

Rick suddenly cursed. "Damn it. Protection is still packed in my suitcase."

"I'm on contraception," she said throatily, dizzy with want.

His gaze caught with hers. "I want you to know I've gotten a clean bill from my doctor. I would never put you at risk."

She licked her lips. "Same goes for me."

They looked at each other for a moment, neither moving, savoring this moment.

And then Chiara held her hand out to him. "We're not going to make it to the bed, are we?"

He gave her a lopsided smile. "Stuntmen can do it everywhere."

Chiara followed his gaze to the nearby long leather ottoman, which doubled as a coffee table. *Oh.* As she bent to sit on it, Rick followed her down, giving her a long, sweet, lingering kiss.

When she embraced him, he entered her in one fluid movement, rocking her to her core. Joined to him, Chiara gave herself up to sensation, following the pace that Rick set.

When she felt Rick tighten, nearing his climax, she ran her hands over his ripped arms and bit back a moan.

"Let me hear you," Rick said as the air grew thick with their deep breathing.

"Rick, oh…now."

And just like that, as he thrust deep, Chiara felt herself coming apart again, dazed with her release.

Rick gave a hoarse shout and buried himself in her, collapsing into her embrace.

Chiara had never felt so at one with someone…exposed and yet secure.

As she walked by, Chiara glanced in her hallway mirror and resisted the urge to pinch herself. She looked happy…relaxed…and yes, sexually satisfied. Filming was over, so the main item on her agenda today was reading a script for a role that she was considering.

Ever since she and Rick had returned to LA from Welsdale two days ago, she'd been in a lovely cocoon. She flushed just thinking about what they'd done yesterday. Foreplay on the weight bench, but the exercise mat and even the jump rope had come in handy…

Walking into the den, she plopped herself on the couch, feet dangling off one end. She began reading the script on her tablet. Moments later, Rick walked in.

After an extraordinary bout of sex this morning, he'd gone out to run errands and she hadn't seen him in the two hours since. He looked just as yummy as earlier, however. They were both dressed in sweats, but somehow, he managed to make his look sexy rather than casual. He hadn't bothered shaving this morning, and she'd come to like the shadow darkening his jaw. Contrasting with his wonderful multihued eyes, it lent him an air of quiet magnetism...

Rick nodded toward the device in her hand. "Have you checked the news yet?"

"No, should I? I just sat down." She belatedly realized he looked more serious than usual.

Rick folded his arms and leaned against the entryway. "Well, the good news is your temporary restraining order came through, so your bad fan can be arrested for getting too close."

"Great." She hadn't given much thought to Todd Jeffers in the past several days, though now that she was back home and he knew her address, she supposed she did feel an undercurrent of more stress. She asked cautiously, "What's the bad news?"

"Your father has gotten himself arrested."

Chiara leaned her head back against the pillows and closed her eyes briefly. "In Sin City? What could he have possibly done? The police turn a blind eye to practically every vice imaginable there. Even prostitution is legal in parts of Nevada, for heaven's sake."

"Apparently he argued about a parking ticket."

"Sounds just like him. Responsibility has never been his strong suit."

"You have to deal with the daddy problem."

"I've never called him *Daddy*," she scoffed, straightening. "Sperm donor, maybe. Daddy, no."

"Whatever the name, you'll keep having the same pesky PR problems if you don't address the issue. And your next big movie might not come with a stuntman willing to double as the star's boyfriend."

"Hilarious." Still, she felt a pull on her heartstrings at the reminder that their arrangement was temporary and fake.

Rick dropped his arms and sauntered into the room. "We may have had some success in distracting the press from your father recently, but you need to turn around and face the issue."

"I don't run from anything," she scoffed again.

"Right. You're a daredevil. Guess who gave you the risk-taking gene?"

She shrugged off a sudden bad feeling as she got up. "I don't know what you're talking about."

Rick's gaze was penetrating. "What do you think gambling is? It's a high from taking risks. There's a rush from the brain's rewards system. You like risks, your father likes risks. Different species of risk, but same family."

She had *nothing* in common with her father. How dare Rick make that connection? Even worse, it was one she hadn't seen coming. So she was in a profession with big highs and lows… So she did some of her own stunts…

Rick folded his arms again. "The funny thing is the only situation where you won't take a chance is arranging a meeting with Michael Feran."

"I don't have anything to say to him."

Rick tossed her a disbelieving look. "Of course you do. You have a lifetime's worth of questions to grill and cross-examine him with," he said pleasantly, "but let's just stick with the issue at hand, which is getting him to stop attracting bad press."

She jutted her chin forward. "And how do you propose I do that?"

"I've got some ideas...ones that might appeal to his own self-interest."

"Oh? And since when have you turned into a psychologist?"

Rick braced his hands on his hips. "People management is part of the job description for a Hollywood producer. And stunt work is about getting your mind ready to conquer fear about what could happen to your body. Mind over body."

"Thanks for the tip."

"I also found your Las Vegas showgirl ventriloquist's dummy on the chair where you left her. She had plenty of insights about you," he joked, "but mostly she was content to just sit there and listen."

"She's trashy."

Rick choked on a laugh. "Great. She'll be popular."

"You like them that way," she accused.

"I like you. The dummy is just the repository for the part of your personality that you're afraid you might have inherited from your father."

"Oh, joy."

Rick suddenly sobered. "Your father has a gambling problem, and I understand addiction. Hal went back to drinking too much after Isabel's antics sent him into a spiral."

"You never mentioned there were consequences from Isabel's media stunt." She caught herself at Rick's droll look at the mention of the word *stunt*. "Sorry, bad choice of words. I meant her diva moment for the press."

Rick dropped his hands and shrugged. "Hal is sober

these days after a stint in rehab. Or so I hear through the grapevine…since we don't socialize anymore."

Chiara was starting to understand more and more about Rick's wariness regarding the limelight, actresses and fame in general. An aspiring actress had not only cost him a friendship but had crushed someone he knew.

"I'll even offer my house for a meeting with your father," Rick went on. "Odele can contact Michael Feran and figure out the details, including flying him to Los Angeles. I'll pick up the tab."

She sighed before asking wryly, "So all I have to do is show up?"

"Affirmative."

"Your house isn't even finished!"

"There's landscaping and stuff still to be done, but it's habitable. And more important, it's neutral territory for a private meeting with your father." He raised his eyebrows.

"Is there anything you haven't thought of?" she demanded.

He gave her a lingering look. "There are still a few fantasies that I'm playing with…"

"You know, it's astonishing you come from such a nice family considering—"

"I'm an ego-driven macho stuntman who doesn't respect the rights of actresses to do their own daredevil acts and knows nothing about the uses of double-sided tape?"

"No, considering your dirty mind."

One side of his mouth lifted in a smile. "Well, that, too. I know plenty of uses for tape and blindfolds and silk ties."

Oh…wow.

Rick's eyes crinkled. "Stunts call for diverse props."

"I go propless."

Rick stepped closer and murmured, "Interesting. No need of any assistance?"

She tossed her hair back as sexual energy emanated off him in luscious waves that wrapped themselves around her. "Yes, I go it alone."

He reached out and took a strand of her hair in his fingers. "Might be more fun if it's two."

"Or three or more?" she queried. "What's your limit? A menagerie?"

He gave a soft laugh. "A couple is good. The number of times, on the other hand…limitless, I'd say."

Her breath started coming quick and shallow. *Oh.*

She swallowed and focused on the faint lines fanning out from the corners of his eyes, and the ones bracketing his mouth.

He lowered his head and then touched his lips to hers, and she sighed. He nudged her—once, twice, coaxing a response. *Open. Open.*

Chiara shivered and felt her breasts peak even though only their lips were touching. She leaned in, falling into something that she knew was bottomless…still relatively unknown…and exciting.

Rick deepened the kiss and raked his fingers through her hair, his hand anchoring at the back of her head. They moved restlessly, unable to get enough of each other.

Then Chiara followed Rick's lead as they stripped off their clothes hurriedly, desperate for skin-on-skin contact. When they were down to underwear, he stopped her.

She drank him in from beneath lowered lashes. He was hot and male and vital. There was the ripped midriff, muscular arms, taut legs…the erection pushing against his boxers. Suddenly she needed to catch her breath.

He lowered the straps of her lacy bra and peeled the garment away from her, and then swallowed. "Chiara."

"Make love to me, Rick."

It was all the invitation that he needed. He kissed her with unrestrained passion, pulling her close as her arms wrapped around his neck. And she responded with a hunger of her own, the feel of his arousal against her fueling her passion.

When she broke away, she pushed down her panties and he did the same with his boxers. And then they were tumbling onto the sofa, reaching for each other in a tangle of limbs and desperate passion.

She grasped Rick's erection and began a pumping motion designed to stoke his passion and hers. He was warm, pulsating male—rigid with his need for her.

He tore her mouth from hers and expelled a breath. "Chiara, we've got to slow down or this is going to be over—"

"Before the director yells cut?" she purred. "There is no director, Stunt Stud."

He gave a strangled laugh. "Stunt Stud?"

"It's the name I came up with when I was objectifying you."

"I was going to say to slow down or this will be finished before you're satisfied."

"Worried I won't be able to keep up with you?" In response, she led his hand to her moist heat, already ready for him.

He stilled, and in the next moment, he was pushing her back against the pillows. Then he sheathed himself in one long stroke that had them both groaning.

As Rick hit her core, she arched her back, taking him in.

She followed his lead and the rhythm he set…building and building until she hit her climax in one husky cry.

"Chiara." In the moment after Rick called her name, he groaned, stiffened and then spilled inside her.

He slumped against her, and she cradled him.

Contentment rolled through her—a feeling that had been too elusive in her life until now…

Nine

When they pulled up in Rick's Range Rover to the nearly completed house, Chiara sucked in a breath. *Wow.*

Nervousness about the upcoming meeting with her father, who was scheduled to arrive within the hour, was replaced by happy surprise.

Rick's home wasn't a house but a castle. It was all gray stone and stunning turrets. She loved it.

She was so entranced that Rick had already come around and opened the car door for her before she thought to get out. She could see there was plenty of landscaping yet to be done, but still the effect from the outside was stunning.

"Want to take a look?" Rick teased as she got out. "I'm sure you've seen plenty of impressive homes belonging to famous people."

None shaped like a castle. She looked at the mansion, and then glanced at Rick. "I'm impressed. You have the castle…were you looking for your fairy-tale princess?"

Rick's lips curved. "Only you can answer that, Snow."

He put his hand at her elbow. "Come on, let's look inside. It's done except for minor details, and is sparsely furnished."

Rick's house—*castle*—made her home look like a small and cute cottage.

Chiara gasped when they entered the foyer. She'd seen this house in her mind's eye.

The double-height entry was airy and sunny but also warm and inviting. Done in light colors, it belied the imposing exterior. A curving staircase led to the upper levels, and various open doorways offered glimpses of other parts of the house.

She followed Rick in a circuit of the ground floor. A warm, country-style kitchen with beige cabinetry and a large island connected to a spacious dining room. An immense living room was bifurcated by a two-way fireplace and was made cozy by coffered ceilings in a warm mahogany wood. A library, den, two bathrooms and a couple of storage rooms for staff rounded out most of the lower level. The only thing missing was furnishings for a family...

When they came full circle back to the entry, Chiara's gaze went to the staircase leading to the upper floors.

Rick adopted a teasing expression. "In case you are wondering, a home office with a built-in desk sits at the top of the principal turret. I haven't stashed a fairy-tale princess there."

"Rapunzel?" She tapped her chest. "Wrong fairy tale. I'm Snow, remember?"

Despite her joking, she felt comfortable here—too at home. It was almost enough to make her forget she was about to have one of the most significant meetings of her life.

She was an actress, she reminded herself sternly. She needed to adopt a persona—a shield—and get what she wanted out of this meeting.

As if reading her thoughts, Rick said, "You and your father can meet in the library. It has two club chairs and a coffee table at the moment."

"Okay." Why had she let Rick talk her into this? She knew he had a good point—dragons must be faced—but she wasn't relishing the chance to slay one of hers. She almost gave a nervous laugh at the thought of Rick cast as her knight in shining armor...

Except of course, she didn't believe in such knights or in Prince Charming—or in fairy tales, for that matter. Though she was having a hard time remembering that these days.

At the sound of a car pulling up, Rick said, "That must be him. I had a driver pick him up from the hotel where he stayed last night after his flight from Vegas."

"Oh, good," she managed, and then cleared her throat.

Rick looked at her searchingly, and then cupped her shoulders. "Are you okay?"

She gave him a blinding smile—one she usually reserved for the cameras. "Never better."

"Remember, you're in charge here. You hold the cards."

"Playing cards are what I intend to take out of his hands."

Rick lifted one side of his mouth. "Sorry, bad choice of words. I'll meet him outside and show him into the library."

"Of course." She'd dressed in a navy shirt dress—something she'd pulled out of the closet herself. Because even if Emery hadn't headed off to start her own fashion line, Chiara couldn't imagine asking a stylist about what to wear to a meeting with her estranged father. For some occasions in life, there was *no* fashion rule book.

Rick shoved his hands into his front pockets and nodded, the hair on his forearms revealed by rolled-up shirtsleeves. "Back soon."

When Rick turned away, Chiara walked into the library. And then, because she couldn't think of what else to do, she faced the partially open doorway…and waited.

The sound of quiet voices reached her. Greetings were exchanged…and then moments later, she heard footsteps.

Someone stepped into the library, and she immediately recognized Michael Feran—*her father*.

Her heart beat a thick, steady rhythm. She hadn't expected to feel this nervous. She hated that she did. *He* was the one who should be tense. After all, he'd walked out on her.

She hadn't seen him in person in years, but the media had made sure she hadn't forgotten what he looked like. She wished she could dismiss him as a gaunt and lonely gambling addict wallowing in his misery, but he looked… good.

She silently cursed the Feran genes. They'd graced her with the looks and figure that had propelled her to the top in Hollywood, but they also hadn't skipped a generation with Michael Feran. His salt-and-pepper hair made him look distinguished—a candidate for the father role in any big studio blockbuster.

"Chiara." He smiled. "It's wonderful to see you."

She wished she could say the same. Under the circumstances, it was a forced meeting.

At her continued silence, he went on, "I'm glad you wanted to meet with me."

"Rick convinced me that I needed to have this face-to-face meeting."

Michael Feran smiled. "Yes, how is the stuntman?" So her father read the press about her. *Of course.*

"I met him when I came in. Is he a candidate for future son-in-law?"

Chiara was hit with a sudden realization that left her breathless. She was falling for Rick. She had fallen for him. But they'd never discussed making their fake relationship permanent… She pushed aside the thought that had come with staggering clarity because if she dealt with any more emotion right now, she'd overload.

Instead, she forced herself to focus on Michael Feran. "You're creating unwanted publicity."

"I see."

"Why did you talk to that tabloid about me last year?" It was an unforgivable transgression to add to his list of sins.

"Money would be the easy answer."

She waited.

He heaved a sigh. "The hard one is that I wanted your attention."

"Well, you got it." She folded her arms.

She wasn't going to offer him a seat, and she sure wasn't going to sit down herself, despite the fact that Rick had pointed out this room had comfortable chairs. Michael Feran had to understand this was a halfhearted welcome and not an olive branch.

His gray brows drew together. "I probably didn't go about it in the best way. Believe it or not, it was the only time I took money from a reporter."

"Because you needed to pay off your gambling debts," she guessed.

He looked aggrieved. "It was a mistake. One I don't intend to make again."

She was definitely going to see to it that he didn't spill the beans again.

"Usually I'm winning at the card tables. Enough to pay my bills."

"Naturally. It's what matters in life." She couldn't help the tone of heavy sarcasm in her voice. "But you're generating bad press."

"Chiara—"

"Do you have any idea what it meant for a little girl to wake up wondering if her father had bolted again?" she interrupted, even while she didn't know why she was being so forthright. Maybe it was because, without even realizing it, she'd waited years for this opportunity to confront him about his misdeeds. Just as Rick had suggested.

"Chiara, I know I hurt you." Her father paused. "That's why I stopped showing up after you turned five. I thought that not making a sudden appearance was better than hurting you by coming and going."

He made it seem as if he'd done her a favor. She remembered the betting games they'd played when she was young. *I bet I can throw this pebble farther. Race you to the tree, loser is a rotten egg.* Even then Michael Feran hadn't been able to resist a bet. "You left a wife, a child, a home..."

"You don't know what it's like to walk away from a family—"

"I never would."

"—but you get to reinvent yourself with every film role."

"It's acting." First Rick, now her father. Was there no man in her life who could understand she was just pretending? She *liked* acting.

"You can become someone different, follow your dreams…"

Of course, but… She was so *not* going to feel sorry for him.

Michael sobered. "I can't turn back the clock."

She took a deep breath and addressed the elephant in the room. "Why did you leave that first time?"

She'd never asked because posing the question might be interpreted to mean she cared what the answer was. And she'd spent years making sure she didn't care—ignoring Michael Feran, leading her glamorous life and making sure her image stayed polished. Except he kept putting a dent in it.

Her father looked at her for a long moment, and then heaved another sigh. "I was an ambitious musician and I had dreams to follow, or so I thought."

She could relate to the career and the ambition part. Wasn't that what she'd spent her life pursuing? She loved acting…getting to know a character…and, yes, even getting immersed in a role. Except had she ever gotten to know herself—before Rick convinced her to stop and deal with her problems?

"I had some moderate success. We were the opening act for top singers. But I never broke through in the way you have." There was a note of pride in Michael Feran's voice, before he went on, "You're more successful than I was. Maybe…you always wanted to prove you could be more successful."

Again, she was floored by his observation. Had her drive to succeed been motivated by her need to outperform him—the absentee father? She'd never looked at it that way, but in any case she wasn't about to admit anything, so she said aloud, "You don't know me."

Michael Feran's face turned grave. "I don't. I don't know you, but I'd like to."

"As you said, we can't do a rewind."

"No, no, we can't." His face was grave, sad.

"You'd have to clean up your act if we're going to be any sort of family."

Where had that offer come from? But the minute the words were out of her mouth, her father perked up. *Her father.* Looking at his face, the resemblance was undeniable. She saw herself in the texture of his dark hair sprinkled with gray, in the shape of his face…in the slant of his aquiline nose.

Okay, she did feel sorry for him. He'd done very little for her since she was born, but he'd done even less for himself. Maybe it was for the best he hadn't been in her life. She'd been protected from the gambling…drifting… *Ugh.* It sounded just like life in Tinseltown, except she was committed to clean living even if she was based in Hollywood.

"I'd like to try," he said.

"Well, you're going to do more than try this time, you're going to succeed. You're checking into rehab for your gambling addiction." She felt…powerful…in control…*relieved.* She'd been the helpless kid who'd watched him walk away, not knowing when her father would be back, if ever. But this time, she was calling the shots.

She set down her terms. "I'm prepared to offer you a deal. You get into a facility to help with your problem and agree to stop making headlines. In return, I'll cover your living expenses. The deal will be in writing, and you'll sign."

She had Rick to thank for that bit of inspiration. After their last sexual encounter, they'd sat in her garden and watched the sun set. He'd revealed himself to be more than a lover. He'd shown himself to be a partner and skilled negotiator who'd helped her come up with a plan for this meeting.

"And if I relapse?" There was a hint of vulnerability in her father's eyes that she hadn't expected.

"Then back to rehab you go…for as long as it takes."

He relaxed into a smile. "That's a gamble I'm willing to take."

"Because you have no choice."

"Because I want to improve if that means having a relationship with you, Chiara." As if he sensed she might argue, he continued in a rush, "It's too late for me to help raise you, but I hope we…can be family."

Family. Wasn't that what she'd yearned for when she'd been around the Serenghettis? And now here was her *father* offering the ties that bind. Choked up by emotion, she cleared her throat. "Fine, it's a role I'm willing to take on, but I'm putting you on notice, I expect an Oscar-worthy performance from you as a family member getting a second chance."

An unguarded look of hope crossed her father's face before he responded gruffly, "I have faith that the acting gene runs in the family."

Trouble for Chiara Feran and Her New Man? Sources Close to the Couple Admit That Blending Two Careers Is Causing Stress.

Chiara looked up from her cell phone screen and at Odele's expectant gaze. Her manager was clearly waiting to hear what Chiara thought about the web site that she'd told her to pull up.

They were sitting sipping coffee in the Novatus Studio commissary. Chiara had met Rick here earlier, where postproduction work had begun on *Pegasus Pride*. As an actress, she wasn't involved in picture and sound editing, but since Rick was a producer on this film, she'd tagged along when he'd said he was interested in checking in with Dan to see how things were going. Afterward, she'd made her way to the commissary to wait for Odele, so they could discuss business.

"Well, what do you think?" Odele asked in her raspy voice, nodding to the cell phone still clutched in Chiara's hand.

"You fed this story to *Gossipmonger*?"

Odele nodded. "I needed a way to hint at a possible end to your dalliance with Rick now that your father is going to rehab, while still keeping you in the public eye."

"I'm still wrapping my head around the fact that you didn't know Rick was a wealthy producer!"

Her manager shrugged. "He's a wily one, I'll admit. I thought I knew everyone in this town, but I guess I can be forgiven for not being acquainted with every silent investor in a film production company. Once you told me about the pile that he built in Beverly Hills, I realized I should have had him on my radar, though, I'll give you that."

"We don't need to rush to bring the ax down on the Chiara-Rick story, do we?" Chiara set down her phone, her heart heavy.

Odele was right. She no longer had to worry about her father making bad headlines, and she had Rick to thank for helping to engineer the resolution to that situation. It also meant she no longer *needed* Rick. Wasn't the entire purpose of their fake relationship to divert attention from her father's negative publicity?

Odele gave her a keen look. "No rush…but planning ahead wouldn't hurt, sweetie. Drop a few suggestions in the press that all might not be happily-ever-after. So when the story does end, it won't seem abrupt and it'll be a soft blow."

For whom? Chiara stifled the question even though she couldn't tell if Odele was referring to the hit to her or to her public image. Did it matter? The two were intertwined. She and Rick weren't a *relationship*, after all, but a *story*.

Chiara worried her bottom lip with her teeth. "Has Rick seen this headline?"

Odele adjusted her glasses. "Of course. I ran into him earlier when you'd momentarily left his side. He knows the script. He's known it from the beginning."

Chiara blanched and glanced down at her coffee cup. So he had seen it, and judging from Odele's expression, it hadn't ruffled him. He knew the bargain they'd struck.

Chiara squared her shoulders, seeing with clarity the road ahead—the path that had been there from the beginning. If she made the first move for a clean break, it didn't even have to damage Rick's reputation. She was familiar with how these things worked. A face-saving explanation would be issued. She could even see the headline: *Snow White and Prince Charming Go Their Separate Ways.*

She was doing Rick a favor. He'd never wanted to be tied to an actress…a *celebrity*. He could take his bow and retreat behind the curtain to his nice quiet life—on his large estate in LA. She was being fair.

But the two of them definitely needed to talk. *Soon. Right now.* Before she fell apart…or at least deeper into the warm cocoon of their relationship, where it was *her love* and his…*what*? He'd never come close to saying he loved her. Her heart squeezed and she blinked against a sudden swell of emotion.

She was a highly rated actress—she could do this.

She had sudden flashes from interludes in his arms.

They'd been wonderful…but there'd been no promise of forever, and tomorrow started today. The next chapter.

Chiara looked at her watch. Rick was supposed to meet her here when he was done. And now she had more than enough to say to him…

She forced herself to continue her conversation with Odele, but twenty minutes later when her manager left to make her next meeting, Chiara was relieved…and then nervous as she waited for Rick to show up.

After a quarter of an hour, he walked in, looking casual…relaxed…happy. And as attractive as ever in gray pants and a white shirt.

Chiara swallowed when he gave her a quick peck on the lips.

He sat down across from her at the small table and then lounged back in his chair.

"How did your meeting with Dan end?" she asked brightly.

"Fine. The editor showed up and we discussed plans for the rough cut." He cracked a grin. "Dan's grateful to you for not needing many retakes and keeping us on schedule. Everything's looking great, and with any luck, the box office receipts will reflect it."

They talked about the postproduction work for a few more minutes. Then when the conversation reached a lull, she jumped in and said, "So you must be relieved." He looked at her quizzically, and she shrugged. "Odele's latest planted story in the press."

"I don't give a damn about Odele's PR moves."

His words surprised her, but then hadn't he always been anti-publicity?

"Okay, but we need to talk—" she wet her lips "—because the reason we got together as a couple no longer exists."

She willed him to…what? Get down on bended knee and pledge his eternal love? She'd said all along that she didn't believe in fairy tales.

She smiled tentatively. "Thank you for helping me resolve the impasse with my father. He loves your idea of the two of us partnering to combat his gambling addiction." Her expression turned wry. "Odele likes it, too, of course. She thinks it would be a good way to turn a negative story into a positive one. I could even take it on as a charitable cause."

Rick inclined his head but looked guarded. "Okay, yeah."

"But now that the problem with my father is gone," she said, taking a deep breath, "we no longer have to continue this farce."

Had she really said *farce*? She'd meant to say…

Rick's expression hardened. "Right."

"You disagree?"

He leaned in. "You're still that little girl who is afraid of being abandoned—of someone walking out on her again."

"Please, I know where you're going with this is, and it's not true." It wasn't abandonment she was scared of. She was a grown woman who feared she'd have her heart broken. *Her heart was broken*—because she was in love with Rick and he steered clear of actresses.

Still, wasn't his keen perception what she liked about him? Loved? Yes, *loved*—in addition to his humor, intelligence and daring. They were qualities that appealed to different sides of her personality, even if they made her uncomfortable and yes, infuriated her sometimes.

"What about your overeager admirer?" Rick demanded.

"That's my problem to deal with."

"And mine."

She furrowed her brow. "What do you mean?"

"I mean my role here wasn't solely to play boyfriend but to make sure you stayed safe."

Her eyes narrowed. "Odele hired you?"

"She didn't need to hire me. Do you know how much money I have invested in *Pegasus Pride*? Keeping the main talent safe was inducement enough."

She felt his words like a blow to the chest. All those lingering touches, kisses, and his motivation had been... "You lied to me."

"Not really. You knew I was primarily a fake boyfriend."

"And secondarily a rat."

He raised his eyebrows. "You're offended because I may have had ulterior motives, too, in this game of ours?"

Yes, it had been a game. She was the fool for forgetting that. "I'm annoyed for not being told the whole truth. At least I was clear about my motivations."

"Yes, and you're determined not to rely on any man, aren't you?"

"Was Odele in on this?" she countered.

He shrugged. "We might have had a conversation about how it was in everyone's interest for me to keep an eye on you."

"Everyone's interest but mine," she said bitterly.

Rick set his jaw. "It was in your best interest, too, though you're too pigheaded to admit it."

Her heart constricted. Had he meant those things he'd whispered in the heat of passion—or had she run into the biggest actor of all? Even now, the urge to touch him was almost irresistible.

How had this conversation gotten very serious and very bad so fast? She'd wanted to talk about their charade and give him an out that she hoped he *wouldn't* take. Instead, she was left deflated and wondering whether she'd ever understood him.

Still, she rallied and lifted her chin. "You should be glad I'm setting you free. We never talked about forever, and you don't like fame. You don't want to be dating an actress, even if it's pretend." Two could play at this game. If he was going to cast her as another high-maintenance starlet, albeit one with an aversion to vulnerability where men were concerned, then she could portray him as camera-shy and hung up on celebrity.

He firmed his jaw but took a while to answer. "You're right. Fame isn't my thing." He raked a hand through his hair. "I should have learned that lesson with Isabel."

Chiara held back a wince. In some ways, she understood. The last thing some stars' egos could handle was to be cast in someone else's shade. There were A-list celebrities who refused to date other A-list celebrities for that very reason. Still, it rankled. She was not some random fame-seeker. If she couldn't fall in love with a celebrity, and an anonymous civilian would be put off her fame, who was left? Did she have to settle for a brief interlude with a stuntman with hidden layers? Was that all there was for her?

She lifted her chin, willing it to hold firm. "It's probably best if you moved out at this point. We could do with some space." Then she decided to echo Odele. "It'll plant the seeds for when our breakup is announced."

Rick's expression tightened. "Can't forget to spin it for the press, right?"

Ten

Chiara looked in her bathroom mirror. It had been a month since her breakup with Rick. A sad, depressing but uneventful month...*until now.*

She looked down at the stick in her hand. There was no mistaking the two telltale lines. Two lines that were about to change her life. She was pregnant.

The irony wasn't lost on her. She'd been wrestling with how to combine a career with her desire to start a family. Now the decision had been made for her.

As she disposed of the stick in the bathroom's wastepaper basket, she thought back to the last time she and Rick had been intimate—and her mind whirled.

She'd recently discovered that she'd expelled her contraceptive ring. It had probably gotten dislodged during rigorous sex, and then gone down the toilet afterward without her knowing it. Preoccupied with her breakup with Rick, she hadn't dwelled too much on it. But now...

Chiara looked at herself in the bathroom mirror as she washed her hands. She didn't look any different—*yet*.

She'd spent years trying not to be pregnant. She had a career to tend.

But while it wasn't the best of circumstances, it wasn't the worst, either. *A baby*. She was in her early thirties, financially independent, and had an established career. She'd always wanted a child, and in fact had started worrying that she couldn't see how it was going to happen. It had finally come to pass, but in a way she hadn't planned or foreseen. She'd been drawn to the Serenghettis, and now she was pregnant with an addition to the family. If things had been different—if Rick had loved her—she'd have been overjoyed right now instead of shadowed with worry. Still, she let giddiness seep through her. *A baby*.

She walked into her bedroom and sat on the bed, taking a calming breath. Then she picked up the phone receiver, toyed with it and replaced it. She had to tell Rick, of course…but she just needed time to process the information herself first. This wasn't avoidance or procrastination. At least that's what she kept telling herself…

She got up, paced, went downstairs to poke around in her fridge and then came upstairs again to stare at her phone.

When she couldn't stand it any longer, she called Odele and spilled all to her manager.

Odele was surprisingly equanimous at the news.

"Don't you know this means I'll be too pregnant to take on another action movie?" Chiara demanded, because she knew career suicide was at the top of Odele's list of sins.

"You wanted to stop doing them anyway."

Chiara lowered her shoulders. "Yes, you're right."

"What was Rick's reaction?"

"I haven't told him yet. I've been working up to that part."

There was a long pause on the line as Odele processed this information. "Well, good luck, honey. And remember, it's best to eat the frog."

"We fairy-tale types are supposed to kiss them, not eat them," Chiara joked weakly. "But okay, I get your point about doing the hard stuff first and getting it over with."

"Exactly."

"I just…" She took a deep breath. "I'm not sure I'm prepared to make that call to Rick." *Just yet.*

"I'm always here to help."

"Thanks, Odele."

The next day, Chiara wasn't feeling calm exactly, but she'd come down from her crazy tumult of emotions. She ventured out to her doctor's office for a consultation, having gotten herself an early appointment after there was a cancellation.

She didn't go into detail with the staff on the phone. She knew how juicy a piece of gossip a pregnant actress was, and medical staff had been known for leaks despite confidentiality laws. Out of an abundance of caution, she wore sunglasses and a scarf when she showed up for her appointment—because the paparazzi also knew that staking out the offices of doctors to the stars was a great way to get a scoop, or at least a tantalizing photo.

Dr. Phyllia Tribbling confirmed she was pregnant and assured her that everything was fine. She told her to come back when she was a few weeks further along.

Chiara found she was calmer after the doctor's visit, no doubt due to the obstetrician's soothing manner.

She spent the rest of the day researching pregnancy

online. She didn't dare visit a bookstore—and certainly not a baby store—because of the risk of being spotted by the press. Instead, she stayed home and took a nap. She should have read the signs in her unusual weariness lately, but pregnancy had been the last thing on her mind.

When she woke late in the day, she checked herself for any sign of morning sickness, but didn't feel a twinge. With the all-clear, she fixed herself a salad and a glass of water. Walking into the den, she sat on the sofa and placed the food on a coffee table.

After a few bites, she scrolled through the day's news on her phone.

When she came across a headline about herself, it took her a moment to process it, but then she nearly collapsed against the cushions.

Chiara Feran Is Pregnant!

She scanned the article and reread it, and then with shaking fingers, called her manager.

"Odele," she gasped. "How did *Gossipmonger* get this info?"

"They probably saw you exiting the doctor's office, sweetie," Odele said calmly. "You know, paparazzi like to stalk the offices of celebrity gynecologists and obstetricians."

"I just got back! Not even the gossip sites operate that fast." Chiara shook her head, even though her manager wasn't there to see it. "I should have worn a wig."

"I don't think that would have done the trick," Odele said drily. "Now, not getting knocked up to begin with, that would have done it."

Chiara's eyes narrowed. "You didn't feed them this story, did you?"

"No."

"But did you slip someone a tip to watch the doctor's office?" Chiara pressed.

"You have a suspicious mind."

"Did you?"

"I might have mentioned Dr. Tribbling has seen a lot of business lately."

"Odele, how could you!"

"Why don't you call Mr. Stuntman and let him know he isn't shooting blanks?" Odele answered sweetly.

"Why?" Chiara was close to wailing. She'd done it enough times on-screen to know when she was nearing the top of the emotional roller coaster.

"Better to squelch the rumor fast that you've broken up with Rick. Otherwise we'll be putting out fires for months. The press loves a story about a spurned pregnant woman going it alone."

Chiara took a breath. "Rick and I are broken up. Period."

"Not as far as the press is concerned. They're going to love stringing your two names together in real and virtual ink."

"And that's the only thing that matters, right?"

"No…it isn't." Odele sighed, softening. "Why don't you talk to him? Then reality and public perception can be aligned."

Chiara steeled herself and took a deep gulping breath. "Odele, you're fired."

They were words she'd never thought she'd say, but she'd had enough of manipulation…of public scrutiny… of Hollywood…and yes, of one stuntman in particular.

"Sweetie, you're overwrought, and it can't be good for the baby. Take time to think about it."

"Goodbye, Odele."

Yes, she'd calm down…right after she burst into tears.

* * *

Rick spit out his morning coffee. The hot liquid hit the oatmeal bowl like so many chocolate chips dotting cookie batter.

He prided himself on being unflappable. A cool head and calm nerves were a must in stunt work, particularly when something unexpected happened. But as with everything concerning Chiara, levelheadedness walked out the door with his better judgment.

He looked around his West Hollywood rental, still his home since Chiara had canceled his roommate privileges and his Beverly Hills place wasn't finished. The rain hitting the windows suited his mood. Or rather, it fit the rest of his life, which stretched out in a dull gray line in front of him. He got the same adrenaline rush from being with Chiara as he did from stunts, which probably explained the colorlessness of his days since their breakup.

Except now… *Chiara was pregnant.*

Rick was seized by turns with elation and shock. A baby. His and Chiara's. He was going to be a father.

Of course he wanted kids. He'd just never given much thought to how it would happen. He was thirty-three and at some point he'd be too old for stunt work. Sometime between now and then, his life would transition to something different. He figured he'd meet a woman, get married and have kids. Except along the way, he'd never foreseen a fake relationship with a maddening starlet who would then turn up pregnant.

Suddenly someday was now…and it wasn't supposed to happen this way—knocking up an actress tethered to fame when they weren't even married, living together or talking about forever.

Chiara infuriated and amused him by turns, the combustible passion between them feeding on itself. They were good together. Hell, he'd thought things had been heading to…something. But never mind. She'd made it clear he'd served his purpose and now there was no role for him in her life.

Now, though, whether she liked it or not, he had a place. She was pregnant.

He wondered whether this announcement was a public relations ploy, and then dismissed the idea. Chiara had too much integrity. He knew that much even though they were no longer a couple.

Still, she hadn't had the decency to tell him, and his family would be reading the news online and in print, just like everyone else. Her handlers hadn't yet sent out a second volley in this juicy story, but already he was looking like a jerk. *He just broke up with her, and now his ex-girlfriend has announced she's pregnant.* That's what everyone would think. *Maybe he left her because there was a surprise baby.*

There was one thing to do—and he wasn't waiting for an invitation. He still had the passcode to Chiara's front gate, unless she'd changed it.

Rick got his wallet, keys and phone, and then made a line for the door. He'd woken up this morning moody and out of sorts—more or less par for the course for him since his breakup with Chiara, but that was even before realizing he'd been served up as delicious gossipy dish for his neighbors to consume along with their morning coffee.

He cursed. "Moody" had just given way to "flaming-hot pissed off."

He made record time on the way to Chiara's house, adrenaline pumping in his veins. He knew from experience working on stunts that he was operating on a full head of steam. He needed to force himself to take a breath, slow down, collect his thoughts… *Hell.*

A baby. And she hadn't told him.

When he got to Chiara's front gate, rationality returned enough for him to pause a moment and call her from his cell. The last thing he needed was for Chiara to assume her surprise visitor was her stalker.

"It's Rick, and I'm coming in," he announced when she picked up, and then hit the end button without waiting for a response.

When he got to the house, the front door was unlocked and he let himself in.

He found Chiara in the kitchen, dressed in an oversize sweater and leggings, a mug in one hand.

His gaze went to her midriff, before traveling back to her face. Not that she would be showing yet—but she did look weary, as if she hadn't slept well. He resisted the urge to stride over and wrap her in his arms.

"I assume you unlocked the door for me when I called from the gate and that you don't have a standing invitation for your overeager fan to walk in." It was a mild reproach, much less than he wanted to say.

She set the mug down. "What do you think?"

"You're *pregnant*." The last word reverberated through the room like the sound of a brass bell.

Chiara blanched.

"I found out the news with the rest of the world."

"I didn't have time to call you first." She wrung her hands. "The story broke so fast."

"You could have called me when the pregnancy test came back positive."

She hugged her midriff with her arms. "I wanted to be sure. I only went to the doctor yesterday."

"How did this happen?" he asked bluntly.

She raised her eyebrows. "I think you know."

"Right." *Mind-blowing sex.*

"My contraceptive ring accidentally fell out, and I didn't notice. I didn't give it much thought when I realized what happened." She shrugged. "I've always wanted kids. I guess it's happening sooner than I anticipated."

A very real sense of relief washed over him at her words. She wanted this baby, but birth control failure had led to very real consequences for the both of them. "You're going to announce we're still together."

She blinked. "Why?"

"Why? Because I don't want to look like a first-class jerk in front of the world, that's why."

"That your reason?" She appeared bewildered and a flash of hurt crossed her face.

"Aren't you the one who has been all about public image until now?" he tossed back. "Maybe this pregnancy is another PR stunt."

She dropped her arms, her expression turning shocked and offended. *"What?"*

"Are you saying Odele didn't plant the story in *Gossipmonger*?"

"I didn't know anything about it!"

He let another wave of satisfaction wash over him before he turned all-business. "Anyway, it doesn't matter. We're going to start acting and pretending like we never have before—the happy couple expecting a bundle of joy."

She lifted her chin. "I don't need your help."

He knew Chiara had the resources, but that was beside the point. "Sweetheart," he drawled, making the endearment sound ironic, "whether you want it or not, you've got it."

"Or?"

"Odele will be needing medication to deal with the ugly media firestorm."

"And will a wedding in Vegas follow?" she asked sarcastically. "I'll need to put Odele on retainer again."

"Whatever works."

She threw up her hands. "It's ridiculous. How long do you plan for this to go on?"

Until he figured out his next steps. He was buying himself time. "Until I don't look like a loser who abandoned his girlfriend the minute she turned up pregnant."

Rick paced in the nearly empty library of his multimillion-dollar new home. Raking his fingers through his hair, he stared out the French doors at the blazing sunshine bathing his new property in light. He'd just met with a landscaper and walked over the grounds. This morning, his appointment had been uppermost in his mind…until he'd checked the news.

Still, what was it all for? He'd bought and renovated this house as a keen investor…but now it felt insignificant. Because what really mattered in his life was half a city away. *Pregnant. With his baby.*

His gaze settled on the two upholstered armchairs. He'd brokered a cease-fire and even a rapprochement between Chiara and her father, but he couldn't figure out how to dig himself out of a hole—except by muscling in on Chiara earlier and ordering her to get back together until he figured things out. But then what?

His cell phone buzzed, and he fished it out of his pocket.

"Rick." Camilla Serenghetti's voice sounded loud and clear.

Rick hadn't even bothered to look at who was calling. He hadn't had a chance to figure out what to say to his family, but it was showtime.

"I read I'm going to be a grandma, but I know it can't be true. My son would have told me such happy news."

Of course.

"I told Paula at the hairdresser, 'No, no, don't listen to *Gossipmonger*. I know the truth.'" Pause. "Right?"

Rick raked a hand through his hair. "I just found out myself, Mom."

His mother muttered something in Italian. "So it is true? *Congratulazioni*. I can't believe it. First Cole has a surprise wedding. Now you have a surprise baby."

"You still have Jordan and Mia to count on." His remaining siblings might go a more traditional route.

"No, no. I'm happy...*happy* about the baby." His mother sounded emotional. "But no more surprises. *Basta*—enough, okay?"

"I'd like nothing better," he muttered, because he'd gotten the shock of his life today.

When he got off the phone, he texted his siblings.

The gossip is true, hang tight.

He knew he had to deal with stamping out questions—or at least holding them off—until he figured things out. Before he could put away his cell, though, his phone rang again.

"Rick."

"What can I do for you?" Rick recognized the voice, and under the circumstances, Chiara's father was the last person he wanted to have a conversation with. Michael Feran had his number from when he'd helped broker the meeting with Chiara, but he'd never expected the older man to use it.

"This is an odd request."

"Spit it out." The words came out more harshly than Rick intended, but it had already been a hell of a day.

Michael Feran cleared his throat. "I can't get in touch with Chiara."

Great. "What did you do, Michael?"

"Nothing. I called her at eleven, when we'd agreed to talk."

Rick knew Chiara had opted to periodically touch base with her father now that she was paying his bills.

"No one answered."

"I was heading out, and I'm not far from her house. I'll swing by." He didn't examine his motives. Michael Feran had given him another excuse to see Chiara, and maybe this time they could have a more satisfactory meeting— one that didn't end with her turning away and him walking out.

Besides, she was pregnant. His gut tightened. She could really be in trouble.

"Good." An edge of relief sounded in the older man's voice. "And I understand congratulations are in order."

"To you, too."

"Thank you. I just got an invite to be a father again. I didn't expect being a *grandfather* to be part of the bargain. At least not so soon."

"I'm sure," Rick replied curtly. "But one thing at a time. I'll go check on the mother-to-be now."

After ending the call, Rick made for the front door. For the second time that day, he found himself racing to Chiara's house, adrenaline thrumming through his veins.

She was fine. She had to be fine. She was probably dealing with pregnancy symptoms and in no mood to talk to her father. In the meantime, he might have another opportunity to set things to rights between them.

Marry me. The words popped into his head without thought, but of course they were the right ones. Right, natural...logical.

Exiting his house, he got behind the wheel of his Range Rover for the drive to Brentwood. Fortunately, traffic was light, and he reached Chiara's house faster than he expected.

When he reached her front gate, he tried calling her again. And when she didn't answer, he stabbed in the security code, jaw tightening.

Moments later, he pulled up in front of Chiara's house and saw her car parked there. His gut clenched. *Why isn't she answering her phone?*

Noticing the patio door open at the side of the house, he strode toward it...and then froze for a second when he realized there was broken glass on the ground.

Stepping inside the house, he could sense someone was there. Then he saw a man reflected in a mirror down the hall. The intruder crouched and ducked into the next room.

Rick's blood pumped as he raced forward. Damn it, he'd be lucky if this was an ordinary street burglar. But the brief glimpse he'd caught said this guy resembled Chiara's stalker.

Chiara came out of the marble bath in her bedroom suite and then walked into the dressing room. She pulled underwear and exercise clothes from a dresser and slipped into them.

In order to help her relax, she'd just taken a shower— and intended to take another after her workout. Her doctor had cleared her for moderate exercise in her first trimester.

After her argument with Rick earlier, she'd been torn

between wanting to cry and to wail in frustration. Her life had been a series of detours and blind turns lately...

She went downstairs to her home gym, and then glanced out the window at the overcast day. It suited her mood. Even the weather seemed ready to shed some tears...

Suddenly she spotted a hunched figure darting across the lawn. Frowning, she moved closer to the window. She wasn't expecting anyone. She had a regular cleaning service, and a landscaper who came once a week, but she didn't employ a live-in caretaker. There was no reason to, since she was often away on a movie set herself. Still, thanks to her fame, and now a sometime stalker, she had high fences, video cameras, an alarm system and a front gate with a security code. Even if she no longer had a bodyguard...

How had he gotten in?

As Chiara watched, the intruder slipped around the side of the house and out of view. Moments later, she heard a crash and froze. She ran over to the exercise room door and locked it.

Spinning around, she realized how vulnerable she was. Her workout clothes didn't have pockets, and she'd left her cell phone upstairs. She'd also never put a landline extension in this room, because there'd seemingly been no need to. The gym was on the first floor and faced a steep embankment outside. While it would be hard for someone to get in, it also meant she was trapped.

She heard the distant noise of someone moving around in the house. Her best bet was to stay quiet. She hoped whoever it was wouldn't look in here—at least not immediately. In the meantime, she had to figure out what to do... If the intruder wandered upstairs, perhaps she could make a dash for freedom and quietly call 911.

She heard the sound of a car on the gravel drive and almost sobbed with relief. Whoever it was must have known the security code at the front gate. Her heart jumped to her throat. *Rick?*

He didn't know about the intruder. He could be hurt, or worse, killed. She had to warn him.

Only a minute later, voices—angry and male—sounded in the house, but the confrontation was too indistinct for her to make out what was said.

"Chiara, if you're here, don't move!" Rick's voice came to her from the rear of the house.

She heard a scuffle. Something crashed as the combatants seemed to be fighting their way across the first floor.

Ignoring Rick's order, she wrenched open the door to the exercise room and dashed out in the direction of the noise. The sight that confronted her in the den made her heart leap to her throat all over again. Rick was pummeling Todd Jeffers, and while Rick appeared to have the upper hand, his opponent wasn't giving up the fight.

She looked around for a way to help and found herself reaching for a small marble sculpture that her interior decorator had positioned on a side table.

Grabbing it, she approached the two men. As her stalker staggered and then righted himself, she brought the sculpture down on the back of his head with a resounding thud.

Jeffers staggered again and fell to his knees, and Rick landed a knee jab under his chin. Her stalker sprawled backward, and then lay motionless.

Rick finally looked up at her. He was breathing heavily, and there was fire in his eyes. "Damn it, Chiara, I told you not to come out!"

As scared as she was, she had her own temper to deal

with. "You're welcome." Then she looked at the figure at their feet. "Sweet heaven, did I kill him?"

"Heaven is unlikely the place he'll be," Rick snarled.

"So I killed him?" she squeaked.

Rick bent to examine Jeffers and then shook his head. "No, but he's passed out cold."

She leaped for the phone even though what she wanted to do was throw up from sudden nausea. "I have to call 911."

"Do you have any rope or something else we can tie him up with?" Rick asked. "He's unconscious but we don't know for how long."

With shaky fingers, she handed him the receiver. While Rick called the police, she ran to get some twine she kept for wrapping presents. Her uninvited guest needed to be hog-tied, not decorated with a pretty bow, but it was all she had.

As she passed through the house, she noticed some picture frames had been repositioned—as if her stalker had stopped to admire them—and some of her clothes had been moved. Chiara shuddered. Likely Jeffers's obsession with her stuff had bought her time—time enough to stay hidden in the gym until Rick arrived.

Eleven

Chiara sat in her den attempting to get her bearings. Todd Jeffers was on his way to prison, not least because he'd violated a restraining order by scaling her fence, taking advantage of the fact that her alarm system had been off and she'd been ignoring the video cameras. Breaking and entering, trespassing... Thanks to Rick, the police would throw the book at him.

While Rick walked the remaining police to the door, she called Odele. She needed someone who would deal with the inevitable press attention. And even though she'd uttered the words *you're fired*, she and Odele were like family—and there was nothing like a brush with danger and violence to mend fences. She filled in her manager on what had happened, and Odele announced she would drive right over—both to get the fuller story, and perhaps because she sensed Chiara needed a shoulder to lean on.

Because Rick wasn't offering one—he continued to look mad as hell.

She knew she was lucky Rick had shown up at the right moment. She'd been in the shower when her father had attempted to reach her, and because he was worried she hadn't picked up, he'd called Rick. Michael Feran had done nothing for her...until today, when he may have saved her life. The ground beneath her had shifted, and there hadn't even been a major seismological event in LA. Forgetting about her scheduled call with her father had been a lucky break because minutes later she'd had an intruder in her house.

When Rick walked back in, Chiara hugged her arms tight across her chest as she sat on her couch.

He looked like a man on a short leash. The expression on his face was one she'd never seen before—not even in the middle of a difficult stunt. He was furious, and she wondered how much of it was directed at her.

"Thanks," she managed in a small voice.

"Damn it, Chiara!" Rick ran his hand through his hair. "What the hell? I told you to get extra security."

"You were it. I didn't have time to replace you...yet."

"You didn't have time? There's been a court order in place for weeks!"

She stood up. "Sarcastic stuntmen willing to moonlight as bodyguard and pretend boyfriend are hard to come by."

"Well, you almost gained an unwelcome husband!" Rick braced his hands at his sides. "According to the police, your Romeo had picked a wedding date and drafted a marriage announcement before he showed up today."

Chiara felt the hairs on the back of her neck rise. As a celebrity, she'd gotten some overzealous adulation in the past, but this was beyond creepy. "Don't lecture me."

She was frustrated, overwhelmed and tired—nearly shaking with shock and fear. She needed comfort but Rick was scolding her. It was all too much.

Rick crouched beside her. "We need to resolve this."

She raised her chin. "My stalker is behind bars. So that's another reason I don't need you anymore, I guess."

Except she did. She loved him. But he'd offered nothing in return, and she couldn't stay in a relationship based on an illusion. She'd learned this much from Tinseltown: she didn't want make-believe. She didn't want a relationship made for the press, and the false image of a happy couple expecting their first child. She wanted true love.

Rick stood up, a closed look on his face. He thrust his hands in his pockets. "Right, you don't need me. You'll never need any man. Got it. Your father may be back in your life, but you always stand on your own."

She said nothing. In her mind, though, she willed him to give her the speech that she really wanted. *I love you. I can't live without you. I need you.*

He braced his hands on his sides. "We're stuck playing out this drama, the two of us. The press junket for *Pegasus Pride* is coming up, and we don't want to be the story instead of the movie. I'll move back in with you here until my house is ready. We'll do promo for the movie and then nest until the baby arrives. All the while, we're back to Chiara and Rick, the happy expectant couple, as far as the press is concerned."

She lifted her chin again. "Got it."

The only thing that saved her from saying more was Odele breezing in the front door and descending like a mother hen.

"Oh, honey," her manager exclaimed.

Chiara looked at her miserably and then eyed Rick.

"I'm glad you're here because Rick was just leaving to pack. He's moving back in with me."

"I'll be back soon."

She'd dreamed about their getting back together, but it wasn't supposed to happen like this.

Rick looked around his West Hollywood rental, debating what to pack next. The movers could do the rest.

Chiara's stalker may have been arrested, but the threat to Rick's own sanity remained very real. He'd always prided himself on being Mr. Cool and Unflappable—with nerves of steel in the face of every stunt. But there was nothing cool about his relationship with Chiara.

"So the first Serenghetti grandbaby, and it was a surprise." Jordan shook his head as he taped a box together. "Mom must be beside herself."

His brother happened to be in town for another personal appearance, so he'd come over to help Rick pack. Together, they were surrounded by boxes in the small living room.

"Last I heard, she was trying three new recipes." Rick knew cooking was stress relief for his mother.

Damn it, he wished the news had broken another way. Yet, if Chiara was to be believed, it wasn't her doing that the cat was out of the bag.

Jordan shook his head. "Of course Mom is cooking. First Cole throws an unexpected wedding, now you hit her with a surprise grandchild. She's probably trying to figure out what went wrong with her parenting recipe— was she missing an ingredient?"

"Hilarious," Rick remarked drily. "She's got two more kids she can hang her hopes on."

Jordan held up his hands as if warding off a bad omen. "You mean, she has Mia to help her out."

Rick shrugged. "Whatever."

His brother looked around. "You know we could just throw this stuff in a van ourselves instead of using movers."

"Yeah, but I've got more pressing problems at the moment."

Jordan cocked his head. "Oh, yeah, daddy duty. But that doesn't start for another...?"

"Seven months or more," Rick replied shortly.

Chiara had gotten pregnant in Welsdale or soon after. There'd been plenty of opportunities. Once the floodgates had opened, they hadn't been able to keep their hands off each other.

"You know, I was debating what housewarming gift to get you. Now I'm thinking you need one of those dolls they use in parenting classes...to practice diapering and stuff."

"Thanks for the vote of confidence."

"Well, you and Chiara are definitely in the express lane of relationships," Jordan remarked.

"The relationship was a media and publicity stunt."

Jordan's face registered his surprise. "Wow, the work of a stuntman never ends. I'm impressed by your range."

"Put a lid on it, Jordan."

His brother flashed a grin. "Still, a publicity stunt... but Chiara winds up pregnant? How do you explain that one?"

"I was also supposed to protect her from her stalker friend. That was the real part."

Jordan picked up his beer and toasted him with it. "Well, you did do that. I suppose one thing led to another?"

"Yeah, but it could have gone better." The nut job had

already been in Chiara's house when he'd arrived. As for the relationship part…

"Or worse."

Rick's hand curled at his side. Damn it. Why hadn't Chiara listened to him and taken more precautions? Because she was hardheaded.

Jordan shook his head. "I can't believe I had to get the news from *Gossipmonger*."

"Believe it. Chiara's team has a contact there."

"Still, I figured I'd hear it from you. I thought the brotherly bond counted for something," Jordan said in a bemused tone.

"You didn't need to know it was a publicity stunt."

His brother shrugged. "It seemed real enough to me. So what are you going to do?"

"For the moment, I'm moving back in with her. What does it look like I'm doing?"

Jordan nodded, his expression blank. "So you're muscling back into her life. Do you know an approach besides caveman-style?"

"Since when are you a relationship expert?"

"This calls for a grand gesture."

Rick nearly snorted. "She's practically announced she doesn't need a knight on a horse."

Jordan shrugged. "She doesn't need you, you don't need her, but you want each other. Maybe that's what you have to show her." His brother's lips quirked. "You know, upend the fairy tale. Show up on a horse and tell her that she needs to save you."

Rick frowned. "From what?"

Jordan grinned. "Yourself. You've been bad-tempered and cranky."

"So says the Serenghetti family philosopher who only does shallow relationships."

Jordan placed his hand over his heart. "My guru powers only work with others."

Rick threw a towel at his brother, who caught it deftly. "Get packing."

Still, he had to admit Jordan had given him some ideas.

"You look like a miserable pregnant lady," Odele remarked.

"My best role yet." Chiara felt like a mess…or rather, her life was one. Ironically the situation with her father was the only part she'd straightened out.

After yesterday's drama, Odele had stayed over, feeling Chiara needed someone in the house with her. And Chiara was thankful for the support. She'd let herself cry just once…

Chiara toyed with her lunch of salmon and fresh fruit. Outside the breakfast nook, the sun shone bright, so unlike yesterday. Her mood should have picked up, too, but instead she'd been worried about spending the next months with Rick in her house—falling apart with need, so unlike her independent self.

"I hate to see you make a mistake," Odele remarked from across the table.

Was that regret in her manager's voice? "You sound wistful."

"I'm speaking from experience. There was one who got away. Don't let that be your situation."

"Oh, Odele."

"Don't *Odele* me," her manager said in her raspy voice. "These days there's a fifty-three-year-old editor at one of those supermarket rags who is just waiting for a date with yours truly."

Chiara managed a small laugh. "Now, that's more like it."

Odele's eyes gleamed. "He's too young for me."

"At fiftysomething? It's about time someone snatched him out of the cradle."

"I'll think about it…but this conversation isn't about me, honey. It's about you."

Chiara sighed. "So how am I supposed to avoid making a mistake? Or are you going to tell me?"

"I've got an idea. You and Rick are meant to be together. I've thought so for a long time." She shook her head. "That's why—"

"This pregnancy is a sign from the heavens?"

"No, your moping expression is."

Chiara set down her fork. "I guess I'm not as good an actress as I thought."

"You're a great actress, and I've lined up Melody Banyon at *WE Magazine*. She can come here for an interview tomorrow." Her manager harrumphed. "My second attempt at making you and Rick see reason."

"Another of your schemes, Odele?" she said, and then joked, "Haven't we had enough of the press?"

"Trust me, you're going to like this plan better than my idea of lighting a fire under your stuntman with the pregnancy news, but it's up to you what you want to say."

When Odele explained what she had in mind, Chiara nodded and then added her own twist…

By the next morning, Chiara was both nervous and excited. She felt as if she was jumping off a cliff—in fact, it was not so different from doing a movie stunt.

Sitting in a chair in her den facing Melody Banyon, she smoothed her hands down the legs of her slacks. It was almost a replay of her last interview with the reporter... except Rick wasn't here.

"Are you pregnant?"

There it was. She was about to give her confirmation to the world. "Yes, I am."

"Congratulations."

"I'm still in my first trimester."

"And how are you feeling?"

Chiara sucked in a shaky breath. "Good. A little queasy but that's normal."

Melody tilted her head and waited.

"Even though this pregnancy was unexpected," she went on, "I've always wanted children. And, you know, I've learned you can't plan everything in life."

"You were dating a stuntman working on one of your movies. Rick Serenghetti?"

"Yes. Rick did me an enormous favor. It started as a PR stunt. Rick was supposed to pose as my boyfriend to distract the press from stories about my father and his gambling. I know celebrities aren't supposed to admit to doing things for publicity, but I want to clear the air."

This was *so* hard. But she had to do it. Odele had convinced her to talk honestly about her feelings for Rick, but Chiara had thought it was important to come clean publicly about the whole charade. Risky, but important.

"You say *started*..."

"Even though I didn't know it, Rick signed up for our make-believe because he also wanted to protect me from a stalker. It was a threat that I wasn't taking seriously enough."

"But Todd Jeffers is now charged with serious crimes. Are you relieved?"

"Yes, of course. And I'm so grateful to Rick for tackling Jeffers when he broke into my house."

"And how is your father doing?"

"Great. We met, and he agreed to go into rehab for his addiction. I'm proud of him." She had Rick to thank there, too.

Melody leaned forward. "So with your father addressing his addiction, and your stalker behind bars, you and Rick are…?"

Chiara gave a nervous laugh. "Somewhere along the way, I fell in love with Rick. I love him."

Melody leaned forward and shut off her voice recorder. "Perfect."

Chiara blew a breath. "You think so?"

The reporter gave her a sympathetic look. "I know so. A headline will appear on the *WE Magazine* site in a few hours, and then we'll go to press with the print edition for the end of the week."

Hours. That's all she had before Rick and the world would know what lay in her heart.

Best to keep occupied. She still needed to put in motion the last part of the plan, which she'd suggested to Odele.

Rick nearly fell out of his seat. *I love him.*

He'd followed the news link to *WE Magazine* in Odele's text and got a sucker punch.

Looking around his now nearly bare and sparsely furnished rental, he felt the swoosh of air that he normally associated with a high-altitude stunt.

His cell phone rang, and it was Melody Banyon from *WE Magazine.*

"Do you have a public comment on Chiara Feran's interview with us? She confirmed her pregnancy."

Yes. No. I don't know. "I won't ask how you got my number."

"I think you know the answer," Melody replied, amusement in her voice.

Odele, of course.

And then with sudden clarity, he realized going for broke was the thing to do. His concerns about privacy, getting manipulated by the press, or even publicity-hungry actresses, flew out the window. He didn't have time to think about whether this was another of Odele's PR moves. He was done with charades, make-believe and pretend.

"Anything you'd like to say for the record?" Melody prompted again.

"Yes. My feelings for Chiara were real from the beginning. There was no pretending on my part."

"And the baby news?"

Yeah, wow. Somehow tomorrow was today…but he couldn't be more elated with every passing day. "It may not have been planned, but I'm happy about it."

"Are you Prince Charming?"

He laughed ruefully. "I've enjoyed my privacy up until now. And I've liked keeping my aliases under wraps, but things are becoming public knowledge."

Melody cleared her throat. "Okay, off the record now… I wouldn't let Chiara get away if I were you. She's scared, but I've seen you two together. You belong together."

"And here I thought Chiara and I had done a good snow job convincing you that we really were a couple."

"Not as good a snow job as you two have done on each other," Melody replied.

Yeah. And suddenly he knew he had to follow through on the idea that Jordan had given him…

"Give me until tomorrow before you publish my comment, Melody. I want Chiara to be the first to know."

"Of course!" the reporter responded with a smile in her voice.

Rick barely heard her. His mind was already buzzing with ideas for props for his next stunt.

Chiara was tense. Controlling one's image was paramount in Hollywood, and she'd just blown her cover. *I love him*... And the entire world knew. There was nowhere to hide.

She wrung her hands as she stared out her kitchen window. *WE Magazine* had published parts of her interview online late yesterday. It had been hours...and still no word from Rick.

He could humiliate her. He could issue a stunning rejection that handed her heart back to her.

Picking up the phone, she made a lifeline call to her manager.

"Oh, Odele, what have you gotten me into?" she moaned.

"Have you looked at social media?"

"Are you kidding? It's the last thing I can bring myself to peek at."

"Well, you should. The confirmation of your pregnancy has taken the internet by storm, of course."

"Great," she said weakly.

"Yup, but the viral storm is turning in your favor, sweetie. People are applauding your honesty."

"About being a fraud?"

"You were honest about the phoniness of celebrity culture."

Chiara closed her eyes. She'd gone viral as a recovering liar...and people loved it. "I'm afraid to leave the house."

"You weren't scared when you had a stalker, but now you are?"

Of course she was. She hadn't heard from Rick. The ax could still fall.

Then a distant sound reached her, and she frowned. "Hold on, Odele."

It sounded like hoof beats. *Impossible.*

She peeked out the window. A rider on a white horse was coming up the drive.

The *clomp* of hooves sounded louder as horse and rider came closer. It couldn't be...but her heart knew it was. "Odele... I've got to go."

"What's the matter, honey?" Chiara could practically hear the frown in her manager's voice. "Do I need to send the police?"

"Um, that won't be necessary. I think I'm being rescued..."

"What...?"

"It's Rick on a white horse...bye."

"Well, I'll be damned. And he didn't even give me a heads-up so I could send a photographer to snap the moment."

"We'll do the scene over for you."

"Great, because romances are my favorite."

"I'd never have known from the way you've pushed me to do action flicks—"

"And you met a hunky stuntman in the process."

"Odele, I have to go!"

Her manager laughed. "Good luck, honey."

Rushing to the front door, Chiara took a moment to glance at herself in the hall mirror. Her eyes were bright, but she wished she could have looked more polished than she did in stretch pants and a T-shirt. Still, at least these clothes continued to fit her.

She took a deep breath and opened the door, stepping outside.

Rick stopped his horse in front of her, a smile playing at his lips.

Chiara placed her hands on her hips. "You got a horse through my front gate...really?"

"I still have the code. You've got to change it if you don't want to keep having unexpected visitors."

She nodded at the animal that he sat astride, her insides buzzing. "And you rode him along canyon roads to my house?"

"Hey, I'm a stuntman."

She met his gaze head-on. "And this is one of your stunts?"

"Jordan told me to get on a horse. Before I could do it or go with the backup plan of coming by with a wood boyfriend for Ruby, you had your interview with *WE Magazine*," he said, not answering her directly. "But I thought I'd...accommodate you anyway."

She tilted her head. "Accommodate how?"

He swung down, all lithe physique, and then pulled her into his arms and kissed her.

She leaned into him, kissing him back.

When they broke apart, he said, "I love you."

She blinked back sudden emotion, and joked, "You should if you rode a horse here."

"It took me a while to recognize it, but then you were put in danger by Jeffers." His face blazed with emotion. "Damn it, Chiara, I could have lost you."

She nodded, swallowing against the lump in her throat.

"I let my experience with Isabel color my perspective even though it was becoming increasingly obvious you couldn't be more different."

She gave a watery smile. "Well, you can be forgiven

for that one. Thanks to Odele, I was using you to manipulate the press, too."

"In the beginning, yeah. But you had guts and determination. Plus more and more layers that I wanted to uncover even though I kept trying to pigeonhole you as just another evil starlet."

"Who, me? Snow White?" she said playfully.

He cracked a smile and then gave her another quick kiss.

She braced her hands on his chest. "Thank you for tackling Jeffers...twice. I didn't take the risk seriously enough because I wasn't going to let you tell me what to do. But you helped me save my father from himself." When he started to say something, she placed a finger on his lips to stop him. "Thank you for coming into my life and dealing with all the craziness of fame. I was so afraid of being vulnerable and getting hurt."

He grasped her wrist and kissed her hand.

"I love you. I was falling in love with you and it scared me to feel so much," she finished.

"We're getting married."

She gave an emotional laugh—happiness bubbling out of her. "Before or after the baby is born?"

"Before. Vegas, even. Your father can give you away."

"He doesn't want to give me away. He just got me back! And I can't be an actress eloping to Vegas. It's too clichéd," she protested.

"You're a pregnant Hollywood actress who'll be a few months along at the wedding. You're already a cliché." He winked. "We'll leave people guessing about whether we're taking our stunt to the extreme by actually getting married."

"So our love isn't real?"

"Snow, if my feelings were any more real, they'd be jumping around like the Seven Dwarves."

"Funny, Serenghetti."

And then he proceeded to show her just how real they were…

Epilogue

Two months later...

Chiara mingled with other Serenghettis who'd gathered for Serg's sixty-seventh birthday barbecue on a hot August afternoon in Welsdale. She was still getting used to these family get-togethers. They were a world apart from her past experiences with her own family. Serg and Camilla's home brimmed with animated voices and laughter.

Still, her relationship with her father had come a long way. Her father was in rehab, but he'd already announced he'd like to become an addiction counselor. And Odele had been and continued to be like a second mother. She'd already started shopping for baby clothes. And now, of course, Chiara had the Serenghettis, as well.

"The food is delicious," Marisa announced as she stepped onto the patio bathed in late-afternoon sun. "I feel even more like an overstuffed piñata."

Chiara smiled at her sister-in-law. "Now, there's a metaphor for being pregnant I haven't heard before."

In a nice surprise, shortly after her own pregnancy had gone public, Cole and Marisa had quietly announced they were expecting, too. Her sister-in-law was only a month further along. Naturally, Chiara thought, there'd be another female Serenghetti to take this journey with.

Marisa sighed. "I know what a chicken cordon bleu feels like."

"A ham?" Jordan asked, having overheard.

His sister-in-law shot him a droll look. "Funny."

"Just don't have a surprise birth," Jordan teased. "Mom wants a chance to plan for a big event for once."

Chiara bit back another smile, and then looked down at her plain platinum wedding band and large canary diamond solitaire engagement ring. She and Rick had had a quick wedding in Las Vegas with just immediate family present. It had been small, intimate and private, just like they'd wanted. There'd been no press, though they'd given Melody an exclusive after the fact.

Now as Marisa and Jordan stepped away, Rick came up and settled his hands on her shoulders, kneading them gently. Chiara nearly purred with contentment.

"How are you feeling?" Rick asked in a low voice.

"Like my next role should be as a pregnant stuntwoman," she responded.

"You'd be great. I've got just the vehicle."

"I feel like a starlet who has slept her way to the top with the studio boss."

He chuckled. "Snow, we're partners now."

At home and at the office. She and Rick were starting their own production company. He'd vowed to support her career in any way he could, and that included helping her find appropriate acting roles. For her part, she wanted to respect Rick's preference to not be in the glare of celebrity. She'd done interviews herself, but he'd insisted that as her prince, he needed and wanted to be her escort to public events.

Just then, Serafina, Marisa's cousin, stepped onto the patio and then frowned as she spotted Jordan.

"Uh-oh," Rick said in a low voice for Chiara's ears only. "Trouble."

As if on cue, Jordan gave a lazy grin, and then sauntered toward Serafina with a gleam in his eye.

Chiara smiled. "Only the best kind for those two." Then turning, she snuggled against Rick as he draped an arm around her shoulders. "Don't you agree?"

Her husband winked and gave her a kiss. "Definitely. You're the best trouble I ever had, Snow. And then love had walked in for us."

* * * * *

MILLS & BOON®

Desire™

PASSIONATE AND DRAMATIC LOVE STORIES

A sneak peek at next month's titles...

In stores from 15th June 2017:

- **The Baby Favour** – Andrea Laurence
  and **His Unexpected Heir** – Maureen Child

- **Lone Star Baby Scandal** – Lauren Canan
  and **Pregnant by the Billionaire** – Karen Booth

- **Best Friend Bride** – Kat Cantrell
  and **Claiming the Cowgirl's Baby** – Silver James

Just can't wait?
Buy our books online before they hit the shops!
www.millsandboon.co.uk

Also available as eBooks.